Looking Glass KILLER

Volume II: The Matthew-Matt Trilogy

floyd merrell

ISBN   Softcover   978-1-950596-98-0

To order additional copies of this book, contact:
Bookwhip
1-855-339-3589
https://www.bookwhip.com

Araceli on my mind. Somehow ensconced within each line?
Playful she is. Flitting from portmanteau to portmanteau.
Gazing at me from fleeting moments to tangential dubitability.
I know not how to go on but I must. Aware my mind is hers.
Reminding me I am duty-bound to get it on.
Pecking it out here and there.
In whatever way I can.

By way of a confession ...

I owe an inestimable debt to Matt Jones—formerly going by Matthew—who gave initial form to the following story. While many of the creative acts of feeling and thinking on these pages are Matt's, many of the words behind them are mine. Matt's process of feeling is the flowing, fluctuating becoming of his thinking, consisting of perpetually changing thoughts. Mere words fail in their effort to capture the feeling and thinking behind his thoughts. As they stream by, meandering, lazily creating rivulets and whirlpools. Briskly rushing along and occasionally cascading with reckless abandon. Attempting to link the appropriate words to Matt's feeling and thinking as well as my own was my inordinately difficult task. Unfortunately, my failures are here for all to see. Fortunately, Matt is spared the agony.

floyd merrell

JABBERWOCKY DREAMS

DETECTIVE Lucia Vieira with badge in hand hollers at the growing crowd, "Police! Make way. Move aside. People, you'll have to clear the area. Right now! Move it!"

The verbal hubbub surrounding Lucia and Mike Rafferty pours out with machine-gun cadence: "Who the hell would do this?" "Oh my God!"—"Poor little lady, she's"—"I heard a shot, and it scared me to death." "Jesus Christ!" "I've said it before and—" "What a monster!" "I can't believe"—"Violence in this city is coming straight out of hell!"

A reporter appearing out of nowhere shoves a microphone in Lucia's face, saying, "Detective, is this"—

"Hey! Get behind the rope," Lucia yells. "I've got a job to do. You over there! No pictures and put your mobile away. This is no Christmas parade."

"Where the hell did everybody come from at this time in the morning?" Mike yells.

"They turn every crime into a circus," Lucia frowns. "Three rings becoming a chaotic One," Mike scowls.

THE crime occurred on Tenth South Green Street at 5:00 A.M. on the sidewalk outside a rundown Victorian home partitioned into six dwellings some fifteen years ago.

Carol Martin, the victim, lived in one of the apartments. She was a recently widowed woman of seventy-three years. Small of stature, around five feet tall, and less than a hundred pounds.

Ms. Martin was removed from her small flat to the sidewalk and executed. With a .38 caliber slug that penetrated her left eye, traveled upward at a forty-five-degree angle through her brain, and shattered her skull.

"Ma'am," Mike says to a blue-haired stooped lady who lives in the building, "a person over there told me you knew Ms. Martin well. Can you tell me about her?"

Tearful words reluctantly come forth, "She was a sweet friend who never harmed anybody. She rarely left her home except to buy groceries and participate in activities at the Wells Senior Center. Young man, find who did this and put him in jail for life."

"We will, Ma'am."

Lucia and Mike interview other residents. The stories reveal nothing new.

There is no evidence of forced entry into the apartment. No indication of abuse, rape, or robbery before or after the execution. No apparent motive. Jewelry in a drawer is untouched. An unopened purse on the table contains credit cards and cash. No fingerprints. No trace for possible DNA samples. Nothing left behind other than an unintelligible note on an end table in red ink obviously printed out with an aging piece of electronic equipment. It reads, Drealorless grue coms retuously impest.

Two pairs of eyes squint. Heads shake. Below a halo of unanswered questions.

The two detectives check the area one more time to be sure. Then they head back to the car.

"What the hell was this note? Some kind of joke?" Mike asks.

"I'm sure it has some purpose behind it, no matter how strange it might seem at the outset. Decipher it, and hopefully, a motive will begin revealing itself."

"I doubt it," Mike responds. "It borders on madness."

"Madness? We're all mad, Mike. No matter how logical we think we are, there's a bit of crazy illogic in our thinking. There's also a special form of logic among the criminally mad minds, just as there is honor among thieves."

"How do you figure we're mad?"

"We must be. Otherwise, we wouldn't find ourselves in this loony profession."

"Come on, Luce. This is serious business."

"To give you an idea, get this. Three days ago, when I entered the office and checked my e-mail, I found an anonymous e-mail message from a strange address, madmadmadmadworld@gmail.com. It said, *Hell to pay; the third day; one hour away; do not delay.* I tried to send a response, asking what was going on. It bounced. Later I tried another response. It bounced.

"I ignored the message. Until now. When I searched and by sheer luck found it. The e-mail was sent at 4:00 A.M three days in in the past. Today, apparently around 5:00 A.M, a murder takes place a quarter mile straight down the road from headquarters. That's no coincidence."

"Creepy."

"Anyway, I'll take this wacky note to Leonard and mention my message of three days ago. He can crack any puzzle you put to him."

MIKE pulls a frown, "Leonard Binroy? He's in forensics, isn't he?"

"That's him. Forensics," Lucia responds. "A romanticized profession that fascinates a public nurtured on TV and movies. But Leonard keeps a level head about the fantasizing public."

"Is a forensic specialist the right person?"

"Len is a jack-of-all-trades. He'll come up with something."

Mike says, "Still, I'm sure this screwball note will have him flabbergasted. Because"—

"Don't be so sure," Lucia is quick to reply. "The assassin had something in mind when he wrote it. This is obviously a well-oiled crime, with everything rigorously planned out. It wasn't the result of a dark, sinister obsession or dream."

"Dream you say? That could be a clue to the note."

Lucia squints at Mike. He hands her the enigmatic note allegedly from the perp. She reads it again and says, "You'll have to explain yourself."

"The sentence begins with *drea* and the third word ends with *ms. Dreams.* And the third word begins with *co,* and the first one ends with *lorless. Colorless.*"

Lucia looks at the note again for a few seconds, then says, "Quite perspicacious if I might say so, Mike. I remember reading Noam Chomsky the linguist. He used 'Colorless green ideas dream furiously' to show how sentences can be *grammatically correct* yet *semantically meaningless*. The killer might be giving us a variation on Chomsky's theme."

"I also noticed the sentence could read 'Colorless *grue* dreams rest impetuously.' If we unscramble the fourth and fifth words, we have 'rest impetuously.'"

"Remarkable," Lucia goes on. "You picked that up in a flash. I'll give you full credit for deciphering this memorandum in my report to the chief."

"It might have been no more than dyslexia on my part."

"Don't be modest."

After a pause, Lucia adds, "Actually, the murderer's phrase is an admirable piece of poetic imagery cited as a meaningless sentence that is at the same time an attractive bit of irony. Chomsky exhibits his sentence as nonsense, but he does it with a dose of poetic license."

"What I can't get is the gist of the word *grue*," Mike puzzles.

"I was thinking about that too. Confusing."

"Yeah. Could it be the combination of two words, like *green* and *blue*?"

Lucia blurts out, "Hey! That must be it! I recall a Harvard philosopher, Nelson Goodman. He wrote an article about the frailty of our inductive reasoning by using *grue* as the color of emeralds in the language of inhabitants from an exotic land."

"*Grue?* The color of emeralds? How's that?"

"The story goes like this—if I recall it correctly. We naturally assume emeralds are invariably *green*. But for those strange people from a strange land, emeralds are in their language *grue*.

"There's a world of difference between their color words and ours. *Grue* for them is like *green* for us. But only up to a certain point in time. Thereafter, their *grue* becomes what would ordinarily be *blue* for us— which is *bleen* for them.

"In other words, their *grue* is as unstable as can be as far as we can tell. In contrast, they consider *grue* inalterable."

THEY enter the car. Mike puts it in motion.

He says, "I don't follow your explanation of *grue*. Could you walk me through it again?"

Lucia laughs and says, "I know what you mean. I had to read Goodman's article more than once before I felt I understood it. Anyway, here's the picture of the *grue* story in greater detail.

"As far as those strangers' perception goes, emeralds are *grue*, a color term for our *green*. They think their emeralds have been, are, and will always have been *grue*. So, as far as they are concerned, *grue* is stable.

"But from our point of view, they consider emeralds the same as *green* in our language, like grass, certain parrots, grasshoppers, and such. But at some arbitrary moment, they begin using *grue* for emeralds as well as the color of things we customarily call *blue*, such as sky, ocean, and such.

"In other words, for them, *grue* is as solid as can be, no questions asked. But for us, their idea of *grue* at some unforeseeable moment undergoes a crazy illogical change from our *green* to our *blue*."

"Ah yes ... I think"—

"There's more to the story. They think we are the nutty ones. Why? Because for them, we label emeralds *green*—their *grue*, blending our *green* and *blue* into one. Then at an unexpected moment, from their perspective, we begin labeling emeralds what in their language is the equivalent of our *blue*, or what they call *bleen*—a word blending our *blue* and *green*.

"So, we see their *grue* as unstable. They see our *green* as unstable."

"Christ! What a vicious brain twister," Mike says.

"Yes, it is. Like going through Lewis Carroll's looking glass."

"What do you mean?"

"Their *grue* suggests change in the way we see things, conceive them, and talk about them. Our *green* suggests change in the way they see, think, and talk. You see? Their color scheme and our color scheme are *mirrorimages* if we look at them from above, that is, from an extra dimension.

"From inside our perspective within one side of the looking glass, their *grue* is absurd, because it flips from one color to another for no reason at all. But from their perspective on the other side of the looking glass, it is our colors that are schizophrenic.

"We call emeralds *green*, which is their *grue*. They call emeralds *grue*, which is our *green*. Later, they still call them *grue*, but it is now the equivalent of our *blue* or their *bleen*."

"Whew! I'm not sure I follow you, but I have a feeling you might have hit the nail on the head. What does it all mean?"

"That's the sixty-four-dollar question, my man. My first reaction is that this riddle might revolve around the idea of perpetually changing language. Which means the murdering predator's MO will strike us as completely wishy-washy. Like *grue* so to speak ... eh? Thus, we're probably in for a wild ride when attempting to solve this crime."

"Why's that?"

"Precisely because the killer's word distortion is something like Lewis Carroll's jabberwocky. You know? *Green* merging with *blue* gives *grue* and *bleen*. It defies ordinary logic and reasoning.

"I'm speculating, but I would venture to suggest that the killer's note probably calls for some screwball form of logic—if we can call it logic at all and not sheer madness."

"Good grief! We have no clear-cut heads or tails but clouds taking on different forms with no rest in sight.

APPREHENSION sets in as Mike parks the car. It's enough to throw a good detective's confidence for a loop. Creating doubt. Notions that reveal incongruities. Uncertainties caught up in a swamp of vague and ambiguous words and concepts.

There is a faint ray of hope, however. In Leonard. Computer guru, math whiz, no-nonsense source of rational answers to virtually any and all questions.

Lucia and Mike enter Leonard's workplace with the idea of unloading their problem on him. To their surprise, he's working on a chess puzzle. Lucia begins by tongue-in-cheek accusing him of cheating on the job.

"Hey, I have to keep my keenest of wits in sharp working order."

"Uh-huh," Lucia responds on a sarcastic note.

Lucia and Mike tell Leonard about Lucia's e-mail message prior to the homicide and their interpretation of the note found at the murder scene. His initial reaction is, "Nifty."

"Is that all you can say?" Lucia eyes him with a critical frown.

"Yes, for now. This is a case of portmanteau-speak," Leonard explains.

"Come again?" Mike pulls a frown.

"Portmanteau words. Like *smog*, a word coined by combining the first two letters of smoke and the last two of fog. We use such words all the time."

"Ah, like *stagflation*, a combination of stagnation and inflation," Mike says.

"Or *sexting*, *sex* plus *texting*. *Squiggle*, *squirm* plus *wiggle*, or Lewis Carroll's own *snark*, which is *snide* plus *remark*," Leonard adds.

"We're not about to enroll in a class on rhetoric at the nearest university. We have a crime to solve," Lucia tells him.

"Yeah," Mike pipes in. "You're a language therapist. We're hoping you can tell us what we need to know."

"It is not a simple matter. With enough analysis and patience, I think we can find a clue to the perpetrator's intriguing message enabling us to proceed. But beware. You are against no mere mortal. Deductive inference tells me your adversary works with some strange manner of thinking that deviates radically from the linear implications of our stock-in-trade logic."

Mike frowns, "What kind of logic?"

"Basically, it consists of *Identity*, *Contradiction barring*, and the *Excluded middle*."

"Please explain," Mike says.

LEONARD turns his eyes toward the ceiling. In thought. Then says, "It follows Aristotelian logic and became lodged in our minds over the centuries. *Identity* says that what *is* must be what it *is* and *nothing else*. *Contradiction barring* says we mustn't take what *is* for something it *is not*, which would entail an inconsistency. The *Excluded middle* principle disallows alternatives that transcend the bivalent notion of either one possible answer or another and no more options.

"I'm afraid whatever this killer's deviant MO may be, it comes from some dark corner in his past and allows for unlimited possibilities along sinewy divergent and convergent paths.

"What I mean is, our world is far removed from your killer's world. Our logic is contrary to his apparent illogic. As if our *green-blue* was his *grue-bleen*. As if our world and his were diametrically opposed."

"Could you say what you just said in ordinary English?" Mike asks. Leonard continues as if he hadn't heard Mike's plea, "Children who are traumatized, bullied, abused, sexually molested, or whatever, often create fantasy worlds. Some kids fail to grow up, and they carry the practice into adulthood. We might have such a case here.

"The problem is that this guy is no simple man-child. He's brilliant. His reasoning faculties are obviously first class. It leads me to believe that if what my intuition tells me is correct, you have a terribly challenging case on your hands. In the manner of *green-blue/grue-bleen* incompatibility."

"You're a genuine confidence builder, Leonard," Lucia says. Mike wrinkles his forehead, "I'm still puzzled."

"So am I," says Leonard. "There must be some rational inference applicable to the conundrum surrounding this note. But right now, I have no idea what it might be."

Leonard fails to console Mike.

Lucia tells Leonard, "If this got *you* stumped, we're in for a rough time indeed. The killer left a printed message. How can we trace it down? He's not stupid. Maybe he bought his printer in a garage sale or whatever. Maybe he ripped it off. Maybe he printed his note at some cybercafe. In whatever case, he can vary the source of his message every time he commits a crime."

Leonard tells her, "You are probably right if he commits any more crimes of this nature."

"Oh, he'll commit another one," Lucia says, "then another, with perhaps no end in sight if we aren't able to catch him."

"How can you be so sure?" Leonard asks her.

"The note he left is a clue. It's a sort of riddle we're supposed to crack. If we can, the implication is that we will have the key to another murder," Mike adds.

"Maybe he's sly enough to make you think it's a clue and that he's the prime example of a serial killer. But perhaps he's not. He's somebody who bears a grudge," Leonard tells him.

Lucia says, "Could be, but we'd best not make that assumption with the expectation that we are right. We want to keep all the options open. Anyway, thanks, Leonard. You can be assured that we will hit you up for more advice as this case becomes increasingly bewildering."

"Any time," Leonard says while walking them to the door.

THEY decide on returning to the crime scene in further search of a clue. Any kind. For they desperately need something that will get them out of the starting blocks with their investigation.

Upon approaching the spot where the murder was committed, Lucia sees a brass-colored object that is almost the same color as its background. She stoops down and picks it up.

"I'll be damned," she says. "A key. And a blank one at that."

"Blank? That's odd," Mike remarks.

"Yes, blank. Which means it can be cut in one of an indeterminate number of ways to open an indeterminate number of locks. A blank key.

It could mean we have virtually an infinite number of possible answers to the clue. This key is what we might call our *zero-degree* clue. From here we either advance and get hotter or digress and get colder. In either direction, the path stretches out indefinitely."

"Good grief! Either you have an imagination gone wild, or you're on track. But the killer isn't of a disposition to yield us much concrete information."

"Yeah, I admit my imagination sometimes flies out of control," Lucia tells him. "This time I would like to think I'm on track, that is, if he left the blank key for *us* and it wasn't simply lost by someone passing through here."

"That's all we need, a dead-end street."

Lucia studies the object with a speculative eye, then says, "Blank. It holds all possible information in simultaneity. But it isn't simply noise, like a group of maximum decibel rock bands blaring at each other. The problem is that all possible keys to the riddle cancel each other out and leave *silence, nothing, zero-degree*."

"Whatever you mean by that, it doesn't sound very promising," Mike mutters.

"No. But it is a key that if used right can open the coffer that holds our puzzling clue."

They look around for a few minutes, then leave the crime scene. Silently. Deep in thought. Lucia somewhat reluctantly offers her estimation of what they're up against, "The killer is supremely confident. He seems to go about his crime as if checking off a shopping list in the supermarket. Methodically and orderly. As if it was a list beginning with produce, meat, milk, bakery, canned goods, chips, cookies, candy, crackers, sodas, and ending with alcoholic beverages. Just like they appear along the aisles in the nearest Wal-Mart or wherever. No nonsense. Straight-forward and linear."

Lucia pipes up, "Our problem is like a set of cause and effect sequences. As if following the rigorously bivalent, either/or logic Leonard was talking about. This and not that, or that and not this. Binary choices. But the whole shebang is dressed up in apparently bizarre illogical clothing with neither heads nor tails."

"Is this what we have to cope with?" Mike asks. "The perp as an obsessed organizer? Washing his hands dozens of times daily? Constantly sanitizing the premises with meticulous care and patience? Shopping for his groceries in the most efficient way possible?

"If so, his moves might seem predictable. Yet, they will be almost impossible to map out. Since every step along our killer's path presents a study in some crazy strategy fixed in his mind but nobody else's."

"We're definitely in for a brain-wracking set of exercises," Lucia concludes.

MIKE agrees with concern written all over his face.

"There's also the problem of the people out there," Lucia adds after a long embarrassing pause. "They think they're as good as the best detectives, profilers, and forensic psychologists.

"Especially those starry-eyed students at the universities who have become obsessed with a degree in criminology, forensics, and profiling. Nurturing the dream of outsmarting psychopaths and serial killers with perverted minds and out-of-sight IQs."

Mike chips in, "Like those bestselling movies, *Silence of the Lambs* and *Hannibal.* And TV shows like *Profiler* and *CSI* promising forensic adventures and dreamy escapades that rarely occur in the real world of tough day-to-day crime solving."

"You're onto it, Mike. At least a few of their professors tell them their chosen careers don't coincide with the charm, exploits, and promise of fame they see in the media."

Their conversation goes on about the populace at once horrified and attracted to gory criminal affairs. Sporting corruption, brutal violence, shootings, destructive explosions, and car pile-ups. Lies and deceit. Sadism and masochism. The criminal investigators' actual job is humdrum in comparison.

This puts them in a dilemma. They feel compelled to go against the grain of public opinion regarding the nature of their job. At the same time, they must appease the people by drizzling out enough information to give them the idea their investigation is getting on.

In other words, since most of what they do is routine, they occasional dress it up a little to impress the public.

What the hell, Lucia thinks, *just get it on*—though she recognizes the impossibility of putting her thoughts in action.

So much for life as an adventurous dream confronting a world of nightmares.

JUST PLAY?

HAVING exhausted their tale of woe regarding the difficulties of their chosen profession, Mike's attention focuses on the city park a block to the right. He suggests that instead of returning to the precinct, they get some java to go at the nearby café, take it to the park, and discuss the sordid murder scene that left them with a rotten taste in their mouth.

A few minutes later, with a Styrofoam cup in each hand, we find them sitting on the nearest bench.

Mike says, "I've only been at this job four months, and I still can't put the gruesome homicide scenes out of my mind. How do you do it, Luce?"

"It affects you that way because you're no psychopath."

"You can say that again. I couldn't in my wildest dreams carry out the bloodthirsty acts I witness in almost every case. But tell me, how do you figure this killer is a psychopath, Luce? Aren't you jumping the gun? Stereotyping him? Putting him in a straight-jacketed profile before the necessary facts are in?"

"What does a cat do with the mouse she's chased down and will eventually gobble up?"

"Play with it."

"Play. See those kids over there playing soccer? They call it play. But watch them closely. You spot those who are bigger, stronger, faster, and have no misgivings about taking advantage of those who are less physically endowed. They push, shove, kick, and holler out orders.

"When the abused victims complain, the answer is 'What d'ya mean it's not fair? That's the way we play the game, and if you can't stomach it, go home to your mama.' They are showing a dose of psychopathic behavior at that tender age."

"Bullies? You mean they will grow up to be psychopaths?"

"A few likely will. Take the cat. The prime four-legged example of a psychopath. She grabs her victim, dangles it in her mouth for a while, and releases it. It sees the chance for a quick escape and takes off. She grabs it again, slaps it back and forth between her paws, and dangles it in her mouth a bit more. Then she lets it go. It tries to escape. And it's *déjà vu* all over again. The mouse is in an uncertain situation, while the cat is in complete control. But it's not simply frivolous play. It's a game. The likes of which must end with either winners or losers."

"Yeah," Mike says. "But the mouse reacts to its context. If it could reason it might think, 'What will this monster do to me next?' It will try to figure her out."

"Sure," Lucia agrees. "Like it's saying, 'I'm just a kind empathetic mouse trying to do the best I can while she's a cold, calculating brute with no feelings at all.' Meanwhile, the cat's thinking, 'I can do whatever I want with this cringing idiot. It's pathetic but amusing.'

"Like I suggested, she's the ultimate psychopath. She enjoys the hunt, feels nothing but contempt for her prey, and reduces it to nothing before killing and eating it. There's nothing personal in her dealing with the mouse. She does what she does because that's who she is, no more, no less."

"Geez, Luce, like a cat, the psychopath's only concern is how the victim will fit into his scheme of things for whatever purpose he has in mind."

"So it would seem."

"If psychopaths are thoroughly inhuman, identifying them should be a simple matter. I see how you can quickly pin the killer down and throw him into the psychopath category."

"You would think so. But ask yourself what distinguishes psychopaths from what we might call normal people."

"Total absence of human qualities," Mike concludes.

"Yes." Lucia says. "They are self-centered to the maximum. They are devoid of what we ordinarily call moral fiber. They feel no responsibility for their actions. No remorse or guilt, no sympathy or empathy, no feelings for others, no sense of fairness, compassion, loyalty, or respect.

"EEG experiments demonstrate this. Show psychopaths and presumably normal people a multimillion-dollar mansion and then show them some good-looking person getting a stab in the chest. Normal people will experience two diametrically opposed reactions. Psychopaths will register no emotion and little substantive difference between the two scenes.

"In fact, there is hardly any response at all. Like the cat, they emotionlessly go about in robot fashion. You recall that silent movie *Un chien andalou* (*An Andalusian Dog*) of the 1920s directed by Luis Buñuel?"

"Never saw it," Mike responds.

"In the opening scene a straight razor is sharpened by a pair of hands. Later, the hands lift a woman's eyelids, revealing as much eyeball as possible. Then the razor slices the eyeball. As objectively, impersonally, and apparently as normally as you could imagine. Shivers go up your spine."

"I can imagine. Because *you* are not a psychopath."

"That's right, Mike. Psychopaths and non-psychopaths are entirely different animals. Our limbic system produces different emotional responses, whereas the psychopath registers no response at all. His limbic system adds up to near absolute zero."

"A coldhearted bastard."

"This makes him narcissistic to the hilt. He thinks of himself as selfsufficient, needing nothing from his victims. Yet he preys on them for his entertainment. He thinks he is of a higher nature than they are. As far as he's concerned, they're nothing but sheep, or mice if you will. They exist to satisfy his cravings. He manipulates them, abuses them, kills them if he wishes, and even eats them.

"Some psychopaths are notorious for drinking their victims' blood and eating their tongues, brains, hearts, kidneys, or whatever. Think of Hannibal Lector in *Silence of the Lambs*. All that matters for psychopaths is their own self-centered, self-contained, narcissistic gratification."

"I can't help thinking about the bullies. I remember some of them when I was in elementary and middle school. I wonder who turned out psychopathic."

"You'd best not make any bets. The psychopaths among us vary widely according to the estimates, from around four to ten percent. One expert claims a third of the men and a tenth of the women are psychopaths. If you have twenty-five friends, chances are one to three or so will have psychopathic tendencies."

"You have to keep your eye out for them. You never know when you will have one of those beasts in your midst."

"Best not to worry yourself. It could drive you to drink."

"Speaking of drink, this is horrible coffee." Mike observes.

"That's your estimate. When I drink coffee, I'm simply after a shot of caffeine. Unless it's Brazilian, that is. Then I go for quality and flavor."

"Whatever."

"There's another thing about psychopaths," Lucia goes on. "They are prone to hurt their victims who for some crazy reason love them. At the same time, they seek their victims' financial assistance and moral support. Then they harp on their own hard luck, their sorry lot in life, and the injustices done them in an appeal for sympathy and pity. Psychopaths are adept at concealing their motives. They often do so by disguising themselves as normal members of society. They convince their victims they are meek and mild.

"But watch out! You could become their next victim. They'll whimper, whine, and bitterly weep in order to get what they're after. They'll charm the pants off you one moment and the next moment make you feel so sorry for them that you will come to their rescue, giving them money and supporting them in every way. Deceiving you while taking advantage of you is the name of their game."

"How do they go about this?" Mike asks.

"They are consummate play-actors. It's a role they play, or better, it's a game, their game, and they are out to win at any cost."

MIKE ponders over Lucia's words for a moment, then says, "The way you put it, people in respectable professions like attorneys, doctors, administrators, CEOs, and politicians ought to fit the bill."

"Right. A considerable number of apparently ordinary people have found success by taking advantage of their associates and clients. As a result, money simply disappears from international corporations, malpractice occurs in hospitals, criminals get off scot-free in the courts, and moral decay, embezzlement, fraud, and corruption seep into politics.

"Much of this is because of psychopathic practices among certain individuals in the professions. Are any of them ready to accept an iota of guilt? Of course not! Meanwhile, their victims suffer the consequences."

"In other words," Mike adds, "while some psychopaths become violent criminals, others take on airs of abiding by the laws, rules, and regulations, while they exploit the hell out of everybody. Like *Wall Street*, that Michael Douglas's movie.

"There's a host of comparable thrillers. *American Psychos, Boiler Room, The Wolf of Wall Street.*"

"Successful, smooth, charming, convincing ... psychopaths all?"

"Yes. They playact their psychopathic roles in order to conceal their real motives. Robert Hare who has written a few books on the topic describes them as 'intra-species predators.' You've often heard it said that we humans are the only animals who feel at liberty to brutalize and kill one another. Well, psychopaths are the most adept at it."

"Ah, then military people must be the most noble of psychopaths."

"So it would seem. The more efficient at the game, the more notorious the four-star general."

"What about the roles actors play in the movies?"

"Correct. The James Bonds and the Dirty Harrys of the law enforcement world. They are often acting out psychopathic roles."

"So we, too, could be psychopaths. Right, Luce?"

"Oh, that I were. I would be considerably better at my job as a detective. Lethal Lucia they'd call me."

Mike guffaws.

Lucia breaks out in a wide smile, "If I were a predator of the first order"—

"Save me," Mike pleads, "I might become one of your victims."

"No chance."

"I've also heard it said that vicious psychopaths come from violent family backgrounds. Where they were beaten, sexually abused, and whatnot."

"Many, but not all. Such were the childhoods of John Wayne Gacy, Ted Bundy, Son of Sam, and others. Hundreds of thousands of children in this country come from broken homes. Many of them grow up and manage to live what we would consider normal lives. Then there are those who grow up and become predators. It's a matter of nature along with nurture.

"There is some evidence of neurological differences among psychopaths that distinguish them from others. But there's also the environmental influence."

Mike nods, "If you're *born* to be crazy, it's who you are and what you do. If they *drive* you crazy, you're one more citizen in the crazy crowd. Is that it, Luce?"

"Psychopathic behavior is not simply mental illness. Of course, psychopaths may suffer from some mental disorder or other. But they rarely respond to methods for curing the mentally ill. This leads some psychologists to believe that it's in their genes and nothing can be done about it.

"The assumption has it today that psychopaths have a cluster of tendencies. Some fall into one set of categories and others fall into different sets. That's why they are difficult to categorize. The problem is further aggravated since psychopathic behavior is a matter of degree not kind with respect to a given set of tendencies. Their common ground lies in the fact that they don't have a heart."

"Unlike that lion in the Wizard of Oz," Mike muses, "they don't have a heart, and they don't want one."

"Yeah."

"A lot of what you're talking about revolves around language use," Mike suggests.

"Language? I never thought of psychopathic behavior that way. But now that you mention it, yes. Psychopaths use words, but they have no sensibility regarding language. They read the lines, but they don't feel the lyrics. They know the tune, but they don't swing with the rhythm. They use and abuse language and, in the process, become masters of subterfuge."

"All the while mooching from others," Mike adds.

"Freeloaders. They suck what they can from people's good will toward them. They crave excitement and get bored quickly. So, they screw others for the sheer adventure of it. They are impulsive. Living for the moment. Saying and doing what is expedient by lying, cheating, double-crossing, duping, and betraying their victims. Then they use language to invent themselves all over again."

"Adults who never grew up?" Mike speculates. "Is it genetic disorder? Or did the devil or society make them do it? Or both? Or neither, but something else? It seems there's hardly any answer."

"Ultimately, I believe it is a matter of control, Mike. It is our job to get into those predators' controlling minds without becoming controlled ourselves. At the same time, they are intent on getting into our minds for the purpose of controlling us.

"The criminal is the creator, and we can do no more than read and interpret what he leaves behind. We are at a disadvantage, and must beware we don't become as monstrous as the monster whose mind we are entering. We stare into the gulf of nothingness, and it stares back at us."

"You're right when you say this is a loony profession, Luce."

Lucia's informative session with her understudy comes to a close. The topic, of course, could have continued for hours.

SIMPLY PLAYACTING?

THE next morning finds Mike at his water cooler gossiping best. He sees Lucia enter the main hall and enthusiastically greets her. She heads him toward her desk, and they sit.

Mike is the first to speak up. Because, he says, something is bothering him, "Have you discussed that predator's strange behavior with the Captain yet?"

"Not yet, Mike. I'm hoping we can latch onto something concrete before I give her a written report."

"We'd better hurry it up. She doesn't like delays. Wants to run a tight ship."

"I'm still reluctant, since we don't have much for her."

"I was thinking," Mike says, "if for some reason this guy's twisted mind isn't that of a psychopath, then what's his problem?"

"He's after something," Lucia says. "But I don't know what. It has occurred to me that he might be merely disguising himself as a psychopath."

"Disguising himself? Why would he want to do that? Psychopaths are loathsome to the extreme."

"To nudge us off track. By leading us to believe he has psychopathic characteristics, whereas he is playing the role for the fun of it. Just to see what the outcome might be. Or he might be full of resentment and wants to get even with somebody or some organization."

"Or could it be that his disguise isn't fake but real and his disguising act is for the purpose of throwing us off track?" Mike suggests.

"That's a cute twist."

"If so, then he is still manipulating us by playing his psychopathic role."

"You may be right," Lucia replies.

"If I am, he likely wants solid control."

"That's what psychopathic behavior is all about. As control goes, so control is, and the same goes for the role," Lucia murmurs as if speaking non-consciously.

"I guess. You're the one who studied up on this. Tell me more about the methods they use to control their victims?"

"A psychopath in a romantic relationship with a new victim builds a castle on quicksand. He has double standards, two diametrically opposed roles. A fake good Samaritan role and an egocentric predatory role. They merge into one. Within a world that has little to do with the victim's pathetic world."

"Doctor Jekyll becoming Mister Hyde and back again."

Lucia nods, "The psychopath mistreats her at will. Soon tires of her and fastidiously tosses her aside. Or maims her. Or in the worst-case scenario kills her."

"It's fake. Nothing but simulation," Mike says, as if he was asking for Lucia's approval.

"Yes. Using his fake personality, he lures a new victim to a secluded spot and slits her throat. If he is a sex maniac as well, he rapes her before killing her. After killing her he might practice sodomy, shove objects into her vagina, slice her body at strategic places, and later dig out her uterus and maybe a few more organs. Then he leaves the scene as if nothing happened. Same as he did when engaged in his fake lover role."

"Inconceivable. How can they so much as stomach themselves?"

"They can and they do," Lucia says.

"Back to our enigmatic killer perp. Could he be playacting that he's playacting a psychopathic role while all the time presenting himself as a charming human specimen?"

"What do you mean Mike?"

"Well, it's like he's doing a playacting job on playacting. So, he puts us in a paradoxical situation. Like saying, 'I'm not playacting.' If he's playacting when he says it, he's lying like a good psychopath. If he's telling the truth, unlike a psychopath, he's not playacting. But since psychopaths are compulsive liars, how can we know he's not telling the truth?"

"Ah yes ... I see. A takeoff on what they call the Liar Paradox. We would have to take his first level playacting as real and his second level playacting as simulation. So, where does that leave him? And where is our place in the scheme of things?"

"It's somewhat of a catch 22 dilemma," Mike suggests.

"So it would seem," Lucia agrees. "We will have to catch him at his playacting. That will be possible only if we have no need to catch him as an actor in a playacting situation, but as the real killer. We can catch the real killer only by playing his game. But what's to prevent him from leaping to another level and entering a playacting role on his playacting on playacting? And we are left with egg on our faces."

"So much circular talk. Why don't we just focus on cuffing him?"

"You're forgetting," Lucia is quick to point out. "We have to play along with his apparently ludicrous game of riddles and playacting. This is not so bad. After all, the fun of the run is in the running, not in breaking the tape, coming in first place, and leaving the other sprinters with their tongues hanging out. We will be having fun and in the end the criminal will find himself in the calaboose."

"We're detectives, not marathoners," Mike protests.

"Of course ... But our present case is a marathon if I ever saw one."

"Or a rollercoaster ride."

"Playacting ... On the back of playacting," Lucia muses. "Knowing you, I have an idea you're onto something."

"Maybe ... I hope so ... Anyway ..."

LUCIA demurs. Her thoughts wander. Lost within a complex wavering syncopated beat.

Mike gives her a quizzical look, "Yes?"

"There's something that once occurred to me, Mike. Look at it this way. Suppose Sean Connery is making his first post-James Bond movie playing another James Bond type of role as Stan Katz. He meets his counterpart. A spy from the enemy nation intent on carrying out its imperialistic plan. The spy just happens to be a beautiful, sexy woman, Melody Bunn."

"Talking about *déjà vu* all over again!"

"Our charismatic secret agent is not meeting with much success. The enemy agent and her cohorts manage to outwit him at every turn. After Katz fails at yet another attempt to outwit his opponent, both in the spy game and in the game of sex, he remarks to his lovely rival, 'If I were James Bond, I'd have had you in bed a month ago.'"

"Oh, I get it! In this post-Bond movie, women are becoming wise to Stan Katz's—that is, James Bond's—outmoded sexist tactics."

"Of course. Now here's the crux of the issue. This is Sean Connery the actor speaking of himself as James Bond in the James Bond movie series and at the same time as Stan Katz in this non-Bond movie. Sean Connery is who he is and he is a post-Bond actor alluding to himself as a Bond actor."

"Yes! And in the movie house populated by popcorn crunchers, these playacting switches go through us as smooth as vanilla ice cream."

"Exactly. They create no insurmountable problem at all. We take in both James Bond's and Stan Katz's worlds through Sean Connery, maybe chuckle a little, and give the conundrum no further thought."

"As if it was as natural as pie"—

"Playacting about playacting revealing real-life situations."

MIKE pulls a frown. Winces. Shakes his head. And says, "Okay. I'll buy into your game. Now, what are you driving at?"

"That the movie script creates *doublespeak* in the imaginary world regarding Sean Connery, James Bond, and Stan Katz."

"Doublespeak? Quick! Everybody grab your assault weapons and defend yourselves against evil! George Orwell's *1984* is upon us!" Mike says with a laugh and Lucia joins in.

Then with a sober face she says, "Think about it. Doublespeak preys on the inconsistency between what is said, what is left unsaid, and what is. It is language's form of cognitive dissonance, rampant inconsistencies. It is communication's downfall. It distorts, misleads, deceives, and lies."

"Hey, are you saying language can also become psychopathic?" Mike incredulously blurts out.

"In a way of putting it, yes. Doublespeak miscommunicates and deceives. It makes climate change out of global warming, transportation counselors out of used car salesmen, preowned cars out of used cars, sanitation engineers out of garbage collectors, pavement deficiencies out of pot holes, strategic misrepresentations out of lies, alleged suspects out of killers."

"What a mouthful! Are you saying we should believe nothing we hear and only half of what we see?"

"Well yes, if you want to put it that way," Lucia somewhat patronizingly tells Mike. "Why? Because doublespeak makes our reality not what it is, but a massive set of misrepresentations."

"In other words, you're saying language is *like* ... psychopathic. Through doublespeak, it charms us to sleep, then it lowers the boom on us. We're victimized before we know it."

"Yes again. Doublespeak turns us into sheep, in *1984* fashion—with a few exceptions of course."

"Ah," Mike says. "But if you want to become a non-sheep upstart as judge of truth about the entire flock, they'll likely run you out of the community. For them you became the enemy, something like a wolf in sheep's clothing."

"Yes. And the psychopath gets around this by posing as just another sheep through playacting. Since this is his nature, he's not really playacting. He's for real. And the sheep take him in as one of their own. According to our job description, we must reveal that the wolf playacting a sheep role is actually a predator. We must cope with psychopaths who are habitual liars.

"There is saving grace however, because if we are all playacting, or in a manner of speaking lying, we don't have to distinguish between truth and lie. We can flip back and forth, however we wish."

"Like a psychopath," Mike interjects. "We're playing his game in order to catch him at his game. We have no problem taking in Sean Connery and his roles without paying any mind to the difference between playacting and what is real. We can do the same with a psycho."

"As if it was all genuinely real. We playact and we see our playacting for what it is. We play along with it, and then at the right moment ... bam! We've got the killer."

"I don't think I follow *you* there," Mike confesses.

"It's like this. Psychopathic language confuses James Bond and Stan Katz and mixes both with Sean Connery. So, it is as if we we're on automatic pilot while flowing along in a murky river that clouds the difference between fiction and what we take as real."

"And my mind's still murky," Mike confesses.

"Think of it this way. While we are in the Stan Katz movie world, we take what we experience for what it is, having suspended disbelief. Level one. Then when leaving the movie theater, suppose we begin interpreting what we experienced while using a lot of abstract language. Level two. Doublespeak takes place between the two levels within the border. It is midway between fiction and reality, movie world and the presumed real, what isn't and what is. Level three."

"All the while, we assume we have control over language at both levels," Mike suggests. "It may be, however, that we remain trapped within doublespeak. Unable genuinely to step into either fiction or fact. Because we are duped."

"If we let ourselves become duped. But if we are aware of the three levels, we stand a chance of tripping the predator up while playacting within his game."

"Still murky," Mike mumbles.

"Doublespeak tells us in so many words 'I am lying'—or as you might put it, 'I am not playacting.' We take it as false, because we are in the misrepresented world. But the sentence tells us it is telling us the truth when it says it is lying. So, the sentence is true, but it's false, and it's false, but it's true."

"It's a language problem, isn't it? The problem of psychopathic language."

"We are not simply dissecting the language problem. We are bewitched by it. Yet, we are not consciously and immediately aware of the deception that engulfs us."

"Yeah. But good grief! If we told Mayor Fitzburger or Governor Chadwick about this tale of language as the supreme psychopath, they would either fire us for incompetence or for wasting time on the job."

"Wait, I haven't told you the whole story yet, Mike."

"I'm all ears, Luce."

"Another way of putting this is by the sentence 'I am not provable.' Because if we're taken in by the lie in a Sean Connery movie while inside the lie, lie and reality merge. We don't consciously and immediately know where one begins and the other ends."

"Wait a minute, Luce. When the movie ends, I ask you how you liked it. You talk about Stan Katz's bumbling and how, unlike him, you'd have caught the international spy. Now you're talking from outside the movie world ... or outside the box as you put it."

"Of course," Lucia responds. "Now I'm outside, in our real world. But while inside the movie, if Stan Katz is almost wasted, I chomp down on a few kernels of the salty stuff more intently. If Stan Katz finally gets Melody Bunn in bed, I smirk and think, *You prehistoric sexist, get real.* During those moments, it's all true, but it isn't. I'm inside the scene, but during certain moments I'm outside it."

"Okay. So, what does this have to do with our killer?"

LUCIA thinks, *Yeah, right. Where am I going with this? Ah, that's where. But should I? Why Not?*

She blurts out, "First things first. I alluded to the phrase, 'I am not provable,' with mathematician Kurt Gödel in mind. You ever heard of him?"

"Yeah, heard of him, but that's all."

"Back when I was studying math, I picked him up and devoured books and articles about him out of sheer curiosity. I read his two theorems on incompleteness ... Well, what I could understand of them. He's damn abstruse. In 1931, when mathematicians still had faith in the truth, provability, and absolute certainty of their proofs, Gödel demonstrated that sufficiently abstract, complex proofs will always be *incomplete*, and in many cases *inconsistent*."

"I imagine that knocked them for a loop," Mike says.

"It certainly did. He showed them they are always in something like a playacting world when they do mathematics. But their playacting is about another playacting world, and that one is about another playacting world, and so on, without end."

"Like Sean Connery, James Bond, Stan Katz, and us and all others as well when drawn into the movie scene showing us another level of playacting and then another."

"Well, as a metaphor so to speak," Lucia suggests. "Our role in the movie theater is like our role within doublespeak and our role as sleuths. We must get inside the criminal's head and his world, as if they were our head and world. At the same time, we must be able to slip into our everyday concrete world at a moment's notice."

"Oh, we are false to ourselves, so we can be true to ourselves. We can be *either* of the two and we have to be *both*. And we must be *neither* of them, because we're trying to bust the case. That is, we're trying to find out something about the criminal we don't yet know. Is that what you mean?"

"I would like to think so," Lucia tells him. "What you are saying is that if there's something we don't know, our case is *incomplete*, and it bears *contradictions* and *inconsistencies*. Even when we solve the case and the criminal is put away for life, new evidence might pop up and tell us in some way or other that he might have been wrongly accused. We can never know with absolute certainty."

"Ah!" Mike is quick to add. "This is to say that since *neither* the accepted playacting world *nor* what it isn't are true. So, we're in a quandary, an *inconsistency*. Thinking *both* the one *and* the other are true doesn't cut the cake. What we need is some other possibility we can take as true, if only provisionally. In order to understand at least a few minor degrees of *completeness*.

"But our real world and our playacting worlds will always have flaws. So, we periodically find ourselves stepping out of the box in search of something better."

"Hey, you put it more effectively than I. In a metaphorical way of speaking, this might be like Gödel's proof. Our knowing was, is, and will always have been basically *incomplete*, and it will often be *inconsistent* to boot."

MIKE rises from his seat with a scowl on his face. Turns around and looks out the door. It's activity out there at a frantic pitch. He mumbles, "They're all doing their thing. Engrossed within their world. As if it was the only world. Criminals and crime busting. As if ..." He shakes his head with a furrowed brow.

Lucia gazes at his silence for a few moments, while saying to herself, *I've thought about this before. Many times. But never discussed it with anybody. And now I revealed it to a wet-behind-the-ears but very capable apprentice. He's probably thinking, "She must be out of her gourd."*

Playacting? How can I put detective work in such an apparently trivial way? It's serious business. It shouldn't have anything to do with makebelieve or whatever.

However, once we look at our job this way, it becomes delightfully entertaining. There's no irresolvable quandary that bends us out of shape at all, but an amusing twist of the sort we run into a few times a day. We live with such situations and cope with them.

We do it to solve our everyday problems by using them to our advantage, including criminal investigation. So maybe we shouldn't take it so seriously after all.

Mike, however, has no problem with Lucia's playacting metaphor. He's thinking, *Doublespeak through playacting? It's likely been with us since the dawn of human cultures. Lucia seems out in left field. But she's probably right. I'll have to think about this some more.*

"Hey, Mike, have I lost you?" Lucia asks.

Mike turns around. Looks at the stack of files on her desk crying out for attention. She looks down at them. Shakes her head while thinking, *I've gotta take care of his godawful mess,* then looks back at him.

"I don't know," he mumbles.

"Anyway, let's get down to earth. We have a case to solve."

"I was thinking that Stan Katz could have said 'Sean Connery' instead of 'James Bond' when addressing himself to Melody Bunn. If so, the characters in question could have played out considerably different roles."

"Whatever ... What we've been talking about is just that. Something to talk about, nothing more."

"Wait a minute, Luce. You've piqued my curiosity and now you want to drop it?"

"What I mean is ... well, it's something we ought to keep in mind."

"In that case ... I guess ..."

THEY leave. Without an additional word. The Captain intercepts them while on her way to lunch. She asks them about the case. They mumble a few unintelligible words. She shakes her head and goes her way.

Lucia thinks, *What can I say? That Sean Connery, that is Stan Katz, couldn't get Melody Bunn into bed? Case closed? I'll become last in the pecking order around here.*

Life in the precinct meat grinder is calling. From the withering heights of airy speculation, it is time to get down to the nitty-gritty.

Lucia and Mike take leave of the precinct and head for the street. Where to? They don't know. The recent verbal encounter has left them empty handed and empty headed. They decide they should get some lunch. What else? There's no inclination to engage in anything more substantial.

Hot dogs at the nearest stand. They eat in silence, as their favorite boulevard chef gives them a few passing glances and says something now and then.

Doublespeak? Reality and make-believe? Incomplete and inconsistent answers? Who's to say? They chow down on their minced animal organ mini-submarine sandwiches. Then mosey on. Thinkingly. Doublespeakingly.

"When do you think the killer will strike again?" Mike asks.

"Who knows," Lucia drawls back, deep in thought, failing to conceal her English as a second language with a slight Texas accent. "It will be a surprise, for sure."

A surprise? she thinks. Then says, "Hey, Mike. I got one for you. It's like a bombshell paradox. Suppose the killer decides to surprise us and strike again within the next fifteen days and tells us so. If he strikes on that day, it can't be a surprise.

"So, there are fourteen days left. By the same token, if he decides on another homicide on that day, it can't come as a surprise either. And so on, down to this very day. If he finds a victim to kill today, it won't surprise us in the least. So, he cannot commit any more murders. End of riddle."

"What do you mean he can't? He can whenever he wants to."

"Pragmatically speaking, yes. But within the closed, timeless, logical confines of his contrived situation, he can't. However, we live in time.

Where there is no prison house of logic. We are always becoming someone other than who we are.

"So is our world, that is, our idea of the world. Time changes, and with it everything changes. As you said. the psychopathic bastard *can* kill whenever the impulse moves him."

"I think you're going too far in your fiction-reality game," Mike says.

"I'm not so sure. It seems that we humans are hardwired to understand logic of the *Identity, Contradiction prohibition*, and *Excluded middle* sort as Len puts it. Armed with these tools, we dictate decisions of *either* this *or* that sort. But understanding vagueness and ambiguity and the hows and the whys, we feel what we feel and know are different issues entirely. Someday I'll have to try and explain my crazy ideas on these issues. But that's another story for another time."

"Yeah. I would like to hear them … Someday … I think … If they don't end up confusing me more."

Lucia says, "I said what we were talking about in the office was no more than something to think about. Now my intuition tells me that it has relevance for our investigation."

"Really? If it does, get it out."

"Ask yourself about that quirky message the killer left. Why the use of rhetorically burdened portmanteau words?"

"I'm game. Tell me."

"There's ordinary language at one level, and there's a second level, consisting of uncustomary rhetorical verbiage that must be deciphered like a riddle. Then there's the riddle itself at yet another level. It is comprehensible only with proper deciphering.

"At these three levels we have *true, false,* and *meaningless* or *nonsense,* until we crack the code and become aware of what there really is. We must complete the message, unravel the riddle, get the punch line, and resolve the apparent inconsistency. We must grasp the gist of the playacting. Sean Connery or James Bond or Stan Katz? They flow into one another.

They coalesce. They are becoming One. One, yet Three. Three, yet One. Dependent on the mysterious magic of Threeness."

"Ah, so you're back to our playacting."

"It's something to ponder. And just maybe, it might be real in the killer's twisted mind."

"You could be right, Luce."

"We need to invent the significance of the word *key*—you know, the blank key—then proceed to that peculiar message the killer left at the scene. Maybe think *blue* and *green* that make up *grue* and *bleen*. Like looking at the problem from another perspective ... or metaphorically speaking from another dimension.

"Could our psychopath be alluding to the bar northwest of here going by the name of Blue Skies. In other words, work out some hypothetical temporal framework about when he will appear and where. Then hopefully we can decipher his MO."

"Easy to say, but doing it is by no means a dance in the park," Mike mumbles. "We will undoubtedly need at least a second homicide before we have enough details. The devil is in the details, as they say."

"Park ... Hey, they call that artificial lake there the Blue Lagoon, don't they?"

"It proves the point I made before," Mike responds. "The idea of blue skies, rhythm and blues, blue Monday, or whatever, are a few possibilities among a mountain of others."

"You're right," Lucia concedes. "It's complex."

"No piece of cake."

"Yes, I know."

"What's the alternative? Just sit around and twiddle our thumbs?"

"That might be the only option."

"Not very promising, is it?"

"No."

They continue ambulating. Where are they now? Oh yes. Starbucks. Coffee, after that pasty hot dog. Sounds level-headed. They enter. Have coffee. Make small talk. Head back to the precinct. And shortly thereafter call it quits for the day. Much painful speculative thinking, few concrete gainful results.

PRESSING THE CASE

LUCIA finds herself at headquarters in her office the next morning with a strange feeling. She hardly has any recollection as to how she got there. She left the apartment, took the bus, walked to the precinct, and entered her office.

But it's all a blank. She was deep in thought. As if not in this world. As if she had been playacting, so to speak, unthinkingly, and was then abruptly jerked into her real world, whatever that is ...

I've got to get this case behind me before it drives me to drink or to the nut house, she thinks to herself.

She checks her e-mail. And ... *What's this? The subject is "Dearest"? Most likely spam or scam. Should I delete it? No. Better check it out. You never know.* It says,

U 'R my Nfatuashun & my joy. We must stay connected.

So it's you! I know your signature. Garbled language using strange rhetorical combinations and texting tricks—how did you know my e-mail address? Stay connected? You and me? You're trapped in your own illusions! And better still, you're beginning to reveal yourself.

Can't resist it, eh? Self-centered bastard. A few more moves like this *and I'll be onto you, soon doing an in-your-face slam dunk.*

The Master in Chief enters, saying, "The press is out there on the street. Soon they'll be banging on the door to get in. We have to give them something."

"And a good morning to you too, Fay. The press? Be my guest," Lucia remarks with a slight giggle.

"You notice I'm not laughing. You also know you're the one best qualified to field their questions."

"Forget them. We must focus on what few facts we have for now. And besides, you're the chief. You should represent us peons," Lucia tells the Captain.

"What are you saying? That I send them off? They'll crucify me. And my superiors will egg them on! Entertain them. Just do what you must. I can't send them away. There would be an outcry you could hear from here to Timbuktu."

Lucia thinks, *Spineless Fay, as always. How in the world did she make it to the top?* "Okay Fay, will do."

She gives Fay a curt salute. Fay scowls, turns, and walks briskly toward her office. Lucia leaves for the front door. She has determination written all over her face. She viciously opens the door.

The din reminds her of hens cooped up at the chicken pen back home. She raises and lowers her arms, asking for silence and calm. Pushing and shoving breaks out. The customary electronic devices extend out and into her face. Anticipating facial expressions. She begins ...

"Good morning. Investigation has hardly begun. Consequently, I have little to say at this juncture. But I welcome your questions."

Lucia extends a hand, "Yes, sir ... You, with the red tie."

"Inspector Vieira, Don Stern speaking."

Lucia: "Yes?"

"Knowing a serial killer is a psychopath can influence how law enforcers carry out their investigation. To what extent have you followed this route?"

Lucia: "We don't know if the person who committed the crime is a serial killer or a psychopath. Our forensic crew is working on it. If the need arises, we will call on a profiler, and if not, we will wait until further evidence is collected. At this moment we can make no decision until more facts are in hand ... Yes, Barbara ..."

"Thank you. Psychopathic personality traits include charm, charisma, coolness under pressure, and lack of empathy, remorse, or a sense of guilt. Do you find these traits in the criminal under investigation?"

Lucia: "I have no idea at this point. We have found the victim but we have not yet received a forensic report. I can say no more. Yes ..."

"Paul Mortensen."

Lucia: "Go on please."

"What have you gathered from the note the perpetrator of the crime left?"

Lucia: "I have nothing to say regarding your question ... How do you—"

"I understand the language he used is bizarre, straight out of Alice in Wonderland. Have you deduced anything from the nature of the message?"

Lucia: "I am not at liberty to divulge any information about any alleged note. Yes, Nick ..."

"Was the note left at the crime scene comparable to anything the department has investigated in the past?"

Lucia: "I have nothing to say ... Yes ... your name?"

"Walt Wycliff."

Lucia: "Let's hear it."

"Is such a note of the type a psychopath would leave in order to taunt those investigating the crime?"

Lucia: "I have nothing to say. Read the literature on psychopathic behavior. You, sir ..."

"Mark Johnstone. Do you think your being a female investigator has anything to do with the reason the killer left this type of message?" Lucia: "That's irrelevant. Next ..."

"Chad Lewis. Psychopaths can reveal a warped sense of humor. Are you taking this into consideration?"

Lucia: "We do not yet know whether the perp is a psychopath, so I have no opinion."

"Then why haven't you called in a profiler. Could he not give you an idea about what you should be looking for?"

Lucia: "The time has not yet come for effective profiling. We need more evidence. Yes ... Madeline, I think ..."

"Thank you. Inspector Vieira, psychopaths don't procrastinate. Yet, they act on the spur of the moment. Consequently, aren't you expecting another crime within the next few days?"

Lucia: "I have no opinion since we do not have sufficient evidence on the basis of which we can make predictions."

"But do you not expect the next crime to occur soon and do you not believe it will reveal the perp's MO?"

Lucia: "With little evidence, we have no reason to believe there will be another homicide. John ..."

"People in some professions, like CEOs, lawyers, salespersons, police officers, surgeons and civil servants in high positions manifest certain psychopathological tendencies. Have you considered the possible professional background of the assassin?"

Lucia: "You failed to include media icons and journalists in your list. Have you analyzed yourself, John? If not, I would suggest you do so."

Laughter.

Lucia: "I regret to say that your questions are redundant and of little substance regarding this crime. Please do your homework before the next press conference. Good day ladies and gentlemen."

Lucia makes a hasty retreat as the press erupts into its former hen house din.

FAY is in the hallway. Impatiently anticipating Lucia's return. She gives Lucia a quizzical look. Lucia looks back at Fay with fire in her eyes, "What the hell is going on? Who leaked information about the note that son of a bitch left?"

"I have no idea," Fay replies. "But I will get to the bottom of it."

"Do so? I'll emulsify the bastard!"

"Calm down."

"Calm down? The information is out. Now I'll have to contend with the public reaction. What's worse, the killer is now directly in the spotlight and obviously gloating over the attention he's getting. If he hadn't planned on committing another crime, I'm sure he's seriously considering it now."

"Lucia, do your job, come what may. Pay everything else no mind."

"Sure, like a good psychopath. Worry not about the consequences. Do what gives me gratification and bloats my ego. I'm not like that and you know it. Someone else could get killed because of this goddamn disclosure to the press."

"Yes, I know. But stay focused. If not, you might blow it, because you are up against a shrewd customer."

"Yeah," Lucia says, "and he just got shrewder after watching that damn press conference. You can be assured he was glued to the TV."

"Come on, Lucia. Let's get out of here," Mike says as he approaches her. "I have something I need to tell you."

They enter Lucia's office and sit. Mike fidgets nervously. Lucia anticipates. He says, "Lucia, believe me. I never said anything to anybody."

"I know, Mike. Your leaking the information never entered my mind."

"Thank you. That note left at the scene. I was thinking about it. Obviously, the crime was not a one-time affair. He's up to something else."

"Yes, I've thought about it too."

"And the press. When there are more messages and another homicide, they'll go wild with their 'See there? We told you so' confidence. How will we confront them? They'll hound us till the cows come home as you say."

"You're right, Mike. I don't know what I'll tell them until the time comes. I'd just like to get my hands on whoever let the cat out of the bag and strangle him—or her."

"I'm with you there. By the way, I liked your final words to the press. Their ruthless aggression, their lack of sympathy or concern over the people they trample on when trying to get the first scoop. It's like they've got a little psychopathy in them."

"Could be."

"What do we do now, Luce?"

"Beats me. Let's check with the forensic psychologist."

"Bill Evans?"

"Yes. He might be able to give us a hint."

While on their way, Mike has a host of questions. Lucia has to admire his gumption. He is shrewd, inquisitive, and resourceful. At times, he puts her on the spot. But his queries are penetrating, and in her responses, she often finds herself coming to terms with some of the issues that have her tied in knots.

Entertaining serious discussion with Mike while they're on their way to Bill's place, Lucia says, "If you turn on the TV, go to the movies, or enter a bookstore, chances are you will run across a fictional rather than a factual portrayal of some brilliant serial killer and a forensic psychologist or profiler able to pin down the case with a psychological sketch. It appears so clean, in contrast to the messiness we have to put up with."

"How I'm finding that out," Mike says with a note of frustration.

Lucia goes on, "People think it's as if forensic experts read tea leaves and magically come up with the answers. Truth be told, they rigorously analyze the situation. They don't simply toss a handful of bones on the table and read the signs.

"Forensic specialists also have the unenviable task of assessing the alleged criminal's mental state for the possibility of an insanity plea, incompetence to stand trial, prediction of violence and risk if put on bail, interpreting polygraph data, and analyzing personality. It's by no means a simple matter."

"So why are we going to a forensic shrink, Luce? Shouldn't we do that when we have a suspect?"

"What I want to know is what kind of deformed mind would leave that idiotic message. Maybe Bill can give us an idea."

"I see. After we talk to him, do we consult the profiler and go from there?"

"At this point, I see no need for a profile or answers to legal questions. I want answers to strictly psychological ones. This is a long shot, but Bill might reveal some sort of clue."

LUCIA and Mike spill it all out at Bill's place. What there is at least, for there isn't much. Bill listens attentively without cutting in.

When they finish, he thoughtfully responds, "You certainly have an enigma on your hands. As I see it—and keep in mind I am doing no more than speculating since data are lacking—the person in question appears to be suffering from antisocial personality disorder (ASPD)."

"But, Bill," Lucia cuts in, "tell us something we don't already know."

"I'm getting to that. Well … it's like this. You are familiar with the list of disorders commonly called the hare psychopathological checklist or PCL-R developed by Robert Hare, are you not?"

"Yes."

"Studies tell us that while fifty to eighty percent of the criminals are diagnosed with ASPD, only fifteen to thirty percent make the grade as fullfledged psychopaths when given the PCL-R test."

"I've read something to that effect."

"This would tend to indicate that you are not up against a psychopathic criminal. However, given his communication with you in a written note and an e-mail, he might be psychopathic after all."

"How do you figure that? I had this vague premonition that the predator might be too brilliant to fit the ordinary psycho category. Psychos usually have intelligence gaps, logical deficiencies."

"It seems to me that the guilty party is likely in a dissociative state of mind."

"What do you mean?" Mike asks.

"He leaves his everyday stream of consciousness and ventures into what he thinks is a better world. He is incapable of appreciating the minds of others because he has become depersonalized, or dissociated. He has lost contact with the concrete world around him, and he has distorted it, sometimes grotesquely.

"In other words, he is artificially objectivizing his world and making it over into a different world of his own liking. His incapacity properly to socialize with other humans puts him into this fantasyland where serially killing is as easy for him as playing tit-tat-toe. Consequently, he sees every social exchange as a chance to engage in a feeding frenzy, a test of will power, where he has a distinct advantage."

"What gives him the idea he can always win?" Lucia butts in.

"He knows people will swallow anything if it is liberally seasoned with lavish praise that tweaks their belly button. And he is apparently a master at intuiting what turns people on. If this doesn't do the trick, he'll convince them how he's become the victim of his circumstances. He will make an emotional appeal to their sympathy, and he's a master at that game as well.

"Think of Ted Bundy. He wore a fake plaster cast so he could appeal to women's sentiments, and he persuaded them to help him get around. Then he killed them as a reward for their good intentions."

Lucia speculates, "Serial killers, or psychopaths as it were, live for the moment, taking advantage of every opportunity. They can be counted among society's most proficient pragmatists."

"You're saying that they do it on the fly, improvising as they go along?" Mike says with a quizzical look.

"Basically, yes."

"Then what about the murderer's signature qualifying his crime as particularly his? And what's his own private MO?" Mike inquires.

"Combine them, and you have something like what we would call a heuristic device," Bill tells him.

"You'll have to explain that to the novice in your midst," Mike says. "A heuristic device is a loose rule-of-thumb he uses if he thinks it will come in handy. And if not, he invents some other rule-of-thumb."

"What you mean, Bill," Lucia says, "is that he will likely change his MO along every step of the way?"

"That's a definite possibility, Lucia."

Mike turns to Lucia and says, "This sounds like our killer all right, doesn't it?"

"For lack of evidence to the contrary, I would tend to agree."

Bill continues, "Let me add a generality about the psychopathic mind that might be taken as a matter of degree rather than kind. Psychopaths basically come in three flavors: *organized*, *disorganized*, and *mixed*.

"The organizers are usually of above average intelligence, the disorganized are of average or below average intelligence, and those whose manner of organizing is a mixture can be strung along the spectrum. Your killer is obviously highly organized and of well above average intelligence."

"Oh" is Lucia's obscure response, for her mind is elsewhere. Then she asks, "What if the criminal is not male?"

"A possibility. The criminal might be a black widow predator, as they call them. About a quarter of the serial killers are female. Poison is one of their preferred methods. Others are stabbing, suffocation, drowning, and often as a last resort, shooting."

"And their ethnicity whether either male or female?"

"While the majority consists of white males, psychopathically twisted minds are known among other ethnicities as well. That TV show, *Criminal Minds*, portrays serial killers of all stripes," Bill adds. "Murderabilia is unfortunately a favorite item in the pop culture circuit these days."

"Yes, unfortunately," Lucia adds. "Oh, by the way, Mike and I have entertained the daffy idea that the murderer is, like … if I might say it … playacting. You know, with his note he seems to make a game out of the whole affair. What do you think? Is it just a crackpot hunch or might there be something to it?"

"Hmm … if he's playacting his theater is in a world of his own making, and his game is deadly serious. Keep in mind that he'll go to any length in order to win."

"We are definitely in tune with the idea."

They thank Bill for the info and advice and head off for pastures that turn out to be neither green nor promising. The killer's MO is simply not forthcoming. He offers virtually no clue. The forensics crew has reported that they found no evidence of undue violence, no fingerprints or traces of blood. He has covered his tracks beautifully.

So, at this point, Lucia says to herself, *our hands are empty and our minds are dusty, with a few vague ideas that never pan out. Maybe it's time to consult the profiler after all. Maybe he can provide us with something concrete we can get our hands dirty with.*

"We'll have to give Bill's advice some thought," Lucia concludes, her mind in a swirl.

LATER, Lucia finds herself wandering around the precinct in search of Mike. Again. Seems that's all she's done lately. But Lucia realizes he is diligent, and she is confident he will always conscientiously remain on the job. He is definitely a social animal. Affable, gregarious, and unreserved. At times, he's like a chicken scrambling around after its head has been lopped off. He does his job though, so she can't complain …

"There you are, Mike. Let me catch up with you once in a while, will you?"

"Sorry. I've been down there with the forensic squad. Nothing. Norm the affable nerd has no answers."

"If he doesn't, I doubt anybody does."

"What's up?"

"We're off to see the profiler."

"You're more confident than I am, Lucia."

"We have to go down all avenues and dark alleys while hoping for the best."

They soon enter Jack Russell's cave a few doors to the south. He has an oversize photograph of Freud on the wall with a caption he placed below it, saying, "Sometimes a psycho is just a sicko." Everybody knows he claims a psycho can presumably be analyzed by fast-track Freudian tunnel-minded formulas, but a sicko is simply who he is and resists generalizations.

Jack's watching the video clip of a young hood who tried to rob a convenience store and a buxom female customer knocked him cold with a can of corn, apparently ignoring the loaded gun he had in his hand.

"They ought to have a dame like that in every store instead of some quivering cashier with a gun in hand," he observes. "She's got more balls than a herd of those immature wannabe hoods."

"Your big guy up there, Freud, once said a child would destroy the world if he had the power," Lucia observes. "Much the same can be said of serial killers. I guess they haven't grown up."

"Don't sell them short, and don't sell Freud short. He focused on the brain's topology years before psychology caught up with him. Anyway, what can I do for you? I shouldn't even ask, should I?"

"No, unfortunately," Lucia replies with a heavy sigh after taking a lungful of air. "Why don't you invent something for us and make us happy. That's what you guys are paid for, isn't it?"

Jack gives Lucia a cold, penetrating look, winces, then breaks into a wry smile and says, "Flattery will get you nowhere. It's not just anybody that can invent true lies at the drop of a hat. I'll do my best at any rate. Just for you."

Lucia replies, "That's what we came for, to get entertained. So, deliver one of your best."

"I studied your report. You don't have much to go on, do you?"

"I'm afraid not," Lucia responds with a shake of her head.

"He's obliviously no blundering idiot."

"Not in the least" Mike is quick to note.

Jack gives them a smile as if savoring his observation.

What's behind that derisive smile? Lucia asks herself. Mike thinks, *Is he gloating over our failure to come up with something?*

"Where do I begin when you give me neither evidence nor eyewitnesses?"

"You're the specialist on subterfuge, Jack. All we want is an answer that will put our minds a little bit at ease."

"Too much to ask for," Jack says with the smirk still plastered on his face. "At the very least, I would say he's probably in the top ten percentile with respect to intelligence. Maybe even higher."

"We've guessed that much," Lucia tells him. "What about his signature? Did you notice anything that might qualify him in comparison to other serial killers or psychos?"

"Sorry to say, no. I'll must add that unfortunately I will probably need details from another couple of homicides."

"That isn't wishful thinking, is it?" Mike is quick to ask, with an ironic twist of his own.

"Certainly not. I'm only saying I need additional information before I can think seriously about the criminal's possible signature or MO."

"By the way, how do you even know he's a he?" Lucia asks.

"I don't. Not yet."

"How do you know ethnicity is not a factor," Lucia again challenges Jack.

"I'm not sure of that either."

Lucia wistfully remarks, "Lucky you. I wish I could give Fay answers like that and continue to draw a salary."

Jack gives her another scowl and responds, "It's all in denying your omniscience without sounding out and out stupid."

Mike asks, "Is there anything else you can tell us about the sicko?"— "He's no sicko" Jack is quick to respond. "He's too organized to be anything short of a psychopath, and as a psychopath, he's playing a game with both of you … With us," he corrects himself. "I would venture to guess that his needs include neither sex nor monetary gain. Yet he nurtures some form of deep-seated anger despite the surface appearance of his playfulness. But I can't quite put my finger on it."

"How can you be sure about what you've said after telling us we don't have enough evidence for you to give us an opinion?" Mike ventures to ask.

Jack winces again and quickly reacts, "Who me? Sure of myself? I'm the sociological proof of Heisenberg's quantum uncertainty. I'm sure of nothing."

"Yeah. Despite what you say, I know you are one of the best," Lucia says.

"I begin with a guesstimate which is often wrong," Jack goes on. "Sherlock Holmes once said he never guesses. Not true. He guesses, and he's a master at it. Because he has a prepared mind. That's the key. Still, many of my guesses are wrong.

"But if a guess holds promise, I give it the ol' inductive test and then subject it to some contrary-to-fact conditional or hypothetical situation. Then I think about it, again and again. Finally, if it stands up to scrutiny, I buy into it. But in the final analysis, sometimes you can and sometimes you can't."

"Thoughtful appraisal. Admirable qualities. Anyway, we've gotta ske-daddle," Lucia says. "Much obliged for the tips, Jack."

"By the way, he's probably around fifty," Jack adds. "A Young Turk full of seething hostility would have neither the tolerance nor the time for the type of play your criminal engaged in. An old codger wouldn't have the energy. And someone in a midlife crisis might be either on the pitypot or obsessed with the fountain of youth.

"But your guy? He's charming and perplexing. He's got it all. And he doesn't take himself so seriously. That, my friends, is what continues to confuse all of us."

Mike thinks, *Sounds like he's infatuated with the killer.*

"He's my age!" Lucia observes with surprise written all over her face.

"Yes, he is," Jack says, "and that could be the reason he has figuratively taken you in his arms."

"Holy cow! Spare me," Lucia blurts out.

"I should also mention," Jack remarks, "that when you have more information for me, I would like to tie it together, construct an official report, and send it in."

"We will make every effort to provide the information you need," Mike says.

Jack stands up from behind his desk. Towering above Lucia and Mike, he walks them to the door while telling them they'll probably have trouble with this case since the killer doesn't fall into any of the common categories, but he wishes them luck anyway.

They plod toward the parking garage. In silence. It has become customary over the past few days. Too much to think about. Too many mysteries. Too many journeys into unknown territory. Too much to do.

AFTER they are seated in the car, Mike breaks the ice.

"The way he launches his conjectures into the atmosphere, you would think he has no more than a rampant free-for-all imagination. But somehow he manages to get it more right than wrong. Despite his unconvincing confession."

"My age" Lucia is stuck in that flower of youth fixation.

"Hey, Luce, you with me?"

"Oh ... I mean, yes. You know, Mike? I was wondering. What the hell is the killer's motivation? Human behavior goes along unique paths in response to environmental and biological factors. Whatever this guy's MO might be, from what we've gathered, he can change it at the drop of a hat.

"By the time we think we've figured him out, he will have become someone else with a different MO. I'm thinking he's completely unpredictable, and we don't stand a chance in hell of getting him in our clutches any time soon."

"That's a tough problem. I'm afraid, Lucia, that at this stage of the game, I can't offer an opinion. Besides, I'm too exhausted to jolt my neurons."

"I agree. We've been at it eighteen hours at a whack over the past few days. Let's call it off for now, get some rest, and try to work something out at the office tomorrow."

"Music to my ears."

LUCIA AND BOB

LUCIA enters her apartment. While thinking, *I gotta get this place in order. Not that it's in shambles.* But she's the type that has a proper place for everything and wants everything in its place. A perfectionist. Demanding of herself.

Yet she holds on to her charming Brazilian ways that include confidence in her capacity to improvise when unexpected situations pop up. She is adept at relying on her wits, creatively inventing and concocting as she goes along. She makes do with what she has at hand for the occasion, entering verbal give and take with friends, associates, competitors, and enemies. It's her type of signature setting her apart from many of her leadfoot colleagues whose inclination is to go by the books, and if that fails, they tend to flounder.

Her mobile phone sounds.

What now? she asks as she sticks it to her ear, expecting the worse. *Oh, it's Bob. Wants to go out for a pizza.*

"Please, Bob. Not today. I'm too tired for words."

"In that case, we won't talk," Bob replies. "Just chomp down."

"I am famished, that's for sure," Lucia remarks.

"Pick you up in fifteen minutes?"

"What can I say?"

"Why not yes?"

"I'm sorry. I had a devilish day."

"No rest for the weary?" Bob asks her. "I have to put up with conniving teens, you with hoodwinking felons. We're almost in the same boat."

"You don't know the half of it."

"Pardon my English, but you've never had to cope with thirty scheming underprivileged kids whose goal in life is to empty their brains of informative content."

"And I'm up against lies, deception, guile, fraud, trickery, all outside the law."

"I try to outsmart them and give them what they need to become respectable citizens. They cook up ways to divert me from my efforts with the vast repertoire of charades they have at hand."

"I have to take each and every one of the criminal's charade, decipher their smoke screen of conning, fraudulence, mocking bogus moves, and if I manage to nab them, they go to court, confident that their slick lawyers in expensive suits and Italian shoes will get them off."

"Well, Lucia, my fair lady. Now that we got that out of our system, fifteen minutes and I'll pick you up?"

"Fifteen minutes."

"A drink before we leave?"

"A drink."

"I'll be looking at you, kid."

"Looking at me?"

"Humphrey Bogart in that movie. You remember?"

They disconnect.

No, Lucia thinks. *I don't want to remember.* She sits, staring at nothing. *Pizza? Too heavy. I'll talk him out of it, and we'll go somewhere else,* she thinks to herself. She sits for another minute. *No time to shower. Just clean up and get into a change of clothes. How I would like to trade places with him for a week.* She looks at the clothes hangers. Grabs one. *Jeans? Yes.*

Her head returns to the wire contraptions in the skimpy blouse section. A hand extends, touches a piece of fabric sticking out. Separates the hook out of the rod holding it upright. Looks at the item it holds. *Yeah, good enough. Nothing special.*

She changes. Washes up. Rustles her hair around a bit. Puts on a little make-up. In fact, very little, as usual. *It's what's in my head that counts, not on the surface of this facial wrapping, this facade called skin.* She flips on the

HD tube. Selects MSNBC news. Stares at the screen with nothing on her mind. Customary, after a day of intensive mind wracking.

Suddenly eyes pop wide and face jerks up. "He's here," she literally yells out, "Yeah!"

Door opens—she rarely locks it, assuming she can handle herself come what may with a firearm always close at hand. Bob's head appears. She looks at him as if she might contemplate her two fish in the bowl to the right. He looks at her as if they'd been with each other for the entire day.

Door closes. A quick kiss. His right hand holds a bottle of wine.

"Wine?"

"Wine."

"I'll get some glasses," she says.

"And a corkscrew," he adds.

She enters the kitchen and soon reappears. He reads the bottle's label. She hands him the corkscrew. She puts two glasses on the end table. Sits on the sofa. And turns her eyes to the flat screen. He pops the cork. Pours wine in the glasses and hands her one.

She sips. "Good."

He sips. "Yes."

They say nothing for the next few minutes while tipping the glasses and staring at the tube.

He says, "Ready?"

"I suppose, but let's do something light. Pizza's too gut filling."

"Agreed."

They leave, but not, of course, before she rinses the glasses out, corks the bottle, pats down the sofa, and adjusts her blouse in the mirror.

Everything now in its proper place, they leave for the local deli.

He has a sandwich. She has a Caesar's salad. They take their time. Alone.

The young man behind the counter occasionally gives them a furtive glance.

He's non-present as far as they are concerned. In fact, there might as well be no deli, sandwich, or salad. No small circular table between them. No chairs holding them up. They are just there. Slowly munching. In virtual oblivion, it might seem.

"You OK?" Bob asks.

"Mm, hum."

"Want to go?"

"Uh-huh."

Two bodies rise, and walk. The young man watches. Says, "Have a good evening."

Two heads turn. Nod. She says, "You too."

He opens the door. She goes out. He goes out. He says nothing while putting his arm around her. They enter the car. Bob heads it back to Lucia's apartment.

Lucia knows Bob's ways. Bob knows Lucia's. A schoolteacher. A detective.

One strives to develop young minds that are troubled, often well-nigh directionless, and don't know they don't know their potential.

The other competes with child-like minds that think they are all-knowing adult minds. Confident that the world is theirs for the taking. Because they are smarter, wiser, and shrewder than the idiots out there who work nine to five, fight with a spouse and kids, and struggle to pay the bills.

Two professionals struggling to create a better world, a world that resists their every effort.

As would be expected, psychopaths are not big on entering the teaching profession, though some do just that. Their preference tends toward police work, among other professions.

That's neither here nor there. Right now, there's Bob and Lucia, Lucia and Bob.

They arrive at Lucia's place. Bob parks the car. They get out. Enter the building. Go up the flight of stairs.

Lucia pulls out the key. *Key? ... No. Don't want to so much as think about it,* she thinks.

The door opens. They enter. Sit on the couch. Make small talk. They get up. She walks him to the door. Their kiss is so light their lips hardly touch. He leaves.

She leaves the door unlocked. Enters dreamland minutes after she hits the sack. Another day ends.

NOT that Lucia's life is hopelessly routine. Not that she has no real personal and intimate contact with others, with acquaintances, friends, and a lover. Not that outside her work, her life is uneventful.

It's that today was challenging, demanding, taxing. Inordinately so. Exhaustively so.

The next morning, she's up at dawn. Making mental preparations for the day.

That goddamn killer, fuckin' X-Man, she thinks to herself.

He obviously has her obsessed. It's as if he hypnotized her, bewitched her. In a way, he enchanted her. Not that kind of enchantment that opens the door to a dream world. Enchantment that is magical for sure, but it perplexes, confounds, bewilders, puzzles.

X-Man? Did I call him that? she asks herself. *Yes, I did.*

The thought came to her last night when eating her Caesar's salad with Bob.

X-Man. His life is robotic. He lives in manufactured bliss. Each move is machinelike. Each event is a scheme, part of a plot, carefully engineered.

There's nothing to him other than X, an unknown, unqualified variable. Many possibilities, any one of which might pop up when least expected. Like a blank key. He has no features, no specific character traits. He's just X. Same as all Xs.

Bob, she thinks, *contends with flesh and blood subjects. She struggles with Xs, nobodies who think they are somebodies, but they aren't because they reinvent themselves at every turn.*

A hopelessly pathetic lot, she mulls over in her mind.

"Pathetic," she repeats out loud as if there was somebody around to hear her conclusion. No response.

Par for the course, she thinks. And sits for a few moments. Staring at the ceiling. Then, *Better get my ass in high gear.*

JUST SINGING THE BLUES?

BACK at the office, Mike says, "Lucia? I'm still wondering about your so glibly calling the killer a psychopath."

"I've been speculating over that too. In the note he left us, he used that nonsensical Chomskyan phrase garbled up with portmanteau rhetoric for some purpose. Like a riddle for us to solve."

"He's playing with us, manipulating us. Just like a psychopath. But I sense some sort of ulterior motive unbecoming of the stock-in-trade psychopath ... And by the way, don't call him the killer. From this moment forward, he's X-Man."

"X-Man?" Mike asks.

"X-Man. X, an unknown variable. And a man, I presume, as a nonconstant constant."

"X-Man, something like those guys in the movies? You have to be kidding," Mike blurts out.

"No. X-Man the *exaggerocious.*"

"Come again?"

"You know. What they call a rhetorical portmanteau blend. X-Man the exaggeratedly atrocious, vicious, hideous, monstrous. We might as well qualify him by using his own twisted language."

"Hey, I like it."

"Well, I don't. Having to call him that, I mean. Because he remains so much of a mystery. But we have nothing else to go on. So, X-Man he is. For now."

"We have to find out what he's up to," Mike says. "But he doesn't leave clues around that might help us. By the way, are you now sure he's a man?"

"No. Might be a woman. Female psychopaths are as good at the grubby profession as their male counterparts. Jack said so much."

"I would think a woman is better at the game of covering up her motives than a man."

"You a sexist, Mike? Heavens! It doesn't become you."

"What I mean is that women have to cover their asses more than men, since society has tried its best to make them more vulnerable."

"Whatever ..."

"Think again about the crazy message he left at that crime scene, Luce. 'Drealorless *grue* coms retuously impest.' *Colorless* and *dream* make *drealorless* and so on."

"Yes, and in the final analysis, we have 'Colorless *grue* dreams rest impetuously.' A take on Chomsky's 'Colorless green ideas dream furiously.' Not terribly creative. The important question is, why the diff?"

"You got me."

SHE gives him a glance. Her eyes light up, "I have yet to tell you about something that happened this morning on the way here. I got this message on my mobile phone ... here ... look at it,

> *What force and strength cannot get through; J,*
> *with gentle touch and insertion can do; and many*
> *in the street would not in anguish stand; if J were*
> *not there as a stalwart friend in hand; what am J?*

"That's vulgar! In fact, it's grotesque. Some sick porno psycho. Who else would have sent you such a lewd message disguised as a riddle?"

"X-Man, no doubt. Look how he signed it. 'Your soul mate in crime.' Who could that be other than X-Man?"

"I agree. But what call did he have to send you that filthy crap?"

"The sexual innuendos are no more than surface, I take it. There's some motive behind the message."

"Go figure."

"I sent the message to the technical crew. They tapped into the system and told me the source was from a phone that was reported stolen."

"You don't say."

"Like I said in Leonard's office, X-Man can steal a phone here, a tablet there, a laptop somewhere else, and we'll stand hardly a chance of chasing him down using ordinary electronic means. To top matters off, he can do the same with a printer in whatever cybercafe happens to be at hand in the whole damn city."

"Our only recourse for now is to decipher the riddle and see what we can make of it," Mike concludes with a dejected voice.

"Yeah, I guess."

"It cannot get through, but with a gentle insertion and touch it can. People on the street would be in anguish, except when it's in hand," Lucia says out loud while rolling it around in her mind. "Think, Mike. What does it mean?"

"It's in the street and it's in a hand. A touch, insertion, going through, and performing its trick. It's not X-Man's penis at all. It's a key. Right? Not the blank key, but a key that's been cut and ready for use."

"Hey, you're sharp!"

"Now we have an answer to the riddle," Mike smugly declares. "But the problem is this. What's a key got to do with X-Man's message at the scene? All we have is a blank key, and we must transform the blanks into what could become an inordinate number of riddles."

"The key I found is nothing but blankness, emptiness."

"Oh yes," Mike responds. "And as you put it, there are infinite possibilities before us. No help at all."

"The blank key image explains at least a few things," Lucia tells Mike. "*Grue* dreams. Resting impetuously. Dreams that change from green to blue at some point in time."

"No more than garble if you ask me."

"Perhaps, but if that's so, his primary motive is probably to keep us in a state of confusion."

"If you'll pardon my saying so," Mike tells Lucia, "this so-called criminal investigation strikes me as so bizarre it's beyond words."

"I agree," Lucia remarks as if she was reluctant to do so. "But we have to give everything due consideration. Anyway, let's see ... Change, from green to blue. Maybe that's the clue. So, we must create some sort of portmanteau reality within which we can operate. You recall the first murder was on Green Street. So maybe the next crime will occur someplace where blue is a theme. But where? Well, anyway I'm just grasping at straws."

"As far as I know, there's no Blue Street or Avenue in this city. I'll ask Chris over there. He knows this city like the palm of his hand."

Mike leaves the office looking for Chris among all the people present in his neck of the headquarters. It's a boiling hubbub of activity. Police officers scurrying around. A couple of suit-and-tie men, obviously authorities of some kind or other in search of someone. A lawyer asking to see her client who was taken into custody. A couple of drunks dragged in a few minutes ago with thick tongues protesting their apprehension. A young wannabe hood at the front of a line pulling at the back of his jeans that begin almost at knee level, with a tattoo-laden neck, forehead, and left cheek.

A flustered employee at the front desk trying to answer a host of questions that simultaneously come her way. An officer keeping a close eye on the unruly line at the desk.

Mike's gregarious voice pipes in over the humdrum, "Hey, Chris, is there a Blue Street, Avenue, Lane, or whatever in this godforsaken urban sprawl?"

"Not that I know of!" Chris yells back.

Mike returns to Lucia's desk. "He doesn't know of any."

"No problem, Mike. I might have it figured out. The criminal's original note at the crime scene is self-contradictory in another way, and likely for a reason. Dreams are neither colorless nor green nor blue. That much hardly needs saying. More important, they don't rest, and if they did, they couldn't manifest impetuousness.

"Dreams are always moving on. One damn image after another. So also our ruminations. As we go from the crime scene at Green Street to the northwest. And we're soon thinking the Blue Skies Bar."

"Ah yes, Irving Berlin. 'I was as blue as could be but blue skies smile at me'," Mike sings, terribly out of tune. "Or something to that effect. Anyway."

"You're close, but not quite, Mike," Lucia says with a muffled laugh.

"If Blue Skies it is, then *when* will it be? We know the space coordinates, but the time of the crime escapes us."

"I'm afraid so."

"Besides," Mike adds, "what does that Blue Skies place have to do with our answer to the riddle? Where does the key come in?"

"I haven't a clue."

"This is silly, isn't it? We should be busy solving a crime and we're caught in puzzle-solving entanglements. Almost like Leonard fiddling around with a bunch of chess moves."

"Yes. Silly."

"And Jack didn't help us out much either," Mike adds.

"No. If the reporters and the public knew about this whole mish-mash it would strike them as some kind of wacky joke and us as innocent as a couple of kids playing mud pies."

"Kids don't play mud pies anymore."

"They did when I was a snot-nose urchin in rural Texas."

"If X-Man heard you say that, he would use it in his next riddle."

"If you tell him, you're toast."

MIKE leaves with an ear-to-ear grin on his mug. Lucia says to herself, *He's still green behind that pair of ears and a madcap case like this will be of little help toward initiating him properly. This case seems too comical to take seriously.*

Lucia would have preferred the customary killer thriller lending itself to one of those stock-in-trade stereotypes. But this? She would like to see the guy face-to-face. Confront him directly. Rake him over the coals. Find out what makes him tick.

Yes, what does he have in mind, she questions herself. *Think, Lucia. Why would he go to the trouble of inventing such an off-the-wall MO, if you can so much as call it that? Can he really be serious? Does the idea of a key have some screwball symbolism? Colorless ideas!*

What a comedy! How absurd can this get?

Her mind empties itself of such thoughts, save the absurdity of it all. Frustrated, she goes out for another helping of java. Alone. Lost in empty thought, or better, no thought in the least.

A blank key. Zero-point. Emptiness, she thinks to herself. *You can't say the word because if you do, it's not emptiness, it's not that to which it refers. Maybe that's the answer. Wordlessness. It's beyond words. It's ineffable. Just let it gestate, Lucia, and see what surfaces at some unexpected moment.*

She recalls mathematician Henri Poincaré's essay over a century ago about his solving a mathematical problem that had plagued him for some time. First, you must create a lot of input. Then struggle with the internalized ideas to find the answer. If that fails, take a few days off and let it wind around in your head. It gestates.

Then, during the most unexpected of moments, lo and behold, it surfaces. The Eureka! moment. Poincaré writes that his solution struck him with such force while he was boarding a trolley that he almost stumbled on the steps and fell in a heap.

That's it. Let those offbeat ideas and happenings gestate for a while. Can't do any harm.

Lucia catches a glimpse of the passersby on the sidewalk across the street through the window of the café. A panhandler has his hand out to a senior lady who is fumbling around in her purse, obviously for some change. She can't find it.

He becomes impatient and sticks his hand in her purse. She slaps his hand. He jerks back and says something, likely with indignant outrage in his eyes.

A well-dressed man in a business suit stops, pulls out his wallet, and tries to give the panhandler a bill, saying something to him and nodding at the lady. The panhandler makes a lewd gesture at the three-piece suit and leaves.

The world's a stage, and we are all actors in a massive comedy of errors, Lucia muses.

Lucia turns back to her coffee. Amused and somewhat at ease with herself, *Yes. There's no harm in letting the set of equally comical fortuitous conjunctions prance around in my head for a spell.*

NUMBER TWO

AFTER a rough night's sleep, Lucia arrives at headquarters for another day at the criminal nut case consortium. But this isn't the usual morning's activity. It's a whirlwind. What's up?

Lucia goes through the normal good mornings with a sneaky suspicion that eyes are pointing in her direction behind her back. On her way across the spacious hall to her office, Fay intercepts her.

"You didn't see it on the news this morning?" she asks.

"No. Sordid news reports are no way to start my day. What was I supposed to see?"

"There was another homicide."

"Christ! It happened! Where?"

"Not far from here."

"The psycho knows how to insult us. At least that's for sure if nothing else is."

"Grab Mike and get over there," Fay tells Lucia.

"I'm outta here."

She yells at Mike, who is already walking in her direction, eyes straight ahead and glued to her eyes.

"You got word from the Captain?" Mike asks.

"Yes. She said it's walking distance. He's rubbing it in and we can't do a damned thing about it."

"Yeah."

"Let's skedaddle."

"I'm packed up and ready to go."

"What a piece of shit. That guy."

Lucia recalls her early morning meditation on past, present, future, and the mirror image separating them. She thinks, *Border, it's like a gaping chasm between us and X-Man. But hopefully we will close the space. Will I find myself outside looking in? Fathoming him for who he is?*

They take their unmarked car in case they need to make a beeline for somewhere else.

AN inordinate number of gawkers are standing around. Especially for this early in the morning. Lucia and Mike push their way in, badge at the end of their outstretched arms leading the way. They enter the circle whose periphery is held tight by police officers counteracting the relentless pushing and shoving of the surrounding crowd. And there's the victim.

"My God!" Lucia cries out.

"Decapitated!" Mike says with a scowl.

"Her head is completely separated from her body and staring into the sky as if still connected to her body which is lying on its back beside her head."

Voices from the captivated audience chime in, "I don't believe it"—"My God!" What a monster!"—"I'd like to get my hands on the worm that did this"—"Despicable!"

"I think"—

A woman turns around, pushes her way between a couple of onlookers, and vomits on an available piece of sidewalk. Someone giggles. A man hands her his handkerchief. Another woman closes her eyes and shakes her head. Pain is on some faces. A frown on others. Teeth-gnashing anger on still others. All to the tune of Mike's garrulous voice: "Back ... Get back ... Move on people ... We have to take care of our business."

Lucia and Mike get down on their haunches next to the body so they can inspect the severed head. Exchanging observations in the presence of a recording instrument. Latina female. About thirty-five years. Five feet three inches. One hundred and twenty pounds. No surface evidence of rape or excessive violence. Clothing intact. Unopened purse placed in the right hand. Rings on fingers as well as necklace and earrings. Head sheared off with a sharp instrument.

And so on.

Lucia asks the officer in charge what he removed from the scene. With latex-covered hands he produces a note.

"Well, now we know, number two," Lucia says, with an upset look on her face. "What's got me baffled is how the hell he did this here in the open? Surely there must have been at least a few people around."

"It's the times. People don't see what they don't want to see," Mike observes while waving the eager crowd off, his wildly gyrating hands telling them to get lost.

"If MO there is, his leaving notes for us must be part of it," Lucia says while opening the folded eight and a half by eleven sheet of paper. "Yeah, his MO is shining vaguely through a dark glass cloudily. Get this …"

> *Beware the jabberwocky, my fair sleuth! The metallic jaws that bite, the strangling claws that catch! Twas brilling and the slithy toves. Did gyre and gimble in the wave.*

"Directly from Lewis Carroll," Mike observes while nodding his head as if he knew what the words were all about. "He's killing people in unimaginable ways and playing around with us. Daring us to catch him."

"And doing a bang-up job of it if I might say so. But it's not playing or playacting just for the fun of it. For him it's a game. He's out to win, and so far, we are the losers. Uh, my mobile … Just as I might have guessed. He's texted a message. Look at it,

> *When J'm in my proper place J hide, but my head is in plain view outside; what am J?*

"Holy shit! It's almost as lewd as the last one. At first thought, you spontaneously think penis again. What a sick sense of humor."

"Hides, but his head is in plain view," Lucia ponders. "Plain view."

Their heads spontaneously jerk around toward the facial expressions of the crowd surrounding them. Toward bystanders in the distance. Toward windowpanes in nearby buildings. Even toward tree limbs along the street. Nothing.

"Then what does he mean by his head in plain view?" Mike asks.

"You got me. But we should connect the text message with the note left at the scene. 'Jaws that bite' and 'claws that catch.' What's the relevance?"

"Who the hell knows? Ask the White Queen or Humpty Dumpty. They know everything."

"Or the caterpillar," Lucia adds.

"A worm. That fits the killer all right."

"Anyway, we have to solve this problem. Let's put our heads together for some meaningful reasoning."

"Hmm, let me see," Mike speculates. "A jaguar? Rarely seen but lethal when it shows its head."

"Improbable."

"I know. Sometimes it's better that I remain silent and thought a fool than open my mouth and remove all doubt," Mike says, chuckling over his way with words.

"Well, what about a nail," Lucia thinks out loud. "The shaft is hidden and the head is showing. But jaws, bite, claws, and catch?"

"A claw hammer!" Mike interjects. "When turned around it catches the nail, bites it, and pulls it out."

"Makes sense, but I wonder. Hammer, nail, and blank key. The key ought to enter the picture, somehow."

"I still draw a blank," Mike mumbles. "No key to the clue here."

"Let's leave it hanging. Send the poor victim's remains over to Len James and Jamie Lund's forensic lab. We'll talk to them after they have a look at her."

"Jeez. I can't get her out of my mind."

THEY enter the precinct. Lucia heads directly for Fay's office. The Captain is waiting for some word, any word, about the crime.

"What do you have?" she tersely asks Lucia.

"A lot of nothing ... I'm afraid," Lucia responds while thinking, *She wants total input but she offers zero output. What a klutz!*

"I received a picture of the scene on my mobile apparatus," Fay explains. "It's gory, to say the least."

"Stomach turning."

"Seriously. What did you find? I'm sure you have something."

Lucia shows Fay the note and her text message.

Fay scans them, and says, "Psychopaths often contradict themselves in the same breath. They have no compunction about lying. I remember interrogating a suspected murderer, and I asked him if he had ever committed a violent offense. You know what he said?"

"Tell me."

"'No, but there was a time when I had to kill someone.' I asked him if that wasn't a case of violence. He said 'That sonofabitch lied to me.

Nobody lies to me. So I shot him. That's all. I just shot him without committing any violence.'"

"I follow you," Lucia says. "I once had a suspect tell me, 'I'm no serial killer.' I tell him he's suspected of perpetrating five homicides and that's the mark of serial killing. 'Well,' he says. 'If you think so. But I kill because my other tells me to do it. So, I'm not a serial killer.'"

"They coldly kill and later have no second thoughts. It's like stomping on a cockroach in the back porch. The idea of a moral dilemma is completely foreign to them," Fay remarks.

Lucia thinks, *Is this coming from cold fish Fay? She's never talked to me like this. Almost as if I was a colleague. What's she up to? Why is she suddenly so inquisitive regarding this killer?*

Nevertheless, the conversation continues. Anecdotes run wild. The topic is endless. Lucia ends serious talk with an off the wall dicey thought,

"Humans must be creatures who were created at the end of God's workweek when he was completely exhausted and ready for a cold beer."

Fay chuckles and tells her, "Things will fall into place. I have confidence in my most brilliant detective."

Lucia tells Fay, "I would like your kind of confidence. I look at myself this way. First, God made ignoramuses of all sorts. That was for practice. Then he made evildoers to counter the idiots in an effort to smooth things over. Finally, he made intelligent creatures. I belong to the ignoramuses. Since I know nothing and have to start from scratch, perhaps I can at least see things with a clearer eye than some people." *Including you, Fay,* Lucia says to herself.

Fay chuckles and shakes her head while she turns around and goes back to her office.

Now Fay's back to her normal self, Lucia muses.

LUCIA creates something on her mind, though she's not sure what to make of it. She goes to her office. Sits. And speculates.

At 5:00 A.M. the first murder occurs about a quarter mile from the precinct three days after I received that e-mail message sent at 4:00 A.M. That message, "Hell to pay; the third day: one hour away; do not delay," is disturbingly prophetic, though at the time I couldn't have guessed it.

Three days later the second murder takes place at 5:00 A.M. about a quarter mile in the other direction. That 4:00 A.M. message might have prophesied the second homicide as well. Does this mean a killing every three days, each one at 5:00 A.M.? Likely not. Too predictable. So, what's the connection anyway?

She rises and walks over to a map on the wall in the main hall with a yardstick in hand. Checks out the three spots—headquarters, first killing and second killing—and takes note of the distances. Says, "Zero, One, Two." Then she returns to her office and charts the numbers on a sheet of paper. Says to herself,

It's almost a perfect equilateral triangle. From point 0, headquarters, the first murder at 1 is a quarter mile down the street. The same applies to the second murder at 2, but it angles in another direction at about sixty degrees.

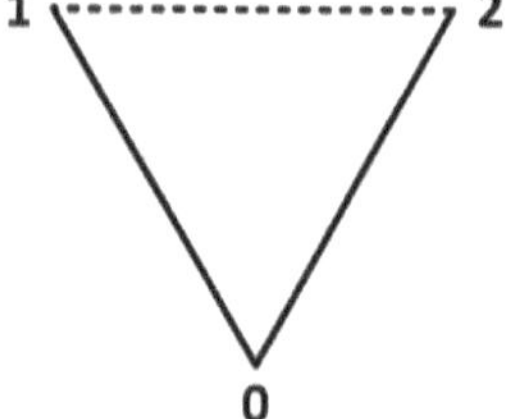

Like the first killing, it is a quarter mile from headquarters. But as the crow flies, cutting across buildings and crossing streets. Distance is the same from point 1 to point 2. Three days and three days and three sides of the triangle.

Jorge Luis Borges's short story, "Death and the Compass," passes through her mind.

Ah yes. In that story, there's a note left after each of the three homicides, the third one stating that it will be the final crime. The crime-busting detective's rigorous logical-aesthetic mind tells him he smells a rat. On an impulse he gets out a compass and draws a triangle connecting the three points, then draws an equidistant fourth point to compose a parallelogram. This, the detective believes, is preferable.

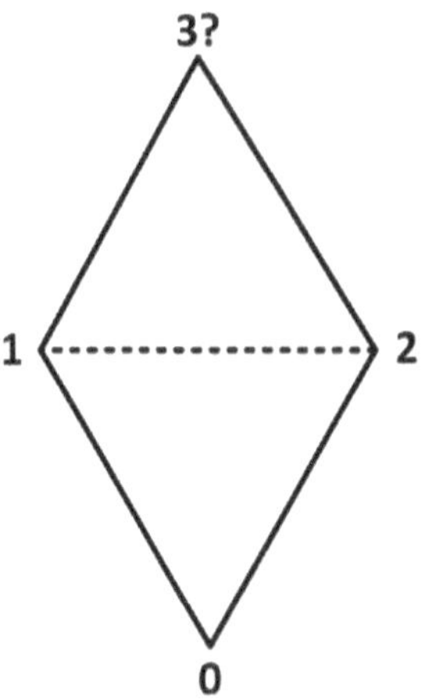

Balance, harmony, and symmetry. Beautiful. A parallelogram is esthetically more pleasing than a triangle, the detective in Borges's story thinks, much like a mathematician or a quantum physicist would gloat with pride over the beauty in her equations. Sure enough, a fourth crime is in the works, the detective concludes.

On the presumed day of the fourth murder, the detective goes to the calculated place, expecting to catch the criminal. To his horror, he realizes he is the chosen victim. And he meets with his own death.

Has X-Man read Borges? she wonders. *If he has, will there be a third murder at the spot where I extend two lines from the two intersections making up the base of the triangle to meet at a sixty-degree angle? The four points make up a parallelogram. Hm ... like the Borges Story.*

But which of the three sides is the triangle's base? 0–1? 0–2? 1–2? Which of the protracted lines will mark the spot? It can't simply be an arbitrary choice. Most likely 1–2 is the triangle's base. If I begin there, the apex will be to the north of 1–2, like this ...

She extends her figure, illustrating the fourth point. Then a thought occurs to her.

The magic number three. Three sides of the geometric figure the corners of which mark the spot where the two murders occurred. And now, will there be a third homicide on the third day at 5:00 A.M.? Will I be XMan's chosen victim if I go there at 5:00 A.M. on the third day? Likely not. Too predictable also. But I wonder ...

The detective in Borges's story would accept nothing other than aesthetically pleasing balance and, above all, symmetry. In other words, perfection. What kind of perfection does X-Man want? In my parallelogram, there are four points—0, 1, 2, and 3.

Will there be a third murder where the lines finally meet? she thinks, but to no avail, deciding her imagination is running out of control.

I doubt the killer may be so ruthlessly calculating. So? Nothing, nada, zilch. *Is that damn murderer born out of society's failures and he can't help how he turned out? Was he born evil, a natural-born killer? Is his brain wiring frozen and he has no options? Is he malicious due to the mode of his nurturing that by chance turned out to be his lot in life? Does he enjoy people's suffering because it gives him some perverted thrill?*

In whatever case, like most psychopaths and serial killers, on the outside he'll likely appear as inconspicuous as anybody else.

Mobile phone again? What now?

She reads,

My dearest sleuth. I have ur imagination out of focus, so ur eyes don't do I much gd. Look round I. Ansrs are many.

Mike is in the vicinity.

"Hey, Mike!" she blurts out. "Get this."

He comes over and reads it, as a frown appears on his face and his eyes turn into a glare.

He says, "The joker's probably trying to make you overcautious. I wouldn't pay him much attention. Knowing what little we know about him, I'm sure whatever we need to know is strategically hidden."

"You're probably right."

"In our hearts we always want to win," Mike continues. "Our disadvantage is that we usually have to go by the rules. It seems to me that psychos are consummate gamers who create their own rules, take us for suckers, and we fall into the trap."

"Yeah, our problem is full of traps. Anyway, I've got to write a report. Fay is getting antsy. Then I think I'll head for my pad, have a stiff drink, and try to get a grip on what we're up against."

"Don't let him play with your mind, Luce."

"I won't," she says, as she realizes he has already begun playing with her mind.

Lucia finishes. Goes to her apartment. Duct taped to her door there's another message,

> *Don't pray for me, my dearest. I don't need it. Nobody prays for Satan either, a sinner beyond the reach of prayers. Pray for yourself. You need it almost as much as I do.*

"What the fuck!" she says out loud. Then she thinks, *The thought never so much as entered my mind. Why would the idea of my praying for him even cross* his *mind anyway? But on second thought, he must have sent this message for some reason. What can it be? Pray for him? A lesser sinner than Satan?*

Was it something that happened during his childhood years? Must have been. Forget it, Lucia, she tells herself. *It's got to be of minor importance.*

She does just that. Lies down on the sofa and is soon asleep. Doesn't awaken until the following morning.

A MELANCHOLY TURN

BEFORE opening her eyes, Lucia is caught thinking while in a dreamy state, half-awake and half-asleep. She torpidly tells herself, *The overriding question is, who is this ruthless killer? He lives in another world. A blank key? It's some sort of game for him.*

He's no little girl making mud pies and pretending they're real. With her imaginary culinary delights, she is playing. Playacting. Not with the idea of duping people, preying on their good intentions. She is in a charmingly entranced world of free play simply for the fun of it.

She imagines mommy makes pies and takes care of her two rag dolls, a boy and a girl. Daddy comes home from work and they sit down at a shoebox table and eat the pies.

Pure play. Nobody wins, nobody loses. They make it up as they proceed. At each moment, a slew of variations presents itself. Mommy and Daddy and presumably the two offspring pick and choose. And the show goes on.

Is it an imaginary work in progress? No. It's process rather than progress. Because it will never come to some predetermined end. It is no tragedy. It is romantic comedy, comedy and romance taken with a playfully ironic grain of salt. It is always open-ended for additions and deletions. Always ongoing.

The next day the kid can resume her playacting. Yesterday it was apple pies. Today it is cherry ones. Yesterday her offspring were squealing with delight. Today they are sound asleep. Always something different. Imagined. They may take their memory back to yesterday and improvise on it as they so desire.

But it's a poor memory that goes backward and expects things to be the same as they were. They can't go back to yesterday because then, their world was different than it now is. As if past and present were separated by a mirror. The past was what it was, but it is now available only by looking into the mirror and seeing a left-hand in the past instead of a righthand in the present.

The past isn't what it was but as it is seen through present eyes. Projecting into the future. Consisting of a zany enantiomorphic mirror-image processing through future moments becoming present becoming past.

EVERYTHING is becoming distorted in Lucia's mind.

Her thoughts meander, becoming somnolent free-flow, *The present is no longer what the past dictated it should be, because there is no rockhard cause that makes the future an extension of what was past. That could become tragic.*

But there is no tragedy. There is spiraling, swiveling, swerving differences created by play emanating from the past image disfiguring the present sliding into an unknown future image.

The mirror between past and future is an ephemeral border. Crossing it takes the play-actor from the past to an imagined present and on to some possible future world.

The mirror? A border? What kind of border? That of my imaginary play-actor's world.

I and my other play-actingly border on lunacy. That's where the action is. At the border we straddle the fence and fleetingly gaze to one side and then the other. Comparing and contrasting our distortion of one side and our imagined world on the other side. Transitorily imagining ourselves coming and going.

While we are for a mere instant here. Straddling the border. Here, there's everywhere and nowhere. We can imagine ourselves as anybody, and as those anybodies accumulate, we are becoming virtually nobody. On the fence. Inside and outside and nowhere.

But the border is no fence at all. It is a rushing, rambling, whitewater cascade. We are in the middle, fighting against the swirling, ongoing pushes and shoves downstream and occasionally toward one bank or the other.

Our becoming temporary fluctuations on the border are no cause for picnic. Though they require a precarious balancing act because at the least expected moment the current can sweep us away.

While the balancing act threatens our need to gain a foothold. Where there is this side now and the other side then. Where there is neither here nor when. Yet there's everywhere and nowhere, everywhen and nowhen.

The ongoing moment of imagining mud pies is as real as can be.

OOPS! *I almost lost my equilibrium ... There, that's better. Now where was I ... Oh yes ... At the border. Between one bank and the other ... Is that side South and the other side North?*

Or is it East or West? Or vice versa ... Or is it all the above or none of the above? ... Steady ... Go with the flow while resisting the flow's cascade striving to whirl you away ...

I'm on one side or the other side ... At least for a passing moment ...

During that moment, if I'm lucky I may see it all ...

See? I see nothing ... At best I get a feel for it ... Following my gut ... Letting it take me wherever it's going ... No? ... No! ... If I go with the flow while here, between one side and the other, I'm lost. Might as well be dead ... Perish the thought ...

OH *my God! I'm losing my hold again ... I'm gyrating in midstream, bobbing up and down. What force ... I'm pushed around within the flow without a paddle ...*

Shit creek? It would be minor compared to this ... There, I'm in shit and I know it ... I have no idea what I am or what's happening here ... Flayed around virtually at random ...

Just gulped a gallon of water ... Just conked my head on a rock ... Feet feel no rocky surface underneath ... No up or down or right or left or forward or backward ... Only pushing forcing me somewhere and nowhere. During some time that is notime ...

HER eyes suddenly fly open. She rockets out of bed. Almost trips on her way to the bathroom.

"Enough of this. Gotta do what I gotta do," she bellows.

She gets dressed and properly presentable. Has coffee and a banana. Then sits and thinks a little more. As if her thoughts were an extension of her bizarre dream, *Oh! So that's it!*

Well, maybe. The murderer is certainly not the typical psychopath. He's playacting and in complete control. Acting out his role beautifully. What is his motive? What's he up to anyway? Where am I going with this? Do I really want to go there?

It's like starting at square-zero again. Unlike square-one. Where I thought I knew the sequence follows a linear marching tune from one, two, three, and onward.

From square-zero, there's an infinite number of possibilities in any direction. And with each step, there's an undetermined number of tangential paths.

No, I don't want to go there. But I must ... I have hardly any other option ... I'll go on ... I'll go there ... Maybe ... Somehow ... Perhaps?

X-Man is playacting for sure ... But why? What a question! I have no idea why ... Think, Lucia! ... I'm thinking, but there's no solid bank in sight.

I'm floundering about!

X-Man? What is it you want anyway? "I want you." What? Did I think what I think I thought? Forget it. I don't want to go there. Heavens no! But I must consider all possibilities.

What if it's true? What if the killer is somebody close to me? To all of us at headquarters? What if he's one of us? Who? Is Fay's strange behavior a clue? That's an abhorrent thought. But what if it's true?

This brings up something else. X-Man? You aren't simply playacting as in spontaneous, loose, and limber play. You're gaming. To win at whatever the cost.

You win, we lose. You gloat, we hang our heads in shame. The end. A closed system with beginning and ending. Spur-of-the-moment extemporaneous free-wheeling play, in contrast, has no undeniable beginning. And if there is what I might call an ending, it stretches out to infinity.

There is no ordered series. It's nonlinear. It can go out in one of virtually countless directions. Or two or three or more directions simultaneously.

X-Man, when you win, you will have neither patience nor empathy for the loser.

If he complains that you cheated on him, you ignore him because you think he's of no account. Or you blow his fucking head off, and it will make no difference.

Silence. Lucia goes to the mirror to comb her hair.

You have no concern for anybody other than yourself, X-Man. Concern for others requires bravery. You have none. Coward! Where are your cojones *you bastard?*

Who are you afraid of? Little ol' Lucia? You know she wouldn't harm a flea. What could you possibly want with her? Look at her in the mirror. What do you see?

Ah. I get it. You're looking through *the mirror. To the other side. Where my right eye becomes my left eye, and my left ear becomes my right ear.*

That might be preferable, since my right eye is a tad higher than the other one. Anyway, what do you see? What are you looking for? On the other side where my enantiomorphic twin resides. What's in it for you?

Oh, that's it. "Twas brilling," and all that. The other side of the mirror where everything's crazy. Where "green ideas" can be "colorless" and can "sleep furiously," and they can become rephrased as portmanteau words.

Rhetoric. Crazy rhetoric. Ha! Crazy like a fox. Eh? It says what isn't so you can know what is.

But if we live in rhetoric, where what is *is always becoming what it* isn't. *"It ain't necessarily so" repeats itself indefinitely.*

Rhetoric. X-Man, you're a bloated bag of rhetoric. And I have the job of figuring you out. Inside the looking glass. Where you reside.

Well then, if we're meant for each other, I guess I'll have to live with it or die with it. Die with it?

Hey, X-Man. Are you some criminal scumbag I once caught up with and you ended in prison and now you're out and you've sworn to get even with me? How about that!

I caught you once and now you think I can't catch you again? Keep thinking, cesspool sucker. My tentacles go anywhere I want them to go. Even down there in the slimy filth where you reside. You'll not elude me.

Time to go to work. Stay behind the mirror with that smirk on your face, X-Man, because it won't last long. Maggot!

Lucia leaves her apartment. Descends the flight of stairs. Decides against public transportation since she's running late. And climbs into her seven-year-old Toyota.

She prepares to fight the morning traffic. Tolerate blaring horns from *macho* men in their BMWs. Cyclists weaving in and out of the linear array of cars. Tractor trailers piloted by beer guzzling NFL and NASCAR enthusiasts. Mothers in their SUVs with squalling kids strapped to their seats.

All the while, Lucia's entertaining the idea that the killer is playacting supremely in order to disguise his game, his identity, and his motives.

LIFE IN THE SPIRALING LANE

SHE arrives, immersing her life in the paranoia gallery. Where everybody brought in claims innocence. They're not simply innocent until proven guilty. As far as they are concerned, they're innocent, period. Blameless. Guiltless.

They think their every word is true blue. Every assertion is golden. Every point of view is diamond clear. None of them have done anything wrong and the world has done them nothing but wrong. They've had a lot of tough luck because they were dealt a lousy deck of cards. They're all in the same boat. They are many and one, one but many.

Yet their persecution complex brings them together. They should be one big happy family. But nobody's smiling. Many of them have gone through repeated incarcerations. Some even solitary confinement. Simply because it was the customary practice.

They imagine they've suffered contempt, insults, and some have been brutalized, sodomized, and tortured. Many of those among them who are psychopaths have killed people. Some in the order of a biologist experimenting with a flat worm in the lab.

They kill, out of curiosity, for the thrill of it, to give them satisfaction, or simply for the hell of it. Yet, they feel no need for justification. Their very existence is their justification. They are within their rights to do what they do. Moreover, they do it simply because that's who they are. Period.

In the final analysis, their justification is their entitlement.

Amazing, Lucia thinks to herself. *Here I am obsessed with bringing XMan to justice. And in his mind, he's completely justified in separating a woman's head from her body.*

Pathetic and outlandish. Horrific and mind-blowing. Blood curdling and at the same time so captivating one can't let it go.

She checks the e-mail in her laptop. E-mail. Garbage in, garbage out. More often than not, something that apparently demands serious reading turns out to be another pile of trash.

Bureaucratic memos and posts sounding authoritative but written by employees who would like to think they are indispensable because vicariously they have something important to say.

Media vultures trying to get a scoop. MSNBC and FOX flashes spewing forth a lot of information backed by few words with substance. Unadulterated junk.

MIKE comes over asking how she is holding up.

"What do you think? At times I feel like vomiting, and at other times my guts are in knots. Wait, what have we here," she says while clicking her e-mail. "Well, I'll declare. Him again, and with an attachment."

Lucia opens it and they read,

> I am precision. It is what I do. It is who I am. I am headed straight to the finish line. But I will not stop there. I'll go on like a meticulously written and an objectively descriptive text. Nothing can alter my relentless push forward. Like a computer's synthesized voice. With neither prosody, rhythm, melody, nor harmony. Like language without vowels, only differentiated staccato consonants. No metaphors, only what is. No irony, only objects pushing objects. No verbs, only substantives. I go straight as an arrow to the target and plunge into the center, which is not every-where but one-where. I evolve out of Os and 1s with computer efficiency. I am in total control. I am I.

"Fuckin' son of a bitch," Lucia screams. Heads turn. Fay stretches her neck to see what's going on. Silent anticipation awaits Lucia's next utterance.

"He sent the most coldhearted, self-centered, presumptuous description of himself imaginable."

"He's a raving madman," Mike adds.

"Pass it around" comes a voice outside to the left.

"Share it with your adoring colleagues" comes another voice.

"Be my guests," Lucia yells at them. She clicks the print button, grabs the document, takes it to the nearest desk, and returns to her office.

"The nerve of that egotistical bastard," Mike says with a contorted facial expression as if he had opened his fridge containing a spoiled batch of salmon cooked up a week ago.

"Yeah," Lucia shoots back. "He's likely one of those spongers who asks for a few bucks because he forgot his wallet and he'll pay you back tomorrow. Who tells his live-in mistress he brought his clothes over to wash them instead of taking them to the laundromat so he can enjoy her beautiful countenance? Who tells her she's his goddess and then goes to the local bar and ends up leaving with a cackling overweight bar-fly at 2:00 A.M."

Mike pipes up, "And he will fill his victim full of lies like, 'I have a graduate degree in English literature,' 'Don't be silly, you're the woman of my life.' 'In a couple of years, I'll be making six figures.' 'You are the best, babe.' 'I'm not around as much anymore because I'm working sixteen hours a day.' 'I'm going to be famous, just wait.'"

Lucia ponders over the possibility of filling Mike in about her triangles, the magical number three, and distances and time between the two homicides. She rejects the idea. Then says to herself, *Just do it, Lucia. That's who you are.*

"Hey, Mike, do you want to know what I've been working on about the killer's MO?"

"You know I do."

"Well, it's like this."

She shows him her scheme and explains it. To her surprise, Mike's impressed. So much that he asks pertinent questions that put her to thinking. Like, "Your scheme is linear. The killer said in his message that his path is linear. But what if his MO takes a turn to nonlinear events in time and space?"

She has no answer.

"Ask yourself why he feels he should go to such lengths."

She thinks, *I have asked myself precisely that*, and says, "If he's so organized and covers the evidence so effectively, it helps explain why he challenges us to try and catch him. Knowing he'll always be a step ahead of us."

"But why the challenge?" Mike asks. "What's in it for him? If he's a psycho, then he's got to be different. Because those bastards want instant gratification. He seems to be in it for play and play alone, without apparent rewards."

"And yet, he's a gamer," Lucia warns.

In view of their unanswerable questions, they decide another trip to Len's place is in the tea leaves.

LUCIA says, "Before we talk to Len, let me show you what I wrote to send X-Man. It's a take on a riddle I told you about the other day."

"Sure."

Two pairs of eyes turn to the laptop screen. Lucia fiddles. Mike patiently waits. A Word document appears containing a long paragraph Lucia had in mind copying and pasting onto her message to the assassin,

The day I apprehend you will catch you by surprise. That day will occur between today, June 20, and September 20. If all the days transpire between now and September 20, you will know you cannot be apprehended on that last day because it will be the only remaining day and it cannot come as a surprise. So, September 20 is not a possibility. Likewise, September 19 cannot be a surprise, since it is hypothetically now the last remaining day. According to this line of reasoning, September 18, 17, 16, 15, and on down to this very day will also fail to catch you by surprise. Thus, you cannot experience a surprising day, and therefore I cannot take you into custody if I remain faithful to my promise. That, my friend, is the inference derived from a timeless linear, logical framework. However, whether you like it or not, we live nonlinearly. Within time, and we will perish within time. Time is the river that rushes us along; it is the wind that pushes us; it is the air that supplies oxygen to our cells and the food that nourishes them; it is the sun that warms us. It is also changing contexts that create pleasure and pain, joy and sadness, and, of course, life and death. You cannot remove the idea of a surprising moment when you will be handcuffed and carted off to jail, tried and found guilty, and left to rot in prison. You cannot forget that on some unsuspected day I will corner you, and though you will lash out in rebellion, your downfall is written in the sands of time.

"Yes! I like it" Mike is quick to remark with his fist lashing upward into thin air.

"Somehow, we've got to break him down, get his goat, let him know he can't play head games with us and win. This might help turn the tide," Lucia says while pasting the message and zipping it off to the e-mail address the killer last used.

"He's as cold as an iceberg," Mike tells Lucia. "But maybe this will put him to thinking. It won't put fear in him because I doubt fear so much as exists in his vocabulary. Yet it could be a beginning toward breaking him down."

"Let's consult Len."

THEY arrive. Len's eyes focus on the headless cadaver on the table before him with a gaze that is slowly oscillating to the right and to the left and back again.

Lucia says. "Morning Len. I sense you aren't exactly full of information to give us."

"Positive," he tells her. "What I mean is, no, I don't have much to say."

"Let's hear what you have, and we'll try to go from there."

"Basically, what you already have from the first victim. No violence, no semen or any indication of rape, and the body wasn't transported from anywhere else.

"The killer apparently caught up with her from behind. Severed her head along the right side. She fell to the ground. He finished decapitating her. Placed the headless body belly up. Arranged her head a short distance away as if she was contemplating the moon. The instrument was a long knife, or a machete of sorts.

"The executioner is male, about six foot three according to the angle of the severance. He must be around two hundred and twenty pounds and in excellent physical condition. There are no fingerprints and nothing that might provide us with a DNA sample."

"Foiled again," Mike pensively states as he separates his eyes from the cadaver with a bitter taste in his mouth.

Lucia says, "What do you suggest we do now?"

"It's a throw of dice. I see hardly anything to go on."

"Very illuminating, Len. Your valuable counsel is exceeded only by your good looks."

"If you're saying I'm completely devoid of good looks, you're accurately qualifying my advice."

Mike gets a good laugh with Len.

"Perspicacious as always." Lucia observes with a slight smile. "We don't expect you to work miracles. Yet, we were hoping."

Mike asks, "Are you suggesting we play tit-tat-toe while we wait around to see what his next move will be?"

"No, play geometry in time and space," Lucia tells him.

"What's that?" Len asks.

"Lucia's alluding to a bizarre scheme she thinks X-Man is cooking up for his future homicides," Mike responds.

"X-Man?"

"Inside shop talk vocabulary," Lucia turns to Len. "We call him X-Man, like an unknown variable. And Mike's referring to the distance between crimes and the time lapse between them. I figure the killer is into hyperstructured time and space coordinates that might give us some clue. But yes, Mike is right to say that we can hardly do more than wait for his next move."

"Frustrating," Len says for lack of any advice.

"Challenging," Mike adds.

"Taxes the mind and ties the gut into knots," Lucia chips in.

THEY leave, silently, pensively. Back in her office, Lucia opens her notebook computer and finds she is not surprised that X-Man has attempted to surprise her with a made-to-order e-mail response,

> My dear counterpart in crime. I'm surprised that you might think your game of surprise will remove the element of surprise from my anticipations. An observation, if you don't mind. You are apparently obsessed with the idea of catching me in order to impress your superiors and expand your fame throughout the city. Unfortunately, catching me will be wellnigh impossible. If, however, you happen to apprehend me due to some slip on my part—since your capacity to trick me is not in the cards— you will release your obsessive animosity toward me. Your implacable violence will know no limits, your claim to impeccable moral standards will be down the gutter, and your fame will be irreparably blemished. Please forgive me, my dear. I wish I could bear good tidings, but your celebrity status is fading in the receding horizon of time.

"Arrogant son of a bitch," Lucia grunts. "He has no idea who he's up against."

She moves papers around on her desk while she fumes over the assassin's words.

How can he be so sure of himself? she thinks. *He can, because as of this moment he's telling himself he's winning. He can tell himself that, because he believes it. And from my point of view? He's right. Much as I hate to admit it.*

So, gotta crack the code. Three days between crimes ... equilateral triangle on the city map ... same time in the morning ... Strike again, X-Man, you piece of shit. I'll get a little closer to you, and soon you'll be mine.

No. What am I saying? Some victim's life is at stake here. Dammit!

How can I prevent it? I can't. What futility!

She's still moving papers around. Runs onto a batch of reports. *Must file these, when I can find some time.* Files from previous cases. *These too.* A candy wrapper, some notes jotted down from days past, memos from the bureaucratic force here and elsewhere, a commendation from the mayor, and another one from a state senator.

What a mess! She turns a sheet of paper over and begins doodling. Big and little triangles. More or less equilateral. One of them duplicates itself, making up a parallelogram. Triangles of approximately the same size add themselves to the parallelogram, creating a tile pattern.

Squares and pentagrams and hexagrams enter the scene. As the pattern grows, the whole concoction becomes nonrepeating, spreading out in all directions. There's no local section that is the same as other sections. The whole collection of sections shows no order to speak of.

Nonrepeating growth, she thinks. *Every additional step of growth is a variation of all the previous steps. What am I creating here?*

Hmm .... Roger Penrose. That physicist who wrote The Emperor's New Clothes. *Penrose puts forth nonrepeating tiling as a visual metaphor of the universe's fabric. He's also creator of the so-called Penrose triangle.*

Lucia carefully draws it in black ink and contemplates it.

An impossible three-dimensional triangular object that needs a fourth dimension for its makeup. Four dimensions. Space and time ... spacetime ... or perhaps better, timespace ... Three dimensions of space and a dimension of time. Wrapped up and becoming one ... The four-dimensional manifold. What's it all about, Lucia?

Zombie-like, she checks her e-mail. Unsurprisingly, X-Man strikes again,

Suppose I say, "The sentence 'It is true that I am not guilty' is true that I am not guilty." If it's

true, then *J*'m not guilty, and if it's false, then *J*'m guilty. *A*m *J* guilty?

She says to herself, *Yes, you God damn maggot!*

Then her better judgment takes over. She calms down. Thinks. Thinks more. Smiles. Clicks Reply. And types,

What would happen if Pinocchio said "When *J* say this, my nose will grow?" *J*f he's telling the truth, his nose won't grow. So, what he says can't be true. But if it is false, then he is lying and his nose will grow. *J*n this case the sentence will be true. But it will be false. But it will be true. So much for Pinocchio. With each e-mail you send me, does your confidence grow? *J*t can grow only if you claim you are not guilty, and you do precisely that. But if you profess innocence, you are lying through your teeth. Consequently, your confidence is in jeopardy because your lie must accumulate with each telling, and you fear that somewhere along the line some mistake, some inconsistency, might pop up because you have failed completely to cover your tracks. *J*f your confidence wanes, then your e-mails will lose their shine. They will become tarnished and eventually bring your guilt into view. Nobody is perfect, my man.

"Cockroach!" she says out loud as she clicks Send.

A couple of heads turn around and peer at her through the window. She smiles and waves them off.

I can't let him get to me.

She recalls that Yogi Berra quip about being careful if you don't know where you're going because you might not get there. She also recalls its parallel with Lewis Carroll's Alice, who asks where she should go from where she is. She's told that it depends on where she wants to go. She says she doesn't care. She's met with the answer that in that case it doesn't matter which way she goes.

Oh yes, Lucia returns to her thinking. *In the fourth dimension, there are possible roads that would contradict one another if taken in a three-dimensional world, like the case of the Penrose triangle. No?*

Yes. The very idea of contradiction. X-Man plays loose and limber with it. Regarding space and time, many contradictions are a problem in three dimensions but not in four. There's something to the threat of contradiction showing its ugly mug, but I can't put my finger on it. In the killer's world, everything appears as so much nonsense.

Back to square-one. Nothing is what it is, because it isn't. Clear and simple. Moreover, in the psycho's world, what isn't in a quirky way is. In other words, what ordinarily wouldn't become in my world has already become what should become in his world.

This is like making an imaginary leap from three dimensions to four to get a more encompassing sense of things. Like stepping back and from a distance contemplating those aliens' grue *and my* green.

At least I would like to believe it's something like that. But what does it mean? Really?

Think, Lucia. Think like X-Man. If everything that isn't, *is,* then anything *should take its place with everything else.*

Outlandish? Anyway, physicists are now telling us there are parallel worlds, zillions of them. X-Man must dwell within one of them.

X-Man! Come out, come out, wherever you are. And let's have our own private duel in the sun.

SHE sits, staring at the computer screen as if it was a gaping chasm threatening to engulf her.

Waiting. For what? For X-Man's next move.

"The horror of it all!" she growls, provoking heads to turn once more in the direction of her window.

Lucia ends her monologue on a series of syncopated notes. The last one is a hesitation that prolongs its silence, its emptiness.

She has nowhere else to go.

WHAT IS BECOMING WHAT WILL HAVE BEEN: MURDER THREE

THREE days after the second homicide, there is no third crime. *So much for time symmetry. Dammit all!* Lucia thinks while feeling like screaming out in exasperation.

The next day she shows dismay over the fact that what she had anticipated turned out to surprise her. Mike is crestfallen. Rich and Berto (Roberto), two detectives who occasionally spell them, have familiarized themselves with the case, and they are disappointed as well.

Rich says, "The perp is surely following some sort of MO, but he creates deviations in it so as to catch us off-guard."

"Maybe he's not as smart as he thinks he is." Berto puts in his two cents worth. "At some time or other, he'll make a mistake."

Mike says, "That's what I've been thinking."

Later that day, Fay drops by Lucia's office. Lucia fills her in on some of the details. But prudence tells her she shouldn't take it too far.

Fay says, "You had better get ready for the unexpected, because you can be sure it will occur at the most surprising moment."

Lucia thinks, *"Yeah, some surprise."* Then she says, "The unexpected consists of the realization of untold possibilities. So how can we ready ourselves for that?"

Fay responds, "I know what you mean. You've got a problem on your hands. By the way, have you seen the morning paper?"

"No," Lucia tells her.

Fay goes on, "It's a column by Leslie Judd. She says you've been tripped up thinking there would be a crime yesterday, and she goes on to make vague allusions about your lingering incompetence."

"What! Another leak! This is becoming character assassination!" Lucia cries out. "Somebody around here is either out to get me or on the take.

I've got a few possible suspects in mind and I'm going to keep a close eye on them. You can bet on that."

"Be careful, Lucia," Fay counsels her. "Don't make any false accusations."

"I'm outraged!"

"You should be. But don't let it affect your handling this case. Things are difficult enough as they are."

"I know," Lucia says while thinking, *What support! And they call this leadership?*

During the next two days, she, Mike, and sometimes Rich and Berto collaborate in checking out possible leads. They end in frustration.

"Where's this thing going?" they ask.

Mike quips, "It's ninety percent mental and fifty percent physical because we have to be constantly on the go to get where nothing helps us in our mental effort to solve the case."

"We're not making any headway, just spinning wheels," Berto says.

"We're making imaginary mud pies and can't eat them because they remain outside real world possibilities," Lucia adds.

THAT afternoon, Lucia and Mike walk over to the park, find a secluded spot, and sit for a chat.

"You know, Mike," Lucia begins, "it is not what we don't know is true about this case that is frustrating and even dangerous. It's what we think we know but it isn't true."

"What do you mean?"

"All we think we know that isn't true, like UFOs, ESP and such doesn't bother us much. Yet our knowing is always incomplete. Give us enough evidence, and, who knows? UFOs might be real and ESP might exist. Yet, our knowing is always incomplete, and a lot of it has some inconsistencies hidden away in the closet. We can never know where the dividing line is between what we know is true, but it isn't, and what we don't know is true, but it is."

"What a bunch of mental spins, Luce! You're beginning to sound like those illogical spin doctors that call themselves politicians," Mike says with a chuckle.

"Maybe it's no more than garble. But there's a problem with knowing something if we don't know what it is we don't know and if what we think we know isn't true."

"Still, we always think we have to know. The mind abhors a vacuum, nothing, emptiness."

"You're right, Mike. We want to think we know and we want to give others the impression that our mind is full of first-rate knowing. Well, halffull or half-empty, according to who's doing the looking."

Mike's skepticism is primed. He begins ruminating, "To fill the mind enough to meet our satisfaction, we see gods and human individuals in star clusters, faces in clouds, the Virgin Mary or Christ in the wood grains of a chopped down tree, basketball players on a roll and making long streaks of baskets, and multiple conspiracy theories bouncing around. What we don't want to know is that a lot of it isn't so, just figments of our restless imagination."

Lucia says, "Yeah I know. We become aware of extraordinary happenings in our world with respect to what we think we know. Then with time our knowing becomes humdrum and commonplace, yet controversial due to its ambiguity opening it to diverse interpretations. You know? We've gone over this terrain before. They call it *doublespeak.* 'Global warming' becomes 'climate change,' which is construed by many people as no more than another natural cycle.

"They say, 'Climate change? It's the same as other cycles during human history.' 'Evolution? There's no proof.' 'Big Bang theory? It's straight out of hell sent by Satan to deceive us.' Or whatever. What flabbergasts me no end is that on both sides of the fence they profess their knowing as if there was no doubt whatsoever"—

Mike chips in, "Everybody's knowing becomes so many stereotypes. All of them are generalities. Taken as absolute truths. As you move outward, they eventually become inordinately vague and ambiguous.

"Arguments regarding these generalities usually degenerate into a simplistic 'he says, she says' affairs. 'It is so,' 'No it ain't,' ''Tis so,' ''Tis not,' and so on. In the final analysis, there are few clear and distinct answers."

"Flip a coin over and over, and theoretically, you will have an equal number of heads and tails. But we live in an imperfect world," Lucia ruminates. "The ideal is always incomplete, and fluctuations in the number of heads to the number of tails will never cease showing up."

"Yeah, I'm with you. But why did you bring it up, Lucia?"

"Because when we have an idea, we would like to convince others that it is valid. In order to convince them, we look for confirmatory evidence. Like 'All psychopaths are A'—where 'A' is some fake quality we would like to believe psychopaths have.

"If we look long enough and hard enough, we find ample evidence to support our idea. We use this evidence to prove our point. And we manage to convince a few people.

"The problem is, by that time our knowing is commonplace. Mindlessly taken for granted, even though it is false. It has become part of what we think we know is true, but in many cases, it isn't."

Mike puts in another two cents' worth, "Maybe it is something like this. We say what we think is true—but it isn't. 'Okay,' they tell us, 'We'll believe it when we see it.' We show them evidence. They see it. And they believe it. Maybe. In the best of all worlds.

"But in order to believe it, they fall under the charm of partly erroneous assumptions. And they run the risk of becoming duped in the manner they think we became duped."

"Well, to a certain extent, yes, Mike. But I was thinking along other lines. It's like they wish to say 'If we see it, it's because we believe it.' The problem is that we often see what we believe we will see.

"But our seeing should be the other way around. We should look for evidence that goes against our thinking. We should say, 'I'll see it when I disconfirm what I thought I saw.'

"Disconfirmation shows us that what we thought we saw and knew isn't so. Like I once read about Einstein. He said theory guides observation more than observation serves to make theory."

"What are you driving at now?"

"We should look for what's wrong with commonplace ideas about psychopaths and serial killers. Then, perhaps we can manage to get into the killer's head."

"Oh, I see," Mike says. "I think. You want to follow your magic number three, distances on the city map, days of the month, times of the day. At the same time, you try to understand why that mad butcher didn't keep it all clear, balanced, and symmetrical."

"You try to understand why what we thought we knew about him was right but it wasn't. And you want to understand how it is that it wasn't?"

"Something like that … I guess."

Mike glances into Lucia's eyes with a frown, "Do you realize you're now sounding more and more like Lewis Carroll?"

"Strange you thought of that," Lucia tells him. "I was thinking the same. It's like Alice. Who got so much in the habit of expecting bizarre events that her out-of-kilter world became so many commonplaces: dull, boring, dreary."

Mike ponders, "We ought to focus on what we don't know, or what we thought we knew but didn't."

"Does that make any sense?" Lucia queries.

"A lot, Lucia."

"We ought to look for what is so common we ordinarily ignore it. What we know and take for granted. But it ain't necessarily so."

"We must keep eyes and ears open," Mike says.

"Like that purloined letter in Edgar Allen Poe's short story," Lucia speculates. "We look for what we don't see, but it's there nonetheless. We don't see it, because it's right there before our eyes and we didn't expect it to be there."

"As some poet once said—was it Gertrude Stein?—there's no *there*, there."

"I know. Using our roving imagination, we have to carve out the *there* in order to see what there is, or what we think there is."

"I don't need to tell you that you should be careful, Lucia. X-Man is still trying to control a zillion neurons in your gray matter."

"I'm aware of that."

The next couple of days, they try bravely and gravely to get into the killer's head and think like him. But fail. Repeatedly.

ON the sixth day after the second killing, a third homicide! A half mile away from the zero-point. About 6:00 A.M. This time the victim is an African American woman. The method? A slit throat.

"Here we go again," Mike says.

"Goddamn him!" Lucia shouts out.

"We'd better get over there quick, Lucia."

"Yes."

They arrive in short order. This time the police have cleared the area of citizens who as usual and for some sordid reason cannot resist pushing their way in so they can gape at the gore. Lucia and Mike make their way directly to the victim and begin comparing notes.

Lucia: "African American, fit-to-kill dressed." Mike: "My God! Don't wax facetious!"

Lucia: "Sorry. I'm not in a mood for this." Mike: "Please go on."

Lucia: "In a skirt, blouse, quality jewelry, and shoes that enhance her height and legs as she walks with the usual discomfort."

Mike: "As we might have expected, no evidence of a struggle."

Lucia: "About twenty-five. Five feet six inches. Around one hundred and twenty pounds."

Mike: "Very carefully and elaborately applied make-up."

Lucia: "A classy dame."

ON par with the first two crimes. Apparently, no struggle. No rape. No theft. No fingerprints or residue. And no further data useful for clearly determining the criminal's motive, signature, or MO.

The customary message is duct taped to her left ankle. Mike removes it. Gives it to Lucia. She unfolds it, careful to prevent tearing it as she separates paper from tape. Reads it,

Twas gushing oil from every pore; tith eared and sad sea and thorth Nawed Pole.

"What the hell?" Mike exclaims.

Lucia says, "That's not all. There's a footnote." They read it,

Tied to a string dangling from the gutter.

"Let's take a look," Mike says.

They search for the closest gutter. Find it. Find a string. Pull it. Revealing a small Ziploc bag with a folded piece of paper in it. Open it. And read,

I run cold and hot; I look blue but I'm not; what am I?

"Oh, spare me," Mike says.

"Let's get over to the office and try to decipher this within the context of previous messages," Lucia tells him.

Fay is waiting for their return.

"What do you have on him?" she's quick to ask.

"No more than a variation on the same theme," Lucia says. "More Alice in Wonderland and a riddle. Take a look."

Fay reads the messages. Rolls her eyes. Hands them to Lucia. Turns around and leaves them trapped within their conundrum without uttering a word.

What a meat-head, Lucia thinks to herself.

"She's a lot of help," Mike ironically observes.

"It's *our* case. At least she gives us full rein to solve it our way."

"Whatever ..."

Lucia glances over at a man headed in their direction.

"Well, well, Norm Carter of the FBI. As if we didn't have enough problems."

"I've been assigned to your case," he begins. "I intend to cooperate fully with you and ask the same of you. For now, I need all the information you have up to this time and expect you to send me all additional information through the Internet as soon as you gather it.

"From this day forward, I will keep in contact with you by phone and e-mail. If I see fit to advise you regarding your investigation with this case I will do so, and if you have any questions or comments, I will welcome them."

Lucia puckers, then replies, "We will cooperate with you every step of the way. Would you like to come into my office?"

The discussion is a one-way affair. Inspector Carter directs his words to them, while inquisitive eyes outside take brief glances through the window as they walk by or swivel around in their seats from their desks. In a few brief minutes, the three investigators stand, shake hands, and the FBI agent leaves.

"Strait-laced and sober-faced." Mike observes.

Lucia says, "He's at least predictable. I hope he doesn't change."

"I can't wait to take another gander at those notes."

Lucia pulls them out of her pocket and they read, silently.

"He includes more of those portmanteau words Len mentioned," she notes. "But they seem irrelevant with respect to our speculations thus far. Perhaps he needs to read Lewis Carroll more carefully."

Mike speculates, "He seems to be hung up on linguistic variations. At least we can make an educated guess that they spell out his signature and reveal some sort of fluctuating MO."

He begins analyzing the note. "Let me see ...'Tith eared' can become 'tired earth.'"

"Do you know you're good at this, Mike?"

"Not really. I'm still dyslexic whether I know it or not." Mike laughs.

"Well, then de-dyslexicize the rest of the puzzle, will you?"

"I'll try. Have you noticed that the first letters of the last two words are in capitals?"

"Yes. Strange, isn't it? I think the two words allude to something special. Like the north pole. But that seems implausible."

Mike says, "Wait! ... Of course, oil. The north pole thawing out, international tension over the new area liberated from its disappearing ice cap, showing abundant oil and mineral wealth."

"My God, you don't suppose we have an environmental terrorist on our hands, do you Mike?"

"Most likely someone who can't get along with women and men can't tolerate, so he became infatuated with puzzles."

"Puzzles and logical enigmas."

"Logical dilemmas, you mean, that create more questions than answers," Mike thinks out loud.

"But for the grace of God go I into this crazy labyrinth," Lucia reflectively mumbles.

"Why do you say that?"

"In college I dreamed of a degree in computer logic until I took a class from a wisecracking prof who made us create logic-based jokes and take turns telling them in class. It was like everybody was doing a Lewis Carroll imitation. That was enough to leave me vomitrocious—portmanteau pun intended."

"Fantabulous! You're really getting into this. But tell me" Mike goes on. "What about the riddle? Running cold and hot, looking blue but not."

"I have no idea."

"Only a brainiac—you know? Brain plus maniac—would be equipped to crack that one."

"Or a cyberdelic freak ..." Lucia struggles to match Mike's rhetorical renditions.

"Or a loquamander—loquacious plus salamander ..."

"Enough of this," Lucia tells him. "I can't keep up with you. Nose to the grindstone."

"Or to the gronestind?" Mike chortles. "Sorry, boss. I couldn't resist."

Lucia ignores him and says, "Hmm ... notice this. Blue and not blue. Salamander? Chameleon?"

"I doubt it," Mike responds. "They're not both cold and hot."

"Well, there are cold-blooded and hot-blooded creatures at least."

"That's it! Blood! You had it at the tip of your tongue all along, Luce.

Looking at our blood vessels through skin and flesh, they're blue. Get a flesh wound, and when our blood hits the air and combines with oxygen, it's red."

"Great, Mike!"

"The victim's slit throat. Homicide three."

"There's no *grue* or *bleen* here like in the first note. There's red and blue *rue* and *bled*. The consequence of a knife wound. What a fuckin' jerk! What tedium!" Lucia remarks with jaded countenance.

"Or opprodium—opprobria plus tedium—no less."

LUCIA looks away while Mike chuckles. Neither of the detectives knows what meaning might be emerging from this charade. Perhaps the killer doesn't either.

After all, he's apparently in it for fun. Perhaps improvising much of it as he goes along. And he obviously has no doubt about who's in control. While Mike and Lucia are at this stage the actors in his puppet show.

They give up, for now at least, in favor of awaiting the coroner's report before going any further.

THE FLOW GOES ON

LUCIA, alone in her office, slips into another stream of dreamy monologuing, What is the upshot of this bizarre tale of standoffs and quandaries?

Is it madness on both sides of the mirror? Is one reflection the reciprocal counterpart of the other? Does the one parallel the other like the positive and negative of those ancient photos?

Alice asks the Cheshire cat how she can know a cat is mad. The cat asks Alice how she can tell a dog is not mad. Alice is befuddled.

The cat informs her that a dog growls when he's angry and wags his tail when he's happy. A cat wags her tail when she's mad and purrs when she's contented.

It is reciprocity. As if the dog was on one side of the mirror and the cat is on the other side.

So much for madness as a transitive state of mind. What about madness as a mentally dissonant condition?

The butcher who killed those three people? Is he mad at the world or is he suffering from madness?

For that matter, what about me and Mike? A reciprocal form of madness on the other side of the mirror? Heavens! Answers! I need answers! Where can I find them?

FRUSTRATED, Lucia calls up some images from the Internet, then sits staring at the two-dimensional, three-dimensional and four-dimensional figures in front of her on the monitor, occasionally glancing at or contemplating the map on the wall she can see through her window.

Answers ... answers ... for hell sakes. Get with it Lucia!

She stares straight ahead.

Then thinks *5:00 A.M. 5:00 A.M. and 6:00 A.M. Three days three days and six days. A quarter mile a quarter mile and a half mile. Some sort of symmetry? Or perhaps syncope? Better, trigonometrical expansion? Can't say. Well, not yet at least.*

But how might it be qualifiable? And besides. What do the riddles and verbal play have to do with it? If anything. Is it some crazy form of psychosis? Or is it sophisticated subtlety of some sort?

Meu Deus! Que confusão! My God! What confusion!

She struggles to think it out.

A semantically nonsensical sentence, a blank key, jabberwocky, a nail clue, and oil and minerals and plenty of blood. No pattern to speak of.

Where will the next crime occur? When will it occur? At what time of the day? No telling.

Reason and logic have been flipped. A lackadaisical walk from the zero-point to the first crime follows a linear, unidimensional path, straight as an arrow.

No walking directly to crime scene two because the linear path cuts across city blocks. Either you follow a two-dimensional route along the city streets that makes a few ninety-degree turns to get there. Or like the crow flies, you enter the third dimension and go up and over buildings until you get where you need to go.

But as far as the map is concerned, there is no there, *there. In dimension three, that will enable you to arrive at your destination. And what about a fourth dimension? How does it enter the equation, if at all? It must be like seeing* grue-world *and* green-world *from a broader more encompassing perspective. By way of some loose and limber logic. If you can call it logic at all.*

Sheer lunacy, no? So it might seem. But what is it about? It? What do I mean by it? It tells me nothing.

Heavens, she thinks. *My two latinated catholicized, properly consecrated languages, Portuguese and Spanish, are influencing my sober secular English.*

She begins deliberating over languages.

There's it, *which has no satisfactory equivalent in Portuguese or Spanish. It* as in *"It rains" ... Strange.* What *rains? Why* it *... What is* it? *... That which provokes an image of raining.*

There's no need for it *in the romance languages. There's simply*
"Chove" and "Llueve" in Portuguese and Spanish. That is, "Raining."

No it ... It *isn't necessary ...* It *is a "nonperson" pronoun. Even an*
"antiperson" pronoun ... Though there's nothing personal about it.

Nothing personal when I say "Nothing personal" either ... It *just is ... A*
sort of all-purpose qualifier? Whatever that means.

It *can be anything and everything and nothing at all.*

Like telling Alice after she says she sees nobody on the road. Amazing. She
can see nobody, and from such a distance too. She sees nobody and she sees it.

Or as Brazilian writer Clarice Lispector puts it, it *is neither somebody*
nor nobody. It *is entirely neutral;* it *is nothing, nothingness, and* it *is*
everythingness ... It *simply* is *what* it is *... Whatever ...*

But if it *is neither somebody nor nobody,* it *is not. Well, then, we might*
wish to say that it *both* is *and* is *not.*

Wrong again ... So it *neither* is *nor* is *it not.* It *just* is. *What's the meaning*
of that line? Is it is *or is* it *ain't?*

It's no wonder there's such difficulty in knowing it is. *No wonder* it *is so*
remote from our concrete sensibilities.

SUDDENLY, Lucia's head fills with an outpouring of geometrical figures
that swirl in time and through space.

Gyrating, vibrating, palpitating, and quivering. She is in a vertiginous
spirilloid free fall to everywhere and nowhere. She is not *it* in this
breathtaking instant. She just *is*, or better, *is becoming*, along with nothing
and everything.

Come to grips with yourself, Lucia, she says to herself. *Snap out of* it *...*
That again. Snapping out of it *is a spontaneous act.*

Can it *be a willed? Consciously willed? ... Unlikely, if* it *is the outcome of*
spontaneity ... Taking this into consideration, now that she's thinking it, *she's*
already snapped out of it. *Spontaneously ...*

Snapped out of what? It *... Anyway ... Back to normal. Normal? ... Like*
a mad cat and a happy dog are normal? Doing the same thing?

Normal? ... Like my normal and the killer's normal? ... Don't be mad, be
glad. For what that's worth ... Sure. Easy as pie.

I must get away from this or it *will drive me to insanity. Or sanity? Perhaps. At this stage I don't really know … All certainty has flown out the window.*

What a bummer! … No, no bummer at all … It's taxing … And exhilarating. Exhilarating? … Yes. Because it *is play, playacting …*

Oh, I almost forgot. Put the impasse in a playacting context and I'm loving it *and fearing* it *… Like entering McDonalds with a terrible case of heart burn … Loving and fearing the consequences, I mean to say …*

With respect to whatever is in store for me.

A PAIN IN THE NECK, AND
LITTLE GAINED

THE next morning, Lucia has an e-mail from, guess who?

> My dearest counterpart in crime. You are burning the midnight oil. Too much work and too little play makes Lucy a lackluster dame. I saw you drag yourself into your abode a little after one in the morning. You shouldn't take life so seriously. Relax. Life is a dream, if you let it engulf you properly. Chill out—or chillax might I say?—and drift along with it.

"Life is a dream my ass!" she says out loud. Then she takes to ruminating, *He's trying to get my guard down again. Well, I won't let him. I'll keep myself in complete control of my wits at every step.*

Atta girl, Lucia. Keep that stiff upper lip.

Coffee and a bagel. A quick shower. Customarily as cold as she can stand it. Jeans, faded, slightly belled, and a pastel blue blouse. She's off to the blood and guts factory for another day.

Lucia and Mike are back at the scene of the third homicide checking out a few minor details when they get word that police officers scouring the second homicide found two witnesses.

"Good news!" Mike spontaneously blurts out.

"Don't bet on it," Lucia mumbles.

Back at headquarters Lucia gives Mike a cynical I-told-you-so smile when they see the witnesses.

Mike says, "I was afraid of this."

Lucia says, "It's what we should have expected."

THE presumed witnesses are Melissa Jackson and Johnny Castor. A tiny lady of around seventy-five or eighty. And a pale, undernourished mouseface teenager who looks like he spends eighteen hours a day on his computer, smart phone, tablet, and what have you.

Lucia ushers soft stepping Melissa to a tiny room at the left and Mike departs with little Johnny to the right.

Mike says, "So you were at the scene."

Johnny responds, "Uh, yes, I think ..."

"You think? What do you mean? Were you there, or weren't you?"

"Well, I was at home, you know?"

"Where's home?"

"Above that coffee shop. In one of the apartments. You know?"

"No. I don't know. Listen, I want you to tell me exactly what you saw. No ifs, ands, or buts. Do you understand me?"

"Yes ... I think."

"Don't think. Describe the scene to me as clearly as you can. What did you see?"

"Uh, you know? It was like this. I was texting a friend, sitting next to the window, and, uh ... I looked down at the street. There was this woman, you know?"

"No, I do not know and stop saying that. Describe the woman. Slender? Heavy-set? White? Latino? African American?"

"She was like ... dark ... maybe ... but it was hard to tell. I saw a lot of hair but not much face ... and I think she was sort of skinny."

"How was she dressed?"

"I ... I don't know. I didn't look at her clothes. My ma told me not to stare at women."

"For hell sakes! You don't have to stare at a woman to see what clothes she's wearing."

"Well ... I don't know."

"Was there a man around?"

"Yes ... He was tall."

"White, African American, Latino?"

"Sort of, I think. He was like ... white."

"Did you see his face?"

"I guess."

"You guess! Did you see his face or didn't you?"

"Not exactly ... You know?"

Mike looks up to the ceiling, shakes his head with eyes half-closed, and says, "A beard, a moustache, short sleeve shirt, tattoos on his arms?"

"I think he had side burns, maybe, and ... like short hair."

"What color?"

"Like ... black."

"Tattoos?"

"Tattoos ... I didn't see any."

"Was he heavy and well built? Fat? Skinny?"

"Uh ... he looked tough ... Yeah, that was it. Tough-like."

"Was he young, middle age, old?"

"Like ... young. Yeah. That's it. Young ... No. Not young. More like middle age."

MEANWHILE, Lucia asks Melissa, "How are you this morning, Ms. Jackson?"

"Fine. My, you're a nice young lady."

"I would like to ask you a few questions. Will that be okay?"

"Yes. I like talking to nice people. You're not like those rude people in the neighborhood that don't want to give me the time of day."

"If you don't mind, I'll get down to business."

"Down? Where are you taking me?"

"We will stay here. Please answer my questions as clearly as you can."

"Yes. I like people that speak clearly, not like those young people in the neighborhood. I can't understand them. Like they are talking some foreign language."

Lucia closes her eyes and says to herself, *Witness? What a joke.* Then she says, "I understand you witnessed the murder scene."

"Murder? My Gracious! Has there been a murder?"

"Did you see the man who accosted a young woman on Fifty-Second Street?"

"I saw a good-looking young man walk up behind a girl and take hold of her."

"Can you describe him?"

"He was handsome. Tall."

"Light or dark complexion?"

"Oh dear, I don't remember much about him. Only that he seemed like such a nice young man."

"What did he do to the woman?"

"Do? Nothing. He took hold of her. Like he knew her, like he was giving her a hug, from back of her. I think she was his girlfriend."

"He didn't attack her? A woman was murdered at that spot at the time you saw the man."

"Murdered? Is that what happened? Dear me. I can hardly believe it."

MIKE asks Johnny, "Was this man behind the woman slightly to the left of her or to the right of her?"

"Behind ... like ... just behind, walkin' fast. He caught up with her and took out this long sort of knife and ... like, maybe he cut her throat. You got the picture?"

"Cut her throat? That's all?"

"That's all I saw. He ... well, he did it so quick like. I can't really say."

"Then what did he do? What was her condition?"

"I don't know. I was texting. You see? I didn't see anything else because I was texting."

"You had no curiosity? Didn't you want to check out what was happening?"

"Well ... he was my best friend."

"The man on the street?"

"No, the dude I was texting."

"For Christ sakes kid! A murder was occurring and you were more interested in texting somebody?"

"We like to keep connected, you know?"

LUCIA asks Melissa, "She was murdered. Didn't you see him attack her?"

"Heavens to Betsy no! If I did, I wouldn't want to see it. I would turn my head and refuse to look it."

"Did you see him pull out a knife?"

"Knife? No. You mean a knife murdered that sweet child? Oh my, what is this world coming to?"

"Thank you, Melissa. You have been helpful. Let me walk you to the door."

"It was nice talking with you. I hope we can do it again sometime."

With a slight smile on her face Lucia thinks *Life is a dream, X-Man said. That describes this senile old lady to the hilt.*

MIKE asks Johnny, "This world is full of violence, and you sit around texting?"

"Well ... you see? It's like when I'm texting, I'm sort of ... well ... like separated from everything. You know? Nobody can do anything to me, they can't boss me around, push me on the street or the bus stop, yell at me, insult me. I have fun texting."

"Go home, kid. Go back to your life's noble mission."

"Is that all?"

"Yes, that's all."

"Well, if you want to ask me any more questions, you can text me at ..."

"No more questions," Mike says as he points at the exit.

Johnny ambles in that direction, wavering somewhat, unsure of himself at every tentative step.

LUCIA approaches Mike. "What did you get?"

"Absolutely nothing."

"Same here."

"Pathetic."

"Yes."

"A waste of time."

"Yes."

"Let's go to that Starbucks on the corner."

"I'm with you. I'll show you the note I had from the killer when I got out of bed this morning."

They leave.

THE usual waiting line includes a few uniformed police officers. They focus on muffins, cookies, double-chocolate brownies, scones more than on the list of coffee selections.

Yep, they're living up to their reputation, Lucia says to herself.

She and Mike order black coffee. None of the frills. "It's just a lot of foam and candy," they say with a grin.

They sit. Lucia hands Mike the killer's last note. He reads it, and declares, "Life is a dream? Better put, head games. He never gives up."

"Where do you think we can go with this?"

"We're going nowhere," Mike replies, "and if the situation doesn't change, there's no chance in hell we'll get anywhere soon."

"Another unsolved case? No. I won't allow it."

Small talk follows. They have no patience this morning. Especially after those so-called interviews. They agree it's time to do something. What? Who knows? Anything.

What a job. Do what you need to do and solve a case and the press attacks you for some minor mistake. Fail to solve it and the boss is down your throat and the press is up your ass. You can't win for losing.

Speaking of the press, Mike spies a column the guy at the next table is reading. "Serial killer still at large." He mentions it to Lucia almost in a whisper.

"I don't want to read it," Lucia says. "It will pile shit on a day already ruined."

"What day?" Mike asks. "Today and yesterday might as well be a vacuum for all they're worth."

Dejected, they leave for the office. Now what? It's been a week since the last killing.

What kind of pattern is hiding from us? Lucia asks herself.

How can I help Lucia out? Mike thinks. *Her reputation is at stake. That God damned vomit bag!*

FAY is waiting for them when they arrive. She calls them over to her inner sanctum.

"I gather the witnesses didn't pan out."

"A senior lady on the verge of Alzheimer and a zonked-out cyberspace kid totally disconnected from the world," Lucia responds.

"I'm at a loss," Fay says.

Faint-hearted Fay, par for the course, Lucia says to herself.

"We are too," Mike offers in support.

Fay suggests they return to the third scene and look around. Again. Something might turn up. What else is there? They leave. With neither hopes nor meaty speculation.

"Fay was as helpful as tits on a boar hog," Lucia says.

Mike gets a good laugh while Lucia scrunches her nose into a frown. At the site. People on the sidewalk coming and going. Cars whizzing by at a speed just a little over the limit to avoid a ticket and get where they are going with effective dispatch. A siren in the distance.

Birds chirping above. A dog walker pulling on the canine's obstinate neck while it's sniffing around a tree trunk. A small gang of ruffians slapping backs, giving high-fives, and guffawing.

The usual day. Lucia and Mike notice hardly any of it. Too much on their mind. Besides, they know the story all too well. Gang violence, drug violence, terrorist violence, serial killings. Above all, guns.

Too many assault weapons. Too easy to purchase. Too *macho* enhancing. Too easy to justify it. With mindless allusions to that universal placebo, the Second Amendment.

At the scene they stand around and stare. Seeing nothing. After almost an hour of looking and asking around, nothing gained.

And nothing lost. Since there was nothing to lose in the first place. What are they doing here anyway?

Back to the poignant precinct.

A BIFURCATING MO: HOMICIDE FOUR

DAY nine, and it happened. Again. A police officer suggests lethal poisoning might have done the trick. A second officer confirms the idea.

Poisoning! He's experimenting with whatever comes to mind, Mike thinks.

Good ol' X-Man. Keeping us guessing, Lucia humors herself. They strive to articulate their thoughts.

"You know? I was thinking ..." Mike melodically chirps.

"And I was thinking ..." Lucia harmonizes with him.

But they say virtually nothing more as they approach the scene.

That's the way they work. Melody. Complementary harmony flowing along with syncopated melody. Entangled music in the heart, mind, and on the tongue.

Thinking and harmonizingly saying and then saying again as a variation of the theme thought.

Usually remarkably effective. Unfortunately, this time it's getting them nowhere quickly.

ENOUGH conjecturing! There's another murder to solve.

Solve? Lucia thinks. Then she says, "Using our intelligence, experience, and logical expertise to solve murders. What a lot of crap!"

Mike says, "Solving murders by using reason, regurgitating past murder cases, and using our God-given common sense. You said it. So much claptrap!"

They are at the scene. This time it is a white male. In a parking lot. Three quarters of a mile from homicide three at 7:00 A.M. A folded piece of stationary is duct taped to the victim's forehead. Strange. All the victims are left lying on their back. What might be the reason? Anyway ...

Mike: "I would say forty-five years. Five feet ten inches. A pudgy one hundred and eighty pounds. Informally dressed."

Lucia: "Clean shaven. A wedding band. Inexpensive watch. Well-worn medium-priced shoes. Occupation probably in some low-level profession."

Mike: "Like the first two murders, there is apparently no indication of a struggle, nothing with which to identify the crime."

With latex gloved hands Lucia removes the note and opens it,

'Twas Einstein and the end of time; cause it thegan bereafter morphing into spimetace.

"Einstein?" Mike says with a note of disbelief. "Now we've heard it all."

"There's a footnote telling me he's sending me the riddle via snail mail."

"Snail mail!" Mike verbally explodes. "He must be from the dinosaur age."

"Whatever. But poison? X-Man's trying to outdo himself. We'll have to do some heavy talking with Len about this. What kind of poison? What would put this guy out almost immediately and apparently nobody is suspicious until they see him lying on the ground?"

A police officer approaches with a middle-age woman at her side. He says, "This is Ms. Greely. She says she is the first person to see the victim fall to the sidewalk."

"Good morning, Ms. Greely," Lucia tells her while extending her hand.

"Can you describe what you saw?"

"There weren't many people on the lot. Those who were walking back and forth around here would surely have noticed this man if he was sick and weaving back and forth or staggering. As far as I could tell, he was walking along like anyone else.

"Suddenly he stiffened. That's when I noticed him. He went rigid, like a block of ice. Then he fell backward. I walked over. Stooped to look at him. He wasn't breathing. I checked his pulse and felt nothing. That's when I called 911."

"Did you see anyone approach him and come into contact with him in any way?"

"No. The first time I noticed him was when he froze."

"Thank you, Ms. Greely. You have been helpful. Here's my card. If anything else comes to mind, please give me a call."

"Yes, I will," she says. "I hope it wasn't any new virus. They are coming out of the woodwork these days."

"I doubt it," Mike says. "We believe it was homicide."

"Homicide! Is it another of those serial killings?"

"We cannot know yet," Mike tells her.

"If it is, I hope you get the louse that did it."

"We will, Ms. Greely."

They stoop over the victim. Mike observes, "There's a spot of blood on the left side of his shirt."

Lucia unbuttons the poor guy's shirt. It's as if an ice pick had penetrated his heart.

"That's why we thought he might have been poisoned," a police officer tells them. "When I was in the academy, I learned that if a long hypodermic needle with a syringe loaded with certain poison liquids is rammed into a person's heart, he dies with hardly a moment's notice."

"Do you know what kind of poison can do that?" Lucia asks her. "I'm sorry. The name doesn't come to me at the moment."

"That's all right. We will ask our forensic specialist."

"I hope you nail the son of a bitch."

"We will," Lucia tells her, as she turns to Mike. "We must talk to Len and Jaimie about this."

"I agree" comes the response.

LUCIA calls Len and says she and Mike are on their way. They make haste. Soon enter his stomping grounds.

"You have a way of picking eccentric customers, don't you?" Len says.

"We don't pick them. They scream out for our attention like they've been suffering from terminal neglect. What do you have?"

"An injection straight into the heart."

"Gruesome," Mike says through clenched teeth.

"Poor bastard," Lucia says.

"This type of lethal injection is called Abspritzen, so called because it became quite common among doctors at Auschwitz," Len informs his grimacing audience of two.

"The justification was that it relieved the Auschwitz crew of the incurable mentally ill patients as well as those too old to do any useful work. At first, they injected ten to fifteen milliliters of the substance into the victim's vein. Then they discovered that if they emptied the syringe directly into his or her heart, death occurred almost immediately."

"So, the bastard puts his left hand on the victim's back and thrusts the needle into his chest and walks away, leaving him to stagger around and fall within a few seconds," Lucia speculates.

"Ten to fifteen seconds and the guy's off to paradise," Len confirms.

"Good God!" Mike adds to cap off the description.

Lucia suggests, "Might the killer be German. An avid reader of what went on in the concentration camps? A specialist on Auschwitz?"

Leonard replies, "Possibly, though it's a long shot, Lucia."

"I know, but we have to grab at the loosest of threads."

THE next morning, Lucia's snail mail arrives. She opens it, and reads,

> *I never was, am always to be; no one ever saw me, nor ever will; who am I?*

Deadpan alley immediately comes to mind for some reason or other. *Why?* she asks herself. *Death? No way, José. Deadpan? A blank, expressionless mug telling dry jokes.*

Perhaps like X-Man? Hmm. Or maybe it's Deadpan Alley? The musical combo. Their songs. "She Sleeps." Dream? Life is a dream? What could possibly be the relation?

"Goodnight, Lily." Like, goodnight, Lucy? What a runaway imagination you have, Lucia. "I'm lonely tonight." Spare me.

Lucia decides to take the riddle to Mike. While she is on her way to his desk, her phone begins vibrating. *Nuts,* she thinks, *Oh well, I'll see what it is while Mike is reading the riddle.*

"Hey, Mike. Here's the snail mail memo. Do a read of it and let me know what you think."

He reads. She checks her cell phone.

Oh God, it's him again, she complains in silence.

She reads it while Mike inquisitively peers over her shoulder,

those who are guilty go, I allude to their shame, their guilt, and I openly accuse those and only those who do not throw shame and guilt on themselves. Do I throw shame and guilt on myself? Look at it this way. If I say, "I'm lying when I say I am free of shame and guilt," am I telling the truth? Yours truly. (Ah, it bears mentioning that I'll zip another enticing puzzle to your phone in a few minutes.)

"Self-serving narcissism. What a prick," she tells Mike.

"This one's a skull cracker, isn't it?" Mike says.

"What? Oh yes. It's a tough one. What do you make of it?"

"Nothing so far, except that he's the most narcissistic son of a bitch I've seen since I left my ex-wife after ten months of hell."

"I know what you mean," Lucia nonchalantly replies.

"Shall I say we should sleep on it? I'm so bummed out I don't want to think about it, much less talk about it."

"Wait a sec. He promised me a second fugue-riddle. Let's see if it makes its appearance in the next few minutes. If not, we're outta here."

She no longer finishes saying that when the second riddle filters in. The killer tells her,

> *I appear in the morning but am always there; you
> can never see me though I am everywhere; by night
> I am gone, though I sometimes never was; nothing
> can defeat me because I am so easily gone; what
> am I?*

"Holy shit!" Mike exclaims. "I think he's losing it."

"What do you mean, Mike?"

"He's like the Mad Hatter who offers Alice a riddle she can't decode. She asks him what the answer is. He replies that he hasn't the slightest idea."

"The ultimate in frivolous play. With no purpose except to continue playing the play? Is that what you mean?"

"Something like that, I guess."

"I sense you've been rereading Lewis Carroll lately."

"Yeah ... Anyway, I'm beat. Out of sync. A basket case. I need to get away from this psychosis for a few hours."

"Fine with me. Tomorrow?"

"Tomorrow."

DURING the days that follow there's no rest for weary. The press periodically hounds Fay. She puts pressure on Lucia and Mike as well as others in the department.

Newspaper reporters are relentless. The city's mayor and the governor are getting into the act. To top it off, Lucia's cat comes up sick, which means a trip to the vet.

Lucia and Mike are beyond their wits. They often find themselves asking the same questions followed by weary eyes and nonresponses. Out of frustration, they resort to speculation over social issues, human nature, psychological hang-ups, the tenor of current times, and such.

But life must go on. At least they keep that idea stuck somewhere in the back of their mind.

DURING an early morning, Lucia and Mike find themselves speculating.

"Mike, this country cannot heal itself as long as the few become richer and the growing many are barely getting by. It creates dissatisfaction, frustration, ill-will, and resentment that explodes, creating social disintegration and hopelessness.

"Surely this must spawn disorders that culminate in psychopathic behavior among those most prone to violence. Something has to give."

"Tell me about it." Mike says. "Gangs and guns proliferate. Thieving and mugging are on the increase—except for those shining examples like New York City that managed to clean up their act."

"The constant threat of terrorism doesn't help either," Lucia adds. "To say nothing about conspiracy theories that a lot of people believe for some insane reason."

The parallels and consequences go on and on, leading nowhere. Lucia and Mike give up their discussion out of mental exhaustion.

MIKE decides on a change of topic, "Lucia, I remember you once made mention of game theory. You said it found its way and lodged itself in a lot of thinking among economists. For some strange reason might this be a key to the killer's gaming technique."

Lucia says, "Never thought about it. Game theory ... hmm. It involves Economists believe that if we are rational and at liberty to make our own decisions, we will under ordinary circumstances behave rationally.

"The assumption has it that we must be relatively free of those compulsions influenced by the media, folk beliefs, religion, and bigotry of all sorts. Then, we will make decisions according to what we deem will lead to the most desirable result."

"A simple example, if you don't mind."

"Swell, those are the only kinds of examples I can fathom," Lucia concedes.

"I know you better than that."

"Anyway, here goes. If we have a fifty percent chance of winning one hundred dollars or a ten percent chance of winning fifty dollars, we will always choose the first option."

"Life is never as simple as that," Mike protests. "The brain's well-calculated reasons often come in at a distant second place in comparison to irrational responses from the heart and guts."

"I'm getting there," Lucia tells him. "In the messy real world, problems often arise that cause us to make irrational decisions. For instance, if someone sees a lot of movies on TV revolving around violence and reaches the conclusion that violence is more prevalent in society than it actually is, it will likely affect her choices. If we take another step, we can say much the same of criminal minds, probably even psychopaths."

"In other words," Mike says, "we are wired to think rationally, but we often don't, because of our environmental pressures and influences."

"That's pretty much it."

"It is nature versus nurture all over again."

"I'm afraid I'll have to agree."

"Then," Mike concludes, "we are back where we started. With no answers"—

"Wait a minute" Lucia is quick to point out. "In the best of worlds, game theory gives us a zero-sum situation where if you win, somebody loses. If you multiply the process many times, everything eventually tends to balance out."

"Sounds too good to be true," Mike's skepticism tells Lucia. "But"—

Lucia butts in. "As you know, despite that Great Recession, the top one percent and more in this country had it pretty good. While most people barely scraped by. This tells us something was rotten in Denmark."

"If the rich enjoy power, they can go on forever."

"Not really. This condition cannot continue. Eventually, something's got to give."

"How so?" Mike asks.

"Look at it this way. Many of the rich produce things the general populace buys. But if the populace is becoming poorer in part because the rich are becoming richer—through tax cuts, loopholes, and all that—then the middle class and the poor class can buy less and less as the years go by. They will max out their credit cards, fall into heavy debt, and find themselves with decreasing purchasing power. You see? It's not a zero-sum game at all. It's a non-zero-sum game."

"Oh, so if I always win and you always lose," Mike points out. "Your losing eventually reflects on my winning and diminishes it."

"There you go."

"So, more people should have more money in their pockets. The rich will no longer be hauling money in by the tons. But that's no problem since most of them still have more than they deserve. The good life returns to the common people, and they're dancing in the streets."

"Exactly," Lucia adds her support.

MIKE returns to a previous point, "How does this add up to gaming and its relationship to play?"

"I never took that into serious consideration."

"As I see it, the way you describe game theory, it is just that: a game. Winners take their trophy, go to the pedestal with a toothy smile on their place, and bask in their glory. Losers hang their heads in shame and go home empty-handed. This is the result of cut-throat competition. It divides everybody in terms of bivalent either/or categories.

"According to one interpretation, the rich win because they are good at playing the game, and the poor lose presumably because they're lazy, uncompetitive, and lacking in the smarts department. Isn't this too simple? What about conditions the poor kids are born into compared to golden opportunities the rich kids surrounded by abundance enjoy?"

"You're right," Lucia concedes. "In addition, there's an important difference between game and play that comes to bear. It highlights the distinction between winners and losers as far as social games are concerned."

"Social games, everyday affairs."

"Yes. These games are for the most part closed. There are rigid rules and regulations. Think of chess. Or football. You must follow the rules, or you find yourself kicked out of the game.

"Play, in contrast, is open. There might be a few rules and regulations, but they at least some of them are to a degree flexible. Allowing for more freedom. Think of jazz. Or kids playacting in an imaginary world. Or art. Picasso, Duchamp, Warhol, Pollock. A small number of those at the bottom of the economic pyramid can nevertheless excel in certain social games and come out winners. Basketball and professional sports are among the best examples. Music is another one."

"I think I see," Mike says. "Maybe it's like play allows more creative freedom and game demands rigorous rule-following. In the long run, to a certain extent surely they must balance out."

"Hopefully, at least. In a democratic society, maybe. Games are serious business in politics, economics, social values and standards, and all that. Play is the joy of creative freedom where you can fly into the blue with wild flights of the imagination. Games come to an end, most typical in a totalitarian society. Play can go on forever.

"That's why in a democracy the balance must be perpetuated."

Mike is amused and puzzled.

"Okay," he concedes, "but with X-Man, we have a game on our hands. We can't simply play around. We've got to construct the most likely endgame."

"X-Man's world involves a game, for sure. If we can solve it, we will be winners. But to solve it we must use our imagination. And improvise. That's play. Or better, playacting.

"Sober Sherlock Holmes apparently used deduction and induction supremely. He can effectively do this, because he has a prepared mind. He's hypersensitive to anything that might be out of the ordinary, and suspicious of everything that seems too orderly. He anticipates future possibilities to avoid surprises. And he always wins the game magnificently."

"Well, I guess, but this puts us in another arena entirely. Play. Where virtually anything can happen. So, everything might come as a possible surprise, and we have to create as we go along."

"There's more to it," Lucia tells Mike. "We must begin from the zerodegree and create possible scenarios. We must engage in cool calculation of strange and often bizarre possibilities. And we periodically plunge into the depths of our imaginary mind."

"I think it's like we're not building the killer's world from a blue print according to the rules of a game. Because we must wing it as we proceed," Mike surmises.

"Of course. We improvise our play as we progress. Game might be rigorously logical. Play isn't. But play is not simply illogical. It follows its own logic and reason. Of the heart and guts, so to speak. While our mind bows to intuition.

"You get it, Mike? We're creating a world from scratch. From the zerodegree. I believe that's what the mad butcher is doing too. If we wish to beat him as if it was a game, he'll beat us. Beating him requires creatively playing along with him until we catch him. You remember the cat and the mouse?"

"Yeah, but the cat is following her instincts. She doesn't coincide with our means and methods."

"Granted. If it were a game, she would quickly and efficiently latch onto the mouse and eat him. A winner, and a loser. But there's a lapse in the game when she plays with her prey. Her type of spontaneous, gratuitous play."

"You're saying it's back to zero? Last night I couldn't sleep. Thinking of that take-off on Lewis Carroll's lines. Now it's beginning to make sense."

"You too? I looked at the riddle again and came up with this response."

She takes her latest riddle from X-Man out of her pocket and displays it for Mike's eyes. Mike reads it out loud,

J never was, am always to be; no one ever saw me, nor ever will; who am J?

"Make anything of it?" Lucia asks.

"Allusions to time are prevalent. Was, always, ever, never. Put them together, then it becomes timelessness. All there all at once. Like a humongous block. No yesterday. No tomorrow. Only now."

"What does it tell you."

"Hm ..."

"That's not good enough, Mike."

"Uh ... I got it! Everything happens in its own private now. The past is long gone. The future never was, at least not yet. And the now is always on the road toward becoming another now.

"So, the present now is also always becoming something else. In our consciousness. Within our living and breathing world.

"This is to say that each of the killer's homicides is in its own exclusive now. All his homicides make up a staccato series of now-laden blips."

"Mike, you are a genius."

"You're the intellectual playing games. I'm just a humble player trying to solve irrational puzzles."

Lucia laughs and says, "Now let's take a look at the other note."

Lucia reads the second riddle,

I appear in the morning but am always there; you can never see me though I am everywhere; by night I am gone, though I sometimes never was; nothing can defeat me but I am so easily gone; what am I?

"Always there, everywhere, never was, gone at night." Mike ponders over the words.

"Gone at night but everywhere. The sun! It's rays!" Lucia conjectures.

"Hey, yeah! Great intellect won the game this time by playing loose and limber."

"The future and the sun. What does this tell us?"

"That I'm stumped ... No ... Here it is! The future crime will be in broad daylight, unlike the first two killings."

"Timelessness enters the light of day and the crime becomes something other than what it was becoming. Mike? You're an intellectual virtuoso."

"So, I shout 'Eureka!' Fly out in the street naked. And announce my discovery to the world?"

Lucia belches out a hearty laugh. Then soberly says, "Each now appears to our consciousness as if moving forward with each murder. But each virtually instantaneous now will be another now. The next murder.

"The question is, when is that next murder's now? It's interesting that the killer's riddles have so much to do with perception and thinking merging with invisibility, and concealment, isn't it?"

"It's frustrating."

"More than that, it's maddening."

"We're all mad anyhow according to Professor Lucia. So not to worry."

Lucia grins, "Sure ..."

BEGINNING DELIBERATING
IN A NEW CONTEXT

THE following day, Lucia and Mike are not in the highest of spirits for obvious reasons.

During their lunch break they venture out for a fiery chili dog and then it's the usual trip to Starbucks.

On a street corner some religious freak is hollering about Armageddon and the end of the world. Not unexpected, given the circumstances.

They enter the coffee shop, pay for the vice of their choice, and sit at the nearest table. After a few sips they overhear the conversation at an adjacent sitting place.

"Those serial killings are awesome."

"Awesome you say? They kept me up all night."

"Gory crimes always give me jitters."

"I know. When I said awesome, I should have said bizarre, you know?"

"And to think they haven't a clue as to who the killer is."

"The mayor ought to can those poor excuses for detectives."

"I'm with you, and replace them with competence."

Lucia with face registering disgust says, "Let's get out of here."

"I'm on my way," Mike responds with a frown and a bitter taste in his mouth.

They toss their virtually unconsumed caffeine into the trash bin and briskly leave the premise.

Now ambling along the sidewalk, Mike says, "I imagine the whole city is talking like that. It's embarrassing."

"It shouldn't be, since few people recognize us."

"That's the only thing that allows me to show my face in public."

"Do you mind taking a detour to the drugstore," Lucia asks him. "I have a splitting headache and those generic painkillers at the precinct do me no good."

"Sure thing."

They enter the drugstore. Lucia selects her brand. Takes it to the cashier. While handing back her credit card the cashier says, "I've seen you before."

Lucia says nothing.

The cashier spouts out, "Now I remember. On the news. The reporters were interviewing you. Do you think they'll catch X-Man?"

"X-Man? What on earth do you mean?" Lucia says with wide open eyes. "You must have me confused with someone else."

"Oh, pardon me. But haven't you heard of X-Man? The serial killer."

"No. I keep away from a lot of the news. They use a liberal dose of imagination more than hard facts."

"You'd better watch out for that creep. I hear he's mostly after women."

"I'll keep that in mind."

They leave.

"Goddammit to hell, Mike. Nobody can have any secrets in this world."

"This is getting serious. Someone in the precinct continues leaking it out to the public, and the twit reporters are having a heyday spreading it like wildfire."

They enter headquarters. Lucia searches out Fay.

"Good morning. I need to talk to you about a serious issue."

"What is it?" Fay asks.

"I bought something at the drugstore, and the cashier mentioned the killer as X-Man. A cashier! Somebody around here is spewing information all over the city and I insist you get to the bottom of this!"

"I understand. And I apologize for taking so long with this investigation. Whoever is leaking the info isn't leaving any tracks. I'll get John Caperton onto the problem. He seems to know people around here better than the rest of us."

Grabbing at straws, Lucia thinks, as she says, "I would appreciate it. Let me know as soon as you find something out."

"You can be sure."

LUCIA enters her office fuming and foaming. *The next thing you know they'll be speculating over the label of my underwear,* she sizzles. Then she decides a boiling point temper will get her nowhere. She settles her frizzled nerves, and gets down to business.

Let me check out the map. Again? Definitely. The fourth crime was three quarters of a mile from the third killing. 7:00 A.M. Right there.

She stabs the spot with a tack-pin and returns to her swivel seat.

The times, 5:00, 5:00, 6:00, 7:00.

The distances? One-fourth, one-fourth, one-half, and three-fourths miles.

The number of days, three, three, six, nine.

What's the pattern? Timespace. Combine space with time and what do we have?

. . .

Think, dammit! Space plus time. Timespace. Curved space, timeless time within the block that spatializes time.

Isn't that how Uncle George once put it?

What about the riddles? Past, present and future in the static now. The sun's rays that are everywhere, but we bask in them coming from somewhere during the daytime hours.

What the hell has the psycho got packed away in his mind? Maybe nothing at all. Because in cavalier fashion he's simply playing.

Could that be it in a nutshell? He's playing with us rather than gaming? We want to think we're swivel seat warriors rationalizing it all. Meanwhile, he's loose and limber. Nonchalantly giggling as if he had no concerns whatsoever.

Playful mind games. Well, screw you!

Screw you? Is that the limit of my response? Is my agenda that hollow? Am I flying off in multiple directions the sum of which is no direction at all?

SHE stubborn-mindedly carries her thoughts with her when she calls it quits and heads for home. Buys a sandwich, some chips, and a pickle on her way.

Enters her apartment. Changes into sweats. And eats. She watches a bit of MSNBC. *Good ol' Rachel Maddow. If I had her brains, gift of gab, and whatever else,* Lucia thinks.

When Rachel signs off, Lucia activates her computer. And for the fun of it begins writing a narrative of her speculations as a one-act play.

A comedy masquerading as a murder mystery. She imagines herself in a situation like Sean Connery playing a new character in a non-James Bond movie while referring to the other Sean Connery in her favorite James Bond movie.

She's Lucia, hypothesizing about X-Man playacting his psyching her out because he is mad at the world and wants to get even with somebody. Anybody. And she happens to be a worthy opponent for his superior intellect, or at least what he considers his first-class mind.

At the same time, Lucia is secretly playing out her childhood when her father—a sleazy counterpart to X-Man—was in his customary act of controlling her mother. He had the habit of sending her ear warming charm one minute, appealing to her sentiments the next minute, and out of the blue flying into a rage over some trivial detail that put her in complete confusion.

Then whenever the opportunity presented itself, he would grab Lucia, hug her, tell her what a beautiful child she was, slide his hands all over her and fondle her in those "naughty places."

Filthy bastard, she thought as she wrote. *And to think I liked the attention he gave me. Since the kids at school gave me a hard time because I was little for my age.*

The "runt" they called me, a "wart on the frog's back." They taunted me because they told me I was "stupid" and didn't even know how to talk right.

Good Lord! During my early years I lived in Brazil with my Brazilian father and American mother. I knew hardly any English at all when we moved to the United States. They threw me in a classroom with all the others and I had to learn English on the fly. What did they expect?

My teachers put me in the back of the room so they wouldn't have to bother with me. But my dad was nice to me, or so he told me. While his hands did their exploring thing. Hell, I didn't know any difference. I put up with his perversity because at least he somehow made me feel good about myself. What a fuckin' merry-go-round.

She writes. While thinking to herself.

If I were then who I now am, I'd clobber those guys at school. Tell the pathetic teachers what I thought of them. Kick my sick dad in the balls and tell the world what he was doing to me.

She thinks, *Lucia then and Lucia later and Lucia at this moment becoming someone else. Because this new guy in town, X-Man, is glibly poking fun at me and mocking me and at the same time getting into my mind like a combination of my pathetic old man and everybody at school.*

I never thought of it that way. Revolting!

She is Lucia then and Lucia now as well. Her story includes X-Man and those around her during her childhood and her lewd dad who made her life hell.

SHE stops writing. Sits quietly. Hardly blinking. Feeling her heart palpitating. And says, "If I didn't know better, I would likely think I am meditating."

She perks up and says to herself in an uncertain voice, *Did my fuckin' old man have a streak of psychopathic behavior? Is X-Man a psychopath of the same sort? Am I on the road toward becoming his future victim? Can I escape his psychological grasp on my mind?*

Who am I? Really? Still that pathetically helpless child? Or am I who I would like to think I now am?

She sits. And continues sitting. *Nothing else to do. Just rest up before getting on with it tomorrow.* So, she sits. Silently but rigidly. She's tense. But it is no nervous sort of tension. For she's silent land still. As if nothing was going on.

Yet, her sitting is far from resting. In a way, it's free of anxieties. She says to herself. *Time to move over to the couch or remain unmovably here going numb, Lucia.*

She rises. Slowly. Shillyshallies to the sofa. And sits. Tension's still there. So, she passively sits. A half hour later, she slips over on her right side and stretches her legs as far as the sofa's length permits.

She sleeps. Sort of figuratively speaking. Because she dreams she meets up with X-Man. She flips out because he has her dad's face on a huge, massively muscled body. He throws her on a bed. Makes sweet talk. With his hands all over her.

"Kick him in the nuts!" she suddenly says in a heavy *macho* voice as her eyes fly open, and she bolts out of bed. "Fucking son of a bitch," she screams with enough decibels to wake up apartment dwellers in the vicinity.

So much for sleep. She struggles mightily to free herself of her dream state and equally mightily to struggle no more with her childhood memories.

After calming down, she makes coffee. And sits. Waiting for time to pass so she can get ready and head for the sanctimonious law enforcing sanatorium of sweat, pain, and helpless, hopeless questions that have no answers.

PLAYING IT BY EAR

FOR some enviable reason, Mike is in good spirits at the office. "What are you smiling about, knucklehead?" Lucia says. "What a night I had with Elena."

She chuckles, "I'll do you the favor of inquiring no further. But I must say, I don't know how she puts up with you."

"Because I'm irresistible, naturally."

"Well, Mike, you sure had me fooled," Lucia says with tongue in cheek.

"Cheer up, Lucia. Smile and the world smiles with you; frown and you frown alone."

"I'll be damned. I haven't heard that piece of folk wisdom since my old man used it on a daily basis." *My old man? Spare me!*

"My mom was the folksy philosopher."

"What do you say we get to work."

"Work? What is there to do? We've drawn nothing but blanks."

"Maybe not. But I've got something for you."

Lucia tells Mike about what she came up with on the map, then says, "There is a progression of time and space. My gut tells me it corresponds to the psycho-butcher's out-in-left-field allusions to Einstein and timespace.

"To the riddles. To contradictory colorless green ideas morphing into word fusion. To the border between this world and a Lewis Carroll world on the other side of the mirror.

"To the paradoxical situations pervading almost everything he has said and done."

"Geez, all that? My grey matter is flipping."

"I think he's gravitating toward something, and the key is on the map and through time. Indeed, space and time may be giving us the answers we so desperately need."

"A blank key," Mike mumbles.

"Yes, blank. That's the beginning, the zero-point that holds countless possibilities. And we must know which one?

"Here's the scheme I worked up," Lucia says as she pulls a sheet of paper off her desk with a figure drawn on it. "Crimes one and two head off in different directions. The first one is down the street from headquarters, and the second one cuts across city blocks.

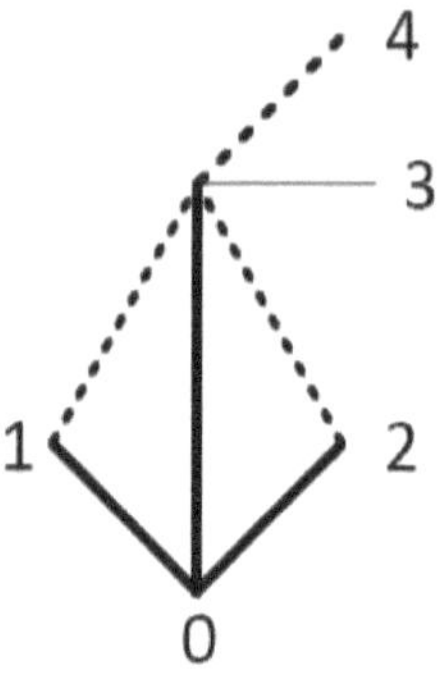

Crime three, of twice the distance, also cuts across city blocks. Crime four, almost twice the distance of one and two, exists along a nonlinear tangential path, like two and three. What does this suggest?"

"That I was never good at geometry."

"Come on. Put the puzzle together. Everything is interconnected. Along linear and nonlinear paths."

"What exactly are you getting at?" Mike queries.

LUCIA stares at Mike staring at her with a grim face for a couple of seconds as if she was seeing nothing at all, then ...

"Uh, nothing, I guess." Lucia finds herself forced to concede.

"Nothing? I thought you had something to show me."

"Now that I'm trying to explain it, I see nothing more than a hollow idea. Pure abstraction unrelated to the concrete world."

"You're sounding once more like Lewis Carroll's Queen who marvels over Alice's ability to see nothing."

"I know. Because I have nothing to see or say. And yet I have a sneaky feeling that this is where it began," Lucia confesses.

"Remarkable that you can have nothing as if it was something."

"Nothing? Something? What's the difference?"

"All the difference in the world. Nothing, at your zero-point, becomes something, and then something else, and then ..."

"Mike, are you implying that there will be one crime after another until we stop him or throw our hands up in despair?"

"Or until he gets tired of the charade, scams a widow out of untold millions her husband left her, and lives happily ever after with an air-head bimbo he convinced he's God's gift to women."

"I'm afraid you are right," Lucia sadly acknowledges.

"There's going to be hell to pay with Fay, the media, the mayor, the governor, and worst of all, the public."

"I know. Because we have nothing," Lucia morosely mutters. "My diagram might as well have remained a blank sheet."

"Nothing," Mike adds.

"Yes. I mean no. You're right. How the hell do you say there's nothing if when you say it you're saying something?"

"Yeah. What can we say?" Mike asks.

"I don't know."

THEY gawk. At the diagram.

"A map is two-dimensional," Lucia observes.

"Offering the picture of a three-dimensional city," Mike adds.

"Space expands, time moves on, while creating a transformation from the map to what is mapped." Lucia observes further.

"Timespace. It's all connected. Somehow."

"Yes, connected," Lucia repeats. "And we remain disconnected."

"Connections must make themselves manifest."

"Out of the blue," Lucia adds.

Perking up and getting them out of their mental lethargy, Mike says, "Does what you call nonlinearity in the two-dimensional diagram push us into the third dimension?"

"On the map, the scheme is two dimensional, but when we interject it into three dimensions, we're in our everyday nuts and bolts physical world. Is that what you mean?"

"More or less ... I suppose."

"Well, then, maybe it can eventually guide us into the fourth dimension where everything is interconnected, and we will be in the murderer's imaginary world."

"If you say so, Luce."

"Let me explain, if I can. Assume the assassin has total information about us from the leaks some rat among us at headquarters passed over to him. With that info it would be as if he was in a 'higher dimension.

"From this higher dimension he can peer down on us in our lowly threedimensional world. Know where we are, what we're up to, and what we are finding out about his crimes. In much the same way that in our threedimensional world we can enter a psychologist's laboratory and gaze at a rat in maze turning corners at random and failing to end up with a morsel of chow in the middle.

"We can see where the rat came from, where he is, and where he needs to go to find his reward. But in his maze, all he can know is that at every juncture he has no alternative other than choosing the left or the right. As if he was in a two-dimensional world."

"Makes sense ... I guess."

"You guess?"

"Well, I still don't know where you're coming from."

"You ever seen those mazes psychologists cook up to run rats through?"

"Yes."

"As far as the rat is concerned, he's moving around on a two-dimensional world between a bunch of narrow walls. We are above him, in three dimensions, and can see exactly where he must go to get the grub."

"Okay! So, we're trapped in three dimensions, and it's like the villain is in the next dimension laughing at our pathetic state of mind. But we have to be careful if we don't know where we're going because we might not get there."

Lucia laughs. "If we could put it in three dimensions and see it from four dimensions, we might be onto something."

"You remember that Penrose triangle you showed me?" Mike asks. "Yes, why?"

"It's an imaginary spatial paradox. It can't exist in three-dimensional space but it can in four."

"In the timespace manifold, you mean."

"How can we get there?" Mike asks.

"We can't. We are like Flatlanders who can't move into three dimensions. We're in three dimensions and can't move into four, because we're three-dimensional objects. You ever read that book by Edwin Abbott, *Flatland*?"

"Never."

"You ought to read it, Mike."

"I will."

"Timespace," Lucia dreamily repeats.

Lucia and Mike's rather empty, somewhat directionless speculation comes to a close. Lucia puts the diagram underneath other papers to hide it from view. As if she didn't want anybody to see it. As if she was embarrassed by it.

Mike gives a laugh and suggests she show it to Fay. Lucia grimaces. Mike laughs again. So much for crystalline speculation and back to the grubby world.

A cuffed suspect enters the premise pushed along by two police officers. He's protesting every step of the way. "Ey, what're you shoving me around for? What've I done to you dudes?"

"Well, well, if it isn't Duke," Lucia calls over to him.

"You know him?" one of the officers asks.

"Yeah. His reputation is exceeded only by his bad manners that precede him. The Duke of Hazard we call him."

The cops guffaw along with Lucia and Mike.

Lucia tells them, "He's a menace, but more of a threat to himself than anyone else."

"He says he committed homicide three," the second officer tells Lucia and Mike.

"Do tell," Mike pipes up. "Hey, Duke, did you also commit homicides one, two, and four also?"

"I don't know about them others, but I slit that bitch's throat."

"Why did you do it," Mike asks him.

"Because she called me the '*n*' word. Nobody calls me that. I had to waste her."

"Horrors. A black woman using the '*n*' word with a black man." Lucia puts on a frightful face. "That's enough motive to kill anybody. Now tell me. Are you sure you aren't confessing to a murder so in your neighborhood they'll think you're a tough dude?"

"What d'ya mean a black woman? She had a white ass?"

"She had fairly light skin but she was black."

"Then she was a fuckin' white black."

"Don't try to kid me. I know who you are. Your squeamish nature wouldn't let you fit in with the *macho* crowd, so you created stories to build up the reputation of a hard-hitting customer. That way you thought you'll be accepted by the bad-ass tough-guy crowd."

"I ain't got no idea what you're talking 'bout, lady."

"Tell us, Duke, what kind of knife did you use?" Mike asks him. "Knife? I used a razor, ya know, them kind the barbers use."

"Where did you get it?" Lucia begins interrogating him in earnest.

"I ripped it off a barber. Stupid mother fucker. Right under his eyes, and he didn't see me take it."

"And how did you commit the crime?"

"Sliced her across the throat. Killed her ass. Didn't even give her a chance to scream."

"From ear to ear?"

"Yeah, that's it. Shhhlish, from ear to ear. She didn't know what happened to her."

"Did you plaster that note on her with duct tape?"

"What note? I split out like that dude from Jamaica. You know? That dude who ran like a bolt of lightning."

"I see." Lucia turns to the officers.

"Take this piece of trash out of here and put him back in his natural habitat."

"What?" Duke shouts. "You ain't gonna book me?"

"No Duke. We happen to know you killed nobody. You are free to go."

"Uuh, shit. I don't wants my face on TV anyway."

"Get him out of here."

After he's out of sight, Mike turns to Lucia. "Why do we have to put up with this crap."

"It comes with the job."

"Yeah, they think our job is like what they see in the movies. If they only knew."

"Even the socially incompetent think they are entitled to their fifteen minutes of fame."

"It's the pits."

"It's no cake walk for sure."

A few moments of silence. Then,

"You know?" Lucia says to bring some light to the issue bothering them, "Scientists have developed what they call *chaos theory*. People who don't know any better take it as literal chaos, randomness, total disorganization.

"Actually, chaos theory has to do with the creation of order out of disorder. Disorder isn't complete chaos or randomness. It contains the means for creating order. And with order, the emergence of life. 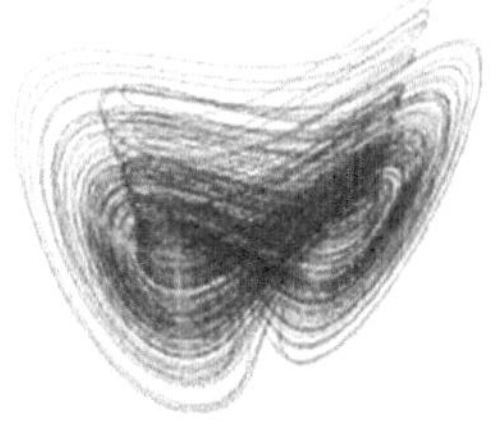

"Wait a minute. Let me see. I copied some illustrations ... Here's one ... See this? It's a visual metaphor of what they call the butterfly effect."

"I guess so, but"—

"See? It's nonlinear. Wavy lines swerving around along different paths. Somewhat in line with what they also call *fractals*."

"Fractals!" Mike perks up. "I've seen them everywhere. Even on T-shirts."

"Order out of chaos. It's the same principle that lies behind life itself. For example, the leaves of a fern are organized based on repetition over and over, but with a slight change each time.

"It creates difference from virtual sameness. Balance that is not quite perfect. Mirror imagery that is slightly flawed. Harmony that, like a Bach fugue, has the pattern altered a little with each repetition."

"I follow you yet, I'm puzzled."

"Bear with me. Repetitions when chaos is becoming order spiral out and out, nonlinearly. Perfect repetition is from A to B to A to B and on and on. Like a vicious circle. Spiraling repetition is from A to B, A_1 to B_1, A_2 to B_2, and so on.

"Within this spiraling whirligig, things repeat themselves. But there's a slight difference after each turn. There is a bit of swerving, swiveling variation of the theme. This makes for the creation of new forms, new movements bringing up surprises.

"Each context is new, and since it is surprising, it can be to a lesser or greater degree puzzling and enchanting. We are caught up in the free play of the universe. Play! That's the key that will unlock the door."

"Stop! My head is spiraling."

"Then you are in tune with what I'm saying. Eh, Mike?"

"No. I'm floundering because I don't know where you're going."

"Just let it flow, Mike. Flow along with it to see where it takes you."

"Go on, Lucia."

"X-Man wants us to cross a border, fall through the mirror to the other side, and into a world where everything is constantly changing. He also wants us to change. Change our idea of him. Notice little differences that make big differences.

"Then he'll slip away and leave us empty-handed and empty-headed. So, we'll have to start all over again. While mulling over the possibilities, the vicious spiral goes on. Virtually without end."

"Ah, I think I vaguely sense it."

"The border is where the person who likes his booze crosses the line into alcoholism because his physical tolerance for the drug of his choice fell to pieces.

"His pancreatic disorder becomes cirrhosis of the liver. His body moves outside the loop, giving up the struggle. It's all a matter of crossing a line, then another, then another ...

"It's like when the magician presents what we see as what there is. Then by a slight of hand, he moves outside the box. And what we thought we saw remains beyond our seeing. We realize we've been duped."

"Okay. And the grand climax?"

"This. X-Man thinks he can trash forensics and criminal investigation. We use scientific means and methods. But he thinks he's smarter than we are. And he's hell-bent to prove it."

"You mean like a psychopath?" Mike says.

"Exactly. He uses logic and reason against us by way of his messages and riddles and at the same time he rejects that same logic and reason. It is like saying 'I am irrational and illogical, and if you don't believe me, prove me wrong.'

"But there is no proving him wrong. He is sort of like that mathematical logician Kurt Gödel, who used mathematical logic to prove mathematics and logic are not always provable. It's as if he was saying 'I am lying.'

"X-Man is telling the truth, but he's lying so we will think he's creating his little games for real. But in a way, they are no more than playacting."

"He's a wily customer the way you put it."

"Indeed he is," Lucia says.

"Has it occurred to you that he could be right? That he's smarter than we are?"

"Quite possibly." Lucia ponders. "It's like he is order falling into chaos, and what will become a new order only he knows."

"Does that mean we have no chance in hell of cuffing him?"

"I hope to God not. We have to wait and see."

"Wait you say? I've heard that too many times," Mike complains.

"Yeah ... It's a kind of waiting game. We wait for him. His next move catches our attention. And we wait some more. But in vain, for he never appears in the way we think he will. It's like waiting for Gödel alias XMan. Gödel, or Göd, as a sign that fails to show up and make itself known."

Mike laughs. Lucia puckers up her lips and furrows her brow.

"You know," Lucia says with a sober face, "it's all a maze created out of playacting. Including us. Using horse-sense. Going with our guts. Following a strange logic that remains outside the bounds of what customarily goes as logic. You know, *Identity*, *Contradiction barring*, and the *Excluded middle*."

"I'm afraid you'll have to explain yourself again."

"You remember what Len told is in this respect."

"More or less. But it's now fuzzy."

"Standard logic tells us that what *is*, is what it *is*, and it can't be anything other than what it *is*. That what *is* can't be what it *is* and something else at the same time. And that there either *is* what there *is* or what there *isn't*, and that's all folks, for nothing else is possible. In other words, there's no third option."

"Oh yeah," Mike grunts.

"In contrast, X-Man's form of logic has everything always changing. What we think *is*, is never what it *was*, because it is always becoming *different*."

"Uh, yes, Ms. Rocket scientist."

"Don't be facetious. I'm serious. Because the psycho-butcher's game is serious. Or better, it's play within a sober nonsensical game. And we have to change along with his MO that is always becoming different."

"Yeah, I somehow think you're right. But I don't know how or why."

Mike and Lucia fall into silence again. Not because they feel like it, but because they can't help it. Then Lucia suggests, "Let's get down to business."

And business goes on in a way that would please Fay. Which is to say, they look busy. They search the Internet possibilities for some clues, visit a few crime scenes once again with the futile hope they might find some new evidence. They consult the forensic psychologist about some quirks that came up in their investigation. They invent something new to tell Fay who is demanding they keep her abreast about what's going on. Above all, they create some new twist that might convince the media it is playing an acceptable good-public-servant's role.

These activities are punctuated by extensive park bench sessions, time spent gazing at variations of Lucia's diagrams, and long sleepless nights.

All told, nothing genuinely ventured, nothing substantially gained.

STRANGE PROFILING

LUCIA tells Mike after they tire of for-the-sake-of-appearances conjuring acts, "I think another trip to Jack's cave is in order."

"Let's do it," Mike responds.

They call to make sure he's there. Then head out. When they arrive, Jack already has info about the murderer on his desk and he's pouring over it.

"Jack," Lucia begins. "Give us your opinion about psychopaths. If the killer we are trying to chase down is indeed a psychopath, some would say he sufficiently fits neither the general stereotype nor enough of Bob Hare's checklist of characteristics. How can we get a handle on him?"

"You know there are a lot of mistaken ideas about psychopaths out there."

"Yes, we do, and we don't want to make any more mistaken assumptions," Mike says.

"Here goes, then. If you have any questions as I proceed, pop them to me. One popular misconception is that psychopaths and serial killers are dysfunctional loners, social misfits who shun the crowd. On the contrary. They usually—though not always—strike you as commonplace social animals.

"They can appear as acceptable members of the community. They can have families, homes, and friends who consider them normal, which is to say they can hide in plain sight. Robert Yates, for example, was married with five children and lived in a middle-class neighborhood in Spokane. He killed seventeen prostitutes.

"Another misconception. They are almost invariably white males. This is simply not the case. True, the percentage of white male psychopaths among the white male population is relatively large. But that by no means discounts a growing number of female and minority psychopaths."

"Our problem is that we know very little about the killer," Mike says as he shuffles in his seat, showing little enthusiasm for the conversation.

"I am aware of that," Jack says with a grin on his face.

Lucia wonders, *Why does he seem to be savoring this disgusting psychopathic talk?*

"Jack," she asks, "can you say anything in this regard about our killer?"

"Not much, save the premonition that he might be a twenty-first-century counterpart to the man in the grey flannel suit, apparently as common-place as they come. These days most everybody is usually out to get what they can for themselves and to hell with everybody else. According to the information at hand, your killer seems remarkably in tune with the times."

"That isn't very encouraging," Lucia says. "Sorry, but it's the way I see it," Jack tells her. "I understand. Please continue."

"Another false stereotype has it that they are geniuses who outwit the best law enforcers around. In the real world, most psychopaths are losers who think they are winners. They think they can do no wrong. If they are caught lying, cheating, stealing, and manipulating others, it is always somebody else's fault. They give the impression they are as clean as a whistle.

"Actually, there is rarely any indication that they are super-intellectuals. Take Ted Bundy, for example. He approached women he decided to victimize saying something like 'Hi, I'm Ted Bundy.' Is this a clever opening or what? He was never caught by super intelligent detective work, but after he was stopped for speeding. He was so intelligent he told the police that he was watching a movie at the time in question, and it wasn't playing in any theater"—

Mike pipes up, "The killer we're trying to nab is obviously intelligent, and he knows it. He flaunts it, and he wants everybody to acknowledge it."

"I have gathered so much," Jack reveals with another broad smile and a nod, and he continues, "Another misconception. Psychopaths are supposed to be motivated by sex. Sometimes true, often not.

"They are usually angry and resentful. Many of them are thrill seekers who want to see the consequences of their sordid acts in the newspapers and on TV. They wish to become notorious, and some of them even want to get caught so they can bask in their own notoriety."

"Now that sounds like our predator," Mike says.

"Another stereotype that does not hold up is the popular notion that once they start killing, they like it, become addicted to it, and cannot stop.

"Truth be told, there are many cases of a few serial killings and then the killer goes back to normal life."

"I'm afraid we draw a blank here," Lucia interjects. "We don't know much about the killer, so we have no idea how long he will be on the rampage."

"Yes, I am aware of that. Your case is intriguing. Your perp is apparently intelligent, cunning, and even playful."

"Interesting you say that, since the killer sends us enigmatic notes, puzzles, and riddles." Lucia observes. "We also think he does this out of sheer playfulness."

"It's like a big joke, and we are the punch line," Mike pipes up.

Jack lets out a muffled cackle that Mike finds annoying, but he says nothing, and Jack quickly moves on, "Of singular importance, many think a serial killer's signature is tied to his MO. The problem is that many serial killers do not repeat their crimes in rapid succession. Some let years go by before committing another crime.

"In the meantime, they've changed, and their MO might be entirely different. Their new crime might be the result of some incident that stimulated them: an accident that left them in physical pain, their spouse cutting out on them, losing their job, becoming the butt of jokes at the workplace, or whatever."

Mike jumps in. "Strange. This doesn't apply to our case either. The killer's crimes have come in quick succession, though the time between them is becoming longer."

Jack ignores Mike, keeping eye contact with Lucia when he says, "This is the proof of the pudding. The fact of the matter is that psychopaths are unpredictable. The most intelligent among them are admirably innovative individuals."

"Jack," Lucia asks, "Serial killers are often psychopaths. To what extent does the one involve the other?"

"Serial killers are not mass murderers, as are terrorists and those frustrated individuals who enter a public place and open fire on a crowd. Serial killers usually commit their heinous acts one victim at a time. They reach their high and then they calm down for a cool-off period. Something like a week-end binge drinker.

"Psychopaths are a particular type of serial killer. Unlike many serial killers, they have a personality disorder that compels them to use charm, intimidation, manipulation and violence to get their kicks and satisfaction. But keep in mind that psychopaths' scores on the Bob Hare checklist make up a continuum. There is no way of knowing at what point a person whose score edges into the psychopathic category qualifies him as either mentally disordered or not."

"Multiple motives, vague signatures, changing identities, deviation from all the stereotypes," Lucia pensively mumbles. "It seems we're up against a brick wall"

"I should mention," Jack tentatively adds with a strange smirk, "that in recent years, nature has been winning over nurture among scholars of psychopathology. Though in my estimation the two certainly go hand in hand in most cases."

"Thanks for the advice, Jack, we certainly appreciate it," Lucia says. "Mike, it's time to boogie. We need to work on our report. Tomorrow's the deadline to please Fay. As well as Norm Carter of the FBI who almost daily presses me for info."

"I hope I've been able to help you out and wish you luck. I have an idea you'll need it," Jack says with a slight twitch of his right eye. "If you have any further questions, feel free to call on me."

AFTER they leave, Mike is quick to say, "X-Man gives us no respect."

"Self-respect is his limit. Narcissism is his nature. Arrogance is his mode. Domination is his goal."

"What is the fiendish monster after, really?"

"I wish I knew," Lucia says with a wince.

"It's been a while since his last strike. When do you suppose he will surprise us with another one?"

"Three days, then three, six, and nine, and we are now in the thirteenth day, that is, after homicide four."

"What does that tell you, Luce?"

"Nothing. We're going nowhere." Mike rolls his eyes, "That again."

"Yes, that. The hour of the day progresses with each crime. As do the number of days and distances on the map. But we're left with nothing. We returned at the zero-point looking out into empty space and timeless time."

Zero, zilch, Mike mumbles.

Empty space and timeless time, Lucia thinks, then she says, "I can't help thinking about time warps, or better, topology, a special form of geometry. A living organism is a bundle of forms in space that morph into other forms with the passage of time. My uncle told me a lot about metamorphing forms in time."

"If you say so, Luce," Mike says with a lethargic murmur.

LUCIA was always good at geometry. She knew it. And she enjoyed the reputation she had among her classmates. Though there wasn't any lack of envy as well as snide comments that included "nerd" "klutz" "stuck up" "snobbish" "teacher's pet," and such.

She thought seriously about majoring in geometry at the university and was encouraged by her uncle, a retired math professor. But she decided against it. Probably due to her dad's constantly insisting that girls are no good with numbers.

Still, she took classes in math whenever she got a chance, and came out with better grades in that area than in her major.

"George," Lucia almost whispers.

"Who's that?" Mike asks.

"Uncle George. I ought to talk to him about my timespace figures. He might tell us something that clicks. Maybe I should wait until after the fifth crime. If there is a fifth crime. Good lord, if there isn't, this killer will surely end up in the unsolved files, and my ass will be cooked."

"Hey, definitely!" Mike bursts out.

"Definitely what? That my ass will also be cooked?"

"No." Mike chuckles. "We should talk to your uncle and find out if he sees any pattern in your sketches?"

"It's on the agenda."

BUT they put George on the backburner. Briskly walk to the parking lot. And drive off to check out a butcher at the packing plant who claims he knows something about the last homicide. *Fat chance*, they think. Probably another dead end.

During the trip Lucia ponders, *Cars and people coming and going. Life as usual. They'll jaw about the murders. Everybody will have an opinion. They'll tell you at the drop of a hat what the investigators should do, and if they don't, they ought to be canned. They'll speculate about the killer, and if you put their speculations in a bag, they will cancel out and leave you with nothing.*

The case ends up in the unsolved files. End of story. What futility, Lucia thinks to herself.

The packing plant looms. They enter and head to Ben Conti's workplace with badge in hand. He is cutting up a slab of beef. Welcomes the opportunity to take a break. They go to a corner of the building and try to talk over the din of machines, guttural shouts, and occasional guffaws.

"Mr. Conti," Lucia begins. "Tell us what you know about the case of lethal poisoning."

"My neighbor was entering his house next to mine and I was doing the same after getting off work. We usually talk a little when we see each other. This time he didn't want to talk. But he knows a lot about plumbing and I had a problem with the toilet and wanted to ask him a question.

"I asked him 'What do you do when that ball in the toilet doesn't prevent the water from leaking. Because I bought two of those sets and put them in, and the water still leaks out. What else can I do?' He didn't want to talk to me. I could tell by that look in his eyes, almost like he was scared. He clutched his bag in his right hand tighter and gave me some advice. But you don't want to hear about that so I'll get to the details.

"Anyways he just turned around and put his key in the lock and disappeared without sayin' good-bye or go to hell. He isn't like that. Now, I know he's also into rat and cockroach killing. A fanatic. Everybody knows he keeps all the nasty bugs and things out of the neighborhood because he has this hatred or maybe it's a fear of them. And he always uses poison. The toughest kind he can get.

"Every time he talks about the different types of poison, he uses he gets this smile on his face like he gets a high from killing rats like a dope fiend gets a high on the drug of his choice.

"I think you outta check this guy out. Not because I have anything against him. I consider him a friend and I have nothing against him. But he's been kind of strange lately."

Mike focuses on the clouds he sees out the window promising a thunderstorm. Lucia tells Ben "Thank you. You've been very helpful, and we will check out all the possible leads."

They leave.

Mike says, "What a mealy mouth. He doesn't talk, he vomits words. Are we going to check on his neighbor?"

Lucia responds, "No. The guy Conti was talking about has a phobia regarding cockroaches and rats. He doesn't lop off heads or slice throats."

"That's what I thought," Mike says.

They return to the precinct and enter their respective places for more fantasy, foible, and frustration.

LUCIA wants isolation so she can pore over and drill in on those geometry facts and fictions that have her obsessed. For some strange reason she is becoming increasingly convinced that they offer the key to the murderer's apparently morphing MO.

She doesn't know why. She feels it in her bones.

Okay, Lucia, if you're such a hot shot, why haven't you figured this out? Stoke up the neurons. Get the fire going inside your noggin? You must tap your imagination so it can come up with something others can't see.

You can observe a lot by just looking, and the gray matter can spew out a lot if you just keep it cooking. A solution involves intuitive conjectures before those highly touted processes. Then induction and deduction in good Sherlock

Holmes fashion. It involves creation out of feelings and intuitive inclinations before settling down to hard-core logical cogitation.

It's an act of creative destruction before there's anything to reason about. Destruction, because the habitual channels of thought must suffer abandonment so you can strike out into the unknown ...

Hey! Where are these rambling thoughts coming from? Enough of this. Get with it, Lucia ...

Yeah, so it's space and time. Gotta think outside the box to understand them. My mind's gotta be somewhere else. Iconoclasm! That's what it's about. Gotta play like I'm a cognitive rebel. Out of the groove and into somewhere else where nobody has gone.

It's not simply a matter of what you see is what you get. It's your imagination letting you see what could have been but wasn't. Then it enters the process of becoming something other than what it was becoming.

It's like falling through the looking glass.

That again? How can you think and go through the looking glass at the same time? You're either going there because your body and mind are unthinkingly thinking and going with the flow, or you're going nowhere because your mind shut down your body and its doing its thinking in an abstract artificial mode.

You must let yourself go with the flow. You can't put your creative brain in high gear if your abstract thoughts keep it churning and grinding with nowhere else to go.

Let go and enter the flow, Lucia. Just do it. Then and only then can you put yourself to thinking seriously about it.

SHE gets out her latest diagram. Gazes at it. Trying to get a feel for it. Then she thinks, *Progression in time must parallel progression in space. Somehow. But how?*

She is aware that a bigger jump in time after the first two crimes somehow corresponds to a bigger jump in space. But she doesn't know what to do about it.

Put time and space together and you have timespace. One-fourth, onefourth, one-half, and three-fourths. Yes.

Five o'clock, five o'clock, six o'clock and seven o'clock.

Okay. After the first two crimes, the distance increases by a quartermile and the time increases by an hour. What if I extrapolate the diagram? ...

There. The next crime should be at nine o'clock a mile and a quarter away from the first crime. On what day?

The first murder was three days after I got a message from X-Man and so was the second murder. The third one was six days later and the fourth one nine days later. So, the next murder should be twelve days later. Right?

Negative. We're now in the fourteenth day. Does this mean the next crime will be greater in time and space as well? If so, where and when?

God dammit X-Man! Give me something I can work with! You're a first-rate coward at heart, aren't you? Paranoia grabs you at every step due to your fear we might trip you up.

She stares at the diagram. Continues staring at it.

Solving this crime will be ninety-percent free-wheeling imagination and fifty-percent thinking it all out. If that could be possible. But it isn't. Like this case.

At any rate, the thinking and reasoning self has a big ego problem. I shouldn't bow down to it, worship it, sing praises to it. I must let imagination do what it does. I must draw from the fire it gives off to light up my mind. Then I can begin seriously entertaining my thoughts.

Is that what going through the looking glass is all about? Is the other side populated with patterns of neuronal firings that combine to form a crazy imaginary world? Then the mind's thoughts cancel and replace this world with what it thinks is logical and rational?

When a child I did childish things by letting my imagination fly all over the place. Then I grew up, left childish things behind, and took up mature cerebral thinking, reasoning, and doing. Now, it seems, I need to go in reverse and become a child again.

Easy to say, painful to do. Back in time, my sorry excuse for a father had this fake smile on his mug, and my mother passively bowed to his every demand. Back then, the other kids were saying "take that brown shoe polish off your face." They called me "nigger" and all that.

What the fuck! I'm Brazilian. That's how we are. We're a grand ethnic stew and Europeans and Africans and indigenous people become the wanted and at times unwanted ingredients.

But now I have to do what I have to do. Stray away from abstract thinking, and get in tune with the images of sight, sound, and sense.

She continues staring at the diagram. Then drops it. Her phone is paging her ...

Dammit! Now we'll likely have to check out another lead that will end in naught.

I won't so much as respond. No. I'd better.

I was right. Another lead.

SHE calls Mike. They meet at the alleged site. Lucia was on the mark. A story about a guy with a syringe from an informant who must have memorized the newspaper reports.

Hell, Mike thought, *half of what they write is a lie and the other half is a long stretch of useless imagination.*

They have to check the remotely possible lead out anyway. Turns out he's a diabetic. A recluse on a TV diet of sports, HBO movies, and sitcoms. He knows virtually nothing about the homicides.

Doldrums threaten once more. They return to the precinct. Mike contemplates Lucia's obsession over abstractions. He leaves his desk. "Lucia?" he says from two yards outside the open door of Lucia's office.

"Yes, Mike, what's on your mind"?

"I got to thinking about your figures, geometry, numbers, and space and time. Then I asked a lot of questions to Google about those topics, and especially number magic, you know? Numerology."

"Come on, Mike. You don't for a minute believe that nonsense do you?"

"Of course not. I was just curious."

"Watch out. Before you know it, you'll find yourself hooked."

"Not at all. It was no more than a bit of snooping. Here, let me show you what I found." He unfolds a sheet of paper he has in his hands. "On the

Internet I saw a book by Martin Gardner, *Magic Numbers of Dr. Matrix*. I went to the library and checked it out.

"Get this. Among other topics, it tells us about Abraham Lincoln and John F. Kennedy. Lincoln was elected in 1860, Kennedy in 1960, one hundred years later.

"Both were assassinated on Friday. A bullet entering their head from behind killed them. Both assassins were killed before they were brought to trial. Both were succeeded by vice-presidents whose surnames were Johnson. Andrew Johnson was born in 1808 and Lyndon Johnson was born in 1908, one hundred years apart.

"Lincoln and Kennedy have seven letters. Andrew Johnson and Lyndon Johnson have thirteen letters. John Wilkes Booth and Lee Harvey Oswald have fifteen letters."

"And?"

"Coincidence or predetermined necessity?"

"Like I've said, I believe nothing is coincidental. Everything happens for a reason. But the reason is not simply a matter of fate. Reason is not guided by fatalism but by an open mind putting data together with crystal clear calculation."

Am I saying this? she thinks, *After my prolonged meditations on imagination?*

"Of course," Mike nods. And you've occasionally said X-Man's strategies don't follow ordinary logic and reason."

"Whoa! If you think I give any credit to that numerology crap you've got another think coming."

"I'm just suggesting that maybe our placing stock in strange combinations of numbers, times, places, and catchy riddles is no more than XMan's gimmickry for keeping us off track. Should we place so much stock in it?"

"The unreasonable effectiveness," Lucia mumbles.

"What was that?"

"A famous physicist once wrote an essay about math and its eerie ability to answer questions about the physical world. He called it the 'unreasonable effectiveness' of math. He said we have no reason to hold such faith in the power of math. But it works, so we ought to use it, whether it is reasonable or not."

"We're not doing physics here, Lucia."

"Of course not. But we have hardly anything else to go on. So, let's use the abstractions with a dose of disbelief until we find some strategy more to our liking."

"Playact, in other words," Mike ventures to say.

"If you wish to put it that way, yes."

"Until something better happens to come along. Will it appear by chance or necessity?" Mike asks.

"We'll have it when we put the details in a bag, shake them up, pull out the results, and invent some new combination."

"Invent?" Mike asks.

"Create if you wish. Using our imaginary faculties. After all, we're playacting. Are we not?" Lucia responds

"Or dreaming."

"Is there any difference?"

"Hmm. I see ... I think."

Mike goes out the doorway on a tenuous note. Lucia observes him and nods her head, thinking, *He's got a point. But imagination merging with logical reasoning is how my mind works.*

I'm Brazilian in gut and heart, Anglo-American in mind. The complementary balancing act between my two ethnicities is fragile.

To hell with that idea of one language, one culture, and one God perpetually blessing America over all other peoples and cultures. This country is also becoming a mixture of ethnicities from all over the world.

There's no One. There's Many. If you wish to call the Many One, it's your prerogative. But the One is Many. We must keep the notion of Many in mind and heart, and the multiple ambiguity of it all, if we hope to make heads or tails of this mind-boggling mess the psycho has cooked up for us.

Another day, while some conjunction, fortuitous or inevitable, is out there awaiting the propitious time and place ...

GIVE HIM A HIGH-FIVE?

DAY fifteen begins like another typical day at the sporadically enterprising enforcement factory. Complying with bureaucratic formalities, mandates, requests, petitions and an occasional ultimatum. Until a little after nine in the morning, that is.

Then pandemonium erupts. Homicide five.

Voices rise to a high pitched crescendo. Bodies jerk themselves around apparently at random. Faces gesture wildly. Arms gyrate. A coffee cup falls to the floor, covering two square feet of the aisle.

Fay appears. To see what the commotion is about. "Five!" she hears, and immediately knows. There's work to do. She sees Lucia. Calls her over. Tells her and Mike to keep their eye on the most minute details. Stick around the scene in case the assassin can't resist the chance to gloat over his most recent criminal masterpiece.

"We have to close this case because the top dogs in their plush offices are giving me a lot of hell," Fay says.

"I know," Lucia tells her, "and the press will probably be at the door by the time we leave because some bastard around here has tipped them off."

"I've got somebody on that. I'll find out who it is. Your job is to focus on that maniac."

Of course, and exactly what is your job, Fay? You ever ask yourself? Lucia says to herself as she tells Fay, "Get that snitch. Please. He's making my life miserable."

"Let's make haste, Luce." Mike gives her a nudge. She turns to Mike and says, "We're off."

THE victim is a Latino male. The murderer is mixing it up beautifully. He apparently jives on ethnic plurality.

The victim was stabbed at the edge of the park and left in plain view in order to be detected without delay. This is part of the criminal's freewheeling MO, it would seem. But how in the world does he do it without anybody getting a glimpse of him? Lucia and Mike ask everybody present. Nobody saw anything suspicious.

Back to the victim. Swarthy, perhaps from the Caribbean. Five ten and about a hundred and sixty pounds. A thin moustache. Tightly curled hair. A dagger tattooed on the left side of his neck and a cross on his right shoulder. Physically impressive. Sweats and running shoes. X-Man must be powerful indeed if he was able to man-handled this victim without leaving traces of violence. A high school wrestling champion perhaps?

Shirt intact. No scratches or contusions. Maybe the killer dragged the victim behind the nearby bush, stabbed him a dozen or so times, and dragged him out at the propitious moment when nobody was around.

They search the bushes in the area. Nothing other than normal scuffing left by traipsing, trampling feet. No shoe prints worthy of note. How can he do this without resorting to violence? Threaten his victim with a gun? Get him behind the bush, pull out a knife, and stab him repeatedly?

The first stab wound would probably be in the back. Then the predator turned him over and finished killing him with multiple stabs to the chest. And left him staring into the sky. Mike and Lucia turn him over. There it is. First stab wound in the back and the others in front.

Nothing unusual on the sidewalk or in the grass. Tell-tale footprints? Negative. Knife? Likewise. Chance of success with a DNA sample? Probably not. The killer undoubtedly used latex gloves.

Lucia removes the note duct taped to the victim's forehead. She hadn't done it prior to this moment because she's tiring of the puzzles. Doesn't want to think about them. Just get it on and get it solved and over with.

She opens the paper and reads,

$\mathcal{J}$was zero sum and $\sqrt{-1}$; orthtesian to the carogonal plane.

The usual information regarding the riddle's whereabouts is included,

Underneath the park table.

Two pairs of eyes look around, spy a table. Go over. A hand moves under the table's surface. Removes the note. Two hands open it. Lucia's eyes read,

You saw me where I never was and where I could not be; and yet within that very place my face you often see; what am I?

"I'm fucking tired of this charade," Mike says.

"You think I'm not?" Lucia asks him, "But we have to decipher his notes. Whether we like it or not."

They sit at the table. Impatiently and zombie-like, they reread the unwanted brainteasers.

Lucia says, "My mind isn't into this."

"Coffee? The usual remedy for TDMSS?" Mike says.

"TDMSS?"

"Terminally Dissonant Mind-Set Syndrome," Mike tells her with a laugh.

Lucia gives him a smirk and says, "What else? We've got Berto and Rich moseying around to check out any suspicious characters in the vicinity. First, coffee, while agonizing over these damned limericks, then we'll go over and see if they found anything."

When they are inside and seated with their cup of black magic in hand, Mike observes. "You notice there's usually a Starbucks around?"

"They're everywhere."

"I know, but it still seems unusual. Could there be any clue here?"

"I doubt it."

"Whatever ... Let's figure out these mindbenders."

They gawk at the message and riddle.

Lucia's thinking, *There's nothing easier than the predator's searching your mind or the Internet for jokes, puzzles, riddles and paradoxes to complicate a series of crimes.*

Nothing easier than torturing a helpless victim and mutilating the cadaver.

Nothing more difficult for us than getting into his mind, understanding how he operates, and why he operates that way.

The question that looms up and hovers over the investigation of such hideous acts is: Why?

Mike thinks, *This is so ghastly, so appalling ... What type of human specimen would invent these horrid acts, carry them out, gloat over them afterward?*

They gape, with nothing of constructive importance in mind.

Lucia asks herself, *How can you get your mind-set in tune with this? In tune? What tune? There's no more than screechy million decibel static. You can't concentrate, can't think.*

Mike wonders, *Fuckin' pervert. If I could get my hands on him. If I could analyze him like Lucia does ...*

THEY return to the park table with the idea of thinking things over for a while before returning to headquarters.

"You know, Mike?" Lucia finally says, "Never before have I had to go back to my days of geometry, math, calculus, trigonometry, and all that."

"No, I don't know," Mike says. "I was the class clown, a numbskull whose main goal in life was getting laughs to attract attention."

Lucia continues as if she hadn't heard him, "Now it is coming in handy. Think about this. Zero-sum games, the square root of minus one on the Cartesian plane. You remember?"

"No. In school I systematically forgot whatever came out of the teacher's mouth as soon as possible. Gone forever."

"*Orthtesian* and *carogonal* in X-Man's vocabulary becomes *orthogonal* and *Cartesian*. This play on words might allude to what is called the Argand plane. Set it up as x and y coordinates on a sheet of paper and what do you have?"

"You tell me, Luce. You're the math whiz."

"Here let me show you."

Lucia draws a set of three axes on a two-dimensional plane suggesting three-dimensionality. And explains, "Along the x axis you have positive integers to the right and negative integers to the left with zero in the middle. Win some and lose some by the same amount and you end up with zero. A zerosum game, metaphorically speaking. Along the *y* axis it's the same story. These two axes make up the familiar two-dimensional Cartesian plane.

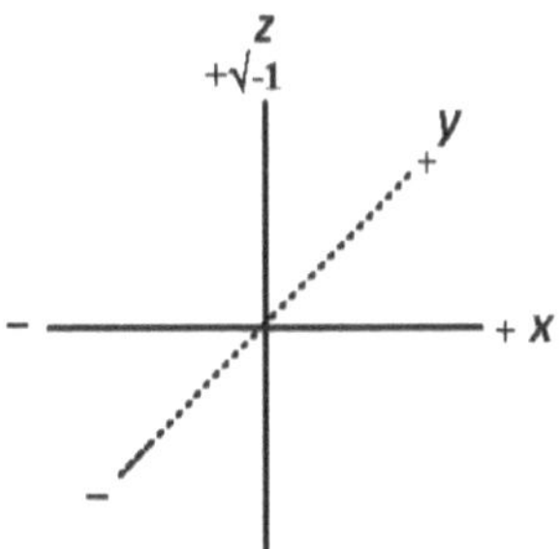

"To construct an Argand plane, delete the *y* axis, leaving you with a two-dimensional plane. It consists of positive integers to the right and negative integers on the left modeled by the *x* axis. Which is crossed by the *imaginary* plane—so called because it sports *imaginary* numbers. The *z* axis has the positive square root of minus one above and the negative square root of minus one below."

"I see it but have no idea what it's about," Mike says with furrowed brow. "What do you mean by imaginary numbers?"

"They are numbers of the nature of the square root of minus one. It's in our latest riddle. It *is* the riddle. What can we say about it? Is the answer ensconced within the square root of minus one plus one? No. One times one is one. Is the answer minus one? No. Minus one times minus one is also one. We're caught in a bind.

"Actually, *imaginary* numbers are no more *imaginary* than any other set of numbers. They defy the normal, rational, logical nature of whole numbers. Yet, they are sort of misfits."

"I'll go along with that. But how do we know it's not flaky numerology, or whatever?"

"Oh ye of little faith. It's a matter of orthogonality. The *z* axis is orthogonal with respect to the *x* axis. When you create the image of a *y* axis, you have three-dimensionality in comparison to the two-dimensional Cartesian plane. The three-dimensional structure is in the riddle. *Orthogonality* blended with the *Cartesian* plane. Or if you wish, *orthtesian* the *carogonal* plane. It is what the riddle is about."

"Message schmessage, scheme schmean. It's so much Greek to me. How does this help us get handcuffs on the killer?"

"Put your mind to it, Mike. You're not thinking."

"This isn't thinking. Sorry to put it this way, but as far as I can tell, it's moving letters and figures and lines around senselessly."

"There's got to be something to it."

"Nonsense. That's what it's about."

"Think, Mike. Read the riddle again. 'You saw me where I never was and where I could not be.' But wherever that is, we can see his face. A mirror, a reflection. You know? The solution to that last riddle. The mirror reflects barbarous killer's image on a flat plane, while he is in another dimension of space.

"Where is that other dimension? It is orthogonal to the mirror's surface, following the Argand plane."

"Reflection," Mike says while he looks around him in all directions compelling Lucia to do likewise.

A park. Trees, bushes, flowers, grass. A pond. A bridge. Mounds and slopes leading down to a pond. Pathway leading to a bridge and moving away from it on the other side. And there's Rich over there, and Berto about twenty yards away.

"What does it mean?" Lucia ponders. "Nonsensical, illogical, absurd," Mike mumbles.

"Can't simply be irrational. There has to be some explanation," Lucia wishes to reason.

"Reasonlessness. *Nada*," Mike mindlessly gargles. "No, wait," he perks up with renewed energy. "The underside of that bridge reflects the pond's flat surface, doesn't it? Then maybe there's a *there*, there."

"Let's look," Lucia says with a drop of new-found encouragement. They head for the pond. Go halfway across the bridge. Mike gets down on his belly, twists his torso to the right, and peers underneath it.

"Bingo. There's something taped with—what's new?—duct tape. Held tight with nails pounded between the bricks."

Mike puts himself in a prone position as he hands the envelope to Lucia. She opens it. They read,

> I am here, I am there; I am burned into the mind of none; I walk on fire and live on ice; my words are meaningless for I talk not; I hate everyone yet fear no one; I have lived for centuries yet I've never existed; what am I?

"What the shit is driving this mind-warped irrational lunatic now?" Mike squawks.

"Not warped at all. He's as astute as they come," Lucia tells him.

"*He* thinks so. *I* think he's insane."

"He dwells on the other side of the mirror. He can see through it. He can see us but we can't see him. Cute, isn't it?"

"Are you still obsessed with Alice through the looking glass? She'll get us nowhere."

"You're the one who said the killer is irrational."

"Because that's what he is and he has nothing to do with Alice."

"Don't forget," Lucia says. "I have Brazil in my blood. We Brazilians thrive on illogical logic, logical illogic. Indescribable combinations. Irrational conjunctions. We have a joke about a guy who asked God why he created a country without hurricanes, tornadoes, earthquakes or volcanoes when everybody everywhere else has to put up with natural calamities. God told him 'Yes, but you don't know what type of people I decided to put there.'"

They enjoy a welcome moment of laughter.

Lucia explains, "Brazilians live in paradise. We are compelled to dream up imaginary paradoxical situations to make life interesting. Otherwise we would die of sheer boredom."

Mike laughs again and adds, "And *we* have to dream up some nutty kind of logic to explain insane criminals' actions and make them boring so people out there will think we rationally solved a crime. Well, Luce, put your best illogical logical or logical illogical thinking cap on and let's go to work. I have an idea this case is going to require your heftiest effort."

Lucia chuckles, shakes her head, and says, "You've got a point, Mike. But I believe you're talking about my dunce cap. I still doubt I have a genuine thinking cap."

"Whatever."

While looking into the sky, Mike tells nobody, "I'll have to say that I see no rhyme or reason to this puzzle. Here and there ... out of mind and out of sight ... mute and meaningless ... neither here nor there ... centuries old and never existed? What the hell?"

"Hell. Is that it?" Lucia asks, "Or is it the killer's heaven?"

"Heaven becoming hell through the looking glass," Mike quips. "There you go again."

"There's nowhere to go because there's nothing to go on," Lucia mutters.

"Nothing reflected, nothing gained, nothing but pain. I give up," Mike says in a grumbling whisper.

"Not so fast," Lucia complains. "We have to invent something for Fay."

"Fay? She's got it easy in comparison to this. Sitting in her office and telling us what we should be doing. Doing what needs to be done is another ballgame entirely."

"Think over another coffee?"

"More? Your Brazilian vice is coming through loud and clear. Anyway, I guess we have nothing else for now."

"Ah, what I would give for a double dose of Rio espresso."

MINDLESSLY sipping java. Simple pleasures after a mind-racking series of futile conjectures and refutations. Mike and Lucia sit and stare at the street through the window. Morning rush. A homeless young man is twisting his hood around to get a look at an attractive woman passing by.

Mike mindless says, "Is he planning a rip-off? Could be. No way to tell. Well, what if we focus on his profile—however politically incorrect, but it pays dividends. White. Loafing. Up to nothing. So, we shake him down and find some mind-altering substance on him. For our effort, the press trashes us for profiling."

"Yeah," Lucia breaks in. "You can't win for losing."

While his eyes are stuck to the hood across the street, Mike says, "You know? If our job was a matter of your zero-sum games, we should at least enjoy some benefit of the doubt before they bear down on us."

"We're nothing in their eyes if we aren't targets for their biases," Lucia offers.

"Yeah, nothing," Mike drones.

"Nothing is nothing is nothingness."

"And coffee is coffee is caffeine is a drug is jittery nerves is a vice is defense against heart failure. Whichever way, you'll be dead and gone before you know it."

"Yes, Mike, that's what it is."

"If it's nothing, it isn't."

"The riddle," Lucia reminds him. "It's everywhere and nowhere. Nothingness."

"Oh, I got you. Now what can we do with it? Nothing."

"The center of the Argand plane, Mike. Zero. Nothing. But everything can possibly come from it. That's something. But what? We have no idea. We're nowhere."

"Yeah, we're nothing *nohow*, as Humpty Dumpty might put it," Mike says with a grin.

"Through the looking glass," Lucia suggests. "It takes us to nothing and creates a completely different way of thinking in a different world. Where there's *grue* instead of either *green* or *blue*, or *bleen* instead of either *blue* or *green*. Remember?"

"That again? It gets us nowhere, anyhow."

"Yeah, but nowhere is anywhere."

"Let's go to the office," Mike suggests. "At least we can shuffle a few papers around."

"While waiting for the next homicide," Lucia says. "Like a chigger clinging to a branch in the tree."

"How so Lucia?"

"It's waiting for its next meal to meander by. When it gets a whiff of butyric acid from the sweat of some furry animal it parachutes onto him and chows down?"

"What a life. About as inspiring as ours right now," Mike muses. "The fifteenth day," Lucia reminisces.

"How many more?"

"From the pit of nothingness, he'll surely strike again, somewhere, sometime. The lion doesn't announce his presence. He pounces," Lucia adds.

"Yeah, I'm afraid so. But, to rephrase Groucho Marx, I intend to live till I solve this thing, or die trying."

"In the meantime, have fun. At least it can be fun if you make it that way, till it isn't."

FUN IT IS NOT

UPON entering the office area Lucia spies the morning's newspaper heading: "Polyethnic Killer Puzzles Police."

She scans the report, then thinks, *The killer lives up to his image. He strikes when they think the iron is cold. He fails to reveal a consistent MO. And he resists all the stereotypes.*

Christ! Is there anybody out there who thinks he can do better than us?

She finds Mike and asks him, "You seen the morning paper?"

"Yeah, our heads are on the chopping block."

"It's impossible to get a debate going. Everybody is talking too much and saying a lot of empty-headed nonsense. How can you respond to everything they keep spouting out?"

"Nonsense. Nothingness. We've gone over all that before," Mike recalls.

"That last puzzle suggests reflection. X-Man says he reflects me. He also says I'm his counterpart. That I reflect him. He's obviously singling me out!"

"How do you figure that?"

"Because he implies that we are like opposite sides of a sheet of paper. What's between one side and the other side? A bit of cellulose. But the matter of the fact is of no account. It's not the cellulose that's of importance. It has nothing to say. What the note says is written on the front side of the sheet or on both sides. The in-betweeness of the sheet is nothing.

"But as nothing, or zero, it offers a host of possible written signs bearing meaning of all sorts. The cellulose is like *nothingness*. Yet it is what makes me me, and X-Man X-Man. Positive integers on one side and negative integers on the other side.

"Like that Argand plane. Positivity and negativity of the irresolvable square root of minus one along the orthogonal axis. In other words, it's the looking glass effect."

"Whatever ..." Mike mumbles with zonked out countenance. And he leaves Lucia to her painfully leavened mental contortions.

LUCIA turns to her brooding, *You fuckin' assassin. Do you have any idea what you are up to? Maybe, just maybe, you don't. But it's my bet you do.*

Fay drops by.

That's all I need this morning, Lucia thinks. Fay says, "You saw the paper this morning?"

"Yes, I glanced at it. Those language-laden leeches know how to rub it in."

"We've got to give them something that will hold them at bay for a while."

"Any suggestions?" Lucia inquires, hoping for some hint and expecting nothing.

"Why don't you scan the murder scenes again. Check out the entire context. Something might turn up."

"That's what I used to think," she says as she thinks *How original, Fay.*

"But I'm not sure I'm sure any more."

"Keep at it anyway," Fay repeats as she moves on.

All this is becoming redundantly predictable, Lucia thinks. *Feckless Fay.*

Lucia's nemesis Jessie Zollinger comes by, obviously to rub some salt into her wounds.

"Hey, Lucia, you got it all figured out yet?"

"If I did do you think I would tell you?"

"Come on now, I was about to give you a little sympathy and moral support, and there you go again, turning on me like a wounded tiger."

"The same Jess as always. If you were as nice a guy as you tell people you are, you still wouldn't be."

"Ha! I see you're having a sour morning. I'll leave you to your misery."

"My misery doesn't enjoy your kind of company."

He leaves. Lucia scowls, *Good riddance.*

HER thoughts turn back to the predator at large. She deliberates, *If he was for real, he might be predictable, and if he were, he would be who we think he could be, but since he isn't, he ain't. Or* contrariwise, *as Tweedledee might put it.*

Is that logic? If it were, it could be, but it isn't, so it ain't. What an unadulterated pile of shit! It's insane. But then we're all mad. Especially X-Man and me. My sanity is his madness and vice versa. I'm mad in his world, he's mad in my world.

Lucia gets her diagram out to make a stab at plotting crime five, *Ah, just as I might have predicted. Crime five, like four, takes off along a nonlinear path to what appears to be a randomly chosen spot. But there's no pattern I can get excited over, no MO.*

So, where do I go from here? ...

Let me see, Lucia begins. Three days, three more, then six, nine, and now fifteen.

Five A.M. five A.M. then six, seven, and now nine. Progression, of some sort or other.

One-fourth mile, one-fourth again, then one-half, three-fourths, and now one and one-fourth. Progression again, but how can I project it into the future?

There are victims of all sorts. Instruments and methods vary as well. The sixth crime. Twenty-five days? Noon or one o'clock? Or two or three? Two and a half miles? Or three or four? Nothing but wild guesses. Random speculation.

Maybe he was a bed wetter as a kid. The punishment became increasingly intense. From slapping him on the head to going without breakfast to no TV the whole day, then tied up in the closet all afternoon.

Now as an adult, in and out of friends and live-in partners' apartments where he smooches until they tire of him and tell him to hit the road, accusing him of leeching and ripping them off and contributing to none of the work around the place.

Then he has the gall to tell them "What the fuck! I didn't have a job and needed some money. How can do anything around here if I spend all my time out there looking for work? What kind of a friend are you anyway? Can't you fuckin' help me out?"

He had a lousy childhood so he makes all the poor bastards around him feel sorry for him for what he says they're doing to him.

Through it all, he has no definite pattern. No stable MO. Everything is always becoming different. He's a study of chaos giving way to some twisted illogical disorder masquerading as irrefutable reasoning.

In other words, game mixed with play or playacting. Iron-clad rules, competition, power, skill, and intellect. Fused with freedom from rules, openness, everybody doing what they can when they can.

Is that the predator? He wants control but there's a play element involved. He has to win, but he creates intriguing situations so you think you have a chance of beating him.

What if I'm right? What can I do about the situation he's creating? I'll have to do what I can so he (my mirror-image other, as he has so deftly put it) can feel he is free to do his own thing. Weaving his acts together so he can elude me at every step.

We mirror one another? What a lot of shit! But he's growing on me. Against my will. I am the "normal" one, the "socially acceptable" one. He needs me so he can also become "normal" by proxy.

Good God! I'm so obsessed with trying to think like he thinks that I don't really know which one of us is thinking these words at this very moment. Me? Or my other who mirrors him? My other? Who might that be? Counterpart to an assassin? God save me!

So be it. I'll have to do what I have to do and hope for the best. At every turn I'll use logic and reason, where A is A and it can't be anything else, for there is no option other than either A or Not-A?

At the same time, I'll have to use some vague. multiply ambiguous form of pliable, amorphous everyday living logic and style of reasoning.

The relation between everyday living logic and strait-laced conventional logic has to be subtle.

Rather than looking for the most probable, I'll tune in to improbability. Rather than hold faith in repetitiveness, I'll flow along with differences.

I'll pursue tiny samples rather than wholesale generalities.

Rather than what is normal, I'll consider bizarre instances. Rather than precision, I'll focus on vagueness.

Rather than abstractions, my interest will rest on concrete happenings within their different contexts.

It's a matter of what is felt more than what is rational.

What is intuited more than what is known.

No stereotypes, but rather, characteristics rough around the edges.

I'll accept little truths rather than hold out for the big truth. Yeah, that's the way to go. *I'll make him part of my imaginary playacting world while knowing full well that part of this world is also in his own imaginary world.*

We're both as sane as can be and we're crazier than loons. My destiny is like madness. And it's my only path back to sanity. So be it.

LUCIA takes a step back and reappraises her mental condition with respect to the details and puzzles X-Man has spread out for her and Mike.

She tells herself, *Is there a flaw in his putting his MO into effect? I can't know what it is, because his MO remains by and large incognito.*

Yet she is certain there's a flaw somewhere.

But where? Since his MO is still in hiding, I can't know. But for certain it's there. The persistent problem is that there is no there *now and no* then *whenever. Where is the* there *and when is the* when *his next move will occur. Eventually there will be a flaw. I know it as certain as I know I live and breathe.*

Maybe his next move will reveal a blemish in his strategy and maybe not.

Maybe he has already failed in some respect and maybe not. Or maybe his weakness will become apparent and maybe not.

In the long run, there will be a tell-tale sign of some error. When the sign appears, I will know it.

How will I know it?

My knowing must come from within. So, in order to know what needs to be known, I can't search either for what I now know or for what I don't know, since what I don't know isn't within me.

Yet, If I know, I know. If I don't know, I can't know. For how could I know what it is I need to know?

Goddamn you! Are you smug with yourself, you haughty bastard? If you are, that will be your downfall. You're arrogant, full of yourself, and complacent. And that will spell your demise. I guarantee it. Nobody is perfect. If you were perfect, you wouldn't be. And when you commit some error or other, I've got you.

And yet, Lucia's stubborn uncertainty continues to prevail.

WHEN IT HITS THE FAN

THE press again. *Why the hell don't they get out of my hair and let me do my job?* she asks herself. *Can't they see the dilemma I'm caught up in?*

Yes, they can, and they're enjoying it to the hilt. While felicitously tapping away at their computer terminals. They have surreptitiously come up with biting headings for their reports. "Has Detective Vieira lost her touch?"

"Has Vieira met her nemesis?"

"Incompetence shows its ugly face at the police station."

"Has the serial killer outwitted them?"

And to top it off there's a cumbersome heading that goes "Will he continue striking and they'll still be caught with their pants down?"

Give me some credit or get off my back, Lucia thinks, as she takes long powerful strides to the lion's den where they're ready to eat her alive.

She confronts them, "Good morning. We are on the perpetrator's trail. But he has thus far revealed no adequately specifiable MO allowing for some notion as to what he's up to. So, as of this moment we have no way to pin him down.

"Nevertheless, our profiler and forensic experts have provided us with an increasing number of specificities regarding the nature of each of his moves and the sort of killer we are up against.

"He is astute, a brilliant criminal mind. But he *will* make a mistake at some juncture. And when he does, we *will* nail him. Now, questions. Yes Mr. Radner ..."

"Inspector Vieira. Have you detected a pattern in the killer's choice of times and places for his successive homicides?"

Lucia: "Like I said, he's astute. And unpredictable. But he is slowly revealing a pattern. No human animal acts entirely on random impulses, including this perpetrator. Yes ..."

"John Stock. Inspector Vieira, is it true that the Police Department has a snitch who is leaking information out to the press and perhaps even to the killer?"

Lucia: "Like all departments, this department does not exist in a vacuum, nor is it absolutely air tight. We have our suspicions. But we can't be certain until we discover whether there have been leaks and who the accessory to the crime is. Yes Barbara ..."

"Good morning. Could you say something about the allegations concerning the department's growing inefficiency?"

Lucia: "I have no idea where that rumor came from and have no comments. Yes, over in the corner, George ..."

"Do you have any idea how many more homicides we can expect." Lucia: "Expect? Catching the alleged murderer and taking him into custody has nothing to do with statistical averages, mathematical certainty, or logical reasoning leading to predictions and expectations. I can assure you that we will have the criminal in our hands before he commits the projected number of homicides he might have in mind. Next? ..."

"Sally Carrington. Ms. Vieira, are you absolutely sure the killer is a man?"

Lucia: "We are never absolutely sure of anything. But at this stage the evidence points toward a large, physically fit male."

"Oh, inspector. Some have speculated that you have met your match. Do you have an opinion about that?"

Lucia: "You are out of order, sir, but let me tell you. This investigation is taking more time than any of us anticipated. However, I have backing from the best investigators, technicians, and psychologists, anywhere. I must say I resent the negative criticism and I would suggest you people get your own acts together and collaborate positively. I have nothing further. Good day ladies and gentlemen."

Lucia turns and recommences her long strides toward the door, leaving the milling, boisterous voices behind. When out of hearing range she bellows ...

"Shit, shit, shit!"

Mike attempts to unruffle her, saying, "Consider the source, pay them no mind, and get back to your work. I have all the faith in the world in you."

"*Babacas!*"

"Excuse me? Was that Portuguese?"

"*Babacas, tolos, idiotas*—nincompoops, fools, idiots! They can all go to hell in a hand basket!"

"Please. Compose yourself, Lucia. Don't let them get to you too."

"Get to me too? Nobody's getting to me. I just need time. That is, *we* need time."

"I'm with you."

"Sometimes I wonder."

"You can rest assured."

"Yes, I know, Mike. I'm sorry. I would just like to smack the dissembling phonies among them down. Just once. For a change of pace."

"They are doing their job. That's all."

"I know that too. They give their readers what they want. The readers? Huh! Many of them would like to think there's some conspiracy going on. That's the temper of the times. Conspiracy theories abound. The people's paranoid tendencies are liberally nurtured by them. What a lot of crap!"

"I know."

A witness appears out of nowhere. Saying he has some information that might be of value.

"Great!" Mike exclaims.

"Let's not get our hopes too high," Lucia tells him. "Merely wait and see if things happen to pan out this time. Anything's possible if that blank key can be cut in an infinite number of ways, right?"

"I guess ... in principle. In principle, we could elect a donkey as president. But there's virtually no chance of it happening," Mike ruminates.

"Or an elephant. You know, Mike, in a city in the interior of Brazil they had a rhinoceros named *Cacareco* at the zoo. Municipal elections were held in 1958 and he was put up as a candidate for mayor in protest against government corruption. He got over sixty-thousand write in votes. Enough to win the election since there were multiple candidates."

Mike lets out a stream of hearty laughter.

"Don't expect much out of our witness, though."

Fay brings the presumed witness in.

"Lucia and Mike, this is Matt Jones. Matt, Lucia and Mike. They wish to hear your story."

Fay leaves. Lucia begins, "Thank you for coming in, Mr. Jones. Tell us what you saw."

"I was jogging in the park and saw it from a distance."

"Yes, go on."

"I was quite a way in the distance. But I noticed a man in sweats with a hood come up behind a smaller male individual. He wrapped his left arm around him and forced him behind a nearby bush. The bush didn't conceal them very well. I could vaguely see what was happening. He stabbed his victim in the chest. The poor guy tried to squirm free but his attacker threw him to the ground and plunged the knife into him a number of times, in the chest."

"Can you describe the aggressor?"

"More or less. He was big, well-built. He must have been at least six feet three and well over two hundred pounds. His hair was dark. No facial hair that I could see. I'm sorry, but for obvious reasons, I didn't want get any closer to him."

"I understand. Do you know in what direction he went when he left his victim?"

"Like I said, I didn't care to stick around."

"Of course. Can you describe the knife? Do you know whether he took it with him when he left?"

"I don't know. He was clenching the knife and I didn't get a good look at it. But I believe the blade had to be around eight inches long, judging by the way the victim's body jerked upward a few times when the killer pulled the knife out and plunged it into him, again. I was vacating the scene when he left, so I don't know if he was carrying the weapon."

"Why did you wait until now to come in?"

"I've only been in this city for a few months. I don't go out much, I watch little TV, and don't frequently buy a newspaper. You see? I'm writing a novel, and it has consumed me over the past few weeks. I got wind of this crime, but didn't think much about it.

"I know I should have come in to give you a report. But I didn't. Then yesterday I got a glimpse of a newspaper on the park bench mentioning the last murder. I checked the article out, and decided I had better come in."

"I understand. But I must say, as a conscientious citizen, you should immediately report a crime as grave as what you witnessed."

"I know, and I'm sorry. Over these past few months, I've pretty much become a recluse."

"If you think of anything else, Mr. Jones, here's my card. Call me."

"I certainly will."

Mike and Lucia see him to the door.

"You were right, Lucia."

"I wish I weren't."

"He at least spits out a few intelligent responses. That's a refreshing change."

"Yes. Well, for now I guess it's back to the drawing board."

"Speaking of drawing boards, have you done any more work with your diagrams?" Mike asks. "At least we have them."

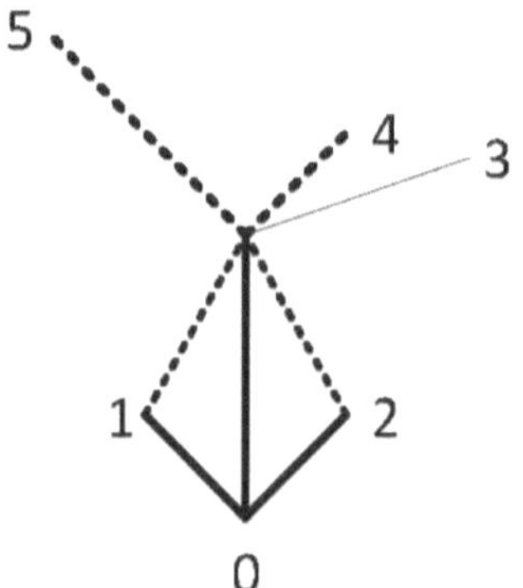

"For whatever they are worth ..."

"And?"

"Yes. I extrapolated the fifth crime on the diagram. I'll show you."

They proceed to Lucia's desk. She pulls the diagram out. Mike evinces an image of intensive concentration. Lucia, now at ease, passively takes turns gazes at it, at Mike, and occasionally at the goings on outside her office.

Finally, Mike says, "There's the progression you've mentioned before. But I see no blueprint that can tell us anything substantial."

"Neither can I. But we have hardly anything else to go on, do we?"

"No. Unfortunately."

"A cup of black stuff and some chatter about this?" Lucia suggests.

"What else? Since it's been a few hours and I'm having a black attack."

"Black attack?" Lucia repeats with a grin.

They leave. Walk over to the nearest caffeine outlet. Lucia observes ...

"Look at that crown in the Starbucks logo. Three prominent points on top, two to the right and the left underneath it. Five."

"Five it is," Mike says. "And there are two more points below. Five plus two. Seven homicides? Care for another dose of numerology?"

"No. It's just coincidence," Lucia tells him. "No more, no less. Like I've said, there are no coincidences of any worth in criminal investigation."

"Yeah. 'Nothing but the facts, ma'am.'"

"Cute."

They enter. Silently thinking, *Seven. Seven? No, it can't be. Two more homicides? Horrors* they both think almost in unison. They mindlessly order coffee. Sit. Remain in thought. Desperately needing a change of topic.

MIKE throws out a few words to smooth the edgy pace, "Are the Patriots going to win this weekend? America's team. They have to be my team since I'm originally from New England."

"Football," Lucia exclaims as if having thought about it extensively. "It's the typical game. Winners or losers. Technically complicated, but the outcome is simple. No more than an either or an or affair."

"In contrast, we are compelled to bring what you call playacting onto center stage. It complicates matters considerably, because we have to make up the rules as we go along."

"Make up the rules?" Lucia asks. "What are the rules of our current game? The killer must enjoy the liberty of making up his own rules. And what is his ultimate rule? Likely it's the rule that there are no rules."

Mike says while cringing, "That's scary"—

"By the way," Lucia is quick to say, "I haven't told you, but last night I got another text message from him. It started out with 'Dearest,' like a few previous notes. Can you imagine? The nerve of that son of a bitch! 'Dearest'!"

"What was the message about?"

"He wrote, 'Dearest, you and I are in this together. Let us team up and make the best of it.' Fuckin' bastard!"

"He does have his nerve."

"Like he's rubbing it in?" Lucia remarks.

They leave after a few minutes of small talk. While crossing the street, Lucia turns around. Looks at the logo. Turns back. Shakes her head with a questioning countenance. Mike notices the gesture out of the corner of his eye, and cannot help showing a slight ironic grin. Lucia gives him a glance. He quickly wipes it off his face.

Fifteen days, she thinks.

BACK in Lucia's office, they open up a bit more.

Lucia says, "The damn press. All they want is a platter full of stereotypes. They want them clean-cut, polished, dished out and spoon-fed to their eager ears so they can copy them down in their columns for their readers who gleefully gobble them up.

"They don't want to admit that stereotypes are laden with all kinds of exceptions. What they don't want to do is what *we* have to do."

"And what is it we have to do?" Mike asks.

"Look for the exceptions. Differences that make a difference. That's where it gets interesting and that's where the case can be solved and the perp put in the calaboose for life."

Mike says, "What I've learned about psychopaths tells me they want order, everything in its place. Their mind is a machine."

"That's the problem. There is no perfection in this world. If the world were perfect, it wouldn't be the world we know. The psychopath's MO—about which we are still ignorant—blinds us to the messiness of the world around us.

"He simplifies. Almost with mathematical precision. But it is not like the real world. Put total order and untidy clutter together and what do you have? Blemishes in the apparent order. We must find the blemishes, the muddles, the sludge. Then we will be on our way toward figuring out the psycho's mind."

"Going back to your playacting," Mike adds, "we should never entirely suspend disbelief when on stage. We should keep an eye tuned in on the differences between what's on stage and our unkempt world. Is that what you're suggesting?"

"You're on target, Mike. Yes. We have to suspend our suspension of disbelief so as not to fall into the killer's beguiling spell."

Mike says, "We ought always to veer away. At least slightly. From whatever stereotype seems to be the case. Otherwise the criminal will slip through the cracks."

"In other words," Lucia wishes to conclude, "we need particularities unique to the context, not generalities applicable to any context. Otherwise our generalities will threaten to become like wild conspiracy tales."

"Oh? How's that?"

"Conspiracy theories take particular coincidences and generalize them to the extreme. This creates in the minds of the true believers an impending threat promising doom, gloom, and apocalypse."

"Well, that's what the people want, though they don't thoroughly know it."

"Exactly," Lucia tells him. "I think we ought to see Bill Evans again. Maybe he can ring our chimes and shake us up a bit."

They leave in that direction.

OPENING the door to Bill's office, they find themselves looking at his back side, studying some papers in his hands.

He swivels around on his seat, sees them, and says, "Hi, I've been thinking about you and hoping you would show up. How goes it?"

"Nothing's going," Lucia responds.

"I was afraid of that. The more I think about your case the quirkier your murderer's moves become. And the press isn't helping you out much."

"You can say that again."

"Ignore them as much as possible. They've been brought up on TV, movies, the Internet, and books showing them how serial killers are tracked down by psychologically sophisticated, astute, and deductively rigorous heroes who can do no wrong.

"The press simply doesn't know what to make of your strange perp. They are like kids who don't know how to cope with a world that leaves them baffled. So they want to create a more comfortable situation with ready-made answers. They are playing a somewhat psychopathic role."

"Interesting you say that, Bill. I've thought the same, but since I'm no psychologist I haven't dared say it."

"You too, Lucia?" Mike says.

Bill tells them, "I'm afraid it's the grave new world we're living in. But back to your case. I must tell you that for now, I can't help you out much. Unless you have some fresh information for me."

On that cue, Lucia whips out her latest diagram, spreads it out on Bill's desk, and explains the progression in detail using her usual mathematical jargon.

"Uh-huh," Bill grunts. "Progression that grows. Trigonometrically, but not exactly. It's less than that. Since it's less, there's no way to predict it. Anyway, that's all mathematics. The question is, why would the perp go to the trouble of creating such an elaborate MO?"

"We came here so you could fill us in," Lucia reminds him.

"Okay, I'll give it a try. As a beginning, serial killers commonly operate along three paths, or some mixture of them. They might be *visionary*. Simply *hedonistic*, lut to fulfill some sort of *mission*. Or they want *power* and *control*. David Berkowitz, called Son of Sam, was *visionary*. He claimed a demon was giving him orders, and that he was on a *mission* to carry them out. These characteristics compose a *mixture*.

"Ted Bundy was more *hedonistic*, and wanted *control* over his victims. John Wayne Gacy, the 'Killer Clown' who was interested in teen age boys, mixed *hedonism* and *control*. Jeffrey Dahmer and Kenneth Bianchi were driven by sexual urges. They were *visionaries*. They were also in it for the *control factor*, by dominating their female victims.

"You see? There's usually some *mixture* or other. The categories aren't of much use except to get a rough idea about the killer."

"What can you say about our killer," Lucia asks.

"It seems to me that he's got an indelible *hedonistic* streak, in view of the messages you've sent me. But he's different. He plays around with *you* rather than exclusively with his victims. He is the tiger. His prey is a combination of you, the object of his play, and his victims, the objects of his crimes. He does this to confuse and exercise *control* not only over his victims, but also over those investigating him.

"You two have become his surrogate victims, whether you like it or not. *Sex* is apparently out of the picture entirely. But he is basically a *visionary*, judging from the nature of his messages and the progression you've illustrated in your diagram. He definitely has a *mission*. But what do we know about his *vision* and his *mission*? Virtually nothing."

"No doubt," Mike chimes in. "My question is why he is obsessed over making fools out of us?"

"Good question," Bill responds, "for which I'm afraid I have no answer."

"How should we proceed?" Lucia asks.

"Do you recall the Great Imposter?"

"Yes," Lucia perks up.

"That Tony Curtis movie?" Says Mike.

"His name was Ferdinand Waldo Demara. The consummate mimic. He played a prison warden, ship's dentist, civil engineer, lawyer, monk, editor, teacher, cancer expert, and many other roles. What is most amazing, for a while at least, he convinced everybody.

"This great pretender knew that in any professional organization there is a lot of available power that can be tapped, if you have the proper charisma, empathy, tact, and common sense. Demara filled the vacuum remarkably well.

"Of course, empathy, sympathy, sentiment and emotion are alien to the psychopath. But your killer, if he has psychopathic tendencies, is a champion in the other categories as well. Like pretending, or acting out a role in a play. This leads me to believe that perhaps he is no psychopath at all. He's a play-actor with Oscar-like qualities."

"Playacting," Mike mutters.

"We have had some thoughts along those lines," Lucia says.

"Great! Then you are ahead of me. Now your task is to separate the real killer from the play-actor."

"Easily said, almost impossibly done," Lucia observes.

"Yes, I know," Bill adds.

"Sean Connery, James Bond, Stan Katz," Mike murmurs almost in a whisper with a pronounced smile on his face.

"What did you say?" Bill asks. "Nothing, just an inside joke."

"Oh."

They bid Bill adieu and leave. Time to call it quits for another day. Lucia and Mike leave for home and a well-deserved break in the routine.

BACK in her apartment Lucia is in no mood to forget about the turn of events after the fifth homicide. There must be some motive to X-Man's madness, she senses.

I'm sure it's right before my eyes, within earshot, under my nose, ready and waiting to be felt out, she thinks. *If I could just put my finger on it.*

She checks her snail mail. Tosses some junk in an available trash can. Notices a multi-colored ad on thick glossy paper.

Win Big! it says. There's a key attached to the ad with a sheet of plastic. The key is cut, but obviously it will open nothing. It is no more than symbolic of the car the ad tells her she can win.

All she must do, after writing down a pin number and the series of digits from a scratched off label, is take the enclosed key and the invitation she has in her hands to the car agent. If three numbers underneath the label match three of the integers she has copied down from the series, SHE WINS.

Ah, now she is led to believe she can't lose. Everybody wins! It's guaranteed! In their pocket! Either she wins the Grand Prize, a new car, a $10.000 cash prize, a diamond studded bracelet, or a vacation to Hawaii.

Sure, she thinks as she nods her head. *Naturally, the numbers will match.*

Naturally, it's a come-on.

Naturally, I will find myself on a list.

Naturally, there is small print at the bottom of the ad that will be a dead giveaway for anybody who reads it.

But who takes the time to read it? It's like the agreement you click before entering a web page. The key might as well be a blank, Lucia muses.

They build you up and then toss you in the garbage. What the hell! I'll stick with my blank key. If I decipher it, I've got it in hand and mind, and there's no further question about it.

She takes the blank key out of her purse where she's had it for good keeping since day one. *The key, she says to herself. Like the so-called empty set as the mathematicians call it. This reminds me of a Paradox named after philosopher Bertrand Russell.*

Russell asks his readers to think of the set of all humans. It contains humans that have lived, are living, and will have lived. An individual human, a hundred of them or a million or billions of them, are members of the set. But the set of all humans cannot be a member of itself. Because it can't contain itself. This is like that Groucho Marx quip that he would never belong to a club (a set) that would have him as a member.

What relevance does this have with respect to the killer? He is author of his invented world. But he is in that world. He can't be outside looking in, nor can he have been outside, creating that of which he is a member.

Moreover, he wants to draw me into his zany world. If he pushes me through the glass, I'm in.

But he gave me a shove from outside.

But he's inside—like I am after I was given a swift heave.

Yet like him, I'm as if outside.

In a manner of putting it, we're both inside and outside. We're neither entirely inside nor outside. Yet, we must be either inside or outside.

Lucia giggles to herself. Then looks around. As if expecting someone is watching.

"X-Man," she says in a firm voice, "we're in this world together. Despite whatever kind of imaginary existence you cobbled up for the purpose of amusing yourself while playacting. Now, it's a matter of my waiting for you. How many days? Twenty-three? Four? Five? Or more? Or less?"

Lucia remains lost in thought until around two in the morning. Then she has trouble falling asleep. Finally, when she reaches a certain peak or threshold, she conks out. Sleeps like a baby for a change.

LUCIA unaccustomedly glares at the TV while downing breakfast. Newscast! Nothing new under the sun. They pick up the latest scandal or incidence of violence, bleed it for all its worth, each half-hour repeating themselves *ad nauseum*.

She turns to her laptop and finds the usual tasteless tidbits, *Bland, but you can at least surf the net and find variety in the virtual randomness*, she says to herself. *What's this? Government conspiracy evolving into tyranny? The CIA in control of over three hundred newspapers and magazines? Including New York Times and Washington Post? What will those paranoid conspiracy-mongers come up with next?*

She reads on. Eyes widening as they become more focused. Head shaking back and forth. A gritty frown making itself known, *Journalists in cahoots with the CIA. Promoting the venerable Company's views. Providing services that include gathering intelligence. Spying in foreign countries. Writing columns at home and abroad in favor of government policies. CIA spin doctors posing minimal threat in comparison to journalists with ties to the CIA and in charge of baring antigovernment exposure.*

They make it sound like Big Brother 1984 is flexing his muscles and will soon be in every home, controlling everybody's minds, Lucia thinks to herself.

Then there's NRA's own Wayne LaPierre. Still around. Saying our Founding Fathers saw the need for protection against King George's tyrannical ways. They wanted guarantee that the people would never again live under a repressive government umbrella.

Today, gun owners welcome strident gun lobbyists fighting to protect the gun owners of America. If there is strict compliance with the Second Amendment, we are saved, LaPierre goes on. We have the means to protect ourselves against a power-crazed government. We are our own militia.

However, we must beware. If background checks are forced down our throat, our weapons will be confiscated, and we will end up like Germany during the 1930s. But we will not surrender. The time to stand up and be counted is now. Our right to bear arms must never be infringed.

Lucia reads that worn-out adage telling us guns don't kill people, people kill people, while thinking, *After all, if guns are banned, murders will still be around. Knives, swords, sledge hammers, poison, chain saws, piano wire strangling, and running them over by car, pushing them off the tenth floor, chaining them and throwing them in the river. Whatever. The guns are not to blame. People are. Get rid of all the sickos. That's the answer.*

Well, she thinks, *I suppose X-Man has a repertoire of weapons. He could just as well have used an AK-47 or whatever. What's the difference? Knifing? Strangling? A hammer blow on the skull? Is he proving the paranoid assault weapons freaks are right? If we all had firearms hanging on our belts, could we defend ourselves against the psychos and sickos of the world? And to boot, defend ourselves against the government when, as predicted, it goes viral and turns the country into a police state?*

So much bunk, she concludes. *Neither we nor the press are in cahoots with Big Brother or any remotely comparable symbol.*

She steps back.

Me and the press? Maybe we are fighting the same fight. Maybe they are out to make sure I keep my nose clean. Should I give them more respect? Are their intentions in the right place? What irks me is when they go overboard, become too garrulous, and want too much control for themselves.

Anyway, I got to go.

ON A DOWNBEAT NOTE

LUCIA enters headquarters. Checks her e-mail. "Oh my God! He's at it again." She focuses on the latest message,

> My dearest Lucia. Fear not. There is no conspiracy afoot, either on the part of the government or any fringe faction among we the people.

Her eyes are on fire as her body tightens, and she sits back in her chair. "Mike!" she screams out. Mike makes haste. "Look!"

He reads the note and says, "I see nothing outside his usual tricks, Luce.

Why the panic?"

"Do you know what?"

"What?"

"This morning over breakfast I was reading on the Internet and watching on TV about the government becoming tyrannical, people holding tight to their guns to defend themselves against all those who infringe on their God-given rights, and various and sundry conspiracy theories. How could he know what I was doing? Is my apartment bugged? I'm going over there right now and check it out."

"It's probably no more than coincidence."

"That again?"

"Okay, Luce. I'll go with you."

THEY leave the precinct, motor over to Lucia's apartment, check it out, and find nothing. Lucia looks out the window at other buildings nearby.

"Was he somewhere out there telescoping me when I was surfing the net? I wonder."

Mike looks out the window. They study the positions of the adjacent windows and decide against that possibility.

"I still have this eerie feeling he knew what I was doing."

"Whatever. I think it was coincidental," Mike says.

Lucia ignores him and speculates, "Could it be that the predator is a veteran of one of our wars since 2000?"

"That's a possibility."

They return to the precinct. In silence. Back in the office, Lucia begins, "I've read that a shocking number of the serial killers running around have had war experience."

"I've also read something to that effect."

"Serial killers are born that way according to recent studies. But the fine art of serial killing is learned, and the military is an optimal training ground. It desensitizes them to the act of taking human lives. When they do so in battle, they are praised, given medals, and enjoy a lot of notoriety for their killings.

"Those who have a twisted mind come to think it is acceptable to kill, and now as serial killers and psychopaths, they want fame for their sordid behavior. Could the killer be one of them?"

"Good point, Luce. Killing becomes part of the soldier's daily life. The enemy, like the serial killer's victim, is not a genuine fellow human but a depersonalized object. That seems to qualify our killer."

"If so, he's living out his military experience during combat situations."

"How can we pursue this idea in view of the killer changing his MO at every step of the way?"

"You got me there."

FAY interrupts them. Trailing along behind her is another FBI agent. Fay introduces Ted Clancy and quickly takes her leave as he enters. Lucia rolls her eyes slightly when Ted glances at Mike.

"Good morning. Just call me Ted. Is Lucia and Mike okay with you?"

"Fine," Lucia responds.

"The FBI is ready to put up to five part-time personnel on your case. Their function will be assistance and collaboration. We by no means wish to meddle with your investigation, and we especially do not want to minimize your effort to put a hand on the perpetrator of the recent serial crimes.

We intend to complement you as a task force, meeting frequently to air out ideas that might lead to solving this case."

"Sounds reasonable," Lucia replies while wandering eyes tell Ted she's less than enthusiastic about his proposition.

"The task force can provide for a flexible framework. Depending on the prevalent needs of the investigation. As you know, they cut our budget. Consequently, our cooperation in the field will be marginal. At least interaction with the task force can offer you a set of options you can work with, aided by our input."

"I welcome your willingness to work with us in this regard. I'm sure your input will be valuable."

"By the way," Ted adds, "I will be on the task force with four agents.

Can we meet with you during the coming week?"

Lucia checks her calendar and tells Ted, "Tuesday will be best, Tuesday morning, at ten."

"Tuesday it is. I look forward to our collaboration."

"Likewise," Mike says.

Ted leaves. Lucia sighs. Mike says nothing. They sit. Lucia finally says,

"I hope to hell their so-called cooperation doesn't turn into a lot of confusion created by changes that always occur in a task force make up."

"Yeah, I know what you mean."

"Or if they miraculously find money laying around to increase the task force operation. Or, heavens! If they enter the field along with us."

"That would be the pits," Mike says.

"Or if the FBI decides on daily e-mail communication and personal briefings a few times a week."

"Good lord!" Mike grumbles. "If that happens, we will be deluged with staggering piles of memos and data that will have to be reviewed and analyzed."

"Whatever leads we might come up with will be lost in all the paper work. What the hell? Here comes Fay dragging somebody else in. Who's this guy."

"Good morning again," she says. "This gentleman is Brad James. Brad, Lucia Vieira, and Mike Rafferty."

"My pleasure," Mike says.

Fay leaves. Lucia invites Brad to have a seat. Mike and Lucia look at him with questioning eyes.

"What I came here for is to inform you that I've seen a suspicious looking person. Male, a little over six feet, about one-hundred-and-eighty welldistributed pounds. He's much like that suspect as reported in the newspaper. I've seen him about three miles from the station, at Sixth and Constitution.

"He always seems to be looking over the buildings, staring intently at the young men around him, and occasionally taking pictures with a mobile phone while hiding it as much as possible. As if he didn't want to be singled out."

"Could you describe his facial features?" Lucia asks him.

"Middle age, good-looking, no moustache or beard, close cropped black hair, and a tanned face with pronounced nose and chin. I also noticed what I thought might be a small tattoo on the back of his left hand but didn't dare get close enough to him to identify it."

"What were you doing in the vicinity?" Mike asks.

"I work close by. During my lunch break, I like to walk briskly along the streets and in the local park. It helps keep me in shape."

"I see," Lucia says. "Your description might help us. We'll keep somebody posted in the area, and if you have any additional information, please let us know. Here's my card."

"Thank you," Brad says, "and have a pleasant day."

Brad leaves. Lucia thinks *Pleasant day? You have to be kidding.* Then she says, "Well, Mike, what do you think?"

"He seems pretty level headed. But I have a question. Should we reveal everything we find to the task force that will soon be in place?"

"No. If we did, we would be committed to them. We'll keep the most important findings to ourselves. That way we can have closer tabs on the investigation."

"I agree," Mike says. "The more we release, the more control they will exercise."

"Besides, if we fill them in on all the details, things will get complicated. We need to maintain free flowing information so we can promptly respond to our leads. Above all Fay needs to bring closure to her search for the rat who is leaking info to the press. If the journalists find too much out and begin interviewing people who might be key witnesses in the future, they could jeopardize the information coming in."

"I can see it all now." Mike's eyes glaze over as he projects into the future. "Pop singers fascinated by the horror of it all compose songs romanticizing X-Man. Yellow journal publications create fantasies that iconize and raise him to celebrity status. Starry eyed authors write poems and pulp fiction about him. Fan clubs come out of the woodwork. Presumed personal possessions and memorabilia appear on *eBay*. What's worse, a third-rate movie about him hit the screens."

"Abhorrent. All we need is the darker side of society entering mainstream," Lucia observes.

"There ought to be a law against sharks profiting from other people's humiliation, suffering, and even death."

"Anyway," Lucia says on a contemplative note, "if we reveal all we have to the FBI, the press, and the general public, there's not much they can do with it because thus far they'll have next to nothing."

"You're right there, Luce."

"At this point our investigation reveals only the tail of the tiger. We ought to pull him by his tail, and shoot him in the ass."

Mike laughs. Lucia joins in with a chuckle.

SHE becomes speculative. Mike takes the clue and follows suit.

"Knowing is what you have from experience," she begins. "That is, after you forget everything you learned in school, at home, and with your peers. You're on your own. Learning from your experience. You ordinarily see what everybody sees. And in addition, you begin thinking what nobody thinks."

"But, Luce. A lot of people can see the evidence, put the facts together, and draw up conclusions."

"It's more than that. Most people who spout out facts are parrots who have a lot of trivia in their heads. They are by habit social climbers. They want to impress the boss, or whatever. If in contrast we think and say what virtually nobody does, we're on the outside, marginalized. But we give meaning to our ideas. We don't simply spout out information."

"Don't they have ideas too? They offer more than disconnected facts, don't they?"

"Their problem is that they think whatever ideas happen to be around are sacred and must be kept pure. But they are not consecrated. They have a life of their own. And we must creatively act on them. But in the final analysis, like them, we are nothing more than ideas. Responsible for attaching words to our ideas and giving them meanings."

"Careful, Luce, you'll become philosophical on me and spend your time doing a lot of talking in place of just doing it."

"No chance. Talk for us is speculating, intuiting, appraising, and scrutinizing. We should ask ourselves whether, if we were psychos, we would have arranged our world of crime in such and such a way. In other words, we must get inside criminal minds. That's the only way we can hope to understand them and eventually nab them."

"I see. So, you're on your way into X-Man's mind."

Lucia rolls her eyes, "Hardly."

Her phone sounds the familiar signal. It's Fay, who left a meeting with Mayor Fitzburger in a tussle. She tells Lucia, "We have to come up with some answers to create the image that we are making progress. Get out there and make some noise. Get yourselves in view of the public. Tramp around, ask questions, look like you are doing something. Anything. As long as you are being seen by people."

Lucia thinks *Yeah, feckless Fay, we'll do it all for you and you'll do nothing for us. Is that it?*

She conveys Fay's message to Mike. He's game. They leave. *I suppose we gotta look like we're doing our job,* Lucia silently observes. *Bail Fay out. Since she has neither the* mojo *nor the* cojones *to take effective command of the situation. Oh well.*

THEY enter the vicinity where Brad said a suspicious customer hangs out. "Let's pose a lot of questions and the people should be favorably impressed," Lucia says with an ironic grin. Mike nods in agreement.

They ask people if they've seen anybody behaving suspiciously lately.

They are met with strange looks, shaking heads, and a lot of "No, not me."

If they had seen anything would they admit it? Probably not. It's the mind-set these days. Keep to yourself. Act normal. Commit yourself to nothing and nobody. Be wary of everybody and everything. But don't tell anybody about it. What a context for police work!

What's going on across the street? Looks like a drug sale. Mike and Lucia ignore it. They are out after bigger game. The ultimate predator. There's a middle-age lady with a penetrating voice boisterously accuses a man of giving her a shove who has his hands out with palms up, claiming innocence.

Vendors holler. Cars honk. A siren whines. A truck roars. Cyclists threaten pedestrians. Briskly stepping citizens frantically move along in robotic fashion. Gaudy store fronts entice shoppers. A homeless man can't decide whether to collect the trash around him and put it in his ripped-off shopping cart or panhandle for a few cents. No big game the pair of detectives can lay their hands on. Everything's normal.

"What are we doing here?" Mike asks. "Following the boss's orders," Lucia responds. "Coffee?"

"Coffee. As usual when we find ourselves against a brick wall."

"Geeze, Luce, your Brazilian vice will be the death of me yet."

"It's the elixir of the gods."

"Whatever ... The mandate is, if you come to a fork in the road, take the one to Starbucks," Mike quips.

They approach a franchise a block away while they're loaded down with premonitions that they'll have no chance of finding any answers at the espresso bar. But when in doubt, do it again.

That seven-point image, Lucia thinks. *Who knows? Yet, I keep thinking there might be something to it after all.*

As if Mike had read her mind, he points at the logo and says, "Look, Luce, it's your favorite symbol."

She isn't amused. Mike gets a scowl for his effort.

They enter. Order the usual. Plain and black with no sugar. Routine. What's new? One day and then another. Garbage into the left-hand bin and non-garbage on the right-hand tray. It's all bureaucratic rigmarole and protocol anyway. Check a lead out in the street and toss your notes in the mental trash can. Routine.

SOMETHING worthy of their attention pops up after they leave the java guzzler and begin ambulating along the sidewalk. Mike notices a person fitting Brad's description leaning against a restaurant wall talking on a cell phone. He brings it to Lucia's attention.

"Keep your eye on him while I cross over to his side of the street," she tells him.

She crosses. The suspect signs off his phone and holds it up as if to take a picture. Lucia takes the cue. Pulls her badge out. Approaches the stranger. Shows him her piece of metal symbolizing authority. And says she would like to hear a few words from him. He scats, with Lucia in hot pursuit.

Mike is across the street running in the same direction, ready to cut the suspect off if he plans on crossing the street on Mike's side.

It bears mentioning that Lucia ran the hundred and two hundred-meter dashes in high school and was on the university track team. She's certainly no slouch. But this guy is fast. She is hard pressed to keep her distance with him, let alone catch him. He's yelling at people to get out of the way, shoving bodies aside, jumping at low and high spots and curbs, dodging cars with cat-like quickness despite his size.

Why that's Jed, Lucia realizes. *I know him, since some scrapes with the law he had a few years ago—and I'm aware of his athleticism. What a waste. All that talent and he didn't even finish high school.*

She's losing ground and looking around for some possible shortcut to reduce the advantage he enjoys. Mike is still on the other street parallel with Jed.

Lucia tells herself, *Run, goddamn it, Lucia! You can't let this mother fucker get away from you.*

He's too fast. She continues losing ground. A car! Brakes screech. Barely misses him. Jed has to cut his momentum short. During the lapse, Lucia gains some ground. In a few quick lunges Jed is at top speed again.

His eyes dart over to the traffic on the right. He sees an opening. Turns on a dime. Makes his way to the other side amid blaring horns and a couple of drivers sticking their head out the window shouting unintelligible profanities.

Mike is there waiting for him. He trips Jed. Pulls out his gun. Warns him that if he moves, he will be dead meat. Jed is motionless. Mike tells him to slowly get up with his hands over his head. Jeb does so. Mike is fixing to handcuff the suspect when Lucia arrives.

"Sorry," she manages to say while struggling to cram hefty quantities of oxygen into her lungs, "there was no hole in the traffic I could slip through."

"No problem," Mike says.

Lucia catches her breath somewhat. Turns to Jeb and says, "Long time no see Jed ol' boy. Where've you been hanging out?"

"Around."

"We're taking you to the station for some questions."

"I ain't done nothing."

"Save it until we get to the precinct."

They escort him to the car, take him to headquarters, and direct him to one of the interrogation rooms.

Lucia says, "You have been identified as a suspect for the recent serial killings."

"I don't know what you're talkin' about."

"Where were you three days ago between eight and ten a.m.?"

"Three days ago. I must have been home. Yeah ... that's it. At home. You can ask my ma."

"We'll do that. There was a murder during that time in the city park."

"I ain't killed no one."

"Then why did you run from us?"

"Because I saw you coming with a badge in your hand. I know you people. You profile me and everyone like me, black or white. You rough me up for no reason at all and then lock me up until you decide I ain't done nothing. What do you want me to do? Just stand there and get pistol whipped?"

Mike says, "Did anybody put a hand on you?"

"No. But you could have. Like you cops usually do. Anyway, I ain't done nothing. You can't keep me there."

"You are free to go for now," Lucia tells him. "But stick around. We might have some more questions for you. And you can be sure we will be talking to your mother."

"Do it. I ain't got nuthin' to hide."

Jeb leaves. Disgruntled, and mumbling under his breath. Making a hand gesture as he went through the doorway that might be taken as a bird if anyone had been looking closely.

Mike asks, "What do you think?"

"He's innocent. I know him."

"I gathered so much."

Lucia says, "He's incapable of those killings. Worthless, squeamish, gutless Jeb. He couldn't possibly be up to it. X-Man is most likely programmed to kill and do it without a moment's thought. You did well in pointing him out however."

"Why do you think X-Man has killing in his hard-wiring?"

"Given the type of assassinations he's committed, he has to be emotionless, ruthless. A first-class monster. With eyes like that white shark in the *Jaws* movie. Typical of a serial killer. With each crime, he is left wanting. He's never satisfied, and must have more. Killing is his nature. He's naturally born for it."

"I'm somewhat familiar with all that brouhaha over serial killers," Mike says, "but I'm not really convinced when the experts get on their hobbyhorses and start exaggerating crimes and their perps. What's more, I'm still not convinced X-Man kills because it's in his genes."

"I've thought about that too. But I believe there's more than an ounce of truth to nature taking priority over nurture."

MIKE changes the subject, "That brings the FBI to mind."

"Do they want to collaborate or do they want to keep an eye on what we're doing. The fact of the matter is that the FBI doesn't care much about rapists, child molesters, or serial killers. So why are they so keenly interested in our case?"

"I'm with you. I think the FBI's interests revolve around their obsession with classifying character types and especially those who turn criminal despite themselves. It's nature over nurture again."

"Yeah, you're probably right," Mike concedes.

"Speaking of nature, did you ever hear about the frog transporting a scorpion across a flooding river?"

"No. But I have an idea you're going to fill me in."

"The scorpion wants the frog to take him on his back across the river. The frog's response is negative. How does he know the scorpion won't sting him? The scorpion says he has no wish to sting him if he takes him to the other side. The frog lets the scorpion hop on, and he begins negotiating the flooding stream.

"About halfway to the opposite bank, sure enough, the scorpion stings the frog. The frog cries 'Now look what you've done. I will soon be dead, and you will drown. Why did you do sting me?' The scorpion responded

'I couldn't help it, I'm a natural-born stinger.'"

Mike guffaws.

Lucia is pleased she interjected a light touch—and with a relevant message—in the otherwise morose moments that engulfed them.

In the very least the day ends with a fizzy light.

THE NOTE SOURS, THEN
PICKS UP AGAIN

LUCIA is home. Staring at the wall. That is, at nothing at all. "What do I think I'm doing?" she says out loud. "Criminal investigator? What a joke. Apparently, I have neither the brains nor the balls for it.

"If I was Sam Spade, I would have that butcher in jail. Sam Spade? Sean Connery alias James Bond or Stan Katz? Playacting? This job is not on stage for a bunch of sadistic customers who paid to witness blood, guts, and gore on the screen. People, real people, are ending up dead. And I'm acting like it's play. Who do I think I am? A standup comedian?"

She checks her e-mail. "What's this?" She opens it. Begins reading,

> My lovely Miss Marple—or should J say Angela Lansbury? Aren't you a charming younger version of those crack detectives?

"Now what?" she blurts out while she opens the second message,

> Lovely. You are my enantiomorphic counterpart, my charming other, my spitting diametrically opposed complement. Beguiling and enticing accompaniment aiding and abetting my criminal beingness.

"For God's sakes!" she literally screams out. "Does he know about our playacting metaphor? That's all it is. A metaphor. The outcome of a frivolous theater of words between Mike and me? Meant to exist between the two of us only?

"Is Mike the rat who's been leaking info to the press? And now to the killer? Wait till I confront him. I'll get the truth out of him if it kills me. No. I'll not. He's as clean as they come.

"Or is the criminal—or perhaps his accomplice—a supreme hacker. Me and Mike have sent a few e-mails back and forth about playacting, like some literary conceit. Just between Mike and *moi*. Maybe that's it. A hacker. I trust Mike. It couldn't have been him."

She turns back to the e-mail,

We are equal but opposite, you and me. Opposite yet one, one yet opposite. Let us, then, break bread together, for we deserve each other. A fine restaurant? Good food and great wine? What would you suggest?

"We're one? Deserve each other? Get off my back you fuckin' lout!"

No, she thinks to herself. *This isn't right. He's trying to get to me and he's doing a bang-up job of it. Okay, so I'll play his little game.*

She writes him an e-mail,

> **Well, enthrall my butt off! But I'll have to admit, you have your ways about you. If I was as perverse as you, I might think seriously about getting it on with you. Just for kicks. Then wasting you and cutting your balls off and feeding them to the hogs. But this is no playground we're in. Unlike you, I have a job to do. And rest assured ass-hole, I will do it.**

Will he take the bait? She nervously busies herself by putting a few knick-knacks in place around the room. Straightening a picture on the wall. Passes her finger across the coffee table and contemplating the line she made in the coating of dust. *Gotta clean this place up.*

She viciously grabs a magazine, *Vogue. Vogue?* Yes. She likes gazing at the bimbos, the mind-numbing ads, reading the ludicrously trivial accounts. She doesn't have to think at all, and it puts her mind at ease. She quickly thumbs through a few pages, then checks her e-mail again. *Ah, just like I thought.* It reads,

You have your charming feminine side. Yet occasionally your masculine other comes through loud and clear. But do not despair. I love both of you. A pity you don't hold the same fond thoughts for me. Nevertheless, we must get together, you and me. As one.

She writes back,

Dream on ass hole! I'll soon confront you. I'll have a gun and you'll have none. I'll wear a grin and your lips will be inverted into a sad frown. I'll be crowned Queen of Crime Busting and you'll become a bumbling has-been well past your prime. How's that for enantiomorphic association?

She sends the e-mail and waits at the terminal with hopeful anticipation, meanwhile surfing a lot of nonsense on the Internet. Then,

Lots of luck my Queenie.

That's all? she thinks. Am I to suppose I'm beginning to break him down? Or is his last e-mail designed to put me off guard, lull me to sleep? She responds,

Same to you. Bottled, fermented and spoiled wannabe genie.

What a fuckin' creep she says to herself. *Playacting, splay yakking. Well, it's no more than transitory until reality kicks him in the nuts.*

Yet, Lucia must admit that she's beginning to admire X-Man's penchant for creating a play factor, and she is pleased with herself thinking she has done a slam-dunk on him. Underneath all the glitter and glitz, she now thinks he's a weakling who can't stand up to the real world and must hide behind a set of masks. He can't face the music when things aren't going his way.

It's a matter of time, she tells herself.

ON *second thought,* she thinks, *I'll phone Jack and ask him about the killer's last move. He'll be home. He hardly ever goes out in the evenings.*

She calls. The phone rings once, and Jack's voice rings out. As if he had phone in hand and was anticipating Lucia's call.

"Jack. How're ya doin.'"

"Fine. What's on your mind?"

"A couple of questions."

"I'm all ears."

"The killer just sent me a note. Addressed me as Miss Marple and Angela Lansbury. He seems to be getting chummy with me. Uses words like *dearest, lovely, charming,* his *partner* in *crime,* and *Queenie.* He even said we deserve each other and invited me out to dinner. As a psychologist how does this grab you?"

"Tell me first. How does it affect you?"

"It makes me furious!"—*why does he respond to my questions with more questions?*

"Furious? Why should you react that way?"

"I don't want any man I don't know talking to me that way. Especially a psychopath. But Jack, I need some information from you. It's not me on the couch. It's him."

"Of course. It seems to me he is fixated on you. I would suspect either he had a possessive mother or his lover jilted him. Now he wants revenge.

It could be your looks. Perhaps either his mother or lover was Latina, or at least someone of rather dark complexion. Consequently, he senses some identity between you and the woman who is the object of his resentment. The words he uses like *dearest* and so forth are ambiguous. They are terms of endearment and at the same loaded with irony.

"What I would suggest is that you hold your temper and go along with him. I have an idea his motives will eventually become transparent."

"Is that all, Jack?"

"For now, I can hardly say more. If you give me more context for his messages, perhaps I can give you some additional insight."

"I'll try to cook something up and call you back. In the meantime, stay tuned, because this is getting interesting."

"Interesting? But I thought you were outraged."

"I am. But I try not to let it show or let it get to me."

"You might do well to let it all out occasionally. Get it off your chest. I'll be here if you want to talk."

"Thanks, Jack. I'll keep that in mind."

"My pleasure, Lucia."

Lucia signs off, and thinks *That's strange. Why so much interest in how I feel when I receive those messages? And his words about the killer are sophomoric. Could have come from an undergraduate's term paper. Anyway, so much for Jack. I've got more pressing issues.*

BACK TO THE GRIND

LUCIA looks for Mike. Finds him at the watering tank. Where else? Asks him to give his opinion regarding what she has in her e-mail. They sit at her desk. He reads the killer's messages and her rebuttals.

"What the hell," he says, "you mean to say he knows about our conversations?"

"That's the way it looks. He or somebody else has apparently hacked into us."

"He's flattering you to high heaven. What does he have in mind?"

"Don't ask *me*? Ask *him*."

"By this time, he's probably got another user name and address."

"Probably. Anyway, I have another reason for wanting to talk to you. Last night I recalled a story I once read by Borges about the inhabitants of a strange planet called Tlön. I pulled his *Labyrinths* off my shelf and took another look at it the story.

"The Tlönians's world is not a collection of enduring objects in space and time like ours. It's a series of independent appearances and disappearances of imaginary things, acts, and happenings in time.

"For this reason, they have little use for nouns. Their language consists of verbs and adjectives that more adequately flow with time. If they want to say the equivalent of our English sentence, 'The moon rose above the river,' they would say something like, 'Upward behind the onstreaming it mooned.'"

"Fascinating. I suppose ... Anyway, what's the point."

"The Tlönians are idealists. Much in the sense of philosopher George Berkeley. The idea that if a tree falls in the forest and nobody is around to hear it, it won't make any noise, because it didn't fall.

"In Tlön, prisoners were sent to work on some archeological diggings. They couldn't find anything. Then the bone specialists told them what they were supposed to be looking for. They returned to their excavation. Looked for what the archeologists had in mind, and they found the artifacts.

"Idealism says that what we see is what we get because we saw it. It's not a simple matter of our seeing what there is."

"The point is?" Mike asks.

"This. I have a vague premonition that X-Man creates images through his portmanteau rhetoric—we've talked about this. Given his infatuation with rhetoric, the e-mails he sends me are becoming so much word play. Yet they are—or they become if you prefer—as if physically real. This is like a twisted counterpart to the Tlönians' idealism. Now get this. You recall the perp's message where on no uncertain terms he writes with godlike words?—such as when I declared, 'I am that I am.'"

"Yeah."

"Well, now his idealism falsifies those words. Such that he begins pontificating about his language consisting of a sparsity of rhetoric nor verbs. And about his world as densely populated with nouns. Becoming replacements for verbs and adjectives. Why and how? Because he's interjecting playacting into his world. Playacting, and his world eventually becomes ... like ... objective idealism ... like ... idealized physicalism. Or something of that sort. Sporting a lot of verbalized, adjectivized nouns."

"You might be on track. Because we must admit he's playacting su- premely."

"Yes. And he changes his idealized MO at every turn," Lucia adds.

"So, he's playing to the tune of chance happenings. Like throws of the dice," Mike speculates. "Every time he throws the dice, neither we nor he knows what the outcome is until he takes a gander at them. Then he goes about constructing another imaginary world."

"Yes. You know I don't believe in mere chance, but now I'm having second thoughts."

"X-Man, philosopher of idealism." Mike reflects.

"It's all imaginary, but when interjected into the physical world it becomes real as far as he's concerned."

"So, we have to take it as if it was real."

"Right," Lucia acknowledges.

"All the while, everything's always changing."

"So it seems."

"Then how in hell will we ever catch him?"

"The dice have a limited number of possibilities. Throw them at will and you meet with repetitions. The killer, like all of us, is an animal of habit. He will repeat himself whether he knows it or not. Then we'll know where he's going and we'll have him in our grasp."

"Okay. I'm game. What's the next step?" Mike asks.

"That's the sixty-four-thousand-dollar question."

"We have the solution, but we have no way of knowing whether it's correct or flawed or how to take it to its logical end. Is that what you're saying."

"I'm afraid so."

"Then we have no recourse but to wait for his next move. What's new?"

"Well ... I guess you've said it rightly. It's like that paradox Zeno concocted. In order to get to the goal-line you must cover half the distance, then half of the remaining distance, then half that distance. Again and again. You will never reach your goal, since there will always remain some distance between you and the end of the race."

Mike grins, "Unless I cover an infinite number of steps."

Lucia sends him an eye rolling smile, "There is no series of steps trailing off to infinity. Anyway, our problem is that we don't even know where the goal-line is!"

Mike cries out in sudden desperation. "But Luce! We must do something, and quick. People are threatened by the guillotine."

"I know."

"I think we should quit playing games and get down to the nitty-gritty."

"Right, but how?" Lucia asks.

Mike has no answer. In fact, Lucia and Mike spend the next few days doing nitty-gritty work, tracing down leads going nowhere. It's day twenty-two, and nothing has happened.

Mayor Fitzburger's presence on Fay's back is weighing her down. Governor Chadwick is trying to appease the people who are suspecting police corruption. Conspiracy theorists are recommending a few guns in every home. Mike and Lucia are becoming the brunt of multiplying sarcastic innuendos, snide remarks, and biting jokes. Some are suggesting Lucia is not a true-blue American but an illegal alien who has no loyalty to the country.

TWO days later, mayhem. Homicide six. Mike and Lucia are off like bats out of hell.

This is the twenty-fourth day. Nine more than the last killing. Temporal progression.

The crime is two miles away as the crow flies. Okay, the expected spatial progression.

It occurs at noon. Ditto. Progression in time.

The facts are moving along in marching order. But what, precisely, is the order?

They arrive at the scene. Strangled with piano wire that is left deftly twisted around the victim's neck. White middle-age male. About five feet ten inches—the perp is still mixing up gender and ethnicity. Pudgy and around one hundred and eighty pounds. Blond hair. Green eyes. Scar on the left check but no other markings of noteworthy importance.

The victim's on his back as usual. Staring at the sky. Dressed in a suit, tie, and expensive Italian shoes. How did the predator do this during the light of day? And at the beginning of lunch hour to boot? Could he drag the victim over there at gunpoint and cut off his oxygen without causing too much ruckus? Did he kill his victim elsewhere and somehow bring him here?

He's probably strong enough to hold the poor bastard up with his right arm and talk to him while he pulls him along as if giving a friend a hug and some advice. Anyway, that's yet to be determined. For now, wallet and identification are missing, but there are folded bills in his left back pocket. And, of course, a message, found in the right pocket of the victim's pants,

> 'Twas such fun when on the run; us natorn bural cullers and pat's no thun.

At the bottom of the page there's a footnote that reads,

> Up high, on the lamp post across the street, your anticipated words of wisdom.

Two pairs of eyes dart over on the other side of the street and move up the slender pillar to the top. There it is.

"How did the son of a bitch get up there without raising suspicion?" Mike asks.

They call the firefighting crew. The vehicle arrives. A burly firefighter shinnies up the pole. Rescues the note. And hands it to Mike. He gives it to Lucia. She opens it, and reads,

> Ripped from my mother's womb; beaten and burned; I be- come a bloodthirsty killer; what am I?

"I knew it!" Lucia is elated. "He had a traumatic childhood."

"The question, like all others, is, '*What* am I'?" Mike tells Lucia. "It's not *who*. Maybe we ought to think up the answer to the riddle before jumping the gun."

"You're right. Birth, beaten, burned, and becoming bloodthirsty. Four Bs. Does that ring a bell?" Lucia asks while groping in the dark.

"Not really. It says ripped from the womb. That doesn't exactly suggest human birth."

"Maybe he's speaking figuratively."

"Could be. Still, from the outset he wants us to think birth, and when we think it, we usually conjure up the human variety. He might be trying to put us on the wrong track."

"Could be," Lucia repeats Mike's words in absence of anything else to add.

Lucia has a message on her phone. Not surprisingly, it's him. His text message reads,

B as U appear to B. That is, as U are Becoming. Never imagine Urself not to B otherwise than what U appear to others to B or would B if U were other than what U B (recall Alice in Wland, my sweet honey B).

"*Cafajeste, filho de puta!*" Lucia vociferates her frustration and pain.

"Come again?"

"Bastard, son of a bitch. Well, more or less."

"You can say that again."

"He isn't even worth it. So much for my idea of the four Bs. Birth, beaten, burned, and bloodthirsty as clues. Let's turn to your notion that he's not referring to human birth at all. What do we have?"

"Abuse a dog and he becomes roguish," Mike ventures to guess.

"But a dog isn't ripped from the mother's womb, ordinarily."

"Could be something inanimate. But in that case, there is no mother's womb, literally speaking."

"On the other hand, what other than living creatures do we call mother."

"A hurricane as the mother of all hurricanes. Or saying the same of a rainstorm, freezing temperature, blistering heat, drought ..."

"They aren't bloodthirsty ... Except perhaps metaphorically speaking, and the killer has done plenty of that. Anyway, let's go to the mother message. We have, 'Us natorn bural cullers and pat's no thun.'"

"Hm." Mike's eyes become an almost blind slit. "Na-t-ural, *natural*, born, *born*"

"Oh yes," Lucia chimes in, "and we have th-at's, *that's* and p-un, *pun*. But what can we make of cullers?"

"Cullers," Mike repeats. "Cull, cull out, remove, waste, negate, *kill*, 'Us natural-born killers.' Got it?"

"Mike, you're a mastermind."

"Just sloppy imagination that happens to hit the mark once in a while."

"Natural-born killer. That's what we discussed with Leonard and Jamie.

What does it have to do with the riddle? Natural born isn't ripped from the womb. It's natural born ... natural born ..."

"Like from mother earth," Mike says rather unthinkingly.

"I give up for now. Back to the sweatshop to write up nothing genuinely new."

"Unfortunately." Mike sighs.

NOT surprisingly, Fay is waiting for them with a pile of questions.

"Anything new?" she asks.

"No."

"Nobody around as a witness?"

"No."

"A different gender, different ethnicity?"

"Yes. White male."

"Old? Young?"

"Middle age well-dressed professional."

And so on. Fay doesn't appear in the least perturbed by the curt responses, as if she had expected them.

Lucia and Mike take their leave on the pretext that they need to write up their report so they can go out and check a couple of leads.

That's our cherished leader. Lucia sighs.

Mike says, "This is become too embarrassing for comfort."

Lucia agrees. Mike goes his way and Lucia does likewise. She sits here. Mike sits over there. As if hypnotized. They're attempting to go through the process of thinking things out. But nothing comes up.

I must help Lucia out, Mike thinks. *She's so ... in the doldrums.*

He tries to concentrate on the riddle. As if it might do any good. He doubts it. But he feels he must solve it, just in case. It's a lead of some sort. Perhaps.

So, he thinks, *I must pursue it to its logical end, or its irrational end. Whichever the insane case may become. Let me see ... Womb, beaten, burned ... and bloodthirsty killer ...*

Lucia simply sits ... and would like to convince herself she's thinking. *Useless speculation. Inconclusive thoughts. As time goes by,* she *reckons.*

Humphrey Bogart and Sam in *Casablanca* come to mind. *It's into the pit of despondency* she concludes. *How will we pull ourselves out of it?* Nonetheless, the day goes by, slowly, stealthily.

Mike pops in at five thirty when Lucia is on the verge of dozing off.

"I've got it," he literally shouts, obviously proud of himself.

"Got what?"

"The riddle. Iron ore."

"How do you figure?"

"Out of mother nature's womb, smelted and beaten into ingots, then it becomes an arm of human destruction, a weapon, a bloodthirsty killer."

"You never cease to amaze me, Mike. So now, what did the monster have in mind when he wrote that?"

"I never got to that stage."

"Well, get there."

"Help me out, Luce."

"I'll try. We have to outwit him."

"I'm with you, Luce. But how?"

"Bloodthirsty killer. Iron ore. What's the relationship here?"

"Beats me."

"I'm going home, and meditate on it. While I'm at it I'll extrapolate my diagram to include this sixth crime," Lucia proposes.

"Yeah. See ya tomorrow."

"Enjoy the evening."

"Are you kidding?"

Before leaving, Lucia takes the necessary measurement from the map on the wall and puts it in her attaché case thinking she'll make the extrapolations at home.

HOME. Bob calls. After small talk, he suggests they plan their next night out. Lucia says she's so tied down she doesn't know how she'll break loose for a few hours. Bob says he understands the pressure she's under and asks if she would like him to come over, eat something, chat for a spell, and he's out of her hair.

She asks if he can do it tomorrow. She wants to put the final touch on a scheme she's designed that might help them catch the goddamn criminal.

Bob's fine. Says he'll call her the next evening.

Lucia eats the chow she bought at the carry-out. Then sits down at her computer and prepares to do some light doodling, heavy diagramming, and hopefully dream up something. Anything. For she's becoming desperate.

Okay, Lucia, get with it, girl.

She takes the measurements out of her attaché case and alters her diagram to accommodate it with the fifth crime.

Got it! she thinks to herself. *Now what do I have? As the crow flies, and the proper distance.*

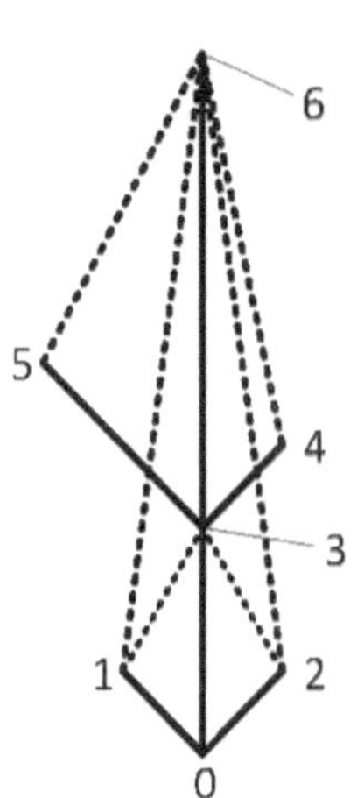

From 0 to 1 straight down the street from the precinct, and from 0 to 2 as the crow flies, catty-corned across buildings and streets. 0 to 3 also as the crow flies. From three to four and five we have connections veering off to the right and the left. And then on to six, connecting four and five in the same way three connects one and two. In this manner 1, 2, 3, 4, and 5 interconnect with 6. Triangles making up elongated rhombus figures.

Geometrically analyzing the diagram *gives closure. Geometrically intuiting the nature of the diagram would suggest that six is the final homicide. Three plus three is six; two times three is six. Wrapped up and tied with a ribbon.*

No? I can imagine so. At least I would like to think so. None of that bullshit about seven points on the Starbucks logo crown.

But on second thought I still can't be certain. So, what do you have that you can sink your teeth into, Lucia? Slip this diagram in front of Mike and he will study it and try to make some positive comment or other. How could he do otherwise? He has to live with me.

Show this to Fay and she'll say I'm out of my mind. For that matter show it to anyone at headquarters, or the mayor or the governor or the public, and ditto. Show it to the press and the ridicule and humor will have no end. So, once again, what do you do with it, lady Lucia?

I'll take it to Uncle George. His mathematical skills will surely lead to some set of interconnections containing time in days and hours and space and directions and the vectors involved in my diagram. The final answer might soon be at hand. "*Graças a Deus!*"—Thank God."

A bit of hope enters Lucia's head. She picks a book off the shelf. *What have we here? Without Conscience by Robert Hare. Some additional info about psychopaths won't hurt me at this stage of the game,* she thinks. *I remember some years ago when I picked up that book in Rio by Ana Beatriz Barbosa Silva,* Mentes perigosas, Dangerous Minds. *She had favorable words about Hare.*

She readies for bedtime. Crawls in. Turns on the bedside lamp with book in hand. And reads.

THE following morning at the office of presentments, pretensions, and pathos, hullabaloo raises its ugly head again. A pair of law enforcers along with detectives Rich and Berto bring in a guy who alleges he committed all six murders.

Skepticism abounds. Especially in view of his unkempt appearance, slurred speech, glazed eyes, and crimson splotched face. A drug addict who sees his only road to salvation through confessing to the crimes and enjoying free treatment and board and room?

Lucia announces, "Bring him on. We can't do any worse than we've been doing over the past few days."

In the interrogation quarters, Mike and Lucia learn his name is Sam Mansfield, or so he claims. His eyes are making wild shifts in every conceivable direction. He is fidgety. Hands are shaking. Body will not sit still. Nasal passages are evidently in terrible shape judging from his wheezing. Eyes are bloodshot and watery. They cannot tell if his pupils are dilating since he averts their gaze. He's obviously on drugs.

"So, you committed those crimes?" Lucia asks him. "Yes, ma'am."

"Why did you choose people of different genders and ethnicity to kill?"

"Ethwhat? I didn't hear you directly."

"Ethnicity, different cultures, different races."

"I ain't no racist."

"I'm not saying you are. But you selected men and women, and white, black, and brown. Why?"

"Well … I killed whoever was there," he answers, slurring his words to the extent that he is hardly intelligible.

"You also used different means for killing your victims. Why is that?"

"Means? I means what I said. I didn't choose nobody. I killed for fun. But don't get me wrong. I'm not really a bad dude because"—

"What I'm saying is, you used a pistol, a knife, poison, a wire for strangulation. Why didn't you kill your victims in the same way? Wouldn't it be more efficient?"

"I killed with what I had. When I did it, I didn't have nothing else."

"What kind of poison did you use?"

"Poison? I don't know what you talkin' about."

"Why did you rape your female victims?"

"What d'ya mean. I never raped any woman in my life. I"—

"We have evidence that two of the women were raped, and we have semen samples and can link them to you with DNA testing. You got that?"

"Yes, but I ain't"—

"Shut up and listen. If you deny the charge and we prove you guilty, you stand a chance of getting the death penalty … Ey? You listening? You had better fess up for your own good."

"They called me a filthy pig. I raped 'em to show them who was boss and then I killed 'em. What else did they expect?"

"You mean you did it in broad daylight with a lot of people on the sidewalk and in the street."

"What if I raped them in the park and took the bodies over there later?"

"What do you mean 'What if I raped them'? Did you or didn't you?"

"Well … It was like this"—

Mike steps back, lifts a five-pound ankle weight he had in his hand when he entered the room, tosses it to the self-proclaimed killer while hollering, "Think fast!" The confessor's reactions are so slow Mike fears the object might catch him in the chest and topple him backward in his chair.

But he puts his right hand up and cushions the blow somewhat, as he screams "Eeeey!" like a stuck sow.

"What you do that for? You tryin' to kill me?"

Mike says, "We have evidence that the killer is about twice your size and very strong. You just proved you are incapable of committing the crimes. Plus the fact that you haven't given any acceptable answers to our questions."

Lucia says, "You are free to leave, Sam."

"What d'ya mean. You not gonna put me in jail? I killed people," he whines.

"No. You're free to go."

"I don't wanna go back on the street. What can I do there?"

"That's your problem," Lucia tells him. "We're looking for the real killer."

"Oh officer," she calls out. "Escort this young man to the door."

"You can't send me away just like that."

"I already have."

The officer takes Sam by the shoulder, pulls him to the door, and leads him away. While Sam voices a stream of garbled protests.

"Poor bastard," Mike opines.

"Is this what our job has now cut out for us?" Lucia asks.

"I wouldn't doubt it," Mike mutters with frustration showing on his face.

Lucia says, "Our only consolation might be found in my revised diagram."

"Oh yeah. Let's see it."

She spreads her *opus* out on her desk. Her expectations ring true: Mike studies the lines, their length and connecting angles, whispers hours and days and spatial increments, then remarks, "You've brought the whole shebang to some sort of closure."

"I hope."

"Shall we show it to Fay?" Mike asks.

"Heavens no. She and the staff would laugh us out of town."

"I guess you're right. Then what do we do with it?"

"I can't quite figure it out, so I'm taking it to my math brained uncle to hear what he has to say."

"Sounds great, I would like to go with you."

"Meet me at seven at my apartment."

THE MACHINE IN THE MONSTER

THEY'RE off to see the mathematical wizard. Hopeful source of a few answers. Lucia tells Mike she sent George the diagram in case he might find time to study it.

Mike becomes enthused over the possibility of finally discovering a smattering of clues. He tells Lucia, "I wonder if he can stomach X-Man's repugnant killing scenes."

"Are you kidding? He worked on the detective force for six years before he took his PhD in mathematics and became a college prof. After dealing with cops who are in it to satisfy their sadistic desire for power, and with criminal misfits of all types, he has plenty of street smarts. You'll see."

They arrive. Go up the steps. Knock on the door. There's a "Hold-yourhorses" holler loud enough to shake the windowpanes. The door opens, and the voice, streaming from a rough, robust male specimen, gregariously vociferates, "Look what the dogs drug in!"

George gives Lucia a tight hug, then a kiss on one cheek and the other. While articulating a few virtually unintelligible words.

"Uncle George, this is my partner, Mike."

"Mike, you're a young whippersnapper aren't you, obviously still a little wet behind the ears."

"I'm new in the department, sir."

"Come sit in the couch. I got some coffee brewin'. Let me fetch it from the kitchen and I'll be back with you."

They sit. George appears in no time at all with coffee pot in one hand and a tray of cups jiggling and chiming with every step. He pours coffee, spilling some in the process, sets the tray on the ornamental table between them and ...

"So, Lucia, I see your name in the newspaper almost daily. They're giving you a rough time. Those damned reporters'll kill to get a scoop. Hell, fifty percent of all those lies they write are false and the other fifty percent are nonsense," he says with an energetic horselaugh. "They wouldn't know the truth if it bit them on the ass. Tell them to go to hell for me, will you?"

"I can't do that, George. My boss, the mayor, and the governor would be down my throat and up my ass."

"Aaaahaaa," George garrulously guffaws. "Still the old Lucia."

"You? What's your name again?"

"Mike."

"Oh yes, what do think of my niece? She's something, isn't she?"

"Yes, sir."

"Did you get a chance to look at my diagram?" Lucia asks.

"Sure did, immediately after you sent it. You're still a geometer at heart. Should have pursued the field, and I could attend your classes at the university to give you hell, ahaahaa."

"I see you're still the same Uncle George. Ornery as a corralled stallion, abrasive as a wood rasp, and a dyed-in-wool son of a bitch."

"Yeah, girl, don't you forget it. And you? Still as stubborn as a mule. Am I right, Mikey?"

"Yes, sir."

"Now, about the diagram." Lucia wants to shunt aside the gab and get down to business.

"Oh that. You want my opinion?"

"That's what we're here for."

"I thought it was because you can't resist my charming ways. Now I'm disappointed, aahaaa ha."

"That too, George."

"Ha, I knew it. Anyway, here's where I am. You said you think your geometrical image is closed with the apex you labeled six. I checked numbers and times and distances, and what do you know? I came up with the Golden Section! How about that?"

"Golden Section?" Mike asks with wide questioning eyes.

"Yeah, the Fibonacci series."

"Amazing," Lucia declares. "Leave it to you to dream up something nobody else thought of."

"That's because my mind is made of pictures, like Einstein and others. Got it? I'm no Einstein, and I gotta do my best with what I have. So, I steal other people's pictures. Eh?"

This guy's more than a little stuck on himself, Mike thinks.

"Fibonacci," Lucia ponders over the possibility.

"Yeah, here, I have an image of it I found in this book. Feast your eyes on her. Beautiful, isn't she?

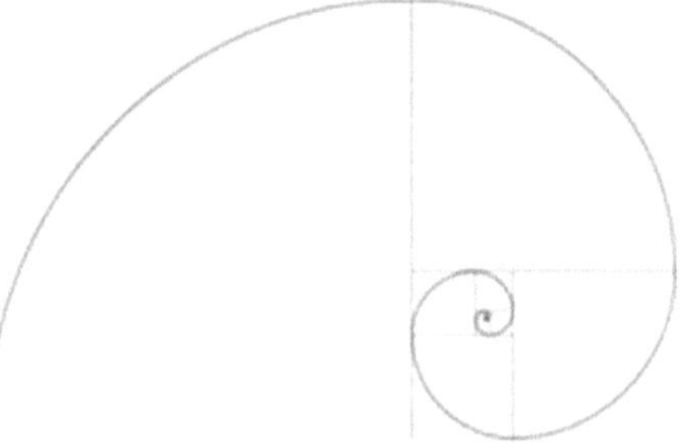

She's found everywhere in nature. Ram horns, narwhale spindles, sea shells of every sort, giant sunflowers, and what have you. In a roundabout way, even the DNA double helix. You get the drift, Mike? It's all based on numbers.

"Starting with zero, you go to one and then one again. You see there, the two small squares. They're one and one. Then you continue. Each new number in the series is the sum of the two before it: 0, 1, 1, 2, 3, 5, 8, 13, 21, 34, 55, and so on. There's much more to it than that. But the important point is that what you have in your diagram follows the Fibonacci series in time and space."

"Amazing," Lucia marvels. "But, George, the murder sequence is: 0, 3, 3, 6, 9, 15, 24. That doesn't coincide with the Fibonacci series."

"Ah, but girl, it does. Your psycho isn't a moron. After zero, begin your numbers with three. Use the same type of algorithm. And what do you have? Old Fibonacci! See there? It works."

"Mind-blowing," Mike utters. "But I don't get it. Lucia's diagram is made of lines and angles connecting them. Your picture is spiral."

"Look at the numbers. Numbers are what make the universe tick. The distances, the times, the trajectories. You start with zero, then you have two threes, three days and three days, like the two ones in the series. You go from there to six days, nine days, fifteen days and twenty-four days.

"The progression is comparable, if not the same. In distance you begin at zero, then one-fourth and one-fourth, then one-half, three-fourths, one and one-fourth, and it's off to the races. In times of the day, it's zero, five A.M., five A.M., six A.M. Do I need to go further?"

"No," Mike sheepishly concedes. "I see it," while he's thinking, *Is this for real or is it another study in questionable numerology?*

"The series takes us to the grand finale! Seventh murder. Hey! Am I great or what?"

"Modesty ought to become you, George," Lucia tells him. "It was Leonardo Fibonacci's idea."

"But I get credit for making the connection. No average Joe could have done it."

"How do you figure there will be a seventh murder?" Lucia asks.

"Here it is," George says, pulling out an alternate diagram. "Feast your eyes."

"Hmm ..." Lucia muses.

"Seven brings the system to closure!"

George confidently roars.

"How is that?" Mike asks him.

"You see young man? It takes two linearly placed connecting lines between six and seven to complete the form. Thus, complementing the linear connections between zero and three. Like you, Lucia,

I found a large map of the city in the municipal library, plotted the murder sites, and discovered that line six-seven is also linear. It is an extension of the line from zero to three. This makes up two interconnected rhombuses. This isn't apparent at first because the rhombuses are elongated. But they're there."

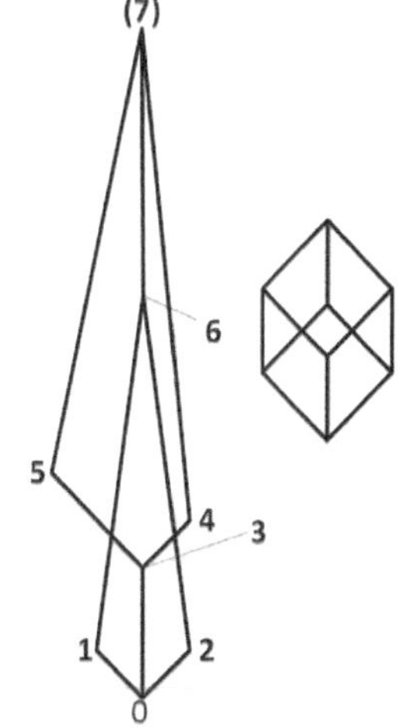

"I repeat," Lucia says, "There's a *there*, there after all"—

Mike butts in, "That's why you have that figure on the right side. It lets us more easily see the connections."

"Right. The figure on the right is a Necker cube. You can see the cube is complete. It gives you a two-dimensional image of a three-dimensional object. In contrast to the cube, our elongated figure on the left lacks a couple of connecting lines."

"So, this is supposed to tell you there must be a seventh murder?" Lucia asks with increasing skepticism.

"Exactly."

"When and where?" Mike asks.

"On the thirty-ninth day—give or take a day perhaps—at six P.M. on Tenth and Brady. It's the six-seven link, straight up from the zero-three link."

"Jesus! You don't actually think X-Man has made all this up do you?" Mike asks.

"X-Man! Where the hell did he come from?"

"It's the name we attached to that bastard predator," Lucia responds. "X, an unknown variable, variable because he has been well-nigh unpredictable, and man because our experts determined the killer has to be a powerful individual and only a six-foot-plus athletic male could pull the murders off."

"What did I tell you?" George roars. "You're still a geometer at heart."

"I feel it in my bones, or maybe it's a premature invasion of arthritis." George's larynx explodes with another hearty outburst.

"George, I have another question for you," Lucia says. "Why the absent connecting lines in your figure when compared to the Necker cube? Why not stick them in? It will make the form complete and balanced. It's a question of geometrical form, you know."

"No. It is a matter of nonlinearity rather than linearity. Linearity is simply *either* one damn thing *or* another. Then it's one damn thing *or* another again, and on and on. Nonlinearity, as in the stretched-out figure, offers many possible connections in different temporal and spatial junctures rather than merely two.

"It is the beauty of vagueness rather than know-it-all certainty. It allows for variations in the form. Nonlinearity accompanies forms that are always changing as they grow, always becoming different than what they were."

"I've called something like this 'illogical logic' when Mike's around and it's driving him up the wall."

George cackles and tells Mike, "Hey, we're Brazilians. We like syncopated irregularity with an off-beat rhythm. What you need is a transfusion of Brazilian blood and you'll be jumping up and dancing the *samba*, haa haae."

"Don't bet on it," Mike quips. "From what I've seen of *samba* I would trip over my own toes with the first step."

George slaps his knees in laughter.

"George, you didn't respond to Mike's question of a few moments ago. Do you really think that sick bastard mathematized his crimes according to your Fibonacci formula?"

"Look. The series follows the Necker cube, except it lacks a couple of lines. That's the beauty of it. If you start at the bottom, you can't go directly to the top. You can get there only by connecting with other lines so that together they can move along. Everything interconnects, and wherever you are in the figure you must depend on your context within the entire figure. That's what makes each move nonlinear and context dependent. You see?"

"No." Mike is quick to respond.

"Anyway," George continues as if he hadn't heard Mike, "I don't know if that psycho intentionally used the Fibonacci series to plot his murders. I do know the formula works. It's beautiful, harmonious, and it works. Kepler said geometry structures the world like the mind of God. I don't know about that, but my philosophy is that if it works, don't meddle with it. Keep it in mind, and it will become instrumental in pouring new ideas into your head."

"Well," Lucia tells George, "I would say that as far as geometry coincides with the killer's MO, it is not certain, and as far as it is certain, it doesn't coincide with his MO. I prefer to maintain a note of skepticism."

After another horselaugh, George says, "Yeah. And you're e a geometer at heart but a detective at work; and you're a detective when working with geometry on your mind. Aahaa."

Mike reciprocates with a harmonious cackle.

Lucia gives them an uncustomary giggle, "Thanks for sharing your wisdom and giving us a few tips, George. We have to get back."

"Hey! Hold on! There's a lot more to say about your diagram."

"Later, George, we have deadlines to meet."

"You've hardly touched your coffee. Wait a minute, I'll refresh it. And I'll bring some chunks of pound cake to flush down the gullet with it. Stick around and chew the fat with me for a while. Hey, Lucia, where's your Brazilian upbringing? Get with the *papo*, eh?"

"*Papo*?" Mike frowns.

"Damn right young man. Talk. Chit-chat. Verbally horsing around. Gossip, jokes, discussion, debate. We Brazilians are world champions at is. After soccer, of course. We"—

"You're right," Lucia butts in. "The pleasures of *papo*. But my job is trying to make myself into a bionic woman, with little *papo* and a lot of action."

"Tell 'em your nimble Brazilian brain can outsmart a bionic brain any day. Aaahaa."

George disappears into the kitchen.

Mike says, "X-Man is like a bionic machine in a hunk of meat. If he's going about mathematizing his killings the way George says, he's got to be the most cold-blooded killer a detective force ever came up against."

"Not surprising you say that, Mike. I was thinking the same thing. Seven homicides. My God! At least I hope George is right and they end at seven. We must intercept him at whatever cost before he gets to eight."

George appears, voicing a song by Gilberto Gil from his reggae CD. It was one of Bob Marley's most successful tunes, and the Brazilian songster gives it a remarkable rendition.

"Here's something to put into your bellies, my sleuthing friends. Now, where were we? ... Oh yes. This character kills white, black and Latino men and women. I'm sorry I have to say this, Lucia, but you're Brazilian. He might get the idea he can terminate two beautiful birds with one stone. You ever thought of that?"

"Yes, but I try to put it out of my mind."

"Don't you forget it. It is a definite possibility."

"I doubt it. He's after easier game."

"I think you ought to stay away from Tenth and Brady streets."

"I cannot. We must canvas that intersection thoroughly. Check out all the details."

"At least never go alone. Mike's a husky lad, tough as nails I bet. I have your best interests in mind, but your safety is in my heart. Be careful, Lucia."

"Rest assured. I will."

"And I'll always be there to back her up," Mike pitches in.

They engage in frivolous jawing, that is, *papo*. Politics, crime, social issues, baseball, basketball, and especially Brazil's prime sport, soccer—which leaves Mike somewhat cold.

They depart, after what seems like an interminable series of recommendations and presentments out of George's vivaciously loquacious vocal cords.

FUNNY PUTTY LOGIC?

ON their way back, Mike makes furtive glances Lucia's way. She feels them but pretends she doesn't acknowledge them. Finally, Mike asks, "What's on your mind?"

"You don't want to know."

"But I do."

"Here goes then. I was thinking of our conversation back there with George. It's the strange conflict about people who disapprove of the United States Congress as a whole. They give their representatives a measly twelve-percent favorable rating or something like that. At the same time, they enthusiastically support the state representatives of their local congressional district. I feel the same way about George's formula.

"It is neat. But too farfetched to take seriously. I would tend to reject it whole hog to save face with Fay and the staff. But when as a rule of thumb it becomes convenient, we can apply it, and ignore it when it isn't."

"Sounds reasonable. Or should I say illogically logical?" Mike chuckles. She gives him an approving nod. He goes on "It occurs to me that our killer's variety of evil should be incompatible with mathematical equations and their god-like truths. But perhaps evil has its own precision, its beauty, and its truth.

"The problem is that as law-abiding citizens we are not familiar with the beauty of what is indescribably sordid, and we can't bring ourselves to see its truth."

Lucia ventures to add, "I still have a cantankerous question in my mind about George's extension of my diagram. Why reject the two lines on the right-side figure that would bring closure to the Necker cube? If he longs for beauty in the equation, why doesn't he connect them? I need to talk to him in more detail about that."

"When?"

"Right now! Turn this vehicle around."

"We just left. Are you sure he won't mind?"

She chuckles, "*Papo* is his favorite pastime."

THEY are back, and approach the door. Lucia's hand extends to give it a knock. It opens before she makes contact. George says, "I knew I would win out over your cheerless existence at headquarters!" he thunders.

"We have more questions," Lucia tells him.

"You think I didn't know that? I left out some details knowing curiosity would get the best of you and you'd be knocking on my door again. Now you have a chance to question me."

Lucia rolls her eyes.

George says, "Step inside and spill it out, my lovely niece."

They enter. Take a seat.

Lucia asks George, "Tell us more about those missing lines. If the killer is so thoroughly obsessed over symmetry, he would have had those lines in mind. So why didn't he connect them?"

"Your criminal wants nonlinear complexity, not the simplicity of either one option or the other. Either/or thinking limits you to two choices. Yes or no. True or false. It becomes too tedious for words. If there are effortless straight lines between the left side and right-side corners of the figure, the journey to the top by any path would be like an ingenuous walk along the city streets.

"This doesn't cut the cake. What's going on with these murders has to be interesting! Challenging! Thought provoking! But it must reveal options. This requires nonlinearity. Between any two options struggling with each other in mortal combat, there's always another one, and then another one, and so on."

"But, George," Lucia protests, "he's a criminal whose goal in life is killing people. Why would he be interested in mathematical intricacies when he could just kill and get it over with?"

"Because it is his nature."

"How can you be so sure of that?" Mike asks.

"I know him. I know a mind whose curiosity knows no bounds when I see it. He's like an Einstein of criminal minds. A Picasso of time and space. A Kafka of a nightmarish bureaucratic social existence. A Bach of fugue counterpoint, the"—

"Yes, George, but give me specific details, not a bag full of analogies."

"Details? The creative mind works with analogies! They are what make our creative world spin. Don't you see? He's a creative genius, a vertiginous intellect, a master mind!"

At that moment, Mike looks at Lucia's uncle as if he wanted to penetrate *his* mind for the first time, *He must have around sixty-five years under his belt, but he's six two and in excellent physical condition. Why his apparent infatuation with the killer's mind? Why all the superlatives? Might he be ...? No. Don't you dare go there, Mike. But still, if George was a psychologist with a geometer's view of the world ...*

Lucia says, "Yes, George. I follow you. But we have to work with concrete details capable of convincing a judge and jury."

George carries on as if he hadn't heard a word Lucia said, "Look at those corners along the two sides of the two squares of the Necker cube (he draws it again as he speaks). There's one above and one below on the right and left sides. Or vice versa depending on how you look at it. They are linearly structured.

"Hence, you can go up the left side and I can go up the right side and we may never meet until we get to the top. When we reach the top we are still disconnected, isolated in our own worlds.

"That's not the way the world works *Lucinha* (diminutive for Lucia).

Like I said, everything interconnects, and what you see and think depends on where you are and when. Look at this," George rants while he grabs pencil and paper and quickly jots down a labeled figure.

"We start at the bottom, zero. Then you move up on the left to L1 and I begin on the right-side and go to G1. It seems that we are completely disconnected.

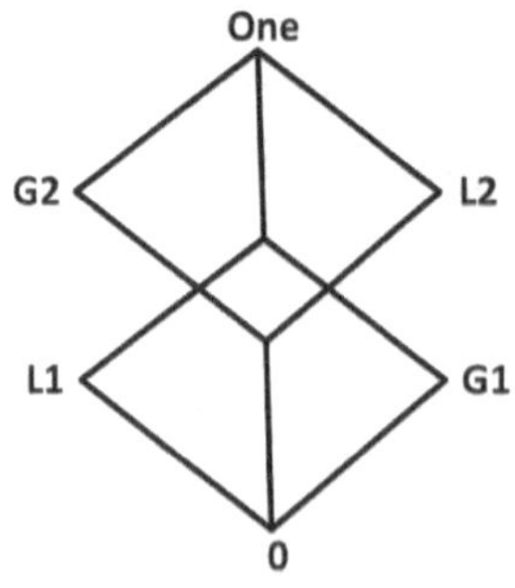

Like aliens living on separate planets.

Like you on one remote side and me on the other side of the Necker cube.

"Then suddenly you find yourself at L2 and I'm at G2, on the other side of the upper square. How did we get there? Magic? No! We made a leap. Like a quantum leap. I say quantum leap *Lucinha* and Mikey, because this figure is relevant to the quantum world! We find ourselves in completely different contexts. We are becoming different. We are becoming somebody else. Read Wolfgang Smith's *The Quantum Enigma* and you'll see.

"Anyway, you are now in L2 and I'm in G2. We changed our place in the lattice. From left to right and from right to left. We jumped from our previous self to our present self that is now different, even if to an almost insignificant degree. But it still seems that we are alienated with respect to one another. Not so Lucinha?

"No, not at all. We realize that from One, at the lattice's top, I can see you leaping to my side while I'm leaping to your side. We are *interconnected, interdependent,* and *interactive.* Our leaping reveals that we are Two and at the same time we are One. Because we *complement* one another from the broader view. Like a two-dimensional plane complements three-dimensionality in a Picasso cubist painting."

Lucia says, "How did we blend into *One?* How can our *interconnectedness* become part of our living world? At the top of the lattice?"

"Right there! At *One?* There, we are still *Two* but we are *One.* For at least an instant our minds merge. We are becoming *One.* Then in the next instant we split off, and once again we are *Two.* Yet we remain *One.*

"Extra lines to the left and the right of the figure making it like a Necker cube would destroy the reason for our becoming interconnected. It would destroy the importance of our sameness in our differences and our differences in our sameness."

"Good lord! My mind's fuzzy with all this. Could you be more specific?" Lucia queries him.

"I already explained it for you!"

George yells with gyrating arms.

Mike tells her, "Hey, Luce, think of your rat in a maze example."

"I know. But I would like George to go over it once more. I'm a little dense. Could you George?"

"You aren't dense. This is new for you and it takes a while to sink in. Think of the Necker cube again. I'll make it easy for you. Look at it," he says as he grabs the sheet of paper he drew the lattice and Necker image on, adds numbers to the image, and places it in front of them.

"I start at the bottom, which you labeled zero on your stretched-out figure to the left of the Necker cube. I can move laterally either to the left or to the right, or straight up to three.

"Then I have a linear choice either to the left or the right or straight ahead. You can then make binary choices all the way to the top, which represents the seventh homicide. To make the story simple, all the paths in the Necker cube are linear, with no breaks. You okay so far?"

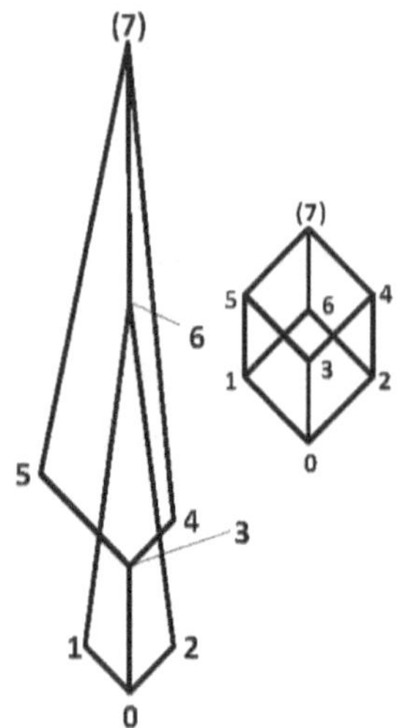

"Yes," Lucia and Mike say in unison.

"Now look at our elongated lattice. You see? If you begin at zero, you can proceed to the left, to the right, or straight ahead. If you go to the left or the right, you have no choice but to head for murder number six and on to seven. If you go straight, with another step you're on the top of the world. But you can't go from two to four or one to five in linear fashion. You must go to six and then straight ahead to seven. Yet, all the lines and junctures can become interconnected."

"How's that?" Lucia asks. "The lines seem more disconnected than in the Necker cube."

"We make the connections! From our three-dimensional view above the diagram. We can see the whole affair all at once. So, including time into the equation, in a fleeting moment we can take that magic leap from two to four or one to five. Then move on to seven. Beautiful isn't it?"

"What are the implications of this?" Mike hesitatingly ventures to ask. "The easy answer is, logical implications. But it's logic of a different kind."

"Then it must be illogical," Mike says with apparent doubt.

"If you want to put it that way, okay. I'll explain it. But keep in mind that I will be repeating myself for emphasis. Moving along the Necker cube lines is a matter of linear, context free operations. But moving along our lattice to the left involves nonlinear, multivalent, complementary and context dependent operations. The lattice includes *both* nonlinear discontinuous jumps from two to four and one to five within four dimensions, including time, and *neither* of the two jumps, since we might linearly have slid from one to three within three dimensions."

"What do you mean when you say 'context dependent'? It's just lines on a blank page. What does context have to do with it?" Lucia asks.

"Ah, you're making the obvious assumption. You're thinking of the line and numbers on a flat plane. I'm thinking of them on a map. There, they aren't limited to two dimensions. They are three dimensional, and time introduces a fourth dimension."

"Please explain."

"Any move up the lattice demands a different form of logic. You know what usually goes as logical principles. There's *Identity*—what is, is, and it can't be anything else. *Noncontradiction*—what is, is eternally divorced from what it isn't and the twain shall never meet. And the *Excluded-middle*—there is either what is or what isn't, and no third possibility. Anyway, I'm oversimplifying in order to get to the point."

"Which is?" Lucia asks.

"The incomplete lattice's logic knows no *complete* and stable *identity*. It allows for occasional *contradictions* or *inconsistencies*. And it always presents many *possibilities*."

"But," Mike wishes to protest, "from zero on the Necker cube we have three choices, not two."

"Ah yes. However, you are beginning from zero. At the zero-point, all possible choices are open, with no problem at all. At the beginning you have the lattice limiting you to three. But actually, there are more alternative possibilities. Many more. A virtually countless number of them. Like this."

George takes pen in hand again and traces out an image. "See? The lattice can become incomprehensibly complex when we begin with zero.

It's smarter than I am, because of its mindboggling multiplicity. And it's certainly smarter than that mechanical monster you call X-Man.

"That's why he simplifies matters tremendously. If he understood the complexity of what he is doing, his megalomania might turn him into a mass killer. But he isn't. He's a psychopathic serial killer. He takes things one step at a time"—

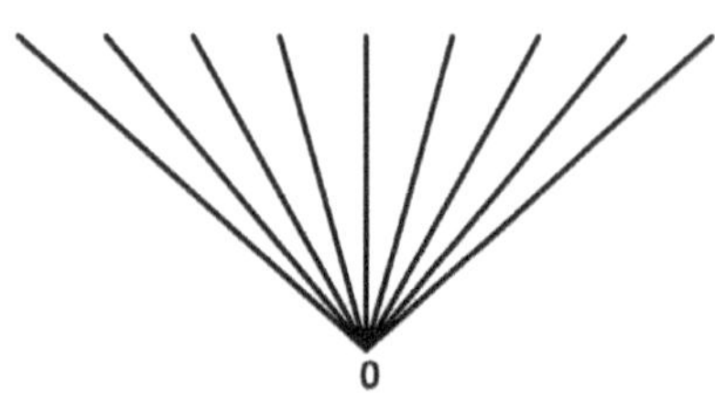

"Wait a minute, George," Lucia pipes up. "Suppose the murdering maniac had taken your lattice in all its complexity into consideration. We would have to survey the whole range of contexts in the city. We would have to be aware of the entire scheme depicting all the possible homicides before we could know what he is up to.

"We would have to know the nature of all those possibilities before we could effectively appraise the nature of whatever choice he happened to make for each of his crimes. Is that it?"

"Exactly. But you're lucky. He made it relatively easy for you. Because he often thinks like a robot of mediocre intelligence. In linear fashion."

"Hm ..."

"Now," George nods, "go out and work your tails off. But relax while doing it. If not, you might miss a lot of details. More coffee?"

"We would like to sit for a while, but we have to get our noses back on the grindstone," Lucia responds.

"Thanks for enlightening us," Mike says as he vigorously shakes George's hand, saying to himself, *If the killer thinks along the lines George recommends with his clever tricks, then who is he? Could it really be someone close to home? ... in the department? ...*

Lucia gives George a healthy hug as he kisses her on each cheek, Brazilian style. Mike is amused. They leave.

"Geometry. Like I said, I was never any good at it," Mike mutters as they get in the car. "What intrigues me is this," he turns to Lucia with an inquisitive eye. "How in the world did you manage to come up with your scheme ... or what you and George call a lattice? How can you be so sure you're on the right track? How can you prove what you created?"

"You're guess is as good as mine. I never gave up thinking about it. When I was so exhausted, I couldn't hold myself together any longer, I conked out—sometimes on my sofa. I had dreams about it. Then it finally came to me out of the blue. From things I learned in college, from George, and from readings over the years. There was lightning and thunder, and suddenly it was there.

"Somehow, I knew I had it. But I didn't know how ... or why. To this moment I can't say by what series of steps I got there, or how it works. It defies words. Yet, I feel it. In my gut."

Mike says, "This feeling of knowing without the ability to say it is a mystery. It seems so absurd, but if you don't follow your feelings when you feel there is something important about what they are telling you, then how can you find a proper answer? If you don't follow your feelings, then what you'll end up with will be humdrum."

"Yeah ... well ... when you have the rest of the mystery figured out, clue me in."

"Fat chance, Lucia."

GETTING UNDER HER SKIN?

ON their way to home base, Lucia says, "Back there I felt my second phone vibrating impulsively, but I didn't want to interrupt George. Let me check it out."

She rolls her eyes, "Who would have guessed it?"

Mike shakes his head, "He doesn't miss a trick. Does he?"

Lucia reads,

> *Ah, my fair lady. 'Twas a wondrous day when I had my first high. A nice woman, but too old. So, she had to pay the price. This brings up a question. What if I had made you the target of my first encounter in a previous time? Before you became the notorious detective you now are? But if you had not yet become notorious, then why would I bother to target you?*

"Lucia," Mike looks at her with concern all over his face. "That's precisely what George was worried about."

"He's still trying to get my goat. But he won't. I'll see to that."

"He has me worried. How can you know he's not seriously thinking about targeting you?"

"I don't know, but I doubt it."

"Well, you're tougher than I am."

"Not really. I just try to put him out of my mind when he gets personal with me. And focus on getting the son of a bitch. That's all."

"I wish I had your self-control."

"Focus on his words, not his person. His words are nothing but hollow signs, because his head is empty of human sentiment. Notice how he twists everything around and creates contradictions and quandaries, if not to say paradoxes. He says he wouldn't have targeted me before, because then I merited no notoriety. This implies he targets notorious people so he will become equally notorious in his own way. Well, were all his victims notorious? Hell no. Ordinary people. What he says is nothing more than wishful thinking."

"Because he's playacting?" Mike asks.

"Yes. Where's the real X-Man? There is none. He is who he is only in the play context."

"Like in a movie where there is either James Bond or Stan Katz, but no Sean Connery. Is that what you mean, Luce?"

"Yes ... but no. Sean Connery knows who he is. X-Man has been playacting for so long I doubt he any longer knows he is nobody. He's played so many roles he is nothing but his roles. He lost his own private self."

"Then what is his role as a real person?" Mike is still groping.

"As a human animal he's terribly incomplete. Because if you put all his roles in one bag, they cancel out, and you have nothing but inconsistency. Once again, it's like pronouncing the simple assertion, 'I am lying'."

"I see," Mike says. "If it's true it's false, and if it's false it's true. And it's both true and false, and it's neither true nor false."

"That's our X-Man," Lucia says. "He thinks he's somebody but he's nobody. Or perhaps he's like Alice through the looking glass. The difference is that he can't go back to who he was because then, he was somebody else. He is now an alienated self. And he can't project into the future because if he does, he will become somebody else alienated from who he now thinks he is."

"Is he living in some imaginary doublespeak wonderland? Where *true* becomes *talse* and *false* becomes *frue*? Where *green* becomes *grue* and *blue* becomes *bleen*? This is where we've been since square-one. So Like George said, from zero, *grue* and *bleen* are possibilities, like *green* and *blue*. Everything *is* interconnected. Isn't it, Luce?"

"In a way of putting it, yes." Lucia concedes. "The killer entered a world where everything is becoming different, and he's confused. He wants clear-cut answers and tries to cut his world up accordingly. But it's a muddle."

"Sort of schizophrenic I'd say. Within his psychopathic world he still wants to think he knows what he's doing and can do no wrong."

"Schizophrenia? You're probably right. His condition reminds me of *Macunaíma*, a fictive character without clear and distinct characteristics in a Brazilian novel. He is a combination of native Brazilian Indian, European, and African. A grand multi-chromatic mixture. He is supposed to embody all Brazilians. But who is he? Everybody and nobody. An imaginary character. That's all."

"Ah, something like Robert Musil's unfinished novel, *The Man without Qualities*," Mike chips in. "But X-Man is no character in a novel. He kills real people."

"Unfortunately. We live our lives in a mixture of the imaginary and the real. That's the problem. Imagination can absorb reality like a cosmic amoeba. It becomes the only reality."

ENOUGH *useless contemplation*, Lucia thinks. *It's nothing but mind spinning metaphysics.*

Mike is numbed by the verbiage that poured out of his and Lucia's mouth. He's paying more attention to his driving. It is rush hour mayhem.

Despite herself, Lucia contemplates her surroundings. A bag lady toting her bag at the side of a business suit. Three teen girls in their gaudy outfits. Two cosmetically transformed women coming out of a clothing store. Two white teens joking and slapping each other while they briskly ambulate along. A taxi driver hollering obscenities in well-nigh unintelligible English at the adjacent driver in a Jaguar. A hooded twenty-something ambling at a lackadaisical pace.

Talk about gender, ethnic, and occupational, social, and financial mixture! Fuse them together and what do you have? Everybody? Yes. But no. Nobody, nothing, nada, emptiness. Like *Macunaíma*.

"Or like X-Man. Or like all these people composing George's diagram momentarily becoming One," she says in a muffled voice.

"What?" Mike asks. "Nothing, literally nothing."

She thinks, *X-Man. Thinks he's somebody but he isn't. Picasso once said, "I'm still an atheist, thank God." X-Man is still X-Man, thanks to his victims and the press and TV and the public and me and Mike. Other than that, he's nothing. And yet, all that nothing is in a playact world becoming something.*

If I succeed in my effort to get into his mind, dwell within his head, will I become nothing as well? Will I be me and X-Man and nobody? Do we ever cease our playacting? Or becoming who we genuinely are? Becoming, but never completing our becoming in order to just be? *Does "be" have no way to just "be"? Is "being" always in the act of "becoming"? The "being" of "becoming" and the "becoming" of "being"?*

What confusion!

LUCIA cringes, then says, "You know, Mike?"

"What?"

"I was thinking."

"What's new? I've never seen you unthinking. Unless you're unthinking your thinking or thinking your unthinking," Mike says.

Lucia chuckles and tells him, "Witty, and you put your finger on what I had in mind."

"Oh? What's that?"

"Thinking is always unthinking previous thinking because it's always thinking anew."

"Come again?"

"Portuguese and Spanish, the other two widely spoken languages on this continent, have two verbs for the English 'to be'."

Mike emits a disinterested, "Oh." Then he feigns a passive degree of interest and asks, "How's that?"

"There's *ser*, to be, as a presumed relatively permanent condition. And there's *estar*, to be, as a temporary or transitive condition, which is never the same as what it was. Of course, I'm simplifying a complicated quality of the two languages for the purpose of illustration."

"Of course," Mike voices, as if he was into the conversation.

"X-Man is nothing but transitive. He's always becoming different. Like *Macunaíma* I mentioned earlier. Or like your *Man without qualities*. He's never who he was and he'll never be who he is because he's always a different play-actor."

"Then who is he?"

"There you go. English. 'Who *is* he?' as if there were something enduring about him. But there isn't. Whoever he now *is*, he *isn't*, because he's always becoming somebody else. He can be labeled in the manner of *estar*, but never *ser*. Because he has no stable self. In other words, there is no static *is* with respect to X-Man."

"Something like Alice you mean?"

"Right."

Mike nods, "This means we'll never catch up with him. Him, who he *is*. Because when he's nabbed, he'll have become someone else. So, he can't be completely guilty. Yet, he may become like a true-blue psychopath," Mike chuckles. "Always becoming someone other than who he was becoming. Devoid of sympathy, empathy, sentiment, moral fiber, and ethical composure."

"Yes." Lucia agrees. "Is this not to say that we, all people, are of the same nature? Playacting? Always becoming somebody else? But we cannot *be* who we *were, are*, and *will have been*? Because we're always becoming someone other than who we were becoming."

MIKE pulls the vehicle to a stop. "Well, here we are" Mike tells Lucia as if he hadn't heard a word of what she was saying. Lucia turns her attention to the task at hand as if she had put her words completely out of her mind.

"Where?"

"Here. You remember? Our next task entailed checking out a possible witness."

"Oh yes, that." *Preferable,* Lucia tells herself. *Because my empty thinking will get us nowhere.*

They knock on the door. Footsteps approach. The knob turns. The door opens. A squirrel faced creep looks at them. They identify themselves in the guise of apparently *being* somebody, detectives. He pulls a questioning face as if he acknowledged what he takes as their *identityless* identity, or *becoming*. And motions them in.

They enter. Look around. A disheveled two-room apartment that probably hasn't been cleaned for a year.

Squirrel-face hasn't said a word. Mike asks if he is Jim Brock. He nods.

Lucia asks if he told two law enforcers he saw the suspected killer after he let go of his victim who collapsed to the sidewalk, dead.

Jim nods.

Lucia asks for a description.

Jim says nothing. Looks at them with expressionless eyes. Mike gets rough.

"Speak up, we haven't got all day. Did you see the suspected killer or didn't you?"

Jim nods, with no more expression than a deer in the headlights.

"Well, tell us about him. What did he look like?"

"I ... No ... I don't know," as if he was in a scatterbrain process of becoming, deprived of being.

"What do you mean you don't know?" Lucia asks him, her voice reaching maximum intensity.

"I ... I didn't see him very well."

"Very well? Then describe him not very well. What did he look like not very well? Speak up or you are going to headquarters with us as a suspected accomplice."

"No ... please."

"Then speak up! Dammit."

"Okay ... he was like big."

"How big?" Mike asks.

"Big. Probably twice my weight."

"Color of hair, eyes, skin, special features?"

"I ... I can't say. He looked at me ..."

"Okay, he looked at you. So what?" Lucia is losing patience.

"I froze. Then he said, 'You didn't see this, punk, and if you say you did, you signed your death warrant.' I was scared!"

"That does it. Let's go to headquarters," Lucia says as she makes a motion to pull out her handcuffs.

"No wait. I think he was white, dark hair, and all that."

"All what?" Mike says grabbing him by the shoulder and turning him around so he could stick his face in Jim's face.

"You know ..."

"No, I don't. Tell me."

"He was, like a robot, with eyes that go through you."

"That doesn't tell us much. Did he have a moustache, beard, what kind of clothes?"

"No."

"No, what?" Mike gives him a shove.

"No moustache ... or beard either. His eyes were big and wide open. Like he was stoned or something ... He wore ... dirty flannel."

"Now we're getting somewhere. How did he walk? A shuffle, like he was drunk?"

"I don't know."

"Didn't you see him walk away."

"No, I turned around and got away from him."

"You pathetic piece of shit," Mike says in a high-pitched shriek, "If you see him again, here's my card. Call me."

"Yes ... When?"

"If you see him again, then," Lucia says. "I hope I don't see him ..."

THEY leave.

"Speaking of nobody who is nothing," Lucia mumbles.

"What a waste of time," Mike mutters in support of Lucia's words. "You were awfully rough on him, Mike. I'm sure that contributed to his panic."

"All I wanted was to get something out of him."

"You ought to go easier on those poor souls."

"I guess. When I see 'I'm lying' or 'I know nothing' written all over their face, I want to push my rough-them-up button."

"Just don't push your sadism button."

"Yeah ... I guess."

And so it goes.

TRUE LIES?

LUCIA asks Bob that evening at his apartment, "What is your experience with high schoolers who turned to drugs, delinquency, and gangs."

"I've had a few run-ins with them. Why do you ask?"

"Mike and I entered so many blind alleys in our investigation of this killer that we have nowhere else to go. I was wondering how the killer might have been when he was between fifteen and eighteen."

"At that stage in life they almost invariably fall into one of a possible number of vague stereotypes."

"Tell me about them."

"I'll try. They begin tuning out of school and extracurricular activities and tuning into the marginal culture. Grades that were usually low take a nose dive. Attention in the classroom vanishes. Participation ceases. When the bell rings they say nothing. Simply put their heads down and slouch out the door.

"Sometimes I dismiss class a couple of minutes early and ask one of them to stay. I ask him if he's okay. But getting him to say something is like squeezing blood out of a turnip. He hangs his head, mopes, and tells me nothing.

"The next day, if I happen to see him on the street, he's with sinisterlooking guys, probably members of some gang. They're all talking, laughing, jabbing at each other. He's now in an entirely new environment."

"Like they've lost their previous human qualities?"

"Yes. Because in the classroom they simply go through the necessary motions. No more. They've become, like ... nobody ... Oh yes. There's something else. I know few of them who really fit into the school crowd, even before the change came over them.

"Since they aren't social animals by nature, other students sometimes make snide remarks about them, ridicule them, mock them, laugh at them. I can tell it bothers them deeply. But they make no effort to defend themselves verbally, though they often resort to breaking out in physical violence."

"Girl friends? Interest in sex?"

"Usually not. At times, I've suspected homosexuality. But I doubt it was that in most all cases. They steal looks at the girls when nobody is noticing. But I hardly ever see any personal interaction with the other sex. Probably due to their lack of social amenities."

"Problems at home?"

"That I don't know. Since I never get them to talk to me, really talk, I learn hardly anything about their home life. I suspect it is considerably less than ideal, however."

"Yeah, well thanks."

"Might I suggest some wine with the pasta I cooked up?"

"Please. Following your observations, I'm now more like the Lucia you would prefer to know."

The evening turns out to be a screaming success. Good wine and pasta. Classical music and smooth jazz. Amiable talk on a positive note. Touching, embracing, kissing, and the best bedtime fun in a long time.

The next morning, Lucia fixes breakfast. She and Bob are all smiles.

HER smile flees once she's at headquarters. It's the same strain and stress sweatshop. Last night with Bob she felt her second phone's tell-tale vibration, but ignored it. Now she takes a look, and,

> Twas CSI and Hawaiian Eye; and fansic fores
> who spoved I loy.

"Now it's limericks by e-mail, and no crime?" she spontaneously evokes. There is a footnote following the memo,

I say my name and disappear; what am I?

Good God! Shall I even so much as share this with Mike? she thinks. *No. Let it fly by and wait to see what happens. Keep your cool. Let me see. This is the twenty-sixth day. How much longer to go? George said between thirty-eight and forty days. Around two weeks.*

What to do until then? What can we work on? No data in, nothing gained. Work on one of the other cases that have been lodged in the computer files? How frustrating!

Shortly thereafter, it's the press again. Lucia fields many of the same questions while she's thinking, *Don't they tire of going over the same terrain time and time again? Don't they learn anything from my unwillingness to divulge information that might rile up the public or inform the perp? Can't they occupy their minds with a few novel news items? They want the latest. But if everybody gets it from the press conference, will their columns not carry a ditto sign with a capital "D"? Why don't they wise up for a change? Get a life?*

Yet she maintains composure in front of the press. She never insults them, chides them, or loses her temper. After all is said, she wishes them the best with a big smile on her face.

"*Well,*" Lucy concludes once she is back in the office, *I might as well pick up a deck of cards and play solitaire for a couple of weeks.*

DON'T *be so negative, Lucia,* she continues. *Right, I need to talk with somebody before I end up in the loony bin. George? Later, when I've thought this out better. April? April Beaumont, my old classmate? Yes.*

Lucia calls April, sets up a time and day. They become later today. She travels across town. And finds April as remarkably vivacious as usual.

"Been a long time," April says.

"Hasn't it. And here I am with the pretext for seeing you when I wanted to get out of that rat race at headquarters. Embarrassing, isn't it?"

"Not at all. You're here. That's what counts."

April rose to full professor of psychology status after four scant years. The screaming success of her recent book did it. Shortly thereafter, she suffered from a divorce that ended up with her the loser. She was the main bread winner, but he demanded high stakes. She caved in and accepted a raw deal just to get rid of him. Fortunately, her rise to fame in the academic world compensated her.

April has coffee and tidbits prepared on her dinette table. After a few additional sociable formalities, customary breeze shooting follows.

She applauds Lucia's reputation as a crack investigator, her citations, medals, and acclaim. Lucia shrugs them off, and changes the topic. Making a ninety-degree turn to the series of crimes she is now working on …

April remarks, "How bizarre. How out of the groove of the usual criminal mind stereotypes? How brash can this psychopath get? What are his hang-ups anyway?"

"He's got me at my wits end," Lucia confesses.

April says, "I've kept up on the details as much as possible. But it's hard to separate the wheat from the chaff. You know? The press stretches the truth as usual. The public's letters to the editor tell you on no uncertain terms what you should be doing. The mayor talks as if the case could be solved over-night. I don't know how you can put up with it."

"I know," Lucia mutters. "I should tolerate them even if their intolerance tends to destroy the possibility of my tolerance. I have to grit my teeth, maintain my composure, and consider the source."

"I think I would tell them to fuck off, turn my back on them, and bug out."

Lucia laughs, "The thought has occurred to me."

"What *are* your thoughts about this case?"

Lucia tells April about the baffling messages, the riddles, e-mails, and texting he sends her. April chuckles occasionally, shakes her head often, emits a few streams of profanity, and in general sympathizes with Lucia.

THEN Lucia puts on a more serious face.

"I'm up against a blank wall," Lucia begins. "Don't know where to turn."

"Tell me about it."

Lucia unloads her dilemma on April in considerable detail. She ends with, "So you see? George gave me this rigorous geometry scheme that I don't dare reveal to the boss or my colleagues at work, much less to the press or public. Yet, I feel I should pursue the idea, no matter how labyrinthine it may become."

"By all means you should."

"I'm becoming obsessed with the killer's foibles and quirks, his doublespeak, the perplexing ambiguity of his talk and actions."

"Doublespeak. You know there are doublespeak whizzes running around these days, and this killer is obviously one of the best. You must become as adept at it as he is."

"I wish I could," Lucia says, "but he's always a step ahead of me."

"Defense is more difficult than offence. In basketball, the offensive guard has all the choices before him while the defensive player can only guess what his opponent's next move might be. In a car chase, the pursued makes unexpected moves, and the pursuer must resort to second guessing him.

"Speaking of doublespeak, your killer has the freedom to make a decision from among all the word combinations and their rhetorical variations. You have no alternative but to wait until he messages you, then you can set up your strategy."

"I know. It's exasperating."

"He's obviously a brilliant artist of deceit. We find deception throughout nature. Fireflies are devious. They mimic and disguise themselves as predators to frighten off rivals and win the lady of their choice. Some spiders spin webs that reflect ultraviolet light unwary insects take as the petals of flowers and they hone in, only to find they have become prey to the wily arachnid. Butterfly's open wings have evolved to look like dangerous predators used to ward off their own predators.

"Charles Darwin took these insects as a key to human origins and our vast array of methods for guile, subterfuge, deception, and out-and-out lies."

"Fits the killer to a T."

"I gathered so much according to the way you describe him. Enlightenment thought told us the universe is a harmonious symphony. Balancing apparently inconsistent notes into a pleasing melody and its complementary harmony. Enlightenment philosophers believed mathematics, logic, and reason could explain it.

"Contemporary physics, mathematics, logic and chaos theory are now telling us that things are not as cut-and-dried as we would like to believe."

"Yes, my uncle has said so much."

"To his credit, Darwin focused on the world's disharmonies, inconsistencies, anomalies, and all the rough spots. Therein, we find the origin of doublespeak. You should look there for answers. Doublespeak can allow you the opportunity to find the killer's weak spots. Perhaps you should resist the desire to find the truth about your murderer.

"It is much easier to find error than truth. Error is almost everywhere. Truth hides. Deceptive artists, whether magician, charlatan, stand-up comedian, crook, and yes, even college professors, are mysteries to be deciphered. Like the punch line of a joke. Or like doublespeak. In other words, look at the differences in terms of errors, deception, and lies."

Lucia laughs, and says, "Yeah, sure. The truth is madcap while a lie reveals its own truth, which is its untruth, but it is truth. Is that kind of what you're suggesting? That the truth I'm looking for contains its own untruth?"

April chuckles. "The way you put it, yes, and no. Forget about truth in the sense of clear, distinct and rational determination. When a new truth becomes tentatively known, it initially presents itself as so dark, ambiguous, and many-sided, that it can't be explained in ordinary language. Only in terms of paradox, inconsistency, and incompleteness.

"Then, after a few generations it miraculously becomes as commonplace as you would like. Think of Copernicus's idea that the sun, not the earth, is the center of the universe. Think of relativity theory."

"Now you're talking like my uncle."

April grins, and says, "You flatter me. But if George says something comparable, I must agree."

"Then truth becomes fiction," Lucia adds. "Fiction, whose lies can contain more truth than truth itself insofar as we can understand the fiction but cannot say exactly what truth is."

"So to speak, yes."

"The same April. Charming, witty, and brilliant."

"More flattery, Lucia?"

Conversation turns to reminiscence about the old days. A couple of hours later, Lucia bids farewell and leaves on a positive note.

What a pleasant break from the usual! she says to herself. *If I had time to do something like this every day, I might become easy to live with.*

BACK in her apartment, Lucia texts Bob and sits down to stare at the newscast on her ancient TV. No big screen NASCAR or football for her. She's all work, and maybe a little play when time permits.

That's the relatively stodgy American in her. But actually, she has assimilated the notion that her work is a small dose of gaming and a massive dose of playing. That must be the ethnically amorphous Brazilian in her. She's pleased with the combination.

However, her syncopated rhythm swerves, as her mind takes a turn toward doublespeak.

Let me see here. You have the front side of the emasculated Necker cube and the back side, the first below and the second above. Or vice versa. The first is a sort of preamble or appetizer to the second, which is the argument or main course. From there you move upward toward a flurry outbreak of interpretations, which can lead to a terrible case of mental indigestion.

Well, Lucia ol' gal, let's work on that. The first square directs you toward belief and presumably truth. The second square reveals it is ultimately a lie. The first is straight-forward language. The second is rhetorical through and through—by way of Frue *and* Talse, *if I might use Mike's example.*

The first garbs itself up as fact. The second provocatively reveals its fiction. The first is one side of the looking glass. The second is the world confronting you after you crash through it. The Cheshire cat's smile, the emperor's new clothes, Nixon's "*I am not a crook*," Clinton's "*I did not have sex with that woman,*" *and so on.*

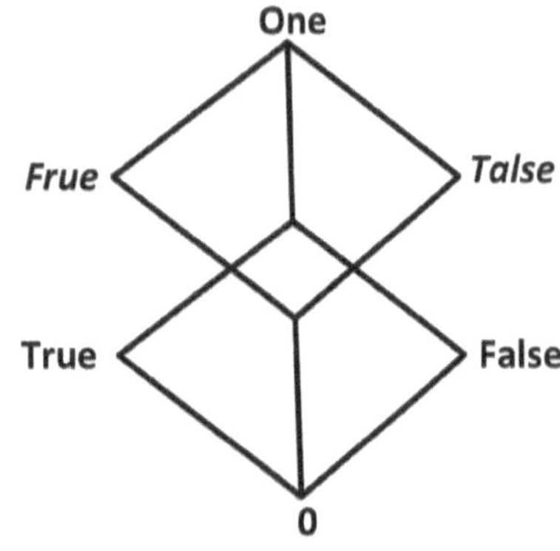

It's a mixing of genuine and sham reality, appearance and artifice, what is expected and subtle sleight of hand maneuvers.

Okay! Now let's look at this from another angle. There's ordinary language at one level and there's a second level consisting of rhetorical verbiage crying out for deciphering as if it was a riddle. Then there's the riddle at that second level, and it, too, is comprehensible only with proper deciphering. At these two levels we have true, false, *and* meaningless *or* nonsense, *until we crack the code and discover what there really is.*

We must complete the message, solve the riddle, get to the punch line, clean up the apparent inconsistency. We must grasp the gist of playacting. Sean Connery, James Bond, or Stan Katz? They flow into one another, becoming fused and confused. They are becoming One, but they are Three.

Her mind takes her to that massive cultural manifestation of mind-boggling coalescent mixture called Brazil when she was young. In 1992 President Fernando Collor de Mello was undergoing impeachment for fleecing the country of millions of dollars. Congress was on the verge of arriving at a decision.

Meanwhile a host of Brazilians were entranced by a wildly popular TV series, *De Corpo e Alma* (Of Heart and Soul). Actress Daniella Pérez played the role of Yasmin, an innocent young ticket puncher on a Rio bus line. She had an obsessively jealous boyfriend, Bira the bus driver, played by Guilherme de Pádua.

Daniella tasted real-world murder while the play was in progress revealing Yasmin's death after a Bira streak of jealousy. Within hours, Guilherme confessed he killed Daniella. Stating it was the consequence of his out-of-control jealousy.

"In the TV public's eyes, it was as if Bira had killed Yasmin, and he later confessed. It was a matter of fiction and nonfiction coalescing and becoming One. So much confusing confabulation.

*Did Bira kill Daniella—*Lucia muses just for the hell of it—*or was it Guilherme who killed Yasmin? The whole scenario was in a* *process of fuzziness becoming. The Brazilian public gravitated toward identity of Bira as Guilherme or vice versa, and of Yasmin as Daniella or vice versa. Mixing fiction with reality.*

Like Stan Katz or James Bond becoming confused with Sean Connery. Or for a stretch of the imagination, the psychopathic killer confused with looking glass X-Man.

To make a long story short, outrage over Daniella's—or was it Yasmin's?—murder went viral. Guilherme—or was it Bira?—became the target of popular culture opprobrium.

At the same time, as far as popular culture went, the Brazilian Senate's project of impeaching Collor de Mello faded into the collective conscious background.

In contrast, the politically inclined public witnessed the President's impeachment process. True to their wishes, it came to pass.

Newscasts blared, headlines highlighted the affair, and foreign correspondents scrambled to get a piece of the action. Elites and much of the middle-class were euphoric. This was the first time a Latin American president was impeached for corruption.

Nevertheless, many of Brazil's working class pushed the event aside in favor of Daniella and Guilherme, Bira and Jazmin. After all, Collor de Mello was merely a politician. Politicians are as they do; they do next to nothing other than practice corruption; ignorance of their crooked doing becomes the choice alternative. Understandably, politics harvested little interest among working class citizens.

Consequently, delirium poured forth during Daniella's funeral. It took place shortly after her murder and Guilherme's confession. A mere few hours after Collor de Mello submitted his resignation while insisting he was innocent of all charges. Onlookers of the funeral paid little attention to the president's demise. Their objective focused on mourning for Daniella-Yazmin.

When the surviving actors of the TV series appeared on the funeral scene, one by one, there was boisterous applause, screams, and whistling. Autographs were signed. People climbed over gravestones to get a better look, often knocking each other down in their attempt to get closer to the action. Photographers and reporters were everywhere. Security police were scarce. To top it all off, the Rio heat was sweltering.

Whether Daniella's murder or the president's impeachment was in the minds of the Brazilians, neither of the two cases was ever completely resolved. Incompleteness and inconsistency continued to rule more than clarity and distinction.

LUCIA also recalls a personal account neurologist Oliver Sacks narrates about a group of aphasiacs. Sacks hears roaring laughter from the patients. His curiosity gets the best of him. He enters the hallway and proceeds to the room where the hubbub is at.

President Ronald Reagan is giving a talk on TV. The great communicator, the actor with his practiced and polished rhetoric, has many of them howling with amusement. Others are bewildered. Some are outraged.

What was going on?

After some thought on the matter, Sacks gets it. While the aphasiacs understand the president's words only to a certain degree, given their aphasia, they understand his nonverbal languages all too well. And they know, or at least they think they know, he is deceiving his audience.

They had some vague feeling for the irony of it all, Lucia reflects. *Irony. Emerging from the facts and nothing but the facts.*

Irony, the use of a words to convey the opposite of what they ordinarily mean. Such as a child looking out the airliner window and saying, "Wow, it sure is high down there." Irony plays havoc with the search for clear and distinct ideas, logical consistency, rational certainty, and hard-rock truth that culminates in the Enlightenment distrust of folk knowledge, common sense, vagueness, ambiguity, and myth.

Irony is usually subtle enough for the observer to know that the whole truth and nothing but the truth is out of reach and can be approached only tangentially or indirectly. It is a form of truth when taken as what is not.

It is words drawing attention to their deception, their frailty, and their limitations.

Irony spoils faith in word use and it avoids naïve belief in language's power. Like lying, irony makes mincemeat of the hopeful security that words mean what they say, with due respects to Humpty Dumpty.

Lucia imagines her ruminations plotted on George's lattice hopefully to shed light on the issue. The first square includes Daniella, Guilherme, and tragic death, or Collor de Mello and impeachment-guilt. The second square involves Yasmin and Bira, or with respect to Collor de Mello, resignation-innocence.

The first square is Reagan on the TV screen. The second is the Reagan of nonverbal cues read by the patients in the aphasiac ward.

Fact in the lower square and fiction in the upper one. Reality in the lower one and imagination in the upper one. The lattice can contain literal language and rhetoric.

Lucia's thoughts return full force, *Oh yes, conventional words and portmanteau renditions, X-Man style! If I put Blue and Green below and Grue and Bleen above, then at the top I have Grue and Bleen and the entire spectrum of possible colors and their names making up One,* she thinks while she grabs paper and pen and draws a variation of the matrix.

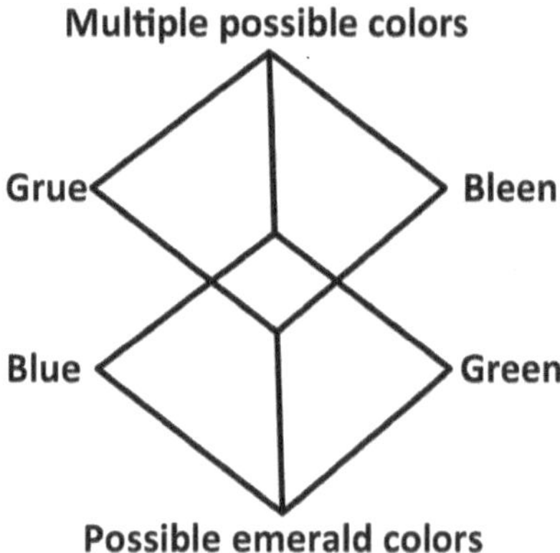

The two colors have coalesced, becoming One, One in George's way of putting it. I can do the same with all the killer's portmanteau words discussed thus far. Becoming Many, but One.

"So, Lucia," she blurts out, "did you solve the killer's crimes with proper dispatch?"

"Through rhetoric?"

"Good grief! I've got to be nuts!"

"Anyway, so much for fiction and fact, inaccessible true reality and faked authenticity, a presumed actual world and imaginary wandering, logic and wavering alogical uncertainty."

MORE GEORGE WISDOM TO THE FORE

THE next morning, Lucia senses she has changed her approach to the killer. Moreover, she's discovering a sense of herself becoming other than who she was becoming. As a consequence, she's becoming more confident.

More confident? she asks herself. *I was at the top of the heap. I thought I had reached the ultimate level of achievement. At least that's what voices and reports led me to believe.*

Now I know my pretentions were a fraud, that I still have a long way to go, that I must strive always to inch a little bit forward, then some more, and more again. I'm not the same Lucia I was.

Her thoughts return to X-Man's last message,

Okay, she begins. "Fansic fores" ... Fanfare? ... No way ... Well, then forensic fans, yes! Spoy ... Proved ... Spy, love ... I Spy, okay! So, it's about TV series and crime busting. Now, the riddle, "I say my name and disappear"?

Uh ... This one's tricky. So ... uh ... disappear after saying his name ... Or his name as a mere word? Don't know. Can't tell. Where to, then? Nothingness? The name ... But it is not what the name says.

A perverted form of irony? X-Man already sent a puzzle the answer for which was nothing or nothingness. I doubt he would do it again. So ... Mike, where are you?

SHE calls Mike to show him the latest riddle. They diddle back and forth by phone for a minute or so. He tells her he will be over in a sec ... Ah, there he is now.

"Luce, you never give up."

"I think we're on the final lap."

"I hope the hell so."

"You got any more ideas, Mike?"

"Not at this moment. Let's put on our thinking caps and go at it."

"I'm game. Why don't you take the baton and I'll follow?"

"I'll try ... Okay. The butcher sporting a psycho mask writes, 'What am I?' not 'Who am I?' It's not about himself but about a name, and the presumed object of the name disappearing. In a vacuum, no less."

"Doesn't make much sense, does it?"

"You are right. But ... What about Heraclitus and the river you can't step in twice. If you can't step in the same river twice you can't genuinely repeat its name. Why? Because it will have become a different river demanding another name. No?"

"Unlikely ... But ... I'm at a loss for words," Lucia admits.

"Maybe that's it. A word. You say it, and it spontaneously disappears."

"It disappears and leaves silence. But it's still in your mind. So it hasn't entirely disappeared, has it?"

"No ... Well then, what about a particular word? Such as, say, "Silence."

"Silence?"

"Yes."

"Ah! Of course! That's it!" Lucia blurts out. "Silence. It demands that once you utter a word, it cannot continue as such. Because of the changing nature of its meaning. By a comparable token, solve the riddle and you miss the boat. Because the object of the riddle is now other than what it was.

"This last riddle complements some of his previous riddles. Resolving this riddle cancels solution of all those previous riddles to which this riddle refers. Why didn't I think of that?"

"Hey. Do you want a monopoly on all the answers?"

"Not at all. But I *would* like to have the answer once in a while."

WHILE Mike contemplates the phrase further, Lucia checks her e-mail, and shouts out, "That perverted fag! Get a load of this."

She shows her iPhone to Mike. He reads it out loud, I go in hard; I come out soft; you blow me hard; what am I?

He looks at her. She looks at him. He discharges a verbal evocation that turns heads sharply toward Lucia's office window. Lucia says, "On top of everything else he's the consummate sexists!"

"Be careful when you say that. He hasn't revealed such an obsession over sex until now," Mike advises.

"He could have been suppressing it."

"True. But we should be working on the meaning of this last puzzle."

"Last?" Lucia says.

"Yes, last. I'm sticking with George's interpretation and hoping for the best until I learn otherwise."

"I suppose so. Well, what do we have here then? In hard, out soft, something you blow up, and it becomes hard again ... Hmm ... Smelting pig iron and turning it into steel? There's some annealing going on."

"But there's no blowing," Mike interjects. "At least in the conventional sense. Billowing yes. In the iron mill."

"I was thinking balloon. But it doesn't go in hard."

"The answer, or clue as it were, will happen while we're waiting," Mike suggests. "How many times have we heard and used the phrase 'Wait around and see what happens'?"

"Oh. Like *Waiting for Godot*.

"What's that?"

"Samuel Beckett's play. You recall? During one of our chats?"

"Oh yes. Waiting for an earth-shaking event that never happens."

"And that bastard thinks he's Godot, God. What a dick head!" Lucia emphasizes.

"You said it."

MIKE departs. Lucia begins mindlessly filing papers. After a couple of minutes, she smiles, snaps the fingers of her right hand, makes a fist with it, and gives with a firm "Yes!"

She goes over to Mike's desk and says, "Gum," with a smile from ear to ear.

"Gum what?" Mike asks.

"You know. Bubble gum. Blowing bubbles."

"Oh, no! I'm losing my touch and you're beating me at my game."

"Bubble gum," Lucia repeats. "God damn. And we're supposed to find some relevance to this muddle?"

"That key goes in hard, gum comes out soft. You remember that blank key?"

"How could I forget it? But what does it tell us?"

"Only the devil could possibly know, or perhaps Godot." Mike says.

"The key, the key, my kingdom for the key."

"Silence and gum. Those are the keys to the last riddles."

"The key to the keys," Lucia adds.

"Where are we going with this?"

"Nowhere," Lucia says on a sour note. "When will we get there?"

"Nowhen."

"We wait?"

Lucia responds ... "No. That's too defeatist."

"Then what?"

"To George's place," Lucia concludes. "I think he knows something he hasn't told us. We've got to squeeze it out of him."

"When?"

"Now."

THEY leave. Mike, struggling for answers to questions that never cease pouring forth, says, "I keep remembering your telling me once that they jail a lot of serial killers for minor infractions. Like Ted Bundy, who was stopped for a traffic violation. Maybe we will get lucky."

"Doubtful," she mutters.

Mike gives it another college boy try, "You know, despite what the authorities say, I think psychopaths think they're a hell of a lot smarter than they really are."

"X-Man has got to be the exception to the rule," she points out.

Mike tries to try again, and again, and fails miserably. His speculations are unanimously aborted. After additional wild ideas and more than a little bit of wrangling, the door to George's apartment meets their eyes. Mike gives the button a ring.

Lucia shouts, "Hey, George. You there?"

"Just a sec" comes a muffled reply.

The door opens. George's face meets them in place of the door. What is left of his face, that is. His right cheek is slashed from ear to chin. Fortunately, it is superficial. He's trying to keep the blood in check with a dish towel.

"My God, George! You look like you've been through a meat grinder," Lucia screams.

"Funny. But you can see I'm not laughing."

"What did they do to you," Lucia s asks.

"Don't say they. Say he. One man. Huge. About two hundred and fifty pounds."

"Did you get a good look at him?"

"Hell no. Do you think I have eyes in the back of my head?"

"It was him!" Mike announces.

"He was strong" George goes on. "I unlocked the door with one hand and I had groceries in the other hand. He grabbed me from behind and held me as tight as a chicken at the chopping block. I heard funeral bells gonging."

Lucia says, "Let me fix you up. Do you have any gauze? Tape? Disinfectant?"

"I'm okay. You came here with some questions, no doubt. So, spit them out."

"I'll do no such thing. Where's your first aid supplies."

"In the upper left drawer in the bathroom."

Lucia disappears. Mike sits George down at the table, then goes to the kitchen to get some paper towels to soak up more blood. Meanwhile, Lucia reappears with first aid supplies in hand.

"You don't have much in that drawer. I'll have to make do with what I have here."

Between Lucia and Mike, George gets his wound dressed up. Despite his protests and uncooperativeness. Then he insists they leave his face alone and get down to serious talk.

"I'd like to get my hands on the person who did this to you," Lucia says. "It has to be him," Mike murmurs under his breath.

"Who?" George asks.

"The serial killer. He did this to you."

"I wouldn't be so sure of it," George tells him. "I wasn't at the right spot at the right time for the seventh killing."

"I have an idea he didn't want to put you away, just give you a good scare," Lucia says.

"Why would he want to do that?" George asks. "Because we're getting too close," Lucia responds. "How would he know, Lucia?"

"He knows everything. He either has a snitch informing him and the press or he's his own snitch."

"Lucia! You're probably his next victim. Be careful."

"I am George."

"You remember Bob Dylan's Rolling Stone?" George goes on. "It's a new world where they got no respect for you and you're on your own where you got nothing to lose, so choose your steps carefully. You remember *Lucinha?*"

"Yes, George."

"Be careful. If you don't know exactly where you're going, you might find yourself where you don't want to be."

Lucia and Mike put grins on their faces. Then Lucia gets down to business.

"You remember my telling you about that blank key, don't you George?"

"Sure do."

"And about those riddles and allusions to Carroll's Alice."

"That too."

"Tell me. Does this have anything at all to do with the zero concept?"

"It sure does, child."

"In what way?"

"Zero came from India and the Arabs brought it to the West. Along with it came two dangerous uninvited guests. The *void,* and the *infinite.*

Zero is like a vast incomprehensible void and infinity looks suspiciously like zero. In fact, zero and infinity are like two sides of the same coin. Something like Yin and Yang."

"My God!" Lucia exclaims with a note of anguish. "The killer alluded to him and me in words that sound suspiciously like what you're saying"—

"Like I said," George cuts her short. "He's got his eye on you. But hold on a minute. I've got more to say."

"Infinity times any other number is infinity. Anything multiplied by zero is zero. Divide any number by infinity and you get zero. Divide that same number by infinity and you are left with zero. Add a number to zero and you still have zero. Add a number to infinity, and it is still infinity according to a school of thought that tells us infinity is never absolutely complete.

"Zero is nothing, of course. And it is everything, since according to its original conception it contains the possibility for generating the infinite series of numbers. Infinity is everything, but we cannot have it in our grasp, so it might as well be zero."

"But, George," Lucia says, "I had in mind that zero you felt compelled to place in your lattice."

Lucia pulls out her figure she has unwarranted faith in and shows it to George.

"Yes. Your zero-point. We discussed this before."

"My question is why do we need zero? Why not begin with crime one?"

"Because, *Lucinha*, zero is the beginning of all numbers. And it mirrors the universe from beginning to end. After zero, number one puts the whole number series in motion. Then, after nothing, or zero, the Big Bang got the universe started."

"Zero is the beginning of what?"

"Of everything. Zero gives rise to one, one to two, two to three, and many. Ultimately an infinite series of numbers, or an infinite mix of everything in the universe."

"Even those strange portmanteau words the killer keeps coming up with?"

"Even those. You were given a blank key, zero. It holds the possibilities for all possible keys. Wager a guess, take the first step, and you're off."

"Off to where, George? You're doing a lot of loose thinking. We want details we can apply to our case."

"You're off along the road toward solving the first crime, then the second, and"—

"Beginning with a wager? Nothing more than a guess?"

"If you want to put it that way, yes."

"So, as we go along, we find ourselves moving up the diagram, and our choices become more and more limited. Is that right?"

"Yes. But keep in mind that no matter how many choices you make, there will still be an infinite number of future choices staring you in the face."

Mike had been a passive bystander. Now his curiosity is piqued. He asks, "That must be why the first crime is on the left side of your lattice and the second is on the right side. Then there's a twist in the lattice—as if through the looking glass—where the half-breed blended words begin. That's where the third crime is, in between, as if it was that looking glass."

"You're in the mark young man. Lucinha, I must say again, you chose your partner well."

"Actually, I had no choice on the matter."

"Gee, thanks, Luce," Mike says.

"Anyway," George continues, "the first three crimes in this lattice—which you, Lucinha, built by a stroke of inspiration—were what we might call a mixed state before they were chosen by the killer and observed by you. They were nothing and everything, the mathematical equivalent of zero and infinity. Once chosen and observed, they entered a relationship with all that wasn't chosen but might possibly be chosen in the future. You see? Interconnectedness!"

Mike interjects, "I'm lost again."

Lucia says, "Are you saying, George, that the variations in time and space from one homicide to the next consist of what was not chosen for a previous homicide but can be chosen for the next one?"

"Right you are Lucinha. When something emerges, it is like that notorious butterfly effect in chaos theory. The butterfly flaps its wings in the Amazon forest and its minute repercussion multiplies over and over with increasing turbulence and finally it causes a hurricane in the

Caribbean. But in your case, it's order out of nothing rather than order out of chaos."

"I get it now," Mike pipes up, "it's colorless green ideas emerging from the vast repertory of possible words, like the meaning of *grue* coming into existence."

"Yes, that's it," George says. "You've seen it in your messages from the executioner."

"That's the game he's playing. And it is definitely a game, not merely play, since he's intent on winning," Lucia adds.

THE analyzing trio remains silent during a few moments. In thought.

Lucia says with a squint, "Keep in mind however, that Chomsky's colorless green ideas involves *syntax*, whereas *grue* is a matter of *semantic* letter scrambling. Syntax is grammar built into context free language use, but semantics is dependent on changing contexts and observer dependence in whatever context."

"This means that syntax is reversible while semantics is irreversible," George clarifies. "And," he adds, "that's why the killer can always be a step ahead of you. He can choose from the virtually random disarray of possible words. It's almost an anything goes situation. You, in contrast, are limited to what he leaves you in specific contexts."

The butterfly brings order out of disorder, while X-Man creates confusion from nothing. Mike ponders. *Is this not just metaphorical talk?* Then he speaks up, "Ah, it's like the criminal can create something from nothing. But we have to reconstruct something out of what he leaves us. Which bears on virtually random possibilities."

George gives Mike a grin, "You've got your thinking cap on and it's working for you, young man."

"Not really," Mike retorts. "You might think there's no order at all in a hurricane. That it's total chaos. But a hurricane follows its own rules, and judged specifically by those rules, it is beauty to behold. You might wish to take *grue* as nonsensical, but given the context from which it emerged, it has plenty of meaning."

Lucia gives a head shake, "The murdering bastard is free to fill in the blanks however he wishes according to his own rules, but we have to understand why he filled them out the way he did."

"Good grief," Mike mutters, "then how can we ever reveal this madman for what he is?"

"Madman he isn't," George suggests. "He's as rational as can be."

"I have another question for you George," Lucia says. "We noticed that wherever there's a murder, there's a Starbucks around. Might this be some sort of clue?"

"Could be. Starbucks might function like an *attractor*. *Attractors* are necessary for bringing order out of chaos. In a metaphorical sense that is. The idea of an *attractor* comes from chaos theory too. Starbucks might be used in some comparable way."

"It could have been Subway, Pizza Hut, McDonalds, Burger King, or whatever, but the killer chose Starbucks," Mike speculates. "Is that it?"

"Might be."

"Well" Mike goes on, "speaking of Starbucks, we've noticed there are seven points on that lady's crown in the logo."

"I'm not sure about that, but it might be of some relevance." George solemnly observes for a change. "You see?" he goes on, "when you are brain-storming like we are, you may be co-participating with your criminal in the creation of his world."

"Christ!" Mike exclaims. "You mean we're collaborating with him? So we are accomplices?"

"Yeah, you might say that."

"Then I'll have nothing to do with him," Mike says.

"Hear George out," Lucia pleads.

"What I mean is that your criminal is creating a world crying out for interpretation, and its interpretation includes a solution of the crimes. The criminal's world without the crimes resolved is incomplete. His world is for you to complete from within the context of each crime and the collection of all the crimes. Of course, then there will be other crimes to solve. The world, the whole world, and nothing but the world of all possible crimes will never become completely solved. It's too big, too much to handle."

Great! We will always have a paycheck coming in. No need to worry. Is that what it amounts to? Mike thinks.

"And there's more, much more," George warns.

"I was afraid of that. This is starting to give me a headache," Mike says.

"Stay with me Mike, I can't afford to lose you," Lucia says.

George begins, "Take another look at *Lucinha's* diagram. Better, let me sketch it out."

He grabs a sheet of paper and draws the image with wavering instead of straight lines to depict ongoing process. Then he says, "In our previous discussion I mentioned

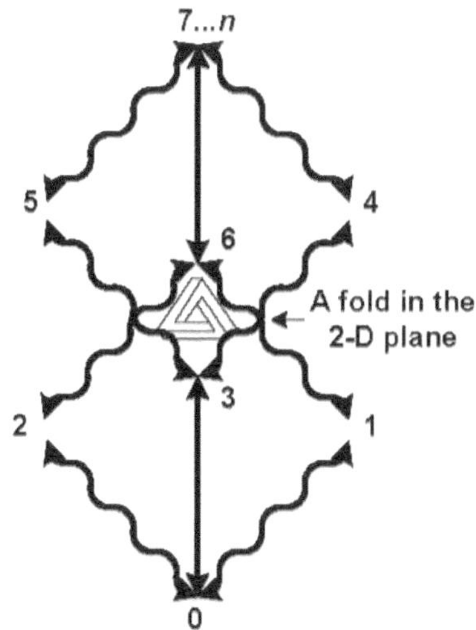

a different form of logic governing the interconnections involved in the lattice. Well, here it is.

Listen closely. If we move up the lattice, there is inclusion of more and more properties that the terms occupying the slots have in common.

"Notice there is an increasingly complex ethnic and gender mixture of the victims, and the perp's murder methods, as we move up the lattice. This implies the possibility of all ethnicities and forms for committing homicide. Moving down the diagram, and that which the homicides and ethnicities have in common becomes lessened. Until it reaches zero.

"Murders one and two, for example, have little in common. But as you move up the lattice, the crimes demonstrate more commonalities. That's what makes up the criminal's signature and MO."

"In the final analysis the relevance is?" Lucia asks.

"That homicide seven will not be the last *possible* murder. Why? Because following number seven, many other alternate *possibilities* will continue to exist. Nevertheless, I predict seven will be the last murder, because the lattice will have covered the basics. It's the end of the rope. Out beyond, there's thin air, virtually nothing. Your X-Man will venture into what has become unknown territory."

"I'm still puzzled," Lucia reveals. "The basics? What do you mean by that?"

"I mean that two cycles have been completed, and that should be sufficient for you to solve the crimes."

"I guess," Lucia mumbles, obviously unconvinced. "But this is beginning to appear too far-fetched for my blood."

Is it no more than voodoo geometry, mumbo-jumbo theorizing? Mike asks himself.

"Well, let me see." George patronizingly tries to soothe Lucia's doubts.

"To be more precise, the lines of the lattice are not set in concrete. They are more like a quivering mass of jelly. They are always changing due to changes of context. That's why I use wavy lines in the diagram."

"Heavens." Lucia can't help remarking. "There's more to your lattice than initially meets the eye. Tell me, why do you have the Penrose triangle in the middle?"

"Here, I have a picture of it."

George opens his desk drawer, fumbles around in it, and pulls out the visual paradox.

"It's an impossible object in a three-dimensional world, but possible in four dimensions," he says.

"Ah." Lucia's eyes light up. "When placed in the middle of the lattice, the triangle gives the idea of a twist in three-dimensions from within a fourth dimension. Our ordinary seeing and thinking tells us that what we see is what we can think and say it is.

"But it's more complex than that. It's like what we can think—for example, the Penrose triangle—is more than what we can ordinarily see and say. It implies the paradoxical nature of our world."

"Precisely," George confirms the suggestion. "This is also one of the conclusions of quantum theory. But that is another story we need not take up here."

"Why the dots and the italicized *n* after the number seven in the lattice?"

Mike asks.

"Because the lattice remains incomplete. In principle it could continue on and on indefinitely."

"I gotta repeat my question. Do you actually think the killer thought about all this?" Mike asks with a dose of skepticism.

"I would like to think so. I doubt that it came out of a vacuum."

LUCIA checks her watch, and says, "Our discussion with you has been enlightening, as always, but much as I hate to say it, our job is calling."

"It has been my pleasure, Lucia and Mike."

"Now that our discussion is over, let me take care of your knife wound properly."

"Wouldn't think of it. I can take care of myself."

"But"—

"No buts. I'll be fine. It's just a flesh wound."

"If you insist, George."

"I insist."

"I think we should go to the ER for some sutures," Mike suggests. "Negative. I'll close it up with a butterfly bandage. It'll be fine. At my age I'm not interested in my looks. I'll not be trying to court women half my age, or any other age. Besides, by sporting a big scar on my cheek I'll recover some of my *macho* image. Aahaaa."

Mike gets a good laugh. Lucia mutters, "Give me a break."

"Taking you to the ER room will be no problem at all. We will have you in and out of there in a few minutes," Mike insists.

"I'll be fme, Mike. Don't worry about me. You two have some serious work to take care of."

Once again, they wish him a speedy recovery, and they are on their way.

TRYING TO PUT THE PIECES TOGETHER

LUCIA arrives home, checks her e-mail. "Who would have guessed it? X-Man calleth!" He writes,

> *We are langpended in susuage,
> & kon't dnow whay wich is
> dop and which is uon,
> & which is forkward & which
> Js bacward.*

What a royal pain in the ass, she says to herself. Then she tries to crack the code and fails. Tries again and fails ... again ... and again. No dice. She forwards it to George. While waiting for a response, she begins cleaning up her apartment. It bores her. She watches the newscast. Becomes depressed. Goes to the grocery store. And returns with a bag full of junk food. Dismayed.

Enough time wasted, she thinks. And phones Bob. "Where have you been hon. I've called time and again."

"Sorry," she says, "I was so tied up I turned my phone off."

They argue for a while. Then he's sorry. And she's sorry. They make up, then hang up. She checks her e-mail again. Among various and sundry messages, there's George. He writes,

> *Didn't take any time at all. Jt is comparable to
> some words by quantum physicist Niels Bohr
> when he said we are suspended in language and*

don't know which way is up and which is down, which is to the left and which is to the right, and which is forward and which is backward.

Lucia says "Oh." Then says no more. Her bed calls her for some snooze time.

What the hell else is there? X-Man, it's thirty-two days since your last crime. What pattern are you following? Something you found in the zodiac?

Are you in tune with George's undecidability or vagueness? Gödel's inconsistency and/or incompleteness? Heisenberg uncertainty? Once I think I have you pegged, you change your trajectory to trip me up? I'll have to hand it to you X-Man. In certain respects, you're a cool customer.

Her bed continues beckoning. She retires, while thinking, *Time is the author of what I'm made of; space is where time makes me. I am that time and that space.*

Good grief! Is this talk no more than mushy-minded thinking? What a waste!

She surprises herself by falling asleep in short order. She dreams of herself as tantamount to an infinite sphere whose center is everywhere and whose circumference is nowhere, and the same description applies to XMan.

She bolts from her bed to the floor and jumps upward. Wide eyed, she tells herself. What in heaven's name is going on? *Are we the same? Is it a small world after all or what? No! Never! I will outlast you, X-Man, or I will die trying.*

"I must say, sweet dreams you experienced, my lovely collaborator in crime."

Did someone say that? Or is my imagination on a rampage?

Her pulse races. Her mouth is dry. Her head is in turmoil. She goes to the fridge for a glass of water. Says to herself, *I'm simply imagining things.*

She returns to bed. Cannot sleep. Rolls and tosses. Finally, her restless mind fades. Night time reluctantly goes its way.

THE next morning, Lucia has another encounter with the media and realizes some cockroach out there is still leaking info. As soon as she dismisses the reporters, she heads straight for Fay's office. Barges in with a growl, "He's up to it again."

"Who," Fay asks.

"The fuckin' stoolpigeon. He's got to be on the take. Do you have anything on him?"

"We think we know who it is, but we need to pile up more evidence before we can take him to court."

"Well, dammit you've got to move, and be quick about it."

"We are doing all we can. By the way, what do you have?" Fay asks.

"I'll give you one guess?"

"I was afraid of that. I saw the mayor this morning and told him you have my full support."

"Thanks. I appreciate it. It's all I have, given the way things are going."

"Positive thinking, Lucia."

"Nothing to be positive about."

"Fake it then."

"You think I'm not trying?"

Lucia leaves. Enters her office just in time to intercept yet another email,

> My gata [sex bomb] gostosa [delicious one]. With an extraordinary bunda [butt]. Can I help you out with your case? You seem to be in such turmoil, my little one. Keep your eyes peeled for further informative revelations. They might help put you in a more favorable frame of mind.

So now you think you're an expert on vulgar Portuguese and Spanish, eh? Well you need a few lessons. Correction. Many lessons.

"Hey, Mike," she hollers out, "come over here."

"What's up?"

"This. Now he's his own translator."

Mike reads the message and remarks, "He's trying to put you down."

"And doing a lousy job of it."

"That's the attitude, Luce."

"Still, his stone age behavior irks me. Wait, here's some more ...Take a look at it with me."

1. I am the only even prime number. What number am I?
2. When you speak my name, some people might become discreet; I become infinite when I'm asleep; I still look the same when I'm upside down; I am the cube of the smallest prime. Add eleven to me, and what number am I?

Mike says, "Now it's number play. Or is it numerology?"

"Numbers. They must have some relevance."

"Yeah, but the problem is that it's a close cousin to lottery." Mike says, "Pick a number and there's one chance in a hundred million you'll hold the lucky one."

"Not funny."

"I'm dead serious," Mike says.

"Concentrate, Mike."

"Well, okay. Even prime number? You're the math mind. You tell me."

"This is an easy one. Too easy. So easy it makes me suspicious."

"Spit it out and we'll see," Mike tells her.

"Two."

"Two?"

"Yes. A Prime Number is a whole number greater than one that can be divided evenly only by one and by itself."

"So much Greek to me," Mike confesses.

"Two is divisible by one and also divisible by itself."

"I got you. And now, my heavenly integer diviner, I beg of you. Reveal the answer to the next puzzle for me."

"That's also a dead giveaway. Two, the smallest even prime number, when cubed, is eight. Two times two times two makes eight."

"Oh, brilliant! Your brain is tops and you know it, but your pretty head doesn't show it 'cause it ain't Einstein's."

Lucia erupts with a laugh. "You're a poet at heart, Mike. But these riddles are not typical of X-Man because they're too easy. He never made anything easy."

They sit looking at the lines on the monitor for a few seconds, saying nothing. Then Lucia offers an observation, "Eight looks the same when placed upside down. When it is in the sleeping position, that is, horizontal, it is the infinity sign. Beautiful. But discreet?"

"In a pool game? The black ball is eight?"

"You're right, Mike. But how would that fit in?" Lucia queries him.

"I don't know. Anyway, we got the answer. So why sweat it."

"Not so fast. We have two and eight. Where does that get us? Nowhere. We have to take the next step."

"You have all the brains, Luce."

"That's it!" Lucia jumps out of her swivel chair so quickly that it goes careening to the left, and she comes close to losing her balance. "Add eleven to twenty-eight and you have thirty-nine. Today is the thirty-third day since the last homicide. George predicted the next one would occur between thirty-eight and forty days, so it must be the thirty-ninth day."

"Now I'm the suspicious one, but I don't know why," Mike admits.

"No matter, we have something. Let's go with it."

MIKE returns to his cave, and Lucia thinks, *I'll be damned. The killer has a sense of humor. Is it possible? Psychopaths are depersonalized, or objectivized. They're not supposed to have any sympathy or empathy, hardly a trace of human emotion or sentiment.*

Something like the consummate scientist who abstracts the universe and observes it, disinterestedly, from a presupposed neutral vantage point. The grand difference is that the psychopath thinks he's literally the center of the universe.

Hm ... Has that not been our goal in Western science in order hopefully to take on some kind of god's-eye perspective of the world out there? Is the grand dream of the knower that of wishing to get the whole universe in her grasp? Is it perhaps in part also the consequence of psychopathic behavior?

Should the psychopath be put on a pedestal? As our hero? Our role model? Whose shining example might scientifically point the way toward giving us the key to the universe? Crazy and scary!

Lucia tries to put these thoughts out of her mind. But she can't. They keep bugging her. The murderer once said she is his mirror-image twin. Could it be that without her knowing it, some non-conscious purpose involves objectivizing herself. Becoming somewhat like him so she can know him? Is that possibly her unaware unknowing aim?

"If it is, count me out," she growls.

What am I saying? Count myself out? Then what is my role? Empathize with him? Agonize with him over the lousy deck of cards he's been dealt? Moan about his childhood traumas, or whatever? Make the sign of the cross and forgive him for his sins because he's not to blame? Because it's his parents? The bullying he suffered? Society's rejecting him? Or whatever?

"Enough of this!" she voices in protest.

But it doesn't stop.

"Am I as evil as he is? For him it's acceptable, because he's on the other side of the law. Is what I assumed was a chasm between him and me no more than a hop, skip, and jump?

"Stop it! Lucia"

ANGUISHED, she dashes out of her apartment, runs down the stairs, jumps in her car, and heads to the fitness place. Huffing, puffing and pouring out streams of profanity. She arrives. Enters. Jogs to the locker room.

Jerks her running gear over her taut frame. Runs out the building to the park and runs lap after lap. Exhausted, she flops into a park bench. Heart racing, lungs pleading, brain struggling to find an anchor point, mind striving to find a leverage point.

An image emerges in her mind, *The Möbius-band. A two-dimensional strip of paper with one end twisted and reconnected to the other end in three-dimensional space. Like the number eight, like the infinity symbol, like the center of the*

diagram according to George's rendition. He is the one who taught me about the Möbius-band. It has only one side. Yet, as you travel along it you metaphorically go from inside to outside and back again, on and on.

Lucia recalls the twist in George's lattice that was a kind of fold at the midpoint where the Penrose triagle appeared. She wonders about putting the Möbius-band in the center of the lattice for illustration. Amazing. As if through the looking glass, the twist enables the coales cence of contraries into Oneness.

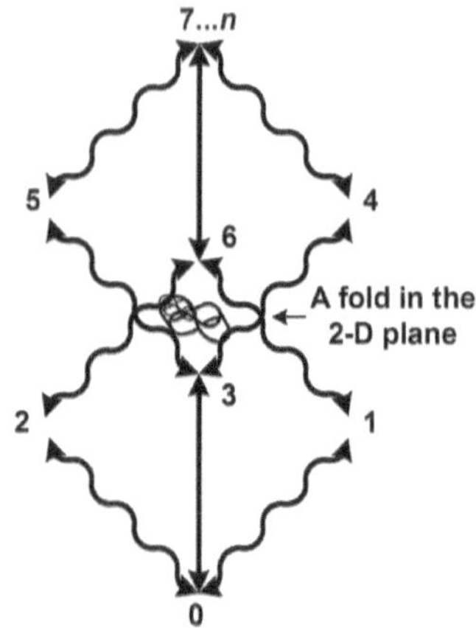

That evil killer and me? One? Repugnant! But on second thought,

for some insane reason, it seems so natural.

She sits. For at least half an hour. It seems to her like an entire day.

I have a lot of work, gotta get a move on.

LUCIA is at work, but it no longer seems like work. It seems more like a natural extension of her monological rumination.

Her thoughts surface anew, *Is my work a mirror-image of the killer's sordid game? Or is it play? No. Can't be. He is definitely out to win at whatever cost. That's why his nature parallels that of a psychopath.*

Wouldn't you like to get your hands on him Lucia? she fantasizes. *Put a slug in him? Or strangle him? Lop his head off? Slice his stomach open? Give him a lethal injection? What a high? What satisfaction? Right, Lucia?*

Lucia doesn't want to think about it. Yet, she can't help thinking about it. It's like saying to an audience "Don't think of a bat." They want to cease thinking of a bat, but at unexpected moments the thought pops into their heads. They must keep in mind what it is they shouldn't think about, and they think about it anyway. They think about not thinking about it, and they think about it. They don't want to stop thinking about it because if they do, they might forget they're not supposed to think about it, and they run the risk of thinking about it.

Lucia murmurs, "Saying a firm 'Stop!' does no good. Nor does saying to myself, 'Just say no' So, where's the answer?"

Stubborn unwanted thoughts. They're within that self-enclosed sack of meat you call your body and a malfunctioning brain enclosed within it that seems in control of my mind.

Right, Lucia?

Right. Wasting him would give me immense pleasure.

Did you think that? Lucia! Are you becoming a monster simulating XMan?

Pleasure. That's all I would feel, that's all I know. Like a psychopath? Horrors! Never!

LUCIA manages to think above the din of whirlwind thoughts telling her she should get her diagram out and try to pinpoint the seventh homicide's location. She does so, while feeling somewhat dizzy, somewhat nauseous.

There. Thirty-ninth day. I should get Mike and go to that very spot.

"Hey, Mike! Front and center." She sticks her head out the door and hollers. He's there and waiting. She says "We're off to locate seventh assassination."

They arrive. The ubiquitous Starbucks nearby. Nothing unusual or noteworthy. A dead-end alley shows itself a half-block from the coffee shop. Must be the spot. Mike thinks the same. They sit in the car and eyeball the area closely for an hour or so. Mike leaves to buy a couple of scones and coffee. And returns. Their eyes roam around for another half hour. Nothing.

It's enough to make a grownup cry. No use sticking around here. They leave.

OTHER THAN WHAT IT WAS BECOMING

BACK at the precinct, Fay is a ball of nerves. Waiting for Lucia. She enters the boss' office. Fay asks her to have a seat. Bad news, Lucia thinks.

"What's going on?" she asks Fay, and then says, "Oh, and by the way, thanks for entertaining the press for me."

"That's what I want to talk to you about. The press," Fay tells her.

"What about it?"

Fay begins, "You know they want you skinned alive don't you."

"Yeah. Character assassination and all. What else is new?"

"This time it's serious."

"They're always serious when they're after my ass."

"This is no laughing matter, Lucia."

"Then what is the fact of the matter in all seriousness?"

"They say you're fabricating the facts of the investigation to make it appear more complicated than it actually is—'intellectualizing the whole affair,' they put it—in an attempt to cover up your incompetence. They say you're losing your touch."

"Well, in that case they can kiss my ass."

"Hear me out, Lucia. They now have the mayor's ears. But since in the general public's eyes you are a pop hero of sorts, he's not willing to make the next move."

"Which is?"

"Your resignation."

"So that's what it has come to? Fabricate the story that I'm fabricating my story so a properly politicized and fabricated replacement can be appointed. Then the psychopathic predator becomes a folk hero. Rap rebels write songs about his ruining my career, killing people and getting away with it by flipping a bird at the cops, and outsmarting the elected officials. Is that what you want?"

"You know better than to ask me that."

"I know. I'm just fucking fed up. That's all."

"You have a right to be disgruntled. But we had better give them something concrete. They are not convinced that the direction you're taking is the best one."

"So, I give them a solution easy enough for the most brain-dead citizens out there. Pick up one of the worthless bums on the street we know is up to no good but we don't yet have anything on him. Beat a confession out if him. Declare the case is closed. And everybody's happy."

"Don't be cynical, Lucia."

"That's all I have left."

"The press wants something they can write about that makes sense to their readers. Your obscure accounts don't cut it for them."

"My instincts go one way and the facts want to go another way. The problem is that the facts don't jibe. They provide nothing I can solve my case with. You know that as well as I do. The press wants simple answers that will make sense to their readers. There are no simple answers. Shall I invent something to appease them? Will that solve the case?"

"Definitely not. I remain on your side. Completely. But I have them on my back, and if I don't come up with something, they'll have my skin too."

"Screw them!"

"For Christ sake, Lucia. *Our* jobs are at stake here. *Mine* as well as *yours*."

"And nothing else matters Fay? This case is as intellectualized as a three-dimensional chess match. And they want me to declare an end game after a few quick moves against a master player. They haven't a ghost of an idea as to how to catch this killer. They're lucky I'm on their side, because if I decided to go psycho, they would stand no chance in hell of catching me and toting me off to jail."

"I know what you mean," Fay says with a slight grin. Then she qualifies her words with a truism, "And yet, psychopaths are more often than not caught by accident."

"Then let's sit here and play computer games while the city burns and hope for an accident to happen."

Fay cannot suppress a spontaneous burst of laughter, then takes on a sober face and says, "A glib demeanor will get us nowhere."

"Once again, that's all I have left. What is the use of having brains in this godforsaken profession? How many people around here have brought as much study and put their talent so obsessively to criminal investigation as I have?"

"I know that."

"But whenever I go out on a limb, I'm given the consideration of a snot-nose kid with an imagination gone wild. This has happened before, many times."

"Agreed."

"What in God's name do you want of me then?"

"Lucia! You are trying my patience. Just give me something."

With that, Fay picks a paper off her desk and pretends she's reading it. Lucia takes her cue and leaves without another word spoken.

ONCE out of the office, Lucia feels eyes on her left side, right side and back side. *Is this real or imaginary?* she thinks. A few colleagues to her left chuckle. She catches a furtive glance. *Does he know something? If so, what?* She overhears talking around the water cooler. *What is the gossip about now? Good God! Am I going paranoid?* She opens the door to her Whoa-Man Cave—as she occasionally dubs it.

Is it in part because I am who I am? A woman? And what does Mike think of me? During his frequent trips to the water cooler is he participating in frivolous gossip about me along with other tasty topics?

Too many negative thoughts. Too much mental wrangling. Enough! Get to work, Lucia. Well, well. Speaking of the water cooler, there's Mike.

"Hey, Mike. What's on your mind?" *What an oaf I am, thinking he's anything less than sincere.*

"I saw you having a word with Fay. Anything new?"

"I wish there was, but she told me what I already know. My ass is on the line."

"And mine too, I guess."

"Not at all. I have the rank. It's my head on the chopping block."

"Which isn't the way it should work," Mike points out.

"What do you mean?"

"Responsibility should be shared."

"That's the democratic way. This institution is no democracy," Lucia shoots back.

"What's on your agenda for today?"

"What's your piece of cake, Mike?"

"Ah, Lucia, decision making is democratically shared, but the responsibility remains on your back. I see I'm occupying the most convenient rung in this broken-down hierarchical ladder."

"You might be righter than you think."

"Either way, it's all in a day's job description."

"Paper shuffling."

"Come again?"

"Paper shuffling's the job description for the day."

"No more?"

"Yes. During the mindless shuffling, jot down whatever comes to mind."

"I usually pay little mind to mind matters when I'm shuffling papers."

"Of course, but when your mind's surface is attending to paper shuffling, assorted trivia, or whatever, your non-conscious mind is at work on what is most pressing. Let it come out in the open, make a note of it, and then we'll compare our notes."

"I got you," Mike says.

"Then when we least expect it, something will click. And bam! There it is, staring us in the face."

"The answer?"

"Hopefully *some* answer."

"Trivia it is, then. My favorite pastime."

Mike leaves. Lucia is in no mood for trivia, so she doodles. *Good therapy. And to boot, it stimulates ideas.* She contemplates the sheet of paper staring her in the face. A squiggle appears here and a flower there and a honeycomb of hexagons somewhere else, and then ... Who knows? If my head is on straight, something will happen.

She thinks *Am I nuts? I don't care what a few psychologists say. Paper shuffling for the mere sake of looking busy. If it works it will undoubtedly be no more than coincidence. Coincidence? My God! To what extent has my thinking deteriorated?*

Lucia had been there, mindlessly, or lost in thought if you prefer, for about twenty minutes, when ...

"Yes!" she evokes a response out loud. *I'll go to that spot on the day prescribed by X-Man's riddles and the time George specified. Six o'clock in the afternoon. And wait. That's the only manner of positive action open to me. It can do no harm. If I run into a stroke of luck, I'll corner the bastard once and for all. Jesus Christ! Is that trifling piece of creative insight the best I can come up with. The press might be right, I'm losing it. Anyway, I'll ask Mike what he thinks.*

She does so. He likes it. She asks him if he would like to go along as cover up. He says he would not have it otherwise. They decide to ask for Rich and Berto's presence as well.

AN INCONVENIENT TURN?

THE time will come, and the method will show its true colors. Whether ending up tried and tested and found true, or flawed and fallacious and proved fake through and through. At any rate, Lucia is preparing herself to visit the presumed right place at the right time for crime seven. Baker Street it is.

She gets a crew cut in order to give her a masculine appearance. Decides to sport jeans, a sweatshirt with a gun concealed underneath it, and a pair of old tennies. A fake skull tattoo on her left hand. She will be leaning against a building across from the alley opening out to the sidewalk. If it happens it happens, and if not, nothing lost and nothing gained.

Everything must appear inordinately flaky, she says to herself, *and it might also appear less suspicious for that very reason."*

She is there and raring to go at 5:30 p.m. Street traffic is beginning to dwindle somewhat. Pedestrians are also fewer in number, but not by much. Nothing suspicious going on. Yet. She melts in, as unassuming as can be. The time? Five-forty. Stand and wait. No more, no less.

Might X-Man have an accomplice? A backup? His own stoolpigeon? Or will he be alone? she asks.

She is not merely a neutral bystander. She is in the habit of taking all thinkable possibilities she can into due consideration. Now is by no means an exception. In fact, she rather passively allows her imagination to run wild.

Ah, Necker cube and Möbius-band and all that. If I inhabited the fourth dimension, I could go completely unnoticed. Naked if I wanted to. Observing the killer without the possibility of his observing me. If I was roaming around in a parallel world, I would also be invisible to him.

What a strange universe we live in. Always here and now. Eternal presence. While I have nothing but my inborn ability and my wits. Will it be enough? Or, holy shit? Does he know through his informer in the department that I am here lying in wait?

What an advantage it would give him! Anyway, I have to be at my wit's best. What's the time? Three minutes until six! What if he doesn't show? What if he's somewhere laughing his head off at my idiocy? How embarrassing!

The stroke of six from some clock a couple of blocks away.

And there it is. Time to jump into action. What action? He'll probably not show. And I'll find myself in secular purgatory. Detective? Intelligence? What a joke! The predator was shrewd to choose this spot. Few people around at six in the afternoon. And an inconspicuous spot as well. Those off from work around here are already on their way home by now.

Then ...

What do we have here? Maybe there's a modicum of brainpower in my noggin after all. Sauntering by the alleyway. In a trench coat. What originality! A little over six feet and two hundred pounds. Smaller than expected, but it could be him. Probably Anglo-American. Ruddy complexion. Smooth walk.

Mike's down the street and can easily spy him. I'm safe as far as it goes. Evidence of an accomplice or a backup? Not immediately apparent. My appearance at this distance? Probably like a man in his thirties, maybe in his forties.

Could be good or bad. Good because I won't be recognizable. Bad, which means he'll have no qualms about putting me away if he thinks it's expedient. Or if he by chance recognizes me. Horrors! Mike, keep your eyes peeled buddy.

The possible perp stopped! Now what? Turns around and looks back. Someone is on the sidewalk walking toward him. Approximating, approximating. He reaches the suspect and passes him. No recognition. The suspect continues looking back from where he came. He turns around and looks this way.

Begins walking. Slowly. Stops near the alley. Two teenage girls go by. No reaction. Then a man in a business suit comes from the opposite direction. No reaction. Time? Almost ten after six. Is it time to make a move, Luce? No. Stay under cover for a few more fleeting moments ...

Time's up! It's now or never. Do it or die trying.

Lucia crosses the street. Stealthily. Heads straight forward. With eyes darting in all directions. The suspect notices she's approaching him.

If he's continuing to mix ethnicities and genders, it's likely he will take me as a Latino male or perhaps the light African American equivalent. That will be good. Chances are he might select me as his seventh victim.

If not, what will I do? Mosey over to the sidewalk and move on like nothing is out of the ordinary. Simple enough.

If he doesn't suspect anything fishy, that is. If he suspects something and makes a move to take me out, go into action. While Mike is rushes in. Takes him into custody. And we carry out no-holds-barred interrogation procedures. No! Don't so much as think about that possibility. I've got to catch him in the act.

The suspect moves into a slight indenture between two buildings at the middle of the city block.

Ah yes. An astute move. Making him even less conspicuous.

Lucia comes to within five yards of him, sees his eyes flit to the right then quickly to the left. She steps up to the sidewalk. Within ten yards of him. She diverts her linear path and begins walking slightly to her right. But ...

Impossible! Is it Jack Russell? Yes, definitely. I hadn't looked him straight in the eye while approaching him. Jack! What the hell's he doing here? Has he given me a good look? Has he recognized me? Surely he has.

Goddamn! This is a most unexpected turn of events! What am I to do now? Drop my disguise? Ask him what he thinks he's up to? Could he be checking out the scene for some inexplicable reason? Or is there a remote possibility ... No ... Can't be ... Yes it can ... Perhaps ...

She stops and says, "Jack? What in the world are you doing here?"

"Waiting for you."

"Why? And how did you know I would be here?" she asks with growing suspicion.

"Because I wanted to share your triumph. I didn't know you'd be here. But I had a hunch. I decided to take the risk. And it panned out. My intuitive aptitude paid off. Wouldn't you agree?"

"Don't be so presumptuous. It doesn't become you."

"And don't talk down to me, Lucia."

"What if I hadn't shown up?"

"The series would have ended with the number six. And in a few years, I'd be living on my pension. Happy as a lark."

"So you would like to think," Lucia says with a slight nod of recognition as she appraises her situation. *Is he or is he not? Becoming or not becoming who he wasn't? Caught up in his own merry-go-round*

"I have a question for you, Jack."

"Shoot."

"Why all the geometry and math making up the MO you so astutely chose?"

"I knew it was in your background. And I knew my contrived set of patterns would click. Especially with your uncle's aid."

"Oh? You've studied math?"

"Not formally. But I read up on it just for you, my dear."

"You're a piece of work, Jack."

"Thanks for the flattery."

Lucia sneers, "You goddamn son of a bitch! You slit George's face. Did you not?"

"He was getting too close. He forced me to do it. I realized later I should have gone further. Then I demurred. He's your uncle. I couldn't force myself to do what I had to do."

"You fuckin' bastard!"

"Careful, Lucia. Such language is not becoming of you."

"Now that I'm here, what do you want of me?"

"The role-model for my last victim."

Lucia's blood turns cold. As her customary cool, unflappable, awareness takes full account of her situation. Has she been so engrossed with the idea of playacting that her thoughts and actions became attuned to it? As if she was dreaming and her life was not really in jeopardy?

Now she fully realizes her intuition was right. Her reasoning and inclinations were on the mark. Mike's gut intuition was right as well. And especially George's reasoning mind. In this, her present now, here he is. In front of her. Jack Russell. Both informer and assassin. And she is the designated victim.

Well, Lucia, you got yourself into this. Now you'll get yourself out of it? By keeping a cool head. She thinks in rapid-fire succession and says, "How did you decide I'm your last victim?"

"It was inevitable. You, a Latino woman. A slight alteration of the sequence. I had you properly fooled. Didn't I?"

"No Jack, you didn't. Your constructing out of kilter antecedents leading up to this last crime gave you away. You're also the fucking cowardly snitch. Aren't you?"

"Convenient, wasn't it?"

"Like I said, it was cowardly."

"Not at all. It was pure genius. Who else in headquarters could have pulled it off?"

"Who's the sick prick that would so much as want to?"

"Don't insult me, Lucia."

"Once again, don't be presumptuous. Why did you do it? I mean really? While playacting as if you were the protagonist in a novel. Becoming a third-rate low-budget movie. Thinking you are who you aren't. Isn't it beneath you?"

"I'm doing it to reap my own private reward when and where reward is due. Look. I'm the one who solved all those crimes for you. And for others over the years. You could never have met with such success without me.

"Yet you're the one who always took the spotlight. What had I done? Tipped you off with a guiding light. A masterful profile. About some poor guy's traumatic childhood. Molesting sadistic father. Neglecting mother. The target of bullying and other social injustices. Or something other. I offered you the whole bag. Kit and caboodle. I did the work. You converted it into notoriety.

"I knew that's what it was. Because I had been victimized in those very ways when I was a kid. But I took it all in my stride. I weathered it. Sucked it up. And fucking survived. I survived!

"Those mother-fucking psychopaths, serial killers, and perverts could do the same if they wanted to. But they don't. Why? They're weaklings. No balls. No zero-sum game in their heads. They don't have what it takes."

"And you do?"

"I'm here, aren't I?"

"Yes. Proving you're no better than they are."

"Wrong. They are now in chains and I'm free."

"Come on, Jack. You know I always appreciated your work. I acknowledged it. And gave you credit for it. Publicly whenever possible. You also know everybody in the department has the highest regard for you. Why the pile of pent-up resentment?"

"Resentment you call it? Resentment when they take me for a zany ESP freak who has no idea what he's doing? Or for a scientist who plugs an equation into his brain and spits out the answer?

"Nobody knows who I am. Profiling requires neither mushy drooling over a criminal's actions nor know-it-all objectivity. It requires years of tough concentration of human behavior and keen sensitivity regarding people's thoughts and attitudes.

"That didn't come simply by acing all the college courses when I was a student. I learned how to get into people's minds. Learn how they think. Why they do what they do. How they do it."

"So, I must say again. You became one of them. A monster simulating monsters. Was it worth spending the rest of your life in jail?"

"You continue to underrate me. Do you think I'll actually be charged with those crimes?"

"I'm not underrating you at all. I want you to know that you are and you've always been an asset to the profession and our department."

"Don't make me laugh. I might as well have been stuffed away in some cubicle responding to text messages when I think about my being almost totally ignored."

"If that's the way you feel, just get it over with, then. Do what you came here to do and be done with it."

"I wish to savor the moment a bit longer. See you squirm."

"In a bizarre way, I guess you deserve it."

"Now you give credit where credit is due. I congratulate you, Lucia."

"Tell me, how did you come up with all the puzzles and paradoxes?"

"Here and there and everywhere."

"As self-centered as always, aren't you, Jack ... But I'm left with a question. How would you have profiled yourself when I first consulted you regarding this case?"

"That's a trade secret."

"I see. Your apprenticeship and years of experience have obviously been effective. But you left something out. If you felt so alienated, why didn't you go into criminal investigation? Your talents would have elevated you to the top of the heap."

"I like what I do."

"Now you sound like a bitter college professor who complains because he's making less than a CEO. Yet, he stays where he is because it's a pleasure trip. I was wrong about you, Jack. I had you—that is, the fuckin' predator—pegged as a cobra. Cool, fearless, ruthless, antisocial.

"Now, I see you for who you are. Nothing but a pit bull. Like a social animal, you and the pit bull always want to please those who take care of your selfish needs. However, if you are given so much as a dirty look, you viciously lash out with the intent to harm. Even kill."

"Okay. Enough is enough. I see I'll get neither whimper nor plea from you. I'll have to say, you're one tough broad. I admire you for it. But this is the end of the line."

"Before continuing, can I ask you one more question?"

"Fair enough. I'll grant you your last wish."

"Out of sheer curiosity, I'm wondering about the seven points on the crown of the Starbucks icon. Are they of any relevance to the number of homicides?"

"Ah yes. I noticed that and wondered if you might catch on. Actually, it was nothing but coincidence."

"I should have known."

"And now, if *you* don't mind ..."

Jack reveals the pistol with a silencer he had concealed under his trench coat. He slowly takes aim. A shot sounds out. Jack clutches his chest. Grimaces. Puts his hand where the slug entered. Pulls it back. Looks at the blood. Looks at her.

The grimace becomes a cruel pathetic grin. He tries to take a step forward. His knees buckle. He falls on his back. His eyes reveal the indescribable shock he senses.

Mike steps up. With the weapon in hand. Jack registers an excruciating jolt of recognition. His eyes flash from Lucia to Mike and back again, as he says, "You weren't supposed to ... Bring a back-up ... I ... I ... thought ... You would consider it an insult to ... Your cool ... uh ... Professional style."

"The reason for your boo-boo is simple, Jack. You didn't bother to profile me."

Jack shows slight traces of a wry smirk on his lips. While he begins struggling for oxygen.

Lucia silently gazes at him. Mike calls for an ambulance.

Rich and Berto shoo away curious citizens invading the scene.

Lucia's eyes remain fixed on Jack. She continues contemplating him as he begins gasping for breath.

He won't last much longer, she says to herself. *Hope the ambulance gets here in time.*

She stoops. Checks his pulse. Gives her head a pathetic shake.

With one hand, she presses on the wound to hold the blood in check and puts her other hand on his shoulder.

She tries to comfort him. Whispers a few words.

A siren sounds in the distance. It soon becomes a screaming, ear-shattering pitch.

The ambulance's brakes screech. Orders sound out. Clanking, clattering and clamor follow.

Lucia steps back to give the medics plenty of room.

She walks along with Jack and the medics to the ambulance. Stands there until he is secure in the rear area of the vehicle.

It rushes off with a banshee scream. As if triumphantly announcing its last victory of good over evil.

Her eyes focus on the flashing lights. Until they turn the corner and disappear.

She remains fixed. Eyes on the convergent point where the flashing lights are no more.

Hazy eyes. Sad eyes. Eyes wishing they weren't seeing what they were seeing.

She slowly turns to Mike and asks with a slightly trembling voice and the hint of a tear in her left eye, "What now, Mike?"

"Call Bob and go out to dinner tonight, Luce. You deserve it."